"I'll have to remember to the next time I stick my ne~~~ a woman."

"Especially if she doesn't require your help," Marianne retorted. "Not all women are as weak and helpless as you seem to think. I don't know what silly girl made you think – "

"Those cuts should be cleaned. Now stay still and let me – provided I have your *permission*, my lady."

Splaying her hands on the rock behind her, leaning back, she vowed not to make another sound, or twitch and wriggle, as he washed her feet. She also wouldn't think about his strong hand gripping her ankle.

When he looked up, their faces were mere inches apart. He wasn't angry any more. He was looking at her in that way he had in the mason's hut just before he kissed her.

The silence stretched between them, taut as a drawn bowstring. The very air seemed to thicken and warm, and pulse with a promise of something sweet and fulfilling. And exciting. Very exciting.

Margaret Moore began her career at the age of eight, when she and a friend concocted stories featuring a lovely damsel and a handsome, misunderstood thief nicknamed 'The Red Sheikh'. Unknowingly pursuing her destiny, Margaret graduated with distinction from the University of Toronto. She has been a Leading Wren in the Royal Canadian Naval Reserve, an award-winning public speaker, a member of an archery team and a student of fencing and ballroom dancing. She has also worked for every major department store chain in Canada. Margaret lives in Toronto with her husband, two children, and two cats.

Don't miss Margaret Moore's

LORD OF DUNKEATHE

in February 2006!

BRIDE OF LOCHBARR

Margaret Moore

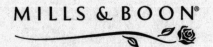

*First published in Great Britain 2005
by Harlequin Mills & Boon Limited,
Eton House, 18-24 Paradise Road, Richmond, Surrey TW9 1SR*

© Margaret Wilkins 2004

ISBN 0 263 84523 0

153-1205

*Printed and bound in Spain
by Litografia Rosés S.A., Barcelona*

BRIDE OF LOCHBARR

With special thanks to
Amy Wilkins and Melissa Endlich
for their excellent editorial suggestions,
and to Tracy Farrell for another
wonderful opportunity.

CHAPTER ONE

Scotland, 1235

MARIANNE WAS in purgatory.

Or so it was easy to believe as she looked out over the sodden landscape from the arched window in her brother's fortress.

Of course it was raining again, the downpour effectively hiding the jagged hilltops surrounding Beauxville like a veil, making the courtyard a mess of mud and puddles, and soaking the scaffolding erected around the half-completed walls of the castle. It had rained every day since she'd arrived in this wilderness at the edge of the civilized world.

If she were in Normandy now, the sun would be shining and the leaves of the trees would be bright green. She'd be beneath their shading branches, whispering with a gaggle of young women her own age, trying to stifle her laughter as the farm laborers went past the convent walls heading home after a day working in the fields. The young men would be singing their bawdy songs, well aware that behind the white walls of the convent, girls would be listening. The nuns would be scurrying about and twittering like a flock of startled birds, chiding their charges and trying to get them to go inside.

If she were back in Normandy, she would be warm. Here, even wearing a linen shift, a gown of indigo blue wool, a bliaut of light red with gold trim and with a bright green woolen shawl wrapped around her shoulders, she was still cold.

If she were in Normandy, she would be warm and happy, not lonely, cold and utterly, completely miserable.

She should have asked more questions when her brother arrived at the convent and told her he was taking her to his estate. Instead, she'd been too happy to be free of the confines of the religious house and too proud of her noble brother and impressed by his bearing and arms to question him. Even the Reverend Mother had seemed intimidated by Nicholas, and Marianne had believed the pope himself couldn't intimidate the Reverend Mother.

Yet if the Reverend Mother had known Nicholas was going to bring his sister here, to this mass of unfinished stone and masonry, where she would live among savages with wild hair and bare legs, surely she would have said that Scotland was the last place on earth suitable for a young Norman woman of noble birth and education. She would have suggested to Nicholas that Marianne be allowed to remain in the place that had been her home for the past twelve years until a suitable husband could be found.

The door to her chamber crashed open. Startled,

she turned from the window and watched as her brother, new-made lord of Beauxville, strode into the room. As always, Nicholas was plainly attired in black wool without a bit of embroidery at cuff or collar. His only ornamentation was the bronze buckle of his sword belt. His scuffed boots were caked with mud, his hair was damp, and his taciturn expression gave no hint as to why he'd decided to visit her here, where he rarely ventured.

"Ah, here you are, Marianne," he said, as if he honestly expected her to be somewhere else. He scanned the small room with its simple, crude furnishings and her painted chest, his gaze lingering for a moment on the embroidery frame neglected in the corner. "What are you doing?"

"I was thinking about the convent."

His response to that was a dismissive sniff, his usual reaction when she mentioned her life there, or spoke of her companions or the sisters. Yet why shouldn't she think of the past and her life in Normandy? Did he think she could forget it? Did he think she wanted to?

Some of her annoyance seeped out. "Shouldn't you be supervising the masons at the south wall? Or entertaining that elderly Scot who arrived this morning?"

"The masons are waiting for drier weather, and Hamish Mac Glogan has taken his leave."

"If the masons need the weather to be dry, they may never finish your castle," she remarked as she glanced out the window again. To her surprise, it wasn't actually raining at the moment, although heavy gray clouds still lingered, like a bad smell. "The delays must be costing you a pretty penny."

"I didn't realize you knew anything about building castles."

"Masons sometimes came to work at the convent, and I once heard the Reverend Mother complaining about the cost," Marianne replied. "You're doing much more than repairing a few loose bricks, so I can only assume—"

"You don't have to assume anything," Nicholas interrupted. "I can afford the masons now that I don't have to pay the good sisters for your care."

His tone was no longer dismissive. It was surprisingly resentful, as if paying for her years at the convent represented serious hardship. Yet her family had never suffered for want of money, and the sisters had never implied that she was there out of charity, like some of the more unfortunate girls. "Was it so very costly to keep me there?"

"Costly enough," he replied. "But I didn't come here to talk about money."

Telling herself his resentment must have another, more mysterious source, she lowered herself onto the stool and thought of a reason he might have come to her chamber. "Have you had word from Henry?"

Crossing his arms over his broad chest, Nicholas frowned. "A soldier doesn't have time to send messages to his family."

From the sound of it, things were still no better

between her brothers. They'd fought constantly as children; indeed, some of her earliest memories involved hiding from them when they argued and wrestled.

"So, what do you wish to talk about?" she asked, confused by his obvious reluctance to come to the point. Nicholas was usually extremely direct, and this prevarication was making her nervous.

Then she thought of one explanation why a brother might seek out a sister. "Is it something about women?" she asked hopefully. "Is there a woman you wish to woo and you came for my advice?"

Nicholas looked at her as if she'd lost her mind. "Don't be ridiculous. I've got more important things to do right now than court a woman, and I wouldn't come to you for advice if I were."

Marianne tried not to feel hurt at his brusque response. "I was only trying to be helpful, Nicholas," she replied. "I was twelve years among girls and women. There's probably not much I don't know about them, so if you ever do want to ask me anything—"

"It's *your* marriage I've come about, not mine."

A knot formed in the pit of her stomach. She'd been expecting this since the day he'd come to take her from the convent. It was, after all, the fate of most noblewomen and she dearly wanted children. Her happiest times at the convent had been helping the younger girls. So what reason could he have for taking so long to tell her that was why he had come to her chamber, unless he thought she wouldn't be pleased?

In spite of her increasing dread, she tried to sound calm when she answered. "Oh? To whom?"

He strolled toward the brazier and studied the glowing coals. "It's a very good match, Marianne," he said after a moment that seemed to last an eternity. "Your husband has great wealth and power."

His words brought absolutely no comfort; they only increased her uneasiness. "Who is he?"

"Hamish Mac Glogan."

She stared at her brother with horrified dismay. "Isn't that the old man who came here this morning?"

"That *old man* is rich and influential, related to the king of Scotland."

Hearing the underlying impatience in his voice, she instantly recalled Nicholas's rages when they were children. He was ten years older than she, and although he never struck her, she'd been terrified nonetheless. She certainly didn't want to rouse that fierce ire.

Clasping her hands, she lowered her voice to a more beseeching tone. "Nicholas, I appreciate that you're my older brother and stand in place of our father. I realize that it's your duty to find a suitable husband for me. But I thought I would marry a Norman. So did the holy sisters, and that is what they had in mind when they taught me."

"I told you, Hamish Mac Glogan is rich, he's noble and he's related to a king. That's all that matters."

She rose and went toward her brother. "But he's

so old, and he's a Scot. I don't know anything about these people, except that their land is harsh and cold and wet, and they wear those odd clothes. Surely there must be somebody else, a Norman nobleman, who—"

"You misunderstand, Marianne," Nicholas replied with a coldness that chilled her to the marrow of her bones. "The agreement has already been made, the contract signed. Hamish Mac Glogan will be a powerful ally, and I need allies here."

He spoke as if she was something for him to use as necessary, no more to him than the brazier beside him.

Anguish filled her as she saw not a brother who loved her, but a man who would do anything to fulfill his own plans.

"The wedding will be in a se'en night," he announced.

So harsh, so cold, so cruel.

Seven nights, and she would be married to that old Scot and forced to live in this wilderness forever.

"Nicholas, I'll willingly marry any man you like, as long as he's a Norman. Surely that's not too much to ask."

"Yes, it is. I told you, Marianne, the agreement has been made, and there's an end to it. Since I'm your oldest male relative, you have to do as I say."

Her dismay and disappointment fled, to be replaced by firm resolution. This was her life, her future, in the balance. If no one else would look out for her interests, she must.

"I have rights, Nicholas. I learned all about them in the convent. Father Damien told us we had to agree to our betrothal. A woman can't be forced into marriage. It's against the law of the church."

Nicholas looked utterly unimpressed. "The Reverend Mother told me you were headstrong and selfish. I see she wasn't exaggerating. No wonder she was relieved to be rid of you."

Marianne wouldn't let his words hurt her. "I'll go to the church for sanctuary."

"Which church? How will you get there?"

"I'll write to Rome, to the pope himself. I assure you I'll do whatever's necessary to see that—"

Nicholas grabbed her shoulders and in that moment, she saw the man his opponents in battle feared—the fierce, determined warrior who had survived when so many others had fallen.

"Are you forgetting who paid to keep you in that convent?" he demanded. "Do you think staying there came cheap? We may be nobly born, but our family's poor and has been for years, since before our parents died."

Refusing to believe him, she twisted out of his grasp. "You're lying. You're lying to try to get me to do what you want. I'd remember if we'd been poor."

"It's the truth, Marianne. You just didn't know it. Our parents sent you away so you wouldn't suffer, and sacrificed much to keep you there, as I did, because before they died they made me promise I would. I kept that promise, and while you were sleeping on clean sheets and eating like a princess, I was risking my neck and killing other men before they could kill me. Wearing secondhand armor. Sleeping in stables rather than pay for a place at an inn. Going hungry more times than I can count. And now I've arranged it so that you'll never suffer from want, keeping my promise still, for which you should be grateful."

Marianne stared at him, aghast, hearing the truth in his angry words. "Why didn't you tell me?"

"I'm telling you now. Scot or not, Hamish Mac Glogan is rich. You'll be living in luxury, while I try to get some income out of this place."

She went to him and put a placating hand on his powerful forearm. "Nicholas, I'm truly sorry you suffered for my sake, and I wish I'd known and been able to do something to help, but please, don't make me repay you with this marriage. Don't make me suffer for the rest of my life because of your ambitions. I can't live in this country."

"*You* can't!" he scoffed, wrenching his arm from her grasp. He strode across the room, then turned to face her. "Maybe that's what I should have said when it came time to send the annual fee to the convent, instead of going without meals and decent armor and a bed to sleep in. 'I can't pay it, Reverend Mother. Throw her out into the streets and let her fend for herself.'"

Marianne clasped her hands together, beseeching and desperate. "Nicholas, please, I'm begging you. I'll marry any Norman nobleman you like. Surely there must be one who'll want me, one just as rich and powerful as that ancient Scot."

Nicholas's expression altered to a sarcastic smirk. "You haven't met many Norman nobles, have you, sister? If so, you'd know they'd try to bed you, but they'd never wed you. You see, my dear beautiful sister, you have no dowry."

She couldn't believe it. "Even if we're not rich, surely there must be something. Why, you've got this estate, this castle."

"That doesn't mean I intend to waste another ha'penny on you," Nicholas replied as he crossed his arms. "What money I have will be used to build and maintain this castle, and my garrison and household as befits my rank. I've spent all that I care to—and more than I could afford—on you already."

"But—"

"But nothing!" he roared, his temper breaking. "I've found a rich, titled man who'll take you without a dowry and by God, woman, you'll wed him and like it! And if you're as clever as the nuns said— although they didn't mean it as a compliment— you'll give the old goat a son or two before he dies. Then you'll have a claim to his wealth and his property."

Her stomach churning, Marianne envisioned a life as the bride of Hamish Mac Glogan. Sharing his bed in a frigid hut somewhere. Eating rock-hard bread. Bearing his children in the mud like some sort of animal. Treated worse than a dog.

A cry sounded from the gates.

"Out of my way," Nicholas snarled as he went to the window. He looked out and muttered a soldier's earthy curse.

"What is it? What's happening?" Marianne asked, fearing some new and different trouble.

"Nothing that need concern you," he retorted as he gave her a scornful look. "We'll speak of your betrothal later, when you've had time to calm yourself and think about where your obligations lie."

Then he went out, slamming the door behind him.

Marianne sat heavily on her bed. No matter what she owed to Nicholas, she wasn't willing to sacrifice her entire life to repay him for what he'd done for her.

Nevertheless, she wished she'd known of his suffering sooner. She could have left the convent and…what?

Perhaps she could have found a husband on her own somehow. A brother of one of her friends, perhaps. She was a beautiful woman, after all, and that was obviously worth something. She'd also been taught all the duties and skills of a chatelaine by the good sisters, and a Norman nobleman would appreciate that, if Nicholas did not.

Yet the chance to find a husband for herself among her friends had passed, and now she was facing a marriage to a Scot.

Telling herself there must be something she could do to prevent the marriage, trying not to give in to despair, she rose and went to the window.

A mounted party of unfamiliar Scots entered the

courtyard through the thick oaken gates bossed with bronze. The man leading them had hair white as freshly fallen snow, and his garment's colors were a reddish brown like dried blood and a green reminiscent of moss. Beside him rode another Scot. He was taller and younger than the other man, with long, dark-brown hair that spread over his broad shoulders, except for two narrow braids that framed his clean-shaven and surprisingly handsome face.

Handsome for a Scot, she mentally clarified. And although his nose was straight, his chin strong and his lips full, he wore that outlandish garment that didn't cover his bare, muscular legs. His sleeveless shirt revealed arms just as powerful. She was relieved to see that he carried no sword or other weapons, yet she suspected he could uproot a small tree with his bare hands, or kill a man with a blow.

Even more unnerving than the physical power of the Scot was his expression as he looked around the courtyard. He was so grimly malevolent, she could believe he wanted to torch everything he saw, and attack every soldier single-handed.

It was no mystery now why her brother had cursed, and she was surprised he had allowed this band of Scots to enter Beauxville at all—unless he hadn't realized the old man had brought his fiercest warrior with him.

Marianne drew back out of sight as the savage warrior continued to scan the yard and surrounding buildings. She didn't want to encounter his venomous gaze directly. She'd endured enough lustful looks from men during her journey here to last a life-time, and she was quite sure this barbarian would react to her beauty like the uncivilized beast he was.

Even so, and in spite of the dread and disgust he inspired, her heartbeat quickened and her body warmed as she continued to watch him. Against her will, she remembered that day she'd climbed the tree and looked over the convent wall. A well-formed young man, wearing only his breeches, and one of the girls from the village had stopped beside a tree near the side of the road, in a spot not easily seen unless one was looking down from a tree. There they'd kissed, in such a way that she'd felt as hot as if the sun was shining directly on her and could melt her like butter.

She hadn't known then what she was feeling, but she did now: lust. And she must truly be losing her mind if she could lust after a brutal, barbarian Scot. Or perhaps this heated, impassioned feeling was merely her heart's protest against marrying an old man, because whatever else this Scots warrior was, he was certainly young and virile.

Nicholas strode out of the hall and for the brief-est of moments, checked his steps as he caught sight of the warrior beside the old man. Clearly her brother had not anticipated his presence and wasn't pleased.

However, his hesitation lasted only a moment before he continued forward and politely greeted the old man, who—surprisingly—replied in Norman French.

She would never have guessed that a Scot knew their language, or could speak it so well. She wondered if that grim warrior could understand what her brother and his leader were saying, and doubted it. Likely all he knew was fighting.

Nicholas stopped talking and gestured toward his hall. The leader of the Scots dismounted, and so did the rest of his men, who followed her brother to the hall.

Whoever these men were, they weren't enemies, at least not openly, or Nicholas would never have extended them that courtesy. If these weren't enemies, but allies or potential allies, Nicholas would also be inviting them to stay the night. Here was a chance to show Nicholas that she deserved to be the wife of a Norman nobleman and chatelaine of a Norman's castle, not the property of a primitive barbarian on the far edges of the world.

She would have to go to the hall and be in the vicinity of the malevolent Scot, though. That was a daunting prospect, but if the ultimate result was the end of her betrothal to Hamish Mac Glogan, she'd set aside her dread and do what she must.

ADAIR MAC TARAN wanted to torch the place. He yearned to set fire to every piece of scaffolding and tear down the walls being built on the sacred soil of Alba stone by stone. He didn't care what reason the king of Scotland had for giving land to the Normans; they were foreigners who didn't belong here, and he hated them all.

"Hark at him," he muttered in Gaelic to his younger brother, Lachlann, as they followed their father and Sir Nicholas toward the Norman's hall, the biggest building Adair had seen outside of York. "Bloody arrogant bastard acts like he owns the whole country."

Adair's friend and clansman, Roban, nodded as he walked beside them. "Or as if he's got a sword up his arse."

"Or as if he's been in more battles than all o' us combined," Lachlann replied, shooting them both a censorious look.

Adair and Roban exchanged knowing smirks. "Aye," Adair said, making no effort to speak softly. "A Scot would have to be all of twelve years old to beat him."

"For God's sake, hold yer tongue, Adair," Lachlann warned. "Did ye not hear what Father said?"

"Aye, I did, and I'll make no trouble, but that doesnae mean I care if that bastard knows wha' I think of him or not," Adair answered. "And it's not as if the man can understand a word we say anyway."

"Aye, it's no secret what Adair thinks of Normans," Roban repeated. "Unless Sir Nicholas is deaf or a complete *gomeral,* he'll already know."

"You make that sound like a good thing," Lachlann snapped. "But it's never good to let your enemy know your thoughts. You've got to learn to guard your tongue, Adair. And whatever happens, don't lose your temper."

Adair regarded his slender, dark-haired brother

with mock indignation, as if such a thing had never happened before. "Who, me, lose my temper with a lying, thieving Norman knight who comes to Scotland and steals our land by stealth?"

"This land was given to him by Alexander and you ought to remember that before you go charging the man with theft."

"I'm not going to charge him with theft. That'll be for Father to do."

Another man spoke from within the group of Scots. "The Norman's not the only one thinking he deserves to rule the world."

Adair didn't have to guess who it was, and he answered without looking over his shoulder. "Not the world, Cormag. Just our clan, as the heir chosen by my father and our clansmen."

Cormag didn't reply, and how could he? That was the truth, and the whole clan knew it. Nobody had ever considered Cormag Mac Taran suitable for taking Seamus Mac Taran's place as chieftain of the clan and thane of Lochbarr, except Cormag himself.

"I'll try not to curse the man outright," Adair said to his brother as they trotted up the steps of the massive stone hall. "Will that content you?"

"I suppose it'll have to," Lachlann grudgingly conceded as they followed the Norman and their chieftain toward a dais at the end of the hall, past the central hearth. The chamber was full of people, including several foot soldiers, armed and armored.

There were also large, scarred trestle tables leaning against the walls, with benches in front of them, and rushes sprinkled with rosemary and fleabane covering the stone floor, muffling their footsteps and lightly scenting the air. Hounds skulked about, studying the newcomers warily, just as the soldiers at the gate had.

King Alexander must have paid the Norman with more than land for his services, or else the mercenary Sir Nicholas had come from a more wealthy family than they knew.

"The rest of us will have to stand like servants," Adair noted under his breath when they reached the dais, where two large and ornately carved chairs stood.

"I feel like one wi'out my *claimh mor*," Roban said, rolling his brawny shoulders as if seeking the huge sword's comfortable weight on his back, where he usually carried it.

"If it comes to a fight, you won't need it. You could probably take half this lot with your bare hands," Adair replied, eyeing his friend who was six foot tall, and weighed fifteen stone after a day's fasting.

"With a dirk, you could likely take them all without breaking a sweat," Roban replied with a chortle.

"'Twas right to leave our *claimh mors* at the gate, since we come in peace," Lachlann said under his breath. "Now be quiet, the pair of you. I want to hear what Father and the Norman say to each other without you muttering in my ear."

"Welcome to my hall, Seamus Mac Taran," Sir Nicholas said in French as the chieftain took his seat.

Then the Norman overlord barked out an order for wine. A female servant, young and pretty, with light-brown hair and green eyes and a mole on her right breast, nodded and scurried away like a frightened mouse, clearly terrified of her master.

Sir Nicholas was obviously fast with a blow or a kick if a servant didn't move quickly enough to suit him, Adair thought, his disgust mounting. And perhaps he used his female servants to serve other needs as well.

The loathsome lout. Any man who forced a woman was no man at all, but a foul beast, and deserved to be treated like one.

"What brings you to call at Beauxville today?"

Adair's lip curled. His father had been a warrior and clan chieftain for thirty years, yet this Norman addressed him as if he were a child. And this place was Dunkeathe, not Beauxville.

"A dozen cattle are missing from the south meadow of our land," Seamus said.

And you and your men have stolen them, Adair silently added.

"How unfortunate," the Norman calmly replied. "Outlaws are everywhere these days."

Including right in front of me.

"Indeed they are," Seamus agreed just as calmly. "But no Scot would steal from the Mac Tarans. They know if they are hungry, they have but to come to my hall and they'll be fed. We Scots understand hospitality."

That honest answer and sly rebuke brought a

smile to Adair's lips. But the Norman, dolt that he was, didn't comprehend. Or if he did, he felt no proper shame.

"What did yer father say?" Roban asked in a whisper. Adair and Lachlann knew French, their father having insisted they learn it, but the rest of their clansmen did not.

"He told the bastard about Scots' hospitality," Adair explained.

"So you don't suspect your fellow countrymen of this alleged crime?" Sir Nicholas inquired of the chieftain.

Adair's temper rose even more at the man's tone, as if Scots should, of course, be the first to be suspected, although it was the Normans who were coming to Scotland and taking everything they could.

"It's possible, I suppose," Seamus said with a shrug. Then he smiled in a way that had chilled many an enemy's bones in days gone by. "But the Scots also know that the Mac Tarans will punish those who steal from them."

"I've heard you people take the law into your own hands," the Norman replied.

At last Adair saw a spark of anger in his father's eyes.

"As a thane with a charter from the king, and chieftain of the clan, I have the right to uphold the law."

"You have a charter?" The Norman sounded surprised. "I thought you Scots didn't hold with such legal documents, that the clan held the land in community."

"I hold the charter *for* the clan, because if I did not, there would be nothing to prevent a foreigner from getting our lands."

"Your own king gives charters. Is that not his right?"

"Of course it is," Seamus said, his voice placid once again. "He gave me our charter, as he gave you your reward. I merely point out that I have it, and because I do, I have the right to punish offenders who steal from me and my clan. So I will, when they are caught."

The servant with the mole on her breast reappeared, carrying a tray bearing two goblets. She offered one first to Sir Nicholas, who frowned and gestured at Seamus.

Her hands, already shaking, could barely hold the tray steady as she turned toward the Scots chieftain. She probably feared a beating for this mistake.

Adair hurried forward and grabbed the tray out of the startled woman's hands. "It's a Scots tradition that a guest serve the first drink in his host's hall," he lied, trusting to the Norman's ignorance of local customs as he handed a goblet to Sir Nicholas.

Who was, judging by his unexpectedly shrewd expression after his initial surprise had passed, perhaps not so ignorant of Scots ways as Adair had assumed. Nevertheless, the Norman accepted the goblet without comment. So did Seamus, who regarded his son with a warning eye.

Paying heed to Lachlann's old woman's worrying was one thing; a look like that from their father's gray eyes was another. But he didn't regret his impetuous act when he saw the grateful look from the serving wench, and remembered the surprise in the Norman's.

Adair handed the tray back to the young woman and returned to his place with the rest of his clansmen.

"You can go," Nicholas snapped at the maidservant.

"This bold fellow is my eldest son, Adair Mac Seamus Mac Taran," Seamus explained to the Norman as the young woman fled. "My clan has chosen him to be thane and chieftain when I die."

As Sir Nicholas ran a measuring gaze over him, Adair wondered if the Norman had heard that Adair Mac Taran had never been beaten in a fight, whether with arms or bare-handed, since he was ten years old—after he had seen what Norman soldiers could do.

Sir Nicholas looked back at Seamus and raised a brow. "Chosen?"

"Aye, although he's my son, we still hold to the old ways. I pick who will succeed me, and my clansmen must agree. I have, and they did."

"And all are happy with that choice?"

"They accept it, and thus it shall be," his father answered with a smile. "Loyalty to the clan comes first above all things."

"Not loyalty to your king?"

"If a chieftain's loyalty is pledged to the king, so is the clan's, without fail. Since I swore my oath to Alexander when he gave me the charter, every man in my clan would die for him."

"Whether there was a reward for such service promised or not," Adair added, earning him another sharp look from his father, and a suspicious one from the Norman.

"My son is a bit hot-tempered, my lord," Seamus said. "Something that stands him in good stead in a fight, but leads to misunderstanding at other times."

"I see. And I sympathize. My brother is the same."

There were two of them?

Seamus smiled as if he and this Norman interloper were good friends. "A trial at times, yet worth the trouble in a fight, eh?"

The Norman actually laughed, a harsh sound like a crow, but a laugh. "If you were to come to Henry and accuse him or his men of theft, he would have his knife at your throat before you'd finished speaking."

And soon after that, he would be dead, Adair silently vowed.

"I haven't come here to accuse you or your men of theft," Seamus replied evenly. "I came to warn you that there may be outlaws afoot. I also came to tell you that we intend to mount more patrols on our land."

His father's intent suddenly became more clear, and acceptable. Not as good as telling the Norman they knew his men had taken the cattle—the hoofprints of the beasts had showed they'd been herded toward Dunkeathe—but his father was a wise and patient man, so perhaps this was the better course, even if it was frustrating.

The Norman's expression hardened. "Are you warning me about outlaws, or that you'll attack any Norman who comes onto your land?"

"Has anyone proof that the cattle were actually stolen?" a woman asked, her dulcet French voice coming from somewhere behind the group of Scots. "Perhaps they merely wandered off."

Adair, and all the others, turned to see who'd spoken. Then they stared at the vision of beauty walking regally toward them.

She was easily the most beautiful woman Adair had ever seen. She looked like an angel, with the merest hint of a smile on her lovely face, clear blue eyes the color of a summer's sky, smooth cheeks and full, rosy lips. Framing her perfect face, her soft blond hair hung in long braids over her shoulders.

She was slender and shapely, too—and wearing the most motley collection of garments he'd ever seen on anybody except a beggar.

So she couldn't be a supernatural being. She was a woman of flesh and blood and bone. A woman a mortal man could woo and hope to win.

Sir Nicholas had no wife. If this was Sir Nicholas's lover, he was a very lucky man, and Adair might finally have found one thing to envy a Norman.

"They were stolen, all right," Adair said, walking toward her. "The herdsman is certain of it, and I would stake my life on his opinion."

She raised a shapely, inquisitive brow. "You would pledge your life on a herdsman's word?"

"That one, aye, I would."

The beauty frowned and addressed the overlord. "I wonder if some of the men of the garrison took the cattle by mistake, Nicholas."

Adair nearly laughed at the stunned look on the man's face.

The Norman quickly recovered, and his cheeks turned as pink as the lady's bliaut. "Marianne, return to your chamber."

So, her name was Marianne. And she was also definitely, unfortunately Norman.

"You would rob us of this charming lady's company?" Adair's father asked, rising. "Here, my dear, please sit down."

It could be that his father was making that offer to goad the Norman, but it was more likely he was merely being kind to a woman, as was his way.

In spite of Seamus's invitation, Sir Nicholas fairly bounded off the dais and came to stand between Adair and the woman. "My sister has other duties to attend to."

Sister, not lover. A thrill of familiar excitement shot through Adair's body, yet because she was a Norman, his excitement quickly dwindled.

Lady Marianne flushed as she addressed his father. "I thank you for your kindness, sir, but my brother is right. I should not linger here."

There had been no need for Sir Nicholas to humiliate her, Adair thought, hating the Norman anew.

"Now if you'll excuse me, I must ensure that we

have adequate food and drink and lodging for our honored guests."

Adair was grimly delighted by the annoyance that flittered across Sir Nicholas's angular face. She'd paid him back for that humiliation, because short of rudely denying them food and drink and a place to sleep, Sir Nicholas had to let them stay.

Still, Adair expected the Norman to be discourteous, so he was taken aback when Sir Nicholas said, "Yes, of course. Off you go, then, Marianne. I'll speak to you about the arrangements later."

The beauty smiled tremulously, bowed and gracefully drifted toward a door at the side of the hall, the hem of her garments swaying as she walked, while the Norman threw himself back into his chair.

The man's anger was no doubt caused by more than having to provide food and drink and lodging. He had to be well aware that a potential enemy could learn a lot about his fortress by staying in it.

Perhaps later, Adair thought with inner glee, he could thank his sister for the opportunity.

CHAPTER TWO

"So HE TOOK the tray right out of my hands and served them himself," Polly said breathlessly. "And handsome? Holy Mother Mary, I've never seen a man so fair. I thought I'd faint when our hands touched, I truly did."

Marianne looked away from the cook to the little group of servants clustered around the very excited Polly, who was describing something that had transpired in the hall before she'd arrived and angered Nicholas even more. She was rather curious as to which man had taken pity on the nervous Polly, but it was time they all got back to work. It was bad enough Nicholas was obviously furious with her; she didn't need a ruined evening meal to make things worse.

"That haunch of venison needs turning," she said to the spit boy. "And the rest of you have other things to do, do you not?"

The lad immediately went back to slowly turning the spit. The scullery maid returned to her pots, and the two other female servants started kneading dough again. Three men hurried out of the kitchen completely.

"Watch out it's not burnt on one side and raw on the other, eh?" Emile, the cook, commanded the spit boy before raising his eyes to heaven as if begging deliverance from the stupidity of servants.

"I'm sure the meat will be fine," Marianne assured Emile, hoping she was right. "Is there anything else—?"

"Non, my lady, *non,"* Emile declared, slicing the air with his hand. "I understand. Twenty more and Scots, too."

He sniffed as he headed for a pot boiling over the fire. He stirred its contents, which were sending forth a delicious smell of beef and gravy. "They will be no trouble. The Scots will eat anything. Even my worst meal will be wonderful to them."

Relieved that Emile wasn't going to panic or lose his temper, Marianne turned her attention to another matter. Gesturing for Polly to join her, she retreated to a corner, away from the bustling of the cook and his helpers. "I heard what happened in the hall."

"Oh, my lady, please, don't be angry!" Polly cried, anxiously wringing her hands. "I couldn't help it. He just did it. Took the tray right away from me. What was I to do?"

"You did nothing wrong in the hall, Polly. That's not why I wanted to speak with you." Marianne delicately cleared her throat. "You, um, seem quite taken with the Scot who helped you."

Polly turned as red as a ripe apple and stared at the floor.

"Of course, that was a kind thing for him to do,"

Marianne went on gently. She knew better than to lecture. The Reverend Mother's lectures had more often had the opposite effect than the one she intended; she'd made sin seem exciting rather than something to be avoided.

"However, I must warn you that many men think a woman's gratitude should be expressed in one particular fashion, and we don't know if that Scot is such a man or not."

Polly looked up, her brow wrinkled, as if she didn't understand.

A year or two in the convent hearing the stories some of the girls had to tell, Marianne reflected, and she wouldn't be so confused. "I mean," she explained, "that he might think you're so grateful, you'll give yourself to him."

Polly's eyes lit up.

This was not the reaction Marianne had expected. "Or that you *ought* to, whether you're willing or not," she added significantly.

Polly gulped and went back to staring at the floor.

"So I think tonight, you should stay away from the Scots. All of them."

"Yes, my lady," Polly murmured, her voice so low, Marianne could scarcely hear her.

Nevertheless hoping the young woman appreciated that she was trying to help, Marianne said, "Now you may go and tell the alewife we'll probably need three more casks for tonight."

"Yes, my lady," the maidservant murmured before she hurried away.

"Marianne!"

At the sound of her brother's enraged voice, Marianne cringed, then turned toward the door leading to the hall.

Nicholas stood just inside the entrance, his hands on his hips, his dark brows lowered, his expression wrathful. He imperiously pointed to the door leading to the yard. "Outside, Marianne, now!"

God help her, this was going to be worse than she'd feared. Yet somehow, she'd have to try to make him understand that she'd only been trying to help.

Once outside, a breeze caught Marianne's garments. It wasn't a chill draft such as she always felt in the castle, but a warm gust of air with the hint of the tang of the sea, some miles east. The clouds parted, giving glimpses of bright blue sky.

Nicholas stamped his way across the courtyard ahead of her. Skirting the puddles, she followed him to a secluded area between the mason's hut and a wattle-and-daub storehouse, away from where the laborers were building the inner curtain wall.

"What the devil was the meaning of that little performance?" Nicholas demanded when they were alone, crossing his arms, his sword still swinging at his side from his brisk pace.

"I didn't mean to offend or upset you, Nicholas," she hastened to assure him. "I was only doing what I'd been taught, to show you that—"

"You shouldn't have come to the hall and you damn well shouldn't have invited those men to stay."

"I didn't invite them. I was sure, as overlord of Beauxville, that you had. That's what the holy sisters taught me an overlord should do."

"Don't quote the holy sisters' ideas of etiquette to me," he retorted.

Clearly, it was wrong to assume even a Norman nobleman behaved like a Norman nobleman in this godforsaken place.

In spite of her mistake, she tried to salvage her plan. "I was only trying to be a good chatelaine to you, and take care of your guests."

"Those men are *not* my guests and this isn't Normandy."

As if she needed reminding. "No, I realize that."

His eyes narrowed.

She hurried on, desperately trying to make him understand why she'd done what she had. "I wanted to show you what I've been taught, at your great expense, to prove to you that the money hadn't been wasted and that I deserve a Norman husband, at the very least."

"You could have spared yourself the effort," Nicholas snapped. "You could act like the queen and it wouldn't make a difference to me. In a se'en night, you're marrying Hamish Mac Glogan if I have to lock you in your chamber and put a guard outside the door to make sure of it."

He stepped closer, glaring at her. "Do I have to put a guard on you, Marianne?"

"No, Nicholas, you don't. I understand," she replied, because to her sorrow and despair, she did.

Her brother's mind was made up, and there was nothing she could say or do that would make him change it.

"Good. And stay out of the hall tonight. Those are the most arrogant, insolent Scots I've ever had the displeasure to meet, and I won't have them staring at my sister."

"I have no wish to be the object of any man's impertinent attention, either," she answered haughtily, her pride roused.

Nicholas didn't look quite so angry. "Good. Now go to your room and stay there."

"Gladly," she said, turning on her heel and walking away from her brother.

And his plans for her future.

THE MOON ROSE nearly full. Marianne had counted back the days from the time she'd last seen it and realized it was waning. If she wanted to flee with the moon to light her way, she dare not delay.

Sadly, she had no choice except to flee, no matter how dangerous it was. It was either stay and marry Hamish Mac Glogan, or escape Beauxville and take her chances.

Clutching a bundle of clothing and shoes against her chest, she left her bedchamber and slowly crept down the curved wall-stairs leading to the hall. She had to get past all the men and hounds sleeping there, and across the courtyard. She'd slip out the postern gate to the river, steal a boat and make her way to a fishing village by the sea. From there, she could purchase passage to York and home to Normandy.

She fingered her mother's crucifix around her neck and hoped it, and her ribbons and perhaps a gown or two, would fetch enough for her journey.

If the postern gate was locked and guarded, she'd have no choice but to climb over an unfinished wall, although that would take more time and run more risk that she'd be seen by the guards at the gatehouse towers.

She reached the hall. Fortunately, her brother was extremely lax in religious matters, so instead of Matins being said, everyone in the castle except the guards on duty were asleep. Unfortunately, in addition to the men who usually slept in the hall—the garrison soldiers, male servants, masons and laborers—she had those Scotsmen to worry about. At least the female servants slept in their own quarters above the kitchen.

She peered into the dark hall. Although the central fire had been banked, she could see the huddled outlines of the slumbering men and dogs. The Scots were easy to distinguish—they'd simply wrapped themselves in the long lengths of cloth they wore as their main garment and lain down seemingly where they'd stood. She quickly and instinctively made a count of their number.

One of them was missing and as she scanned the huddled bodies, she realized who it was—the handsome, muscular one.

Had he been the one Polly was talking about? Probably.

Perhaps her words had been no more effective than the Reverend Mother's, and Polly was expressing her "gratitude" this very moment.

As troubling as that thought was, she couldn't let any concern for Polly's welfare impede her plans. She had to get away, and she had to get away tonight. Keeping to the walls, she sidled toward the side door leading to the kitchen.

The kitchen was just as dark as the hall, and stifling. The lingering odors of smoke, grease, leeks and spices filled her nostrils, and she could feel the sweat dripping down her back as she studied the room illuminated by the moonlight coming in through the high, square windows. She made out the central worktable, and the barrels by the door. The stack of wood closer to the hearth. The spoons and bowls piled on the board at the side. The piscina, a basin built into the outer wall of the building.

The spit boy lay on the floor by the entrance to the buttery, as if he were guarding the ale and wine, which perhaps he was. He rolled onto his back and muttered something.

Fearful he was waking, she swiftly made her way around the worktable to the door, lifted the latch as quickly as she dared and slipped out into the chill air of the evening, which seemed blessedly cool.

There wasn't a cloud in the sky. Indeed, the moon was almost too brilliant, making it harder for her to hide. Nevertheless, she welcomed the illumination.

She didn't know the land, and she didn't want to wander about a dark, unfamiliar countryside.

Most of the walls weren't finished, so there was no wall walk for patrolling soldiers. The gatehouse was nearly complete, though, and Nicholas had set watchmen on the towers there. They would be the ones most likely to spot somebody running through the courtyard.

She watched the towers for what seemed like an age before she could be sure the guards were looking not into the courtyard, but out across the river valley. Then, summoning her resolve, she dashed to the alley between the mason's hut and the storeroom where Nicholas had upbraided her that day.

No one called out. No alarm sounded. She'd managed the first part of her escape undetected.

Taking a deep breath, she leaned back against the small wattle-and-daub storehouse and said a silent prayer of thanks.

Suddenly a man—a broad-shouldered man in the outlandish skirted garment of a Scot and a sleeveless shirt—appeared at the other end of the alley.

Before she could recover from the shock and run or hide, he quietly addressed her in French. "Bit of an odd time for a stroll, isn't it, my lady?"

She recognized that voice. Thank God it wasn't Nicholas, or one of his men—but what was that Scot doing here? And where was Polly?

She froze as a guard called out a challenge.

Had they been seen? Had that lascivious Scot cost her the chance of escape?

Mercifully, another man's voice answered, calm and steady. The guards hadn't seen her, or the Scot.

Yet.

She spotted the open door to the mason's hut to the right of the Scot. Hurrying forward, she shoved him inside, coming in after him.

He never made a sound as the wooden door hinged with leather strips swung shut behind them. The only light filtered through cracks in the wall and the shutters over the window.

The Scot seemed taller in the darkness. Silhouetted against the wall of the hut, his body appeared huge, with his long, bare, muscular legs and strong, equally bare arms.

Perhaps this was a mistake. But before she could leave, he spoke.

"Why, my lady, this is an unexpected pleasure," he said, his deep voice low and slightly husky.

"Be quiet," she commanded in a whisper. "Or do you *want* the guards to catch you here, where you have no right to be?"

"No, I don't want the guards to find me here," he answered quietly. "But unless they can see through walls and hear like dogs, I doubt they will. They're too far away, and too busy looking for enemies beyond the walls."

"Where's Polly?"

"Who?"

"Polly. The maidservant who served the wine."

The Scot strolled toward her. "Ah. The one with the mole on her breast?"

As if he could fool her with his bogus innocence. She knew full well the deceit men were capable of. "Yes. Where is she?"

"I have no idea."

Giving him a cold stare, she backed away from him until her body collided with a workbench covered with masons' tools—chisels and trowels, levels and measuring sticks. She set her bundle down, so that her hands were free. She could defend herself now, if she had to. "I don't believe you. I'm sure you were with her."

"I'm sure I wasn't. I think I'd remember if I were."

Splaying her hands behind her and leaning back, her fingers encountered a chisel. Thrilled that she had some kind of weapon, her hand closed around it. "Then what are you doing skulking about my brother's castle?"

"Searching for the plans to this fortress."

No spy would confess so quickly and so easily, to anyone. "You must think I'm a simpleton."

He strolled closer. "Whatever I think of you, my lady, I don't think you're dim-witted."

She swallowed hard.

Suddenly, his hand shot out and grabbed hers, tightening until she dropped the chisel.

"Were you really planning to attack me with that?" he asked as he let go of her.

She rubbed her sore hand and didn't answer.

"You're quite safe with me, my lady. My taste doesn't run to Normans, even ones as beautiful as you."

She'd never before felt simultaneously insulted and flattered.

Perhaps this was his way of trying to confuse her. "What are you doing outside the hall?" she demanded, although that in itself was no crime. "Answer me honestly, or I'll call the guard."

"You won't do that."

She'd heard some Scots had what they called the Sight, the ability to see things by supernatural means, things they couldn't possibly know otherwise. Yet surely he didn't have such a power. "Oh yes, I will."

"No, you won't," he answered, reaching around her for the chisel, coming so close, she could feel his breath warm on her cheek.

Gripping the edge of the table with both hands, she froze until he retreated.

"You won't because then you'd have to explain what *you're* doing wandering about at this time of night and with a bundle in your hands," he said as he toyed with the chisel. "I'm thinking you had a clandestine rendezvous planned, although sadly not with me." He nodded at the bundle. "And you've thoughtfully brought a blanket to lie on and perhaps some wine to drink."

"What a base suggestion!"

"I didn't mean to be insulting," he replied as he tossed the chisel back onto the table, close enough for her to reach. "I'm impressed you planned so well."

Now she really was insulted. "I am not some hussy of the sort you're obviously used to."

The Scot strolled over to another table and work-bench. "What else could lead a beautiful Norman lady to sneak around alone in her brother's fortress in the middle of the night?" he mused aloud. "Perhaps it's a sign that all is not well with the lady." He turned to regard her steadily. "I could be mistaken, of course. I'd be glad to think I was, and that nothing is amiss with you."

He sounded completely sincere. Yet she'd heard enough stories in the convent to know better than to take any man's words at face value, no matter how sincere he sounded.

So she lied, easily and without compunction. "I couldn't sleep and decided to take some linen to the kitchen to be washed in the morning. I heard noises and thought it was a cat. I wanted to chase it outside, lest it make a mess of the masons' things."

"Really?" the Scot answered. He lazily picked up some other tools one at a time and examined them. "You didn't think it might be somebody up to no good? You weren't bravely coming to confront an enemy?"

"I wouldn't be so foolish as to confront an armed man when I have only a bundle of laundry. And I don't think any intelligent man would attack the sister of Sir Nicholas de Beauxville in his own fortress, or confess a crime to her face."

The Scot put down a trowel. "This place is Dunkeathe, not Beauxville."

"Since my brother has possession of it, he can call it whatever he likes."

"Aye, so he may, and so might the Normans, but to the Scots it is, and always will be, Dunkeathe."

"Proudly spoken, but whatever it's called, I want to know what you're really doing out of the hall in the middle of the night."

He tilted his head and studied her a moment before answering. "All right then, my lady, the truth. It's just as I said. I was trying to find the plans to the castle." He shrugged his broad shoulders. "It has to be obvious I'm up to no good."

Then his full lips curved upward into a devilish smile that seemed to reach right into her breast and set her heart to beating as it never had before. "And since I'm not dim-witted, either, I'm sure that you're doing something you don't want your brother to know about, whether it's meeting a lover or not."

She reached for her bundle. "I told you, I'm taking some linen to be laundered."

"When you're ill? That's what your brother said when you weren't at the evening meal."

"I am recovered."

"And making bundles, which you then carry out of your quarters in the middle of the night, heading for the postern gate. If I were to make a guess, Lady Marianne, I'd say you were running away."

"Why would I run away?"

"I can think of plenty of reasons you'd want to flee. For one, that brother of yours is as arrogant as they come. It must be difficult living under his thumb."

"He's a wonderful brother."

"Well, maybe for a Norman, he is. Thank God, I wouldn't know." The Scot took a step closer. "Whether he is or not, you're willing to risk fleeing his castle and traveling alone rather than stay here."

"Even if that were true—which it isn't—is traveling alone in this country such a great risk? Are you saying I should be afraid of the Scots?"

"There are men who would steal cattle roaming about. Alone on the open road, you'd be very tempting for every outlaw between here and York."

She fought the urge to believe that he cared about her welfare. Most men were scoundrels and liars; even her own brother would use her to further his selfish ambitions. "If I were running away, I'd have enough sense to stay off the open road."

"And not get lost?"

"I need only get to the nearest church or monastery or convent by myself. They would give me sanctuary."

That would also be the first place her brother would look for her, which is why she wouldn't risk doing that. It had to be the village, then York, then France.

The Scot came closer. "If you *were* running away, my lady, I'd think again. Or are you quite certain you'd have nothing to fear from the cattle thieves because they're Normans, too?"

"I don't believe the men who took your cattle came from here," she replied, hoping it was true, although she wouldn't put it past some of the soldiers her brother had hired.

"Then so much the worse for you—or any lone woman—who meets them."

The Scot's gaze searched her face. When he spoke, his voice was firm, and stern. "Does he beat you?"

She instinctively drew back, putting a little more distance between them. "Who?"

"Your brother."

"No!"

"He doesn't…lay hands on you?"

She guessed what terrible thing he was implying. "Never!"

His stern visage relaxed. "So why *do* you want to run away?"

"I don't!"

"I think you're lying. I think you desperately want to get away from here. I just don't know why."

Her reasons simply couldn't be important to him, no matter how concerned he sounded. "You have no idea what I want," she replied, mustering her resolve. "I'm a Norman lady and you're nothing but a…but a…"

"What am I but a man who doesn't want to see you hurt—or worse? Do you really find that so hard to believe?" he asked softly, laying his strong hands lightly on her shoulders, the slight pressure warm and surprisingly welcome.

But it shouldn't be. She should slap his face for daring to touch her. She should raise the alarm. Call out the guards. Shout for help. She should push him away. She shouldn't let him pull her into his arms, as he was doing at that very moment.

Her bundle fell to the ground, the garments and shoes tumbling to the ground like so many scattered leaves.

She shouldn't put her arms around his waist and look up into his handsome face. She should try to get away from him and his deep, seductive voice. She shouldn't feel this thrilling excitement coursing through her body, or allow the images bursting into her head.

Yet in spite of all the inner warnings and orders, and all the things she'd heard about men and their evil ways, Marianne closed her eyes in anticipation and welcomed the first touch of the Scot's lips upon hers. They were as light as the caress of a feathertip before they settled and moved with slow, sinuous deliberation.

This was how that girl under the tree must have felt, except this was no stripling youth kissing her. This was a warrior in his prime, handsome and confident.

Nothing could prepare her for the astonishing reality of his passionate kiss. Not the girl and the boy beneath the tree. Not the whispered descriptions from the other girls in the dark at the convent. Not a troubadour's ballad.

Nothing.

As the Scot's arms tightened around her, a longing as powerful as the need for liberty rooted her to the spot and urged her to surrender to the passion surging through her body, enflamed by his kiss.

He tasted of wine and warmth, his lips soft yet

firm, too, as they slid over hers with excruciating, provoking leisure. Leaning against him, soft and yielding, a whimper of yearning escaped her throat, a little note of longing for something more that his kiss promised.

He shifted, and his embrace tightened. His mouth pressed harder, and his tongue touched her lips, preparing to part them.

A sound interrupted the silence: somebody drawing water from the well. Two women's voices talking about the fine weather.

The kitchen servants, always the first to rise, were already setting about their tasks. Soon, the guards would be changing, and the masons would be coming.

With a horrified gasp, Marianne twisted out of the Scot's grasp. She mustn't be found here—with *him.*

"Let me go or I'll call the guards!" she cried, meaning it, as she frantically picked up her things.

She never should have weakened and given in to her lustful impulses. What would the Reverend Mother and Father Damien say if they could see her now? What would her friends think of her? God help her, what would Nicholas do?

"You won't call the guards," the Scot said firmly, backing away, his body blocking the single exit.

"If you don't get away from the door, I certainly will," she countered, whirling around to face him, holding her clothes against her chest.

His expression hard and as cold as Nicholas's could be, the Scot shook his head. "Oh no, you won't, my fine Norman lady." He nodded at her clothes. "That's no bundle of laundry and you weren't on your way to do washing. You were running away, until we met here. Why, I'm not sure, but *I* am sure you'll never tell your brother that we met, because then you'd have to explain yourself."

"And you thought to take advantage of that, and me, didn't you?" she charged.

His whole body tensing, the Scot spread his hands wide. "I'd never take advantage of a woman, and I'm not keeping you here against your will. I haven't done *anything* against your will."

"Yes, you have!"

"No, I have not, my lady, and you know it."

"You were trying to seduce me."

"If I'd been trying, my lady, you'd have been seduced."

"Of all the insolent, despicable, arrogant—! Let me pass!"

He stepped away from the door. "With pleasure, my lady. But we both know that you enjoyed that kiss as much as I."

Marianne knew nothing of the kind. She only knew that staying with him had been a terrible mistake, and not just because of that kiss. She'd lost her chance to escape, and who could say when she would get another before the week was up?

"Fool!" she muttered, silently cursing both herself and the Scot as she pushed past him and hurried out the door.

CHAPTER THREE

ADAIR BOLDLY STRODE toward the hall, silently daring any of the Norman's soldiers in the courtyard to question or challenge him. He'd like nothing better than to send a few of them sprawling in the mud.

Yet as he headed toward the massive hall, no one—not the workmen, *Sassunach* for the most part, or the soldiers—said a word to stop him. Their master should thank God he wasn't an assassin sent to kill him, if this was how they guarded his fortress.

But what could you expect from men paid to serve you? Scots' loyalty and power came from blood and family, not payment in coin, or the promise of reward.

As for Lady Marianne, she was a lying, scheming Norman like all the rest. Of course she'd been sneaking somewhere, and either she was running away, or taking a change of clothes for some other purpose. She probably *had* been going to meet a lover, and was sorry she'd been caught.

At least at first, because say what she would, she *had* wanted to kiss him. She'd relaxed against him and passionately pressed her lips to his as if she'd like nothing more than to be his lover.

God save him, he'd wanted that, too, forgetting that she was a Norman. There was no excuse for his lustful weakness and he ought to be ashamed.

He *was* ashamed.

Adair shoved open the door to the hall and marched inside the chamber big enough to hold a herd of cattle.

He spotted his father sitting on a bench, his shoulders slumped, not speaking or moving. Adair couldn't remember ever seeing his father quite so still first thing in the morning, and there were circles of weariness under his eyes. Clearly, a night on a stone floor, even one cushioned with rushes, had proved intolerably uncomfortable.

He marched toward his father. "The bastard should have offered you a bed."

Seamus rose, his movements slow and stiff. "It's nae wise to call a man names in his own house, my son," he said as he gave Adair a wry smile. "And he may not have an extra bed."

"The devil he does. He's rich. This place is proof of that."

"This place, my son, is proof that he's spending a lot of coin to fortify Dunkeathe," his father replied, his gaze roving over the high-beamed ceiling and stone walls before returning to Adair. "It doesnae mean he has muckle in the way of beds."

"So you think he needs more money," Adair inquired significantly, thinking of the missing cattle.

"Maybe. But we don't know the man's business, so it's better to make no guesses."

Lachlann nodded. "Especially when we're in his castle."

"Aye, and where the devil have *you* been?" Cormag demanded.

Adair saw no need to explain himself to Cormag. He also saw no reason to tell his father, or anyone else, about his encounter with the Norman's sister. That unforeseen meeting represented no danger to his clan, because he was sure it would remain a secret. In spite of her bravado, the lady wouldn't dare to tell her brother that they'd been alone together. Otherwise she'd have to explain how she came to be in the courtyard in the middle of the night.

"I couldn't sleep, so I went out for a wee walk about the place," he replied, which was true, as far as it went.

He'd left the hall after he'd lain awake for a long time, thinking of this fortress and the danger it represented to his clan and his country. He hadn't planned on meeting the lady, and he should have left her the moment he saw her. Yet she had been frightened and tense, even after she'd pushed him into that hut. His curiosity had been roused enough to try to find out what she was up to, and then if she was in any danger.

He should have known better than to have any sympathy for a Norman, even if the Norman was a woman.

"The bonnie lass with the mole on her breast, was it?" Cormag asked with a sly, disgusting smirk as he adjusted his *feileadh,* pushing and pulling the fabric so that it bunched less around his middle. "Was she grateful that you acted like a servant to Sir Nicholas?"

Adair's lip curled. "I didn't go out to meet a woman," he replied. "And only a desperate lout—or a Norman—would expect a woman to show her gratitude the way that you're implying."

"That's enough, you two," his father said. "I've plenty to think on without you fighting like mongrel dogs."

"Aye," Lachlann seconded. "And we shouldn't quarrel among ourselves while we're here. How will that look to the Normans?"

Lachlann had a point, and Adair resolved to try to ignore Cormag, at least until they were out of Dunkeathe.

His father stretched and glanced at the servants setting up the tables. "That Norman's idea of an evening meal was not mine, and they'll have no notion at all of what a man needs in the morning, so I think it's time we were on our way. Roban, see to the horses."

"Without another word about the cattle?" Adair asked as his friend dutifully headed out of the hall.

His father nodded. "Aye, my son, there'll be not another word about the cattle—for now. We've no proof, and arguing with Sir Nicholas like a hotheaded lad isn't going to provide it. We've warned him and he knows we're suspicious, so that will have to do."

"Aye, Adair. If you can't hold your temper, you'll have us at war with our neighbors," Cormag added.

Adair shot him a look. "I don't mind a fight."

Cormag's hand went for his missing sword. "Are you calling me a coward?"

"I'm saying I don't mind a fight, if it comes to it," Adair replied, trying to control his frustration with Cormag, Sir Nicholas and the Normans in general. "Better a battle than surrender."

"I'll fight when the chieftain tells me to, and not because you can't keep a civil tongue in your head," Cormag retorted.

"It's not your place to chastise my son, nephew," Seamus said, standing between them. "Now let's be gone."

"We're not taking leave of the lady?" Lachlann asked. "It'd be only right to say farewell and give her our thanks for her kindness."

"We'll take our leave of her if she comes to bid us farewell," Seamus answered. "She was too ill to eat with us last night, remember?"

"Aye, poor thing," Adair replied. "Probably sickened from whatever that was they served us. Might have been anything under all that sauce."

The men started to laugh, until Seamus held up his hand to silence them. "Wheesht. Here comes the man himself."

Sir Nicholas strode toward them from the bottom of the curved staircase, carrying himself with the ease of a soldier welcomely divested of heavy chain mail and armor. He was the same height as Adair, and looked as if he could lift ten stone. Some Normans went to fat when they quit going to war or tournaments. Adair doubted this man would.

"Good day to you, Sir Nicholas," his father said in French, his tone jovial, although Adair didn't doubt his father had noted that the man was wearing his sword belt, the bronze hilt of his weapon gleaming in the morning sunlight streaming in through the narrow windows.

"And to you, Seamus," the Norman replied, coming to a halt. "I regret I have no priest in residence to say mass today."

Despite his words, he didn't sound the least bit sorry.

"Oh, well then, I think it's best, my lord, if we take our leave at once. We mustn't be in a state of sin when we break the fast."

His father wasn't being any more sincere. He wasn't a religious man, and the priest of their kirk was notorious for his disagreement with several of the rules of Rome, particularly the one regarding chastity. As for eating before mass, Father Padraig always said God would understand that it was difficult for a man to contemplate anything but his own hunger on an empty belly.

"If you insist upon leaving, naturally I won't detain you," Sir Nicholas said, his expression betraying no hint of dismay or regret, "but I shall be sorry to see you leave without eating and drinking with me once more."

"We really must go," Seamus answered. "Please give our thanks to your lovely sister for her fine hospitality. We hope she'll soon recover."

"I will, and I believe her illness is not overly serious, if wearying. Unfortunately, I doubt she'll have an opportunity to meet you again. She's betrothed and will soon be going to Menteith to be married."

"Oh?" Seamus said, raising a brow. "To whom?"

"Hamish Mac Glogan."

"That greedy, grasping, lecherous old wretch?" Adair cried in Gaelic to his father, aghast at the thought of Lady Marianne married to Hamish Mac Glogan.

"Go and help Roban with the horses," his father said sharply.

It was a command, not a request. Nevertheless, Adair didn't move. "You can't allow this, Father. An alliance between the Normans and that auld lecher. Mac Glogan's lands are too close to our western border. Between the two of them and the sea, they'll have us encircled like a snare."

"I know where Hamish Mac Glogan's lands lie, Adair. Leave us!"

Scowling fiercely, Adair turned on his heel and marched out of the hall.

"WILL YOU NEVER LEARN to think before you speak?" Lachlann demanded as he joined Adair near the stable a few moments later.

Holding the reins of his white horse, Neas, and Lachlann's nut-brown gelding, Adair didn't reply. A little ways off, Roban waited beside their father's black horse, as well as his own feisty roan.

The sun shone brightly, and a warm breeze brought the scent of damp earth to their nostrils, along with wet sand, stone and mortar from the grow-ing walls. All around them they could hear the work-men calling to one another, or talking among themselves in the rough tongue of the *Sassunach*. The mason, a slender fellow who looked as though a strong breeze would blow him away, bustled to and fro, ordering and chiding and complaining as he cre-ated this foreign monstrosity on the sacred soil of Alba.

Lachlann nodded at their father, who marched to-ward his horse without so much as a glance at his sons. "Father's in a right foul mood now."

"So he should be, but not with me," Adair an-swered as he swung into the saddle. "With those scheming Norman bastards and Hamish Mac Glogan. It's not enough the Normans are stealing our land with the king's help. Now they're doing it by mar-riage."

Their father, mounted on his horse, raised his hand to signal his men to head toward the gate. He was at the front of the band, followed by Roban and Cormag and the others, while Adair and Lachlann brought up the rear.

Adair could feel the animosity in the stares of the Norman's soldiers, and he glared right back at the thieving foreigners. Let one of them draw his weapon. He'd be feeling the tip of Adair's dirk at his throat before he took another breath.

Lachlann gave Adair a warning look. "These aren't the men who killed Cellach, you know."

"I know."

"And she died years ago, Adair."

It was easy for Lachlann to put Cellach from his mind. He hadn't been the one who'd found her ravished, broken body.

Lachlann sighed, and changed the subject. "Sir Nicholas's sister is certainly lovely. It's too bad she didn't come back to the hall, but it was obvious her brother was angry with her for inviting us to stay."

He'd been livid, if Adair was any judge. That's why he'd been worried the Norman had hurt her. He wouldn't put it past the man to beat his sister. Yet she'd denied it, and he didn't think she was lying. There'd been no hidden hint of falsehood in her shining eyes. Not then, anyway.

"I think she liked you, Adair," Lachlann noted with a smile. "No surprises there, I suppose."

"She didn't like me." Except, perhaps, to kiss— a notion that rankled.

"Aye, she did. I saw all the usual signs when she looked at you."

"I wouldn't trust any 'signs' she gives, any more than I would her brother."

"Then it won't matter to you that she's watching us right now."

Adair stiffened. "The devil she is."

"Aye, she is, from her window in the apartments beside the hall. She's peeking out as shy as a novice stealing glances at a handsome priest."

Adair glanced up and over his shoulder. Lady Marianne *was* there, standing at the window and watching them. He couldn't see her face well enough to make out her expression.

She was probably delighted he was leaving and taking their secret with him. The duplicitous, deceitful, beautiful, passionate…

Then Sir Nicholas came to stand behind her, looming tall and stern in the shadows behind her, like some sort of judge. Or executioner.

He could well believe that Lady Marianne had been trying to get away from her brother, no matter what she said.

Perhaps she'd been fleeing because she didn't want to marry Hamish Mac Glogan—until he'd stopped her, putting her neck right back in her brother's noose, as if he were Sir Nicholas's henchman.

"Adair!" his father called, gesturing for his son to ride to the head of their party.

He hesitated.

"Adair!"

"What's the matter?" Lachlann demanded in an urgent whisper. "Have you lost your hearing, or do you want to linger longer here among the Normans?"

"Nay, I don't want to linger here," Adair muttered as he punched Neas's side with his heels and went to join his father.

RIDING BESIDE ADAIR at the head of their party, Seamus drew in a deep breath. They were in a pine wood between Lochbarr, their village on a long lake, and Dunkeathe, recently given over to the Norman. Several small streams splashed their way down the rocky, needle-covered slope to the loch.

Lachlann had moved forward, so that now he was behind Adair and his father, and beside Cormag. The rest of the men came after, including Roban, who was robustly singing a bawdy song at the top of his lungs, scaring the birds and sending the wildlife scattering.

The chieftain raised his voice to be heard over the sound of Roban's deep voice and the jingling of the horses' accouterments. "This is better than being in that Norman's castle. A man can breathe out here."

"Aye," Adair agreed. "I felt like my belt was too tight the whole time I was in that place."

"Not too tight to keep you from wandering in the night," his father pointedly remarked. "Where were you?"

"I went to the mason's hut. I wanted to see the plans for the castle."

His father abruptly reined in his horse, causing them all to halt. "You did *what?*"

Adair met his father's shocked gaze steadily. "I wanted to know more about the fortifications he's planning on building. That castle makes Lochbarr look like a farmer's yard."

"You could have got us all killed!" Cormag cried, his anxious horse dancing beneath him.

Adair twisted in his saddle and studied his cousin, catching sight of an equally thunderstruck Lachlann. "I wasn't caught."

Not by the guards, anyway.

"But you might have been," Lachlann said, aghast.

"I had my excuse ready."

"Which was?" his father demanded.

Adair put on a pained expression. "That I was having trouble with my bowels and looking to relieve myself."

His father, Lachlann and some of the other men smiled. Cormag, and those in the band who were his cousin's friends, did not.

"You were lucky," Lachlann said.

"Not that lucky," Adair replied. "I couldn't find the plans. They must have been locked away in the box I saw in the mason's hut."

Beneath the table Lady Marianne had leaned against, watching him warily, as if she was afraid he might bite. He couldn't bear the thought of any woman being frightened of him—another reason he'd stayed, he supposed.

"What a surprise they weren't left lying about for anybody to see," Cormag said sarcastically. "Even your father's tact couldn't have saved you if you'd been found looking over the plans. We might all have been hung for spying. But you didn't think of that, did you?"

In truth, he hadn't. He'd been too keen to find out all he could about the castle. "Don't fash yourself, Cormag."

The chieftain nudged his horse into a walk, as did the others. "Whether you were caught or no," he said to his son, "I have to agree that wasn'a a wise thing to do, especially when you might have guessed that the plans would be kept away from prying eyes."

"Aye, 'twas a fool's errand," Cormag loudly complained. "We don't need to see any plans to realize the Norman's fortifying Dunkeathe in a way that'll make it hard to beat him."

"With one wall, or two?" Adair asked, defending his *fool's errand.* "I've heard that some Norman castles have two curtain walls, and a few even three. They have towered gatehouses and bossed gates, secret passages for escape, dungeons and even a murder hole."

"A murder hole? Losh, what's that?" Lachlann asked.

"'Tis a hole in the roof between the portcullis at the entrance to the gatehouse and the gate at the other end. They can drop rocks through it on invaders, or boiling oil."

"God help us," Lachlann murmured, and a few of the men crossed themselves, or made the sign against the devil.

"Aye. That's why I wanted to see what Sir Nicholas was up to. He strikes me as the sort to have a murder hole. And lots of dark, damp cells."

Perhaps he'd lock his sister away in one if he somehow found out she'd met a Scot in the mason's hut, or was trying to escape his castle.

Adair shoved that thought away. "Father, I'm thinking we should rebuild our own defenses."

"Aye, my son, so am I."

"Especially if the Norman's making an alliance with Mac Glogan."

"That's a bad business, right enough," his father agreed.

"Can you not put a stop to it? You could go to the king. You're a thane and a chieftain. Alexander ought to listen to you."

"Sir Nicholas has Alexander's favor, so any objections will have to be made carefully," his father replied.

"Then Adair'd better stay at home if you decide to go," Cormag said. "Or he'll likely lose his temper with the king."

"Shut it, Cormag," Adair warned.

"If you really want to prevent the marriage, why not seduce the woman, Adair?" Cormag suggested, his voice full of scornful mockery. "Women are helpless to resist your pretty face and *braw* body, are they not?" He grinned and raised his voice, imitating a woman. "Oh, Adair, kiss me! Hold me! Raise my skirts and—"

Adair was off his horse and dragging Cormag from his before any of the other men had time to blink.

"Father!" Lachlann cried as the two Scots wrestled in the mud of the narrow path, all bare legs and plaids and curses. "Stop them before they kill each other."

"They'll not do that," Seamus said as he continued to ride for home. "Let them fight awhile. Then maybe we'll have some peace in our hall tonight. Those Normans weary me something fierce, and I need to think."

CHAPTER FOUR

FIVE DAYS LATER, Neas fairly danced with impatience to be free of the confines of his stall.

Motes of dust and bits of chaff from the hay swirled in the air and about the beams of the stables. The scent of thatch mingled with dung and the leather of bridles, saddles and harnesses. The other horses munched contentedly, or shifted and refooted, some more lively than others because one of their number was going to be leaving as soon as its master could saddle it.

The stable door opened, throwing a shaft of sunlight into the dimmer building.

"Adair!" Lachlann exclaimed as he paused on the threshold. "I wasn't expecting to find you here. I thought you'd be on patrol with Roban and the others."

Partly hidden by Neas, Adair silently cursed. He'd hoped to ride out without having to explain where he was going, or why. "I was, then decided Neas needs more of a run." He threw a fleece over his horse's back. "It's been too long since he had a good gallop."

"Aye. I can't remember a wetter summer." Lachlann strolled closer, studying his brother's face as Adair heaved the saddle onto Neas. "You're healing, I see."

"Thanks to that awful stinking stuff Beitiris makes. Smells worse than a bog, but it works." Adair bent down to buckle the girth. "How's Cormag?"

"His eye's a charming motley of purple and green and yellow, but he can open it now," Lachlann answered. "He's limping yet, though."

Lachlann leaned back against the upright beam at the end of the stall. "Cormag's still some furious. Do you think it's wise to fight with him so much and so openly?"

"What are you getting at?"

"He's never liked you, Adair."

"Nor I, him. What of that?"

Lachlann patted Neas's muzzle. The beast shivered and pranced, so Lachlann withdrew his hand. "It's not good to have enemies within the clan."

Lachlann worried about Cormag too much. "He's my cousin and clansman. He'll stand with me in a battle."

"I hope you're right."

"If he doesn't, you and I both know the fate of a man who'll betray his clan."

"So you're not worried about Cormag at all?" Lachlann asked, his gaze searching Adair's face as if he doubted Adair could really have so little concern for what Cormag thought of him.

"Cormag's our cousin. That's what'll matter when it comes to a battle."

"Then something else is troubling you."

"That damned Norman and his castle," Adair readily admitted. "He shouldn't be here, and that castle'll be hard to capture if the king changes his mind and wants to rid our land of those foreigners. And now he's allying himself with Mac Glogan, who'd sell his own mother for the right price."

"Aye, 'tis troubling. No wonder you've been so quiet lately."

Adair forced a laugh as he started to lead Neas around Lachlann. "You're the one always saying I ought to think more."

And he *had* been thinking, ever since he'd returned from Dunkeathe, about the marriage and the lady and the escape he'd prevented.

"So, where will you be riding?" Lachlann asked as he followed Adair and Neas into the yard.

"The south meadow," Adair answered, not completely lying, for he would indeed be heading south on this fine day. The sky was blue enough to make you think you'd never seen blue like it before. Not a cloud was overhead, nor was there even a hint of mist on the hills around the loch.

"Care for some company on your ride?"

"Not today, Lachlann. I'm not in a mood to talk."

Lachlann put his hand on Adair's arm to detain him. "It's too dangerous," he said in a low and confidential whisper.

"Since when has riding been dangerous for me?" Adair demanded with a raised brow.

"It's not the riding," Lachlann answered, still in that same low, cautious tone. "It's the woman. You can fool Father and the others, but you can't fool me, Adair. You want Lady Marianne—I could see it in your eyes the moment you turned around and saw her."

Adair grabbed his brother's arm and pulled him back into the stable, taking Neas with them. Once they were inside and the door closed behind Neas, Adair tossed his horse's reins over a stall wall and faced Lachlann. "I'm not some lascivious lout."

Lachlann didn't back down. "I saw the look on your face when we rode away from Beauxville—"

"Dunkeathe."

His brother shrugged. "Their fortress."

"It's their fortress and their alliance with Mac Glogan that's got me worried," Adair declared. "I'm worried the Normans are marrying into clans because they're trying to take Scotland over from within, like a plague infecting a village."

"I don't believe that's all there is to this."

Before Adair could refute his charge, Lachlann's expression softened. "It's not just lust you feel for her, Adair. I know that. Ever since Cellach was killed you've had a weakness for a woman in trouble and Lady Marianne's betrothed to Hamish Mac Glogan. No woman could be happy married to him. But it's not your place to interfere."

"It's not *my place* to pretend it's not important, either," Adair retorted, leaving Cellach out of it. "Father hasn't said another word about going to the king to stop the wedding—and it has to be stopped.

With the Norman to the south, Mac Glogan to the west and the sea to the east, we're in a trap."

"The clans to the north are our friends," Lachlann said, his tone reasonable and calm. "And Father's right to be cautious. He has to be sure preventing the marriage is the right thing to do, and plan the best way to go about it if it is."

"Of course it's the right thing to do!" Adair strode a few paces away, then back again. "What if Father spends so much time thinking, she's married before he stirs? Then there'll be nothing anybody can do."

"Perhaps Father has his reasons for not interfering. Have you asked him?"

Adair didn't answer.

Lachlann sighed. "I thought not. Leave it, Adair, and leave her. You'll only make things worse if you go back to Beaux—Dunkeathe."

Adair's impatience was getting difficult to control. "Did I say I was going to Dunkeathe?"

"If you're not, there's no reason I shouldn't go riding with you. I could use the practice. You're always telling me I sit my horse like a bag of stones."

Adair bit back another retort, because he recognized the look in Lachlann's eyes; the lad wasn't going to give up. So he had two choices: lie, or be honest.

"All right, Lachlann, you've caught me," he said, spreading his hands. "I want to ride to Dunkeathe—but just to get a look at Lady Marianne. If I can find proof she's being forced to marry, that'll surely convince Father to go to the king. Father hates to see a woman being used against her will as much as I."

Lachlann regarded Adair doubtfully. "How do you intend to get into the castle? You can't ride up and announce your intentions to Sir Nicholas."

"I'll sneak in."

"Let's say you succeed in getting into the castle. How will you know what's passing between the lady and her brother, or if she objects?"

"I'll find out somehow."

"Hamish Mac Glogan is rich and has influence with Alexander. Maybe she thinks those things outweigh Mac Glogan's faults."

"She's not a *gomeral,* and only a *gomeral* would think anything outweighs that old villain's faults." Adair's voice hardened, like his resolve the moment he'd decided what he had to do. "You aren't going to try to stop me, are you, Lachlann?"

His brother shook his head. "Much as I'd like to, you'd only go another time. And as you say, if she's being forced, that's a good reason for our father to go to the king and try to stop the marriage. So perhaps there's no harm in a wee visit to Dunkeathe—but you have to let me go, too. You need somebody with you who can keep a cool head."

Adair realized he had little choice but to agree, or he would have to waste even more time arguing, and he'd wasted too much already. "Hurry up, then, and saddle your horse."

Lachlann didn't move. "Are you planning to go dressed like that? You'll be a tad *kenspeckle* in your *feileadh.* Should you not make an effort at disguise?"

"Losh, you're right," Adair muttered, looking down at his clothes.

"I'll fetch some other garments while you saddle my horse," Lachlann said, turning to go.

Adair beat him to the door. He didn't want to risk Lachlann revealing their intentions, if only by accident. "I'll fetch the clothes."

Lachlann raised a skeptical brow. "And what will you say you want them for?"

"What excuse will you be giving?" Adair countered.

"I'll think of something, and I'm a better liar."

That was true. Lachlann could lie as cool as you please. "Go, then, and be quick about it. I'll have your horse ready by the time you get back. If you meet anyone, tell them we're going to the south meadow."

"Aye, I remember," Lachlann said. His hand on the latch, he turned back and flashed a grin at his elder brother. "I'm no *gomeral,* either, Adair."

"THERE'S OUR CHANCE," Adair whispered as he peered out of an alley between a tavern and the village smithy outside the castle walls of Dunkeathe.

Coming from the nearby wood, a group of laborers walked past. They were carrying bundles of long poles, probably intended for scaffolding in the castle.

"We'll get ourselves a bundle and walk in, easy as you please."

Dressed like Adair in tunic, breeches and short

cloak, with a hood pulled up over his head and his dirk hidden in his boot, Lachlann didn't look convinced. "Will the guards not realize we're—?"

"They're not even looking at the poor sods. Keep your head bowed and look humble and they'll take no notice, the arrogant oafs. Come on."

Planning to circle around to the wood where they'd left their horses, Adair started back toward the other end of the alley. "Hurry up, Lachlann!"

Lachlann quickened his pace, and soon they reached the clearing where other laborers stacked the bundles and tied them with short pieces of rope.

Adair waited until a group of men returning from the castle drew near. Then he hurried out of the trees and took his place at the back of the line, Lachlann behind him.

With a grunt, he hoisted a bundle onto his shoulder. The sticks were heavier than they looked, or the laborers were stronger than he'd assumed. Regardless, he started to head to the castle, pausing for a moment to glance back at his brother.

Lachlann took two tries to get his bundle on his shoulder. When he finally did, he staggered under its weight, drawing the attention of the woodcutters.

Maybe this wasn't such a clever plan after all.

"Too much ale this morning," Lachlann slurred, belching, sounding so much like a Yorkshireman, Adair could scarcely believe his ears. "I hope that Norman pays well, or I've come a long way for nowt."

The woodsmen laughed and went back to their

work, leaving Lachlann to stumble on his way. Adair slowed his steps, letting the other men get farther ahead, and easing the pace for Lachlann.

"Where did you learn to talk like that?" Adair asked in a whisper when Lachlann caught up to him.

"Listening," Lachlann replied, panting. "I pay attention to people, and not just the bonnie lasses."

"You always were the watchful one. If your load's too heavy for you, I'll take it and go myself."

"I'll manage."

"If you drop it, the guards might get curious," Adair warned. "Unless you want to cause a *stramash,* set that bundle on my other shoulder, go to the tavern and wait for me there."

"You can't carry both."

"I can. Do as I say. I won't be long."

Lachlann didn't immediately agree.

"If I'm not able to see her, you might hear news of her in the tavern."

Lachlann sighed, then hefted his bundle onto Adair's other shoulder. It took a moment for Adair to get the balance right, but once he did, he was satisfied he'd make it into the castle's courtyard without arousing suspicion or undue attention. "Wait until the sun's about a foot above the castle walls. If I'm not back by then, head for the horses. If I'm not there, go home and tell Father he may have to come and get me out of Sir Nicholas's dungeon."

"Losh, Adair, be careful, or there'll be hell to pay, and from more than Father."

"I'll be as careful as can be, and I'd forswear my

loyalty to our clan before I let any Norman catch me. Now go. These bundles are heavy."

"Gur math a thèid leibh," Lachlann said before he hurried away.

"Aye, I may have need of luck," Adair muttered under his breath as he continued on his way, quickening his pace to catch up to the last of the laborers. Silently cursing his damn hood, for sweat was dripping down his forehead and into his eyes, he was still about twenty paces behind the rest when he reached the castle gates.

He kept his head down as he passed the guards.

"There's a strong one, to carry two," one of them said, laughing. "Where're you from?"

"York," Adair grunted, in what he hoped was a passable imitation of the accent, although he didn't sound nearly as convincing as Lachlann.

"Those Yorkshiremen are built like oxen," another guard remarked. "That's why they're so good at hauling."

For a moment, Adair felt a kinship with the common folk of Yorkshire. But he didn't want to make himself any more noticeable, so he continued to follow the laborers until he reached a portion of the wall that was far from completed. The others had put their bundles there and turned back toward the gate.

So did Adair, but instead of returning with the others, he ducked into the alley between the well-remembered mason's hut and the storehouse.

His gaze scanned the courtyard. There was no

sign of Lady Marianne, but it wasn't likely she'd be strolling about the bustling yard full of masons, laborers and servants like a lady in a garden. She was probably in the hall.

Adair scanned the yard again, looking for something he could carry into the hall the same way he had carried the wood into the yard.

There might be such a thing in the storehouse beside him. Aware of the guards and workmen in the vicinity, he strode toward the door of the small building as if not engaged in anything secretive. He put his hand on the latch, hoping it wasn't locked during the day.

It wasn't, and he quickly slipped inside. As his eyes adjusted to the darkness, he realized why the hut wasn't locked.

There wasn't any food in here, or drink. It contained a huge pile of sand, for the mortar, no doubt.

They could make a lot of mortar with that much sand.

Letting out his breath slowly, disappointed in his quest, he wondered why the sand smelled as it did.

Then he realized it wasn't the sand. There were bunches of plants hanging down from the rafters—fleabane and rosemary, to be sprinkled on the rushes that covered the hall floors.

He turned and spotted a pile of rushes in the corner behind the door, perhaps excess from the last time they were swept and replaced.

He had his excuse.

TRYING NOT TO PAY any attention to the huge German mercenary leaning against the wall five feet away, Marianne sat in her brother's hall with her embroidery, a small table bearing a silver carafe of wine and a goblet at her elbow. Polly was seated on a stool across from her, threading the needles with brightly colored woolen strands.

Polly wasn't even trying to ignore the German. She kept glancing anxiously over her shoulder at Herman, who was over six feet tall, with a hideous scar down the left side of his face. It was as if his skin had been wet clay and someone had scraped their fingers from his eye socket to his chin.

"Heavens above, my lady," Polly murmured in Saxon. "Ain't he a horror?"

"He's supposed to protect me," Marianne replied, her mastery of Saxon basic at best as she gave Polly the explanation Nicholas had given her shortly after the Scots led by Seamus Mac Taran had departed.

She'd been afraid he'd discovered that she'd been out in the yard at night, but Nicholas had said nothing about it.

Perhaps Nicholas wisely feared she'd try to flee before the wedding, even if he didn't know she'd made one attempt already, and this German was his means of assuring she would be here when Hamish Mac Glogan came to claim her.

How little Nicholas knew her! It would take more than a guard to dissuade her from escaping, if a marriage against her will was the alternative. She was just as determined as ever to get away, and no unsympathetic brother, or apparently sympathetic Scotsman—even one who'd kissed with such passion and who'd haunted her dreams every night—was going to stop her. Unfortunately, time was running out, and it was but two days before she was to be wed.

She'd considered trying to speak to the priest Nicholas had sent for before the ceremony, to tell him that she was being made to marry, but Nicholas would probably make that impossible.

The only other plan she'd come up with was to feign illness on her wedding day. Yet Nicholas might suspect her of trickery, and insist she attend nonetheless.

Polly shifted nervously. "He looks like something straight from hell."

Marianne couldn't disagree with that. "Pour me some wine, will you, Polly? It's warm today."

Indeed, it was warm enough to make her think this terrible country might actually have a summer, after all.

Polly set down her work and did as Marianne asked. As she handed the goblet to Marianne, Herman suddenly moved, bending down to pat the head of an inquisitive, and very ugly, brown boar hound that was sniffing the fur wrapped about the German's stocky legs.

Polly started with a jerk, sending wine slopping over the edge of the goblet and onto Marianne's embroidery.

"Oh, no!" she cried, immediately setting down

the wine and starting to mop the spill with the edge of her sleeve. Her eyes filled with tears. "I've ruined it! I'm so sorry, my lady!"

"It's all right," Marianne hastened to assure her. "You only got a little on the corner."

Polly didn't seem to hear, either because she was too upset, or because of the noise of the workmen outside. They must be doing something on the wall behind the hall, perhaps finishing the merlons.

"It's nothing to be so upset about. Truly," Marianne said soothingly. She slid a glance at the hulking German, who was still petting the dog and muttering in his native language. "He scares me, too."

The young woman stopped dabbing, raised her red-rimmed eyes and sniffled. "You aren't angry with me, my lady?"

Marianne shook her head and gave Polly a conspiratorial smile. "Once, before I came here, I spilled a whole..." She searched for the right word. "Bucket? No, *carafe*," she amended. "I spilled a whole carafe of wine on the Reverend Mother's head."

Polly stared, her mouth an astonished O.

Marianne nodded and leaned back in her chair. "I did," she confirmed. "The Reverend Mother was very angry. She said I must have been sent by the devil to trouble her, and if I didn't want to burn in hell, I had to pray for forgiveness twice a day and..."

Again she searched her memory for a word. Not finding it, she acted out dipping a cloth and moving it in a circle.

"Scrub?" Polly offered.

"Yes, that's it!" Marianne cried. "Scrub all the floors for a week."

Polly's eyes grew round as wheels. "You never had to wash floors!"

"I did," Marianne confirmed. "So what is a little wine on my sewing? It isn't very good anyway." She studied the stain that was about the size of a coin. "That might even make it look better."

Polly smiled tremulously. "I think you sew very well, my lady. And the colors are very pretty, the red especially. It's as bright as holly berries."

Marianne knew flattery when she heard it.

She didn't sew well because she hated it. She'd only started this because she wanted some excuse to talk to Polly, for a servant knew many things about the running of the household, such as who would be where, when. Polly was also familiar with the countryside and the people who lived outside the castle, as well as the roads leading away from Beauxville.

As Marianne went back to working on her ugly embroidery that looked like miscellaneous blobs of color linked by green strings instead of intertwined roses and vines, two male servants came into the hall and set new torches in the sconces in the wall. A middle-aged serving woman swept out the hearth, leaving some coals at one side to kindle the fire anew in the evening.

Out of the corner of her eye, Marianne caught a movement to her right. Another servant laying rushes.

Whatever for? They'd just been changed yesterday.

There was something odd about that man....

Marianne stiffened and her hand went instinctively to her lips as the memory of the Scot's kiss returned full force.

What in the name of the saints was he doing here? And he had to be up to no good—again—to come in disguise. She should call out the guards or summon Herman.

Yet if she did and the Scot was imprisoned, who knew what he might say to Nicholas? He might reveal that she'd been alone with him. Then Nicholas would surely lock her in her chamber until the wedding, with Herman to guard the door. She'd have absolutely no chance of escape.

She had to get that Scot away from here before anybody realized who he was.

She hastily slipped her needle through her linen and addressed Polly, doing her best to sound as if everything were perfectly normal and there was no need for alarm. "I think I've had enough sewing for today. Please go to the laundry and see if my shifts are dry."

Polly rose, reaching for the tray bearing the wine. "Yes, my lady." She sighed. "I wish you weren't leaving here so soon. Only two more days, and you'll be off to Menteith."

"I'll miss you, too, Polly," Marianne truthfully replied. "Now hurry along. I really ought to begin packing. Oh, and see if there's some extra linen to line the chest, please."

"Yes, my lady," Polly replied before scurrying away.

When she was out of sight, Marianne got to her feet. "You there, with the rushes," she called out. "Come here."

CHAPTER FIVE

AT MARIANNE'S SUMMONS, the Scot slowly straightened. "Yes, my lady," he said humbly, and in a broad Yorkshire accent.

As he walked toward her, she couldn't understand how he'd tricked the guards at the gate. It should have been obvious this man was no peasant, and not only because of his powerful build. He had the same warrior's walk as her brother, a rolling gait of unexpected and lithe grace.

When the Scot came to a halt in front of her, she gestured at her embroidery frame.

"Pick that up and come with me," she commanded, lifting her wooden sewing box. She started toward the curved staircase that led to the bedchambers, glancing over her shoulder to make sure the Scot followed her.

Herman pushed himself off the wall, lumbering after them like a bear just waking from the winter. As always, though, the German halted at the foot of the stairs. Her brother's bedchamber was between hers and the hall, so Herman went no further during the day or the night. The only other entrance to the apartments was at the opposite end of the upper corridor and led to the courtyard. It was always guarded by two men, and had been since her arrival there, lest somebody slip in from the yard and gain entry to the hall, or assassinate her brother in his bed.

"So, he's set his hound to watch you," the Scot said softly in French as he followed her up the stairs. "Does he know about the other—?"

"No. You have nothing to fear about that."

"The only thing I feared is that he'd discovered our meeting and taken his anger out on you. I've come back to make sure you're not suffering for that. Or anything else."

"I'm quite well."

"That's not what I meant. Is he trying to force you to marry against your will? Is that why you were running away when I met you in the courtyard?"

Her heart did an odd little twist. He sounded so sincerely worried. Yet it was impossible that this man, this foreigner, this barbarian who barely knew her, could be concerned about her fate. It was much more likely he'd come back to the castle for other, more devious reasons. "Nicholas isn't the fiend you seem to think he is."

"So you're marrying that old blackguard because you want to? I thought you were trying to run away because you didn't. I'm disappointed to learn otherwise."

She didn't answer as she entered her chamber and put her sewing box on the bed. The Scot put the frame in the nearest corner and threw back his hood, revealing a mottled bruise on his cheek.

Subduing any curiosity about his bruise, she stepped toward the window, yet not so close that she could be seen from the courtyard. Clasping her hands together so that they were covered by the long cuffs of her gown, she mustered her dignity, and her skepticism. "I think you've come back to see the plans and you think they might be in my brother's solar. In that case, you'd best leave, because he keeps that room locked."

"If you had the plans handy, I wouldn't mind a look, but I've told you why I've come—and I still think I'm right to believe your brother's forcing you to marry Hamish Mac Glogan. That's why you've got that delicate new lady's maid waiting below, the one who looks like he can crush a man's skull with his bare hands."

"Herman's supposed to protect me."

The Scot's eyes narrowed. "From what?"

"Scots, I suppose."

He crossed his arms. "You don't believe that any more than I do. Even if your brother doesn't know you've tried to run away once or that we met, he suspects you're going to try to flee, doesn't he?"

"I told you, he thinks I need protection. And clearly, given your boldness in coming into his hall, he's right to be cautious."

"Especially when the prize is a lovely and spirited and very clever woman he can use to further his own ambitions."

Marianne struggled not to be affected by anything this man said, whether good or bad. "You make me sound like something to be won in a contest. I'm not."

"I'd wager your brother treats you as if you are. He seems the ruthless, ambitious sort who'd sell his own mother to get what he wants—just like Hamish Mac Glogan."

"Our mother is dead."

"Sister, then."

She tried not to let the Scot upset her, or think that he was right. "Perhaps you wanted to make certain you hadn't been seen skulking about the castle. If you had, my brother would never have let you leave. He would have thrown you into the dungeon."

The Scot came closer. "Or else he suspected we'd been together and thought it better to say nothing. Hamish Mac Glogan would want a virgin bride, and if your brother confronted me or threw me in his dungeon, he'd have to explain why. He wouldn't want that."

She backed away. "No, he wouldn't, any more than I want my reputation to be damaged by being associated with you—which it will be if we're found here." She pointed to the door. "If you don't leave, I'll call for Herman and tell my brother you were trying to steal the plans for Beauxville."

"Dunkeathe," the Scot muttered as his intense gaze searched her face. "Would you really call the guard?"

"Yes!"

"Even though I'm willing to help you get away from here, my lady?"

She mustn't believe that. This had to be a trick, and he was using his seductive voice and eyes as he probably had a hundred times with a hundred different women, for all sorts of reasons.

"I don't even know your name," she said, refusing to accept that this offer of assistance could be in earnest, or chivalrously intended.

He looked surprised, then bowed with surprising grace. "I forgot we've not been properly introduced. I'm Adair Mac Taran, the eldest son of Seamus Mac Taran, chieftain of our clan and a thane of Scotland. Now will you let me help you?"

He was the chieftain's son?

For a moment, she was tempted—very tempted—to accept his offer. But what then? Where would she go? And, chieftain's son or not, what might he want in return?

Something you might be willing to give.

As she forced away that lustful little thought, his gaze held her motionless and it was as if he was trying to pierce the defenses she was desperately erecting against the feelings he aroused in her.

"One word from you, my lady," he said softly. "Just one word, and I'll do everything I can to stop your marriage to Hamish Mac Glogan and free you from your brother's tyranny."

Oh, God help her, why did he have to sound so sincere, and look at her that way? She wanted so much to trust him, to put her life in his hands, to believe that he would and could help her, expecting nothing in return.

But in the end, she dare not. No matter who he was, or what he said, she dare not trust any man. "I'm quite sure that any offer you make to me is in service of your own cause. Now get out, or I'll call Herman."

The Scot backed toward the door. "I'm willing to help you, my lady."

"Go!"

At last, and with one final, questioning look, he did.

She stood still for a moment, telling herself there was nothing else she could have done. She couldn't trust him, or any other man. She could only trust herself.

Yet in spite of her doubts about his motives, she ran to the window and looked out into the courtyard. Her heart racing, she watched as Adair Mac Taran, warrior and heir to a chieftain, joined a gang of laborers and safely sauntered out the gates.

Whatever his reasons for coming there, she was glad he hadn't been caught. And relieved, too, of course.

"WHAT DO YOU MEAN, you're not going back to Lochbarr?" Lachlann demanded as he faced his brother in the clearing by the river where they'd left their horses. The sun was low in the horizon, and Adair had just arrived.

"I have to stop that marriage," Adair said as he reached down for his dirk, taking it from his boot and shoving it into his belt.

"By yourself? That's a good way to get yourself

killed—or start a war. Leave this to Father, Adair. He's the chieftain."

"It's only two days till the wedding and that bastard's got a guard on her. If he realizes how desperate she is to get away—"

"How do you know she's desperate?"

There was no time for long explanations. "I know, that's all," he said as he went to Neas. "And once Father understands I had no choice, he'll—"

"No choice?" Lachlann cried, following him. "By the saints, there's a choice, a choice between what *you* think is best, and what's best for the clan. I know she's a bonnie woman, but—"

"It's naught to do with her beauty. She's a woman and I can't stand by and do nothing while a woman suffers. Your heart must be a cold one if you can."

"It's not that I don't pity her if her brother's making her marry," Lachlann protested. "But you can't rescue her all by yourself. Come back with me and we'll tell Father."

"Who may or may not do anything." Adair looped Neas's reins over the horse's neck. "It won't be as risky as you fear," he said, leading Neas away from the trees, and trying to sound reasonable, as Lachlann always was, instead of revealing the tumult of emotions surging through him that had been roused by the sight of Lady Marianne's hulking guard. "I saw a way into the castle, little guarded. I can get in and bring her out with me, then we'll ride to Lochbarr."

"And if you're caught?"

"Then I'm caught."

Lachlann took a deep breath. "Adair, please, think again. I agree this marriage isn't good for us, but you can't just take matters into your own hands. Father is a thane, and chieftain. If he goes to the king—"

"Aye, *if* he goes. And if he doesn't?"

"Then that's the way it must be. We can make alliances of our own."

Adair knew that—in his head. But his heart, which saw only a woman in jeopardy, had already decided otherwise. "I'll be making an alliance of sorts. Lady Marianne will be grateful for our help. And once Father realizes that she truly doesn't want Mac Glogan, and the sort of brute her brother is—"

"This isn't some little mishap or misunderstanding, or another fight with Cormag," Lachlann exclaimed. "This could lead to real trouble with the Normans. And even if you do help her, she'll probably go running back to Normandy and forget all about you. She's not Cellach, you know."

Adair threw himself into his saddle and glared at his little brother. "I know she's not Cellach."

But for the sake of the girl he couldn't save, he'd rescue another. "I'm going to Dunkeathe, and there's an end to it."

"Very well, Adair, go back," Lachlann said, throwing up his hands. "But if you're caught, your life could be the price. Are you really willing to rot in that Norman's dungeon, or even hang, for this Norman woman?"

Resolute, Adair looked down at his younger brother. "Aye, I am."

"No good can come of this, Adair."

"I have to do what I have to do, Lachlann. And I cannot wait."

With that, Adair punched Neas's sides with his heels and galloped down the path toward Dunkeathe.

SHE COULDN'T BREATHE.

Startled awake, frantic, too terrified to scream, Marianne struggled against the strong hand pressing against her mouth. Desperately attempting to hit the man holding her even though she couldn't see him in the dark, she tried to get up.

"Wheesht!" the man whispered harshly in her ear. "I've come to help you."

A Scot. *The* Scot—Adair Mac Taran.

His hold loosened and the moment it did, she scooted backward on the bed, pulling the bedclothes up to her chin.

He was dressed in those same peasant's clothes, and he held a sword in his hand. Surely he hadn't fought his way into her room. She would have heard that. "What are you doing here?" she demanded in a whisper, mindful of her brother in his chamber close by, and Herman at the foot of the stairs.

"I told you. I've come to help you. Come, get up and get dressed. We haven't much time."

He rose and held out his hand, obviously expecting her to take it. "The guards I knocked out might wake soon, or somebody might realize they're not at their posts."

She stared at him, aghast.

"Don't be afraid. We can be well away from here before anybody realizes you're gone. Now get dressed. You won't be able to take anything. We can't carry it down the wall."

The *wall?* He wanted to her to climb out the window and down the wall, like some kind of monkey? She could see the end of a rope tied to something metal braced against the inside window frame. He must have thrown it from outside, like a grapple.

She wasn't about to risk falling to her death and she wasn't going anywhere with this stranger, this Scot, for any reason.

She scrambled out of the bed on the side away from him. Her shift was only linen, and when he looked at her, she was immediately reminded that was all she had on. "You must be mad to think I'll go out the window with you."

"It won't be easy, I grant you, but we can be well away before your absence is discovered. My horse is waiting below, and Neas is fast as the wind."

"And then what?"

"And then…you'll be free of your brother."

She eyed him with all the suspicion she felt. "And the marriage, which you so clearly don't want, will not take place."

"I'll not deny I don't want you to marry Mac Glogan, but—"

"But you think I'm some foolish, dim-witted

woman who'll believe anything you say, including that you're selflessly, nobly helping me out of the goodness of your heart. No doubt that's why you kissed me, to ensure I'll fall under your seductive spell."

His expression shifted, and his eyes gleamed with the start of rage. "I didn't kiss you for any reason other than pleasure, and I came back to help you because I was sure you were being forced to marry against your will. Or am I wrong, and you're as greedy as your brother, and all you care about is that Hamish Mac Glogan is rich?"

"I don't have to explain myself to you. I thought I made myself quite clear before that I don't want your help. Worse, you've put me in jeopardy by coming uninvited to my bedchamber in the middle of the night."

More anger flared in his gray eyes, but she told herself she didn't care. His only motive had to be self-interest, like most men.

"You don't believe me?" he demanded.

"I believe you want to stop the marriage," she replied, "but I don't believe you want to do that for the sake of a woman you barely know, unless it serves your own purpose. I also wouldn't be surprised to discover you expect some kind of reward—in your bed."

The Scot's lip curled with disdain. "You don't know *me,* my lady, for if you did, you'd know I'd never do anything for a woman because I expect her to repay me, especially in the way you suggest. That may be why a Norman would help you, but thank God, I'm not a Norman."

She slowly surveyed the savage before her. "No, you're not."

"Aye, and more fool me for thinking you'd welcome the opportunity to get away," he said as he headed for the window. "Forgive me for thinking you might welcome the chance for liberty. I was confusing you with a Scotswoman, I suppose. So now I'll give you good night and be on my—"

She heard something. "Quiet!" she cried softly as she ran to the door and pressed her ear to the wood.

Noises came from the hall below. Voices raised in alarm. Then footsteps on the stairs.

Oh, God, they were going to be found! That Scot was going to be discovered in her bedchamber—and all she had on was her shift.

She ran to him and started shoving him toward the window. "Go! Get out! Get out *now!*"

Her brother's door opened, banging against the stone wall. Then came more agitated voices, Nicholas's among them.

Pushing past her, the Scot raised his sword and started toward her door.

If he encountered Nicholas, he'd surely kill him. She didn't want her brother—or anybody—to die because of her.

She grabbed the Scot's arm and tugged him toward the window. "Go! I don't want your help!"

"Marianne!" Nicholas shouted from behind her door. Fists started pounding on it. "Let me in, Marianne!"

An arrow whizzed through the window into the

room. She jumped as it clattered on the floor at her feet.

The Scot ducked to avoid another.

"Don't you understand?" she cried desperately. "I'll never go *anywhere* with you!"

Finally, scowling, he went to the window. He scrambled onto the sill, then turned to back out. "Farewell, my lady. I wish you all the joy in your marriage you deserve."

With one last, wrathful look, he slipped out of sight.

As shoulders pushed against her bedchamber door, Marianne dashed to the window and looked out. Archers were stationed on the half-finished walls nearby, their arrows nocked as they sought a clear shot at the Scot climbing down the wall. He had to keep twisting to avoid being hit when one of them let fly. Other soldiers in the courtyard watched and waited, their swords drawn.

Below the Scot was a pile of stones that made a sort of bridge between the bedchambers and the inner curtain wall, where another rope was tied around a merlon. Laying sprawled across the stones were two of the guards.

That was obviously how he'd gotten into the castle. To get away, he'd have to cross the pile of stones and climb down the second rope without being shot or captured.

Her door splintered. She spun around as her brother's fiercely angry face appeared in the opening. *"Whore!"*

She staggered backward, as if the word had been a blow. That he could think such a thing of her!

"Who was it? That chieftain's son? I should have known!" Nicholas snarled as he tried to push through the opening. "I saw the way you looked at him, the way he looked at you. You harlot, you'll rue the day you let some Scot steal your maidenhead! And if I have to starve you, you'll marry who I say!"

There was only one thing to do unless she wanted to be a slave to either her brother or that ancient Scot for the rest of her life. She ran to the window and clambered up onto the sill.

"Marianne, stop!" Nicholas cried, pushing his way further into the room as she turned around in the narrow space. "You'll fall!"

"I'd rather be dead than marry that old man!"

Gritting her teeth and gripping the rope, Marianne slipped backward out the window. The soles of her bare feet rubbed on the rough stones as she started down the outside wall. Her hands ached with the effort to hold on. Below, she could hear the sounds of fighting and, with a quick, sickening glance downward, saw the Scot attacking two soldiers. He jabbed at one with his sword, then struck the other with a mighty, backhanded blow that sent the soldier tumbling down the pile of stones.

She had no choice, she told herself as she looked up again. She had to flee. She'd get away. The Scot would fend off anyone who tried to stop them.

Nicholas wouldn't cut the rope. He wouldn't let

her fall. She'd be worthless to him dead. The archers wouldn't dare to shoot her, either.

If she could just get to the pile of stones…

Her shoulders screamed with pain. Her fingers had no feeling left.

Some of Nicholas's soldiers appeared at her window. They started to pull the rope back up. She planted her feet against the rough stones. She couldn't go back to Nicholas, to be his pawn.

Desperate, she looked down again. There were no soldiers near the Scot, although more were scrambling up a ladder that had been set against the stones. He raised his eyes and when he saw her, his face filled with horror and concern.

He had said he would help her. Now, he must.

"Catch me!" she cried.

Then she let go, trusting her fate to God and the Scot.

For one terrrifying instant, the air rushed past her, then, two strong arms caught her.

She wasn't dead.

He'd caught her and she wasn't dead.

She threw her arms about the Scot's neck, clinging to him, breathing hard, joyfully relieved—until she found herself staring into Adair Mac Taran's furiously angry, recriminating eyes.

An arrow shot past them and he quickly set her down and shoved her behind him as he bent to retrieve his sword.

"Stop, you dolts! You'll hit Marianne!" Nicholas shouted.

Seizing upon that, she stepped out from behind the Scot. "Stay close to me," she commanded.

He grabbed the back of her shift. "You stay close to me," he ordered, hauling her against his powerful body.

She didn't protest. All that mattered was getting away safely, and as long as she was close to him, the archers wouldn't dare shoot.

They started toward the merlon and the other rope. She kept her gaze on the anxious archers, aware that Nicholas was probably rushing to the wall as fast as he could go.

"You first," she said when they reached the second rope.

She ignored the fierce frustration in the Scot's eyes as he hesitated. "Didn't you hear Nicholas? They won't shoot at me, but they'll do their best to kill you."

With a parting, angry look, he went over the wall.

What if he abandoned her?

"Wait for me at the bottom," she cried, the words as much a command as a plea.

Nicholas's head appeared at the top of a ladder propped against the stones. She grabbed the second rope and started to climb down. She could barely close her aching hands around it, but she fought her fear and concentrated on gripping it.

"Stop them on the other side of the wall!" Nicholas called out.

More soldiers, some of them holding torches, poured out of the gatehouse like a swarm of bees.

Yet there was still time to get away, if the Scot's horse was close by, and as fast as he claimed.

She was nearly at the bottom when the Scot caught her around the waist. Without a word, he swept her into his arms and carried her toward a horse barely discernible beneath a willow.

She didn't object or demand to be put down; the soles of her feet were too tender and she knew she'd barely be able to walk, let alone run.

"Where are the rest of your men?" she asked, anxiously scanning the trees.

"There aren't any."

He'd come all by himself?

He must be mad...or else he'd realized there was less chance of one man getting caught than if there were many.

He set her on the back of a horse behind the saddle, its cantle jamming into her stomach. Then he mounted swiftly, in one fluid motion.

She wrapped her aching arms around his waist and held on for dear life as the Scot kicked his heels. The horse leapt out of the cover of the tree and before Nicholas's mounted soldiers were out of the castle, Marianne and the Scot galloped out of the village and away from Beauxville.

CHAPTER SIX

SHE WAS LIVING A NIGHTMARE. Her exhausted arms were as heavy as one of the castle stones. Her teeth chattered from the cold, and her bare feet were numb. Of course, it had started to rain, a bone-chilling drizzle that soaked her shift and hair, bare arms and feet. Clouds covered the moon, and Marianne wondered how the Scot managed to see where they were going.

His horse stumbled—maybe *he* couldn't see—and she nearly slipped off its rump.

"I can't hold on much longer," she murmured, trying to grip the Scot tighter about the waist.

"We haven't much farther to go."

Go where? she wearily wondered as they rode along a narrow path through a small cleft in the hills, with sheer rock above and a rushing stream below.

His home, she supposed, wherever that was. She'd never asked Nicholas.

Probably some collection of rude huts. At least there'd be a fire, and a blanket. She hoped.

She moaned softly and leaned her head against the Scot's wet back, the smell of damp wool in her nostrils. She shouldn't have gone with him. She shouldn't have thrown her future away because she'd been afraid of what would happen to her if she stayed.

Surely she could have convinced Nicholas that she hadn't wanted Adair Mac Taran to come to her bedchamber. That they weren't lovers and she was still a virgin. Somehow.

The Scot pulled his horse to a halt at a fall of water about eight feet wide. It rushed into a pool several feet below, where the water frothed and gurgled, the sound loud in the night. A mist of spray filled the air.

"We're stopping here?" she asked.

"Yes."

She grabbed the cantle as he dismounted, but the loss of his body made her sway and she had to fight to keep her balance.

"There's a cave behind the falls where we can spend the night. Your brother and his men won't find us there. We have to go in on foot because the entrance is too low to go on horseback."

She hesitated, unsure if she'd be able to stand on her cold and painful feet, and if she wanted to risk a night alone in a cave with him.

"You still don't trust me, is that it?" he asked, annoyance and frustration in his voice.

"No, I don't," she retorted.

"Then you're welcome to stay the night out here, but heaven help you if your brother's soldiers come upon you and he's not with them."

"My brother's men wouldn't hurt me."

"Maybe not, but I wouldn't count on it. I've seen what Norman soldiers will do to a defenseless girl."

"I'm not a girl."

"So much the worse, maybe. I'm not going to stand here and debate you, my lady. I'll give you my word that I won't hurt you. If that's not good enough for you, you're free to go and I'll leave you to your fate. You decide."

"I'm sure my brother's soldiers wouldn't harm me, but there are those cattle thieves roaming about, and I have no idea where I am, so I'll *have* to stay here until daylight. However, if you attempt to kiss me again—"

"I'll gladly give you my word I won't do that. You may be a beautiful woman, but your heart is as cold as the water in that river, and after tonight, I'll be glad to be rid of you."

"Very well, then, I accept your offer," she said with all the dignity she could muster, despite the circumstances.

Holding the cantle, she eased her leg over the back of the foam-flecked horse. The Scot put his hands around her waist. She wanted to protest, but as she slowly slipped to the ground, wincing when she had to put her weight on her sore feet, she was glad of his support.

Until his gaze raked her body.

With her soaking shift clinging to her, she might as well be naked. She should make him look away, except that without his strength to hold her, she'd fall.

He turned around. "Get on my back. I'll carry you. That way, I can lead Neas, too. He won't come easy. He hates caves."

So did she, but once again, she had no choice, unless she wanted to be left alone and unprotected.

She put her arms around the Scot's neck, gripping her right wrist with her left hand. He put one hand on her buttocks and hoisted her upward. She shifted, wrapping her legs about him as best she could.

Bending over slightly with her weight, he grabbed his horse's reins and started for the waterfall. The way was slippery and he staggered a bit. She immediately envisioned tumbling down the side of the chasm to the surging water below and held on that much tighter.

The Scot muttered something she didn't understand.

"Loosen your hold," he said in French, his voice louder. "I can't breathe."

Against her will, for they were closer to the water now, she did as he commanded.

The clouds parted enough to let out a little moonlight, and what she saw increased her dread. The water was swift, and the floor of the ledge gleamed slickly wet. She could also see the lip of rock the water passed over, and the hollowed-out space behind. Looking at the falls from any other angle, you wouldn't see that indentation.

She closed her eyes and held her breath as he drew closer to the falling water, every step slow and careful. The roar of it was loud in her ears, like a running herd of horses overtaking her. A heavy stream of water washed over her elbow as they passed to the side and beneath the falls. Her other arm grazed damp rock.

What if the force of the water tore her from him, or made him fall?

"You won't slip?" she felt compelled to ask.

"Not if you're quiet and don't distract me," the Scot replied through clenched teeth.

The short journey seemed to take forever and then the sound of the roaring water changed, echoing oddly. She opened her eyes and discovered they were on the other side of the falls, in a passage of gray, wet rock.

The Scot muttered something and tugged on the reins, for just as he'd said, his horse had balked and hadn't come behind the waterfall.

"I'll get down," she said, letting go of her wrist. Grasping his shoulders, she slid to the ground. She managed to lesson the agony of her sore feet by leaning against the cold, slimy wall.

The Scot said nothing to her as she shivered, her teeth chattering; all his attention was on his horse. He was patient with the beast at first, trying to coax it, but soon he was muttering curses under his breath, or so she assumed those foreign words were. Finally, through a combination of soft words, swearing and a consistent pulling of the reins, the horse came under the falls, stepping as delicately as a fine lady dancing.

The Scot said something that sounded like a short

thankful prayer, then led the horse past her. "Come on. Not much farther now."

She wasn't sure if he was addressing her, or his horse. Nevertheless, biting her lip, with one hand on the wall, she followed as best she could.

It was certainly drier than outside, and much darker. Not a ray of light penetrated the charcoal-like blackness. What if there were holes or pits? The Scot seemed confident of where he was going, but she wasn't particularly reassured.

And what if there were bats?

The horse stopped, and so did she, listening. Mercifully, it wasn't the sound of flapping wings she heard, but the Scot feeling around for something above his head, sending little tumbles of stones to the ground.

"Ah, here they are," he said softly, his voice holding both triumph and relief.

In the next moment, she heard a familiar rasping sound, and a spark flashed, telling her he'd been looking for a flint.

The spark flared into torchlight, and the scent of pitch and smoke filled the musty air. She could see past the horse now, to the Scot holding a torch. In addition to the bruise she'd seen on his face before, there was a trickle of blood from a cut beside his left eye.

With his matted hair and injured face shining in the torchlight, his wet clothes clinging to his muscular body, he looked even more like a savage.

She told herself to be brave and proud as a Norman woman ought to be.

"There's a cavern a little way farther," he said gruffly. "It's more comfortable there."

A cavern comfortable? She shuddered to think what his idea of "comfort" must be.

Clenching her teeth so she wouldn't cry out or make any sound at all, she gingerly crept forward. She tried to ignore her painful feet, how cold she was, her wet and clinging shift and her fear of bats.

After going about twenty feet, she rounded a corner and found herself in an enormous chamber, with a pool at one side that had been created by the damming of water that trickled down the wall. The wet wall gleamed as if it was paved with diamonds, and the air was fresher, too. On a ledge about waist-height to her left was a battered wooden chest.

The horse was eagerly drinking at the pool, while the Scot stood waiting for her, holding the torch aloft.

When he saw her, he set the torch in a rusty metal bracket that had been attached to the rock wall. Below it was a circle of stones with the blackened remains of a fire at the bottom. Beside that was a pile of wood, probably as damp as her shift.

She watched as the Scot went to the wooden chest and threw open the lid. He took out some straw and bits of twig. Then he went to the circle of stones and crouched, and made a little pile of the straw and twigs in the center. He pulled the flint from his belt and moved one of the rocks closer to the straw. He struck another spark. Smoke began to curl up from the straw in a lazy swirl. He bent down and started to blow on the small flame. More of the straw and twigs began to burn.

"Bring me some bigger twigs from the box," he ordered as he stayed crouched by the fire.

Wanting to get warm and dry, she hurried to obey, making her way to the ledge as best she could and biting back curses of her own. He glanced at her impatiently.

Then he looked at her feet and frowned. "You're bleeding," he said, straightening. "I didn't realize you'd hurt your feet. Sit down."

He spoke without gentleness or kindness, but she didn't care. She was too tired, too cold and her feet hurt too much to answer, so she simply sank down where she was, perching on a rock.

He went to the chest, pulled out some sticks and threw them on the fire. "You should have said something."

"And what would you have done if I had?" she asked, too weary and miserable to censor her words. "Climbed back to my chamber and fetched my shoes?"

He didn't answer her question as he rummaged in the chest. He pulled out a wineskin and shook it, making its contents slosh. After setting it down, he began to take off his shirt.

She inched away from him. "What are you doing?"

"Making bandages," he said as he pulled the wet shirt over his head. He darted her a suspicious look. "What did you think I was going to do?"

She didn't answer. She didn't want to give him any ideas. And she shouldn't be *getting* any ideas, except for what she ought to do when this terrible night was over.

Scowling darkly, he yanked the knife from the belt around his waist. "Have no fear, my lady," he said. "You're completely safe with me. If I hadn't already given you my word, I wouldn't touch you now for all the gold in England."

She should be relieved, but his tone made her feel…offended.

He frowned as he slit the hem of his shirt, shoved his knife back into his belt and began tearing the cloth into strips with quick, angry motions. "That upsets you, does it?"

Looking up at her, his gaze traveled over her body, more leisurely than before, then returned to her face. "You're used to teasing men, I suppose."

Blushing despite her angered pride at his insolent scrutiny, she straightened her shoulders and wrapped her arms about her body. "I never teased you. I never did anything to encourage you."

"No? I can think of something."

She flushed, sure he was referring to that damnable kiss in the mason's hut. What a mistake that had been! She never should have given in to a moment's desire. "Stop looking at me like that. Did no one ever tell you that it's rude to stare?"

"I can't help it." He strode to the pool. "I'm a man."

He certainly was.

She silenced that mischievous inner voice, the one that also kept telling her she should be relieved he'd come to rescue her and thankful for his help, not complaining and worrying about what the future might hold.

The Scot plunged some of the strips of cloth that had been his shirt into the water. The muscles of his naked back rippled with the effort, and his skin glowed bronze in the light of the torch.

Savage, indeed. But undeniably masculine. Compelling, as no Norman had ever been to her. Her body warmed as she watched him, in a way that had nothing to do with the fire he'd kindled in the circle of stones.

She mentally shook herself as he rose and walked back to her. He wasn't some nobleman wanting to court her; he was the man responsible for putting her in this terrible situation, in this horrible cave.

Still holding the strips of wet cloth, he grabbed the neck of the wineskin and pulled out the stopper with his teeth, then spit it out beside her, making her jump. He poured some of the liquid on the cloth. "Come the morning, I'll take you to Lochbarr. There you can eat and get some clothes, and I'll have someone return you to Dunkeathe."

He made it sound so very simple. But it wasn't. Not at all. "I can't go back to Beauxville. Nicholas thinks you and I are lovers."

The Scot stopped dribbling the liquid onto the cloth and glared at her. "Tell him we're not and never were."

"He won't believe me. I was in my shift, after all, and I never called the guards."

"You mean that even if you swear to a thing, he won't believe you?" the Scot demanded.

She flushed and tried not to be ashamed that her brother would jump to such a swift and hateful conclusion. "Would you believe your sister under such circumstances?"

"If I had one and she swore to me it was the truth, yes, I would," he said with complete conviction. His eyes narrowed. "Is there a reason he'd suspect you were entertaining a lover in your bedchamber?"

She glared right back at him. "I'm an honorable woman," she declared, which is what she should have said to Nicholas instead of fleeing. "I've never invited a man into my bedchamber, and you shouldn't have presumed to interfere."

The Scot said another word that sounded like a curse as he knelt in front of her and took hold of her foot. "I'll have to remember to ask for *permission* the next time I stick my neck out to rescue a woman."

"Especially if she doesn't require your help," Marianne retorted. "Not all women are as weak and helpless as you seem to think. I don't know what silly girl made you think—"

His fingers tightened around her ankle.

"Ouch!"

As she tried to pull free, his hold loosened a bit, but he didn't let go. "Those cuts should be cleaned. Now stay still and let me—provided I have your *permission,* my lady."

She didn't need his insolent sarcasm, or his less than gentle ministrations. She was about to refuse when he put the wet cloth against her foot. She cried out at the stab of pain. Tears started in her eyes.

"Hurts, I know." His expression softened a little. A very little. "But it's necessary."

Splaying her hands on the rock behind her, leaning back, she clenched her teeth and vowed not to make another sound, or twitch and wiggle, as he washed her feet. She also wouldn't think about his strong hand gripping her bare ankle.

When he was finished and the torture concluded, she reached for the dry strips of cloth. "I can bandage them myself."

When he looked up, their faces were mere inches apart.

"If you wish," he said, his deep voice low and his eyes…

He wasn't angry anymore. He was looking at her the way he had in the mason's hut just before he kissed her.

The silence stretched between them, taut as a drawn bowstring. The very air seemed to thicken and warm, and pulse with a promise of something sweet and fulfilling. And exciting. Very exciting.

What did it matter now, after all, if they kissed, and even more? Nicholas already thought she was a ruined woman….

Except that she was not. And she couldn't make this terrible situation worse by letting her lustful desire have its way.

He spared her having to speak when he abruptly got to his feet and went to his horse, taking one of the pieces of cloth with him.

Relieved, she started to wrap the rough bandages about her feet while the Scot removed the horse's saddle. He set it on the ground, then pulled the fleece that had been beneath it from the horse's back. He tossed it to her. "Sit on that."

She eased herself gratefully onto the warm, soft fleece, then picked up the wineskin and shook it. There was still some wine left and she was very thirsty.

She put the opening to her lips and sipped—and gagged. It was the worst thing she'd ever tasted in her life.

"That's not wine!" she spluttered, wiping her chin.

Pausing as he rubbed down his horse, Adair Mac Taran regarded her over his broad, naked shoulder. "I never said it was. It's *uisge beatha*—the water of life. We Scots make it, and it's better than wine."

She curled her lip at that fulsome praise for the horrific beverage.

"I should have guessed you wouldn't appreciate that, either," he muttered as he went back to his task.

"Your drink is terrible, and anyone who appreciates good wine would think so, too."

He didn't answer. He simply continued to rub down his horse.

The horse was surely valuable, as fine a specimen as his master. Whatever else she thought of the Scot, he had a perfect warrior's body—strong, lean, powerful.

He was very handsome, too. And that kiss…

She must stop thinking about that! She couldn't make the mistake of being so weak again. Whatever he said, she couldn't trust him. He was a virile man, and half-naked already.

You can't trust yourself, either, the guilty voice of her conscience whispered. *Even now, in spite of everything, you can't stop yourself imagining being in his arms, as if you're the lovers your brother thinks you are.*

Suddenly, the Scot threw down the cloth and marched toward her. She shrank back as he grabbed the wineskin and took what seemed an enormous swig of the horrible drink.

He'd given his word she'd be safe with him, but she'd heard tales of drunken men and their debauchery, and she was sure that drink was potent.

Adair Mac Taran lowered the wineskin. His eyes gleaming in the flickering torchlight, he gave her a wolfish grin, then smacked his lips and wiped them with the back of his hand. "It warms you."

Trying not to panic, she said the first thing that came to her mind. "If it doesn't kill you first."

He barked a harsh laugh. "Normans!" He took another gulp. "Cold water for you, is it, my fine lady?" he asked. "Very well."

She watched him warily as he stoppered the wineskin and dropped it beside her, then went to the pool. From a little niche in the rock she hadn't noticed before, he pulled out a cup fashioned from a ram's horn. He dipped it in the water and walked back to her, holding it out before him like an offering.

"There you are," he said, giving it to her with a smirk.

Not taking her eyes off him, she took the cup and sipped.

He threw himself down on the ground on the opposite side of the fire, as far away as he could get and still be warmed by the flames. "Are you finished bandaging your feet?"

"Yes. Why don't you use one of the pieces to wash the cut by your eye?"

He reached up and touched the wound, sucking in his breath slightly. He went to the pool and splashed water on his face to wash it.

While he was occupied with that, she reached for one of the logs, now steaming, and moved it within reach. If he tried to attack her, she'd grab it and defend herself. As she'd said, she wasn't as weak and helpless as he seemed to think.

He returned to the fire and sat on the ground. Raising his knees, he rested his forehead on them and wrapped his arms about his legs.

He suddenly seemed as weary as she, and there was a despondency to his attitude that was completed unexpected. But if he was fatigued or dismayed because of his unnecessary efforts, he would get little sympathy from her. Because of him, her future was thrown into turmoil and uncertainty. "What will you do with me in the morning?"

"I told you. I'll take you to Lochbarr. Then…it's up to you."

She didn't believe that for a moment. "Your clan may have other ideas about that. Surely your father—"

"My father didn't know that I was going to rescue you. I didn't tell anybody except my brother."

She stared at him incredulously. "Do you mean to say you came back to Beauxville and risked my brother's wrath without your father's knowledge?"

"I thought there was no time to waste."

He must really be against the marriage alliance…or else he expected her gratitude, just as she'd warned Polly. That would explain why he came back to Beauxville by himself.

He moved so that his legs were crossed, and she was instantly alert and wary.

"Is there any more *uisge beatha?*" he asked.

"You should put what's left on that cut," she said, ignoring his cry of protest as she picked up one of the remaining strips of cloth beside her and poured the last of the drink onto it.

She was sure his next word was a curse, but she didn't care. She'd rather have him annoyed than have to fight off a drunken man.

She held the wet cloth out to him. "Here."

He reached across the fire and grabbed it, but didn't immediately put it to his cheek.

"Why aren't you washing it?"

"I'll do that later."

"Surely you're not afraid of the pain?"

He gave her a sour look. "No." Nevertheless, he still didn't tend to his wound.

"As you said to me, it's necessary. You had no such qualms about washing my feet, and they were much worse off."

"It's not the pain. I hate putting anything near my eyes, that's all. When I was a child, I was running with a stick in my hand, pretending it was a sword, and fell. I nearly took out an eye."

"Oh." That was understandable, if unexpected.

He gave her a sardonic smile. "Perhaps you could do it."

She wasn't going to get close to him again. "No!"

"And here I thought you were brave," he jeered as he closed his eyes and dabbed lightly at the cut, wincing.

Her brother might not be the most arrogant, frustrating and selfish man she'd ever met, after all. "If you came to Beauxville—"

"Dunkeathe."

"My brother's castle, without your father's knowledge or permission, how might he and the rest of your clan feel when you return and tell them what you did?"

He shrugged.

"That's another reason why you shouldn't have bothered."

"I wish I hadn't."

"So do I."

The Scot lay down on the stone floor with his feet closest to the fire and moved his sword away from her, so that he was almost lying on it before wrapping his arms about himself.

Why, oh, *why* had she gone out of the window after this uncouth, barely civilized Scot? If only he'd stayed away. She would have found some way to prevent the wedding.

He muttered something under his breath.

"Can't you at least be quiet?"

He slid her a condemning glance, but she wasn't the one barging into *his* bedchamber and muttering under her breath in a foreign language. "It's rude to say things I can't understand."

"Rude? Oh, my God, can't have that, can we?" he mocked. He shifted, obviously trying to find a better spot to rest his head. "I was saying I wished I had my *feileadh*. Then I'd be snug as a bird in a nest."

"And what, perchance, is a *feileadh?*"

"The wool plaid. These Saxon clothes are damned uncomfortable."

"I daresay it doesn't help that you're lying on your sword."

"You might try to steal it. Or kill me with it. I wouldn't put anything past a Norman."

"Then I'm not so weak and helpless after all?"

His only answer to that was another muttered word she'd never heard before, and clearly not a flattering one.

"If you really feel that way, perhaps you shouldn't sleep at all."

He sat up, the sudden movement catching her off guard. "Are you threatening me, my lady?"

Determined not to let him think he could frighten her, she gave him a smug smile. "How could a weak and helpless woman threaten a big, strong Scot like you?"

"And you told me you didn't tease men," he scoffed. "Stop. It'll avail you nothing."

What did he think she was trying to do? "You're not just arrogant, you're conceited!"

He crossed his arms over his chest. "At least I know how to be grateful."

"Grateful? Why should I be grateful?" she asked, glaring at him across the fire. "I didn't seek your help which, I point out, has made things infinitely worse. In fact, I refused it."

"I'm sorry for not believing you'd rather marry a greedy, grasping old lecher, even if he's rich."

He made her sound greedy and grasping, too. "Rich the man may be, but if I married him, I'd have to stay in this godforsaken, sodden place. I'd rather die—or run away *by myself.*"

"We don't want you Normans here, either," he retorted. "Believe me, my lady, I'd like nothing better than to see you all sent back to Normandy."

"And I'd like nothing better than to go."

"I'm sure my father can help you there."

"It's the least he can do after all the trouble his insolent, arrogant son has caused me."

Glowering, the Scot got to his feet. "Oh, aye, all the trouble I've caused *you.*" He snatched up his sword and turned toward the entrance of the cavern.

"Where are you going?"

"Away from you."

Sure that he meant it, she struggled to stand. "You can't leave me here alone," she said, following him.

He whirled around. "Why not? You can wait here for your precious Normans."

"Because…" She wouldn't admit she was frightened of her brother, who ought to trust her, but didn't, and what he might do to her when he found her. "Because I'm afraid of bats!"

The Scot stared at her. "What?"

"I'm frightened of bats," she said, trying to be dignified, "just the way you're afraid of things coming too close to your eyes."

There was a tense moment that seemed to last far too long.

"All right, I'll stay," he finally said. "But remember that you asked this of me, my lady. I want no accusations come the morning."

She tried not to sound relieved. "If you keep your distance, there'll be none."

CHAPTER SEVEN

EVERY SENSE ALERT for Normans lurking in ambush, and cursing himself with every name for a fool he could think of, Adair tried to ignore the sensation of Lady Marianne's arms around his waist as they neared Lochbarr. He hadn't taken the main road toward home, nor had he seen any signs of Normans pursuing them. Nevertheless, he was ready to send Neas galloping over the hills at the first sign of foreign soldiers.

As for the lady with him…what a mistake he'd made. He should have left her in her brother's hands, as Lachlann had said.

He didn't want to think about what was going to happen when he got back to Lochbarr. He was quite sure Lachlann had already returned and told their father what his eldest son intended to do. They'd all be ignorant of the actual outcome, though, and Adair hoped his father would be so relieved he was still alive, he wouldn't banish him from the clan outright.

To think he'd risked that for this ungrateful woman. This beautiful, defiant, ungrateful woman who hated his country. This defiant, tempting woman who inspired his passion as no woman ever had.

God help him, he *was* a fool. An impetuous, stubborn pigheaded fool who deserved whatever punishment his father meted out.

Adair's gaze scanned the pine woods around them. In the early-morning sunlight, blessedly welcome after weeks of rain, the forest seemed peaceful and calm. Birds sang uninterrupted in the trees as if they were rejoicing. Squirrels scampered, and Adair spotted a rabbit, as startled as he, sitting up under a holly bush.

Perhaps the Normans were faster than he'd thought, and they were waiting for him closer to Lochbarr. Or maybe Sir Nicholas had already reached Lochbarr to complain to his father and threaten to go to the king.

They reached the ridge that overlooked the loch, where the forest cleared and the road led down into the village, with the fortress on a rise beyond.

To his great relief, the village looked as peaceful as the woods. A few of the boats used for fishing were out on the loch near the small island several hundred yards offshore. The deep blue water of the lake was still and smooth as glass.

He couldn't see the fortress well, but he could make out no signs of heightened activity, as if they'd fought off an attack, or feared one.

"Is this Lochbarr?" Lady Marianne asked, her breath warm on his naked back.

The whole way home he'd felt her breath, her breasts and her nipples, through the thin fabric covering them. He'd struggled to ignore the sensations, just as he'd struggled to ignore the arousal he felt whenever he looked at her in the cave last night. Even disheveled and dirty, she appealed to him. Even when she was angry at him and infuriating him, a part of him couldn't stop thinking about making love with her. Imagining those bright eyes shining with desire for him. Having her body beneath him. Being able to touch and caress her, until she cried out for him to take her.

He inwardly gave his head a shake.

"Aye, that's Lochbarr," he answered as he nudged Neas into a walk again. The poor creature had suffered, being forced into the cave.

Unfortunately, there'd been no help for it. If Lady Marianne had come with him as he'd planned, they could have ridden straight on for Lochbarr and not been forced to seek refuge in the cave.

Where he'd discovered her wounded feet, and realized that even her feet were shapely. Where she'd endured his ministrations with a stoic calm that few women—or men, either—possessed.

Where he'd found the *uisge beatha*.

Despite his sizeable gulps, it hadn't helped relax him. But what could he expect, after having his aid cast back at him like a spear to the belly?

As they neared Lochbarr, a group of women at the village well stopped gossiping and stared. By the kirk, a dog sniffed the air, as if he knew a foreigner was among them. A group of children chasing each other halted and gaped and pointed. Two farmers leaned on a stone fence, watching, silent as the rocks under them.

Adair pressed his lips together and tried to ignore their curious scrutiny, although Adair Mac Taran, shirtless and in Saxon breeches, riding through the village with a beautiful, disheveled woman clad only in her shift, must make quite a sight.

If this was humiliating for him, how much worse must it be for her? No doubt she'd tell him so later, in no uncertain terms.

With a sinking heart, he spotted his father waiting at the gates of the fortress, surrounded by warriors and other leading men of the clan who gave him council: Lachlann, to his right, as grim-faced as his father; Barra, the *seanachie,* keeper of the family lineage, most trusted of his father's friends; Roban, looking both relieved and wary; Cormag, triumphant, no doubt anticipating Seamus's anger at his son's act; and others, all looking worried or concerned, including some who shared Cormag's dislike for the chosen heir to their chieftain.

Perhaps they'd get their wish, and his father would suggest another follow him as leader of the clan upon his death.

Marianne held him tighter, evincing the first fear he'd seen since she'd climbed down the wall last night. In the cave, she'd been angry, upset, distrustful, but not, he thought, afraid.

"Who are all those men?" she asked quietly, her voice steady, belying the dread revealed by the tightening of her embrace.

"My father you know," he replied, attempting to pay no heed to the sensation of her arms about his waist, reminding himself of things she'd said last night that ought to make him hate her. "The young, thin fellow to his right is my brother, Lachlann. The others are warriors, or men whose advice my father values."

"They don't look pleased."

He twisted slightly to look at her and tried not to betray any emotion at all when he spoke. "It doesn't look as if your brother's come to fetch you home again, either."

"I didn't think he would," she replied evenly, with no hint of dismay or disappointment. "I told you, he believes I encouraged you."

Adair sniffed derisively. She certainly had encouraged him. Looking at him the way she had. Returning his kiss. Yet she was still trying to wrap herself in the mantle of outraged righteousness.

What an infuriating woman! He'd be glad to see the last of her. And he would hope that some good might come of this yet, if Hamish Mac Glogan refused to marry her. Not for the haughty Marianne's sake, but for his clan's. An alliance between Mac Glogan and Sir Nicholas would be bad.

A few yards from the gates, Adair drew Neas to a halt.

His father's frown deepened as he walked toward them, leaving the others at the gate. "Oh, my son, what have ye done?"

Trying to marshal his arguments, to think the way

Lachlann did—logically and without emotion—Adair took his time dismounting.

"I was helping a lady in distress," he replied as he took hold of Neas's reins. "And stopping a marriage that would be disastrous for our clan."

"Whatever your feelings about the lady, the matter of the marriage should have been left to me."

If his father didn't support him, he was lost indeed.

"Sir," Marianne said in French from where she sat on Neas, her voice ringing out like a clarion call. "Your son has abducted me."

Adair spun around. How dare she make that odious charge? "I didn't abduct you. You came of your own free will."

"I most certainly did not!"

"I never forced you. You came climbing down the wall after me and then called for me to catch you. What was I to do, let you fall?"

"Adair!" his father said sternly. "We'll discuss this in the hall."

Chastened, publicly humiliated, Adair fell silent, for no matter how much he wanted to protest and explain, that tone in his father's voice would brook nothing but absolute obedience.

His father approached Neas and addressed Marianne in French, his manner considerably more genial. "My lady, I can see you've had a difficult journey. Please allow me to extend to you the hospitality of my home, including whatever food or clothing you require." He looked back to the gates. "Dearshul! You will tend to Lady Marianne."

Red-haired and freckled Dearshul appeared among the waiting men as if out of nowhere, regarding Marianne with outright awe as she sidled past Lachlann.

"Now, my lady," his father continued, "if you'll allow me to assist you."

"I thank you, Seamus Mac Taran," Marianne said graciously, and with what sounded like genuine gratitude. "Some water to wash, a comb for my hair and a gown would be most welcome."

Reaching out, she laid her hands on his father's shoulders and jumped lightly to the ground, flinching when her feet touched the earth.

"You're hurt?" Seamus asked.

"My feet are cut and sore. They're feeling better now, and with a little tending, should soon be healed."

"I'll send Beitiris to you—a woman in the village who knows much of medicine."

"Thank you," the lady replied, giving his father a dazzling smile.

As if *he'd* risked his life for her.

"Dearshul," Seamus repeated, gesturing for her to come closer. "Help the lady to my quarters, and see that she has everything she needs."

The young woman hastened to obey, giving Marianne a shoulder to lean on. They made slow but steady progress, and the crowd of men at the gate silently parted to allow them to pass.

All amiability was gone from his father's face when he turned back to Adair. "Now then, boy, to the hall with you."

His father hadn't called him *boy* in that tone since he'd broken Cormag's nose when they were twelve years old.

As his father marched toward the hall, one of the stableboys hurried out to take charge of Neas. The rest of the clansmen followed their chieftain, leaving Adair to trail behind.

Except for Lachlann, who waited for his brother. "You're not badly hurt?" he asked, running a swift gaze over Adair as they walked toward the hall.

"Only the cut to my face. You told them where I'd gone and why?"

"Aye."

"What did Father say?"

"Not much—'twas Cormag and his ilk did the talking. All for banishing you from the clan, they are."

Adair had expected nothing less. "No doubt Cormag thinks he'll be chieftain if that happens."

"Thank God your fate's not up to Cormag and his friends, but Father and the rest. They've agreed to let Father decide what to do, since you're his son."

"That's a mercy," Adair said truthfully.

"Aye. But they like you, too, Adair. You've a way of getting and keeping men's loyalty, no matter what you do."

They reached the hall of Lochbarr and fell silent when they entered. It was much smaller than the Norman's new hall, and smoky from the peat burning in the hearth.

Normally, Adair felt completely at ease in this

chamber, but not now, for seated on benches around that hearth, looking like a grim jury set in judgment upon him, were his clansmen, led by his father, who sat in the center of the semicircle.

Lachlann left Adair's side and went to take his place across from the smug, triumphant Cormag.

Adair didn't have to be told to stay standing in the open space.

"So, young Mac Taran, ye've got yersel' in a pot of boiling water," Barra began.

"Aye, to my everlasting regret," he admitted. "I should never have acted on my own in this matter, without my father's knowledge or consent."

That sent a mutter among the men.

"What, you're not going to stand there in defiance and claim you did right?"

Adair gave Cormag a sour look. "No, although I acted with good intentions, to save a woman from a forced marriage and our clan from an alliance that would mean trouble to come."

Seamus shifted in his chair. "We have no proof Sir Nicholas is our enemy."

"He's a Norman, isn't he? Who else would be stealing our cattle and leading them toward Dunkeathe?"

"If he wasn't our enemy before, he will be after you abducted his sister," Cormag said.

Several of his friends nodded their agreement.

"I didn't abduct her," Adair forcibly replied. "I'd already left her bedchamber when she came after *me*."

"Her bedchamber?" Cormag repeated, as if Adair

had committed a shocking breach of propriety—
this from a man who'd brag about any women he'd
managed to seduce to anybody who'd listen.

Adair's temper flared. "Aye. Where else would
she be in the middle of the night?"

"Waiting for you, maybe."

"She's not my lover. Never was, never will be."

"Then why did she come with you?" Barra asked.

"Because she was going to have to marry Hamish
Mac Glogan and she doesn't want to," Adair replied.

"How can you be so sure?"

"Her brother's set a guard on her, as if he knows
she'll try to run away."

"Oh, so you're reading minds now, is that it?"
Cormag sneered. "Among your many talents."

Adair decided he had to reveal his earlier
encounter with Marianne in Beauxville, or a part of
it, anyway.

Addressing his father, he said, "That night I went
looking for the plans I met her in the yard. I wasn't
sure what she was up to, until I heard about the marriage. She was trying to run away, until I stopped
her."

The men were all duly amazed, as he'd been
when he'd first met Marianne in the alley.

"Why didn't you tell me this before, Adair?" his
father demanded.

"Because at first, I didn't think her troubles were
any concern of mine. Then I learned of the marriage
plans. As bad as that is for us, I realized it would be
worse for her, and that's why she was fleeing. But

even so, since I can't read minds and don't have the Sight—" he shot a condemning glance at Cormag "—I decided to go to Dunkeathe and see if I could find proof she was being forced to wed. When I saw the brute her brother set to guard her, I thought I'd found it. The rest you know."

"I never thought you'd keep secrets from me, Adair," his father said.

Adair flushed with shame. "I wanted to be certain."

"Regardless of your reasons, Adair," Seamus replied, "or what you thought you were doing, great harm's been done."

"Aye, it has," Cormag unnecessarily seconded. He turned to Lachlann. "Why didn't you tell anyone what your brother was about before he went back to Dunkeathe? We could have stopped him."

Lachlann colored as Adair quickly answered. "Lachlann bears no blame in this. He tried to talk me out of it."

"And you wouldn't listen," his father finished with a heavy sigh. "For once, my son, you should have."

"Aye, I'll not deny that," Adair replied, his remorse deep and heartfelt. "But I thought she'd welcome the chance for freedom. Instead, she refused my aid. So I was going to leave without her, until the alarm was raised and she followed me."

"In her shift?" Cormag asked with a sarcastic smirk.

"There wasn't time for her to dress. We'd have

been well away before the alarm if she hadn't balked."

"Oh, so now it's *her* fault the Normans almost caught you," Cormag countered, accompanied by the approving mutterings of his friends. "I suppose you're going to claim she begged for your help, then changed her mind."

"No."

"Yet you went there anyway?"

"How many times do you want me to say I made a mistake?" Adair demanded, his patience gone.

His father rose, stern and commanding. "This isn't some simple misunderstanding, Adair. You've sinned against the woman, and her brother. He has every right to be aggrieved, and bring you before a court of law."

"Father, I swear to you on my life, I didn't force her to come with me. I went to her chamber because I thought she'd welcome my aid."

With a jolt of surprise, he realized nobody was listening to him, not even his father. They were all staring at something behind him.

Marianne had entered the hall and was walking toward them, her movements slow, graceful and dignified. Her golden hair had been brushed so that it was soft and flowing about her slender shoulders. The plainness of her simple gown of doe-brown wool only seemed to accentuate her astonishing beauty and shapely form.

"I assume, sir, that you're talking about me, and what's to be done?" she said, her voice soft and feminine—quite a contrast to the tone she used when she was alone with him.

A woman's wiles, no doubt. The ungrateful, deceitful—

"Yes, we are discussing your fate, my lady," Seamus replied, his whole attitude softening. "I apologize for any trouble or pain my son's caused you. It's often his way, you see, to act first and think later."

Adair tried not to scowl at that description of his character.

"But he's especially impetuous if he thinks a woman's in danger," his father continued.

That was better, although his father's words didn't seem to impress Marianne.

"Or if he thinks his actions will benefit his clan?" the lady smoothly inquired. "Except of course, in this case, his impetuous behavior is more likely to cause greater trouble for your clan than my marriage to Hamish Mac Glogan ever could. My brother won't take kindly to the ruin of his plans."

God help him, how he wished he'd left her there.

"We'll see that you're safely returned to him."

Marianne shook her head. "Unfortunately, because of what your son has done, I can't go back to Beauxville. My brother believes your son and I are lovers."

His father frowned. Lachlann stared at Adair with dismay. The other clansmen looked baffled, clearly wondering what the lady was saying in that soft, deceptively gentle voice.

As Lachlann translated, his voice low, Adair saw a glint in Lady Marianne's bright blue eyes that he recognized all too well. But she couldn't be any more incensed than he was.

"Under those circumstances, my brother will not want me back."

"Then we'll escort you anyplace else you wish to go," his father offered.

There. That should satisfy her. And he'd gladly see her gone.

"I appreciate your generosity," she replied, her voice still unruffled and matter-of-fact. "However, my brother made his accusations loudly and in front of his men. My reputation has been destroyed. I will be notorious. There will be nowhere I wish to go that this scandal will not reach. Also, unless you want war with my brother, we must find a way to stem his angry retribution. I've thought of a way to prevent conflict between you, as well as provide some recompense for me."

His father's white brows rose questioningly, while Adair waited to hear what her idea of recompense would be.

"Your son must marry me."

Adair gasped, dumbfounded.

His father's eyes widened for a moment, then became inscrutable ciphers, as they sometimes did when he was presented with a serious, puzzling problem. Lachlann looked shocked as he told the other clansmen what she'd said. They were obviously as taken aback as Adair.

"Why would you propose such a thing?" he demanded. "You can't possibly want to marry me."

She eyed him as she might a bedbug. "I want children, and I want them to be legitimate. I've seen how bastards are treated. So I must marry *someone.* Thanks to you, I'll be considered unmarriageable by any Norman standard and no Norman will offer for my hand. That leaves you to repair the ruin you've made of my future."

"But I never laid...your virtue is—"

"Now subject to rumor, speculation and innuendo," she interrupted, that glint in her eyes now an indignant glow. "Everyone will believe that either I went with you willingly, in which case you must be my lover, or you took me by force, in which case you surely raped me."

"I would never take a woman against her will!"

"Your moral virtue is immaterial," she said dismissively. "They'll suspect it just the same, and thus my value as a bride is reduced to nothing. The only future I face is the convent, and I have no wish to spend the rest of my life celibate because people think I'm dishonored. Since it's your fault I'm in this predicament, you should do the *honorable* thing and marry me."

Before Adair could protest, before he could even find the words to begin, his father said in Gaelic, "She's right. You made this mess, Adair. You can repair it."

As Adair stared in utter disbelief, the rest of the clan began to express their opinions, some willing to consider the marriage, others clearly against the idea. Lachlann believed the union would be a mistake. Barra, not surprisingly, sided with his father. Roban was silently stunned, looking from Adair to Marianne and back again.

Lachlann and the clansmen opposed to the marriage were expressing but pale imitations of Adair's indignant reaction.

"She hates me," Adair said in Gaelic over the din, addressing his father. "She told me she hates Scots, and she hates our country."

Seamus raised his hand for silence. When the men obeyed, he addressed Marianne. "Adair tells us you don't like him, or Scots, or Scotland. Yet you'd marry him?"

"I want children, so I require a husband," she replied, her voice unwavering, her stance confident. "He's taken that chance from me. And the rest of you should welcome this marriage as a means to avoid my brother's vengeance.

"Nicholas obviously wants an alliance with a Scot," she continued in the same practical way. "If I marry your son, he'll have that. A suitable bride price for me will be welcome, too, I'm sure, and help overcome any further objections on his part."

"Adair will pay the bride price," his father declared.

Now he was going to have pay money for the privilege of marrying a woman he didn't want, a woman who didn't want him, either?

"Why should I have to pay recompense?" he demanded of her. "You broke the betrothal when you ran away."

Her expression was as hard as the rock that made up the hills around Lochbarr. "You forced me to run away when you came uninvited into my bedchamber."

"You were going to flee anyway."

"But I hadn't yet, had I?" she retorted. She faced his father. "For the sake of peace, I'm even willing to tell Nicholas that your son and I were lovers."

She gave Adair a disgruntled look that declared nothing could be further from the truth. "I'll explain to him that your handsome son swept me off my feet and I fell desperately in love with him. Then he won't be able to blame you, or your clan, for what's happened. He can only fault me for my weakness, and your son for his lust.

"*And,* if he takes a grievance to your king, you can truthfully say that you knew nothing about our plans until I had fled Beauxville with Adair."

Of all the reasons he'd ever thought to marry, placating a Norman had not been one of them—and it shouldn't be one now, any more than he should have to part with money because she'd followed him.

"I'm not going to marry a woman I don't want and I'm not going to marry to appease your bastard of a brother," he vowed, glaring at Marianne.

"I don't want you, either," she returned, bold and defiant still. "But I'm the wronged party here, not you. I'm the woman whose life you've destroyed. I meant what I said about children, so much so I'm willing to stay here and marry you rather than face a barren life."

She ran a scornful gaze over him. "You should be grateful for the opportunity I'm offering to prevent bloodshed, too."

"I should be grateful?" he charged, overwhelmed by her incredible arrogance. "Because you deign to marry me?"

When she answered, there was no hint of shame, no implication that there was any chance she'd reconsider, in either her voice or her expression. "Yes."

Of all the haughty, proud, cold Normans he'd ever met, she had to be the worst.

"They could handfast," Barra suggested, his voice sounding loud in the silence.

Adair grasped at the suggestion like a drowning man a rope thrown from shore.

"Aye," he agreed, addressing his father in Gaelic. "And then if we don't suit, she can go back to her brother after the year and day are over."

"I don't think she'll agree," Lachlann said. "She's got everything to lose and nothing to gain by handfasting."

Adair shot his brother a disparaging look.

"What are you saying?" Marianne asked, her smooth brow furrowing.

Despite Adair's silent warning, Lachlann jumped in to explain. "They're proposing you handfast. It's a sort of temporary marriage. If, after a year and a day, you don't wish to stay with Adair, you're free to go."

Marianne coolly raised one inquisitive brow. "Marriage—with all that implies?"

"Yes," Lachlann answered.

"I could leave him, or he might leave me at the end, I suppose?"

"Yes."

"And if there are children?"

"They stay with the father."

The lady gave Adair a scornful smile, as if he'd tried to trick her. "I won't agree to something that has every advantage for him and none for me."

"She won't go for it," Lachlann translated for the clansmen.

"Of course not," Adair growled. "The way you explained it, who would? You should have said—"

"There must be a legal wedding, with a priest's blessing," Marianne declared.

Trying to keep calm and not succeeding very well, Adair said, "There's no shame in a handfasted union. Everyone in Scotland will accept it, and if it ends, there's no shame, either."

"It's not whether a Scot will accept it or not that concerns me," she replied. "It's what a Norman would think, and none of them would see it in such a light. I would have been a mistress, not a wife."

"A word, my son," Seamus interjected. He rose from his chair and gestured for his son to follow him to a far corner of the hall, where they couldn't be heard.

Perhaps his father had thought of some other way to appease the lady and her brother that didn't require marriage, Adair thought hopefully.

His brief hope was dashed when he saw his father's grave expression.

"I know this isn't what you planned when you went to Dunkeathe, my son," Seamus said quietly as they stood in the corner, "yet now it's time to think of the clan. Lady Marianne's right about preventing bloodshed. And whether Sir Nicholas approves of the marriage or not, it's better you marry her than having her wed to Hamish Mac Glogan, or some other Scot who might be tempted to move against us."

He slid a glance back to the stately Marianne. "It could be worse, Adair. She's a bonnie lass."

"Oh, aye, bonnie to look at, but not to live with, I'm thinking. You can see what she thinks of me. How can I be happy with a wife who hates me?"

"You went to her bedchamber, Adair," Seamus replied, his voice firm, although there was some pity in his eyes. "I know why you did, but you've still got yourself in a mess, and the clan, too. Worse, you've left no way out of it, except what she suggests. You're learning a hard lesson, but it's one you must learn if you're to be chieftain—you've got to think things through, Adair, with all the possible consequences. You didn't, and now you've got to pay the price."

"For the rest of my life?"

His father nodded. "Aye, because she's right about

the Normans and how they'll treat her. She'll be like a leper to them, my son, and she doesn't deserve that."

"But she didn't have to come after me."

"Did she not?" his father asked, his gaze searching his son's face.

Adair thought of the shouting, the pounding on the door, the tone of her brother's words that he could hear even on the other side of a stone wall.

He knew then that he had no choice, for she'd had none.

He grasped at something else his father said, something to make him feel he hadn't utterly ruined his future. "You're still willing to have me lead the clan after you?"

His father looked genuinely shocked that he'd asked. "Aye."

Adair let his breath out slowly. "Then I'll marry her, and be glad my punishment's no worse."

Seamus briefly patted him on the back before they returned to the others.

"Adair's agreed," Seamus told them in Gaelic. "They'll be married. Today."

There was some murmuring among the men, and Cormag looked far from pleased, but none of them dared openly disagree with the chieftain's decision.

Seamus smiled at Marianne. "The wedding will be today," he said in French. "I can't promise much of a feast on such short notice, but we'll do our best."

Marianne's only reaction was a lowering of her

brows and a slight flush, as if she hadn't really expected his father to concede to her demand, after all.

If she tried to change her mind now…!

Adair strode up to her and tugged her into his arms. She was taken aback, and that pleased him. Let her be shocked and confused and feeling as if the ground beneath her feet would no longer support her, just as he had from the time she'd made her unexpected, outrageous proposal.

Then he kissed her, his lips moving over hers with sure and certain purpose. If it was marriage she wanted, and children, he'd show her that he fully intended to live up to his husbandly duties. He'd certainly—nay, eagerly—do what he must to get her with child, for that, and the children themselves, might be the only pleasure he'd get from his wife.

Children with Marianne. Blond bonnie lasses with fire in their eyes, and spirit and strength. Dark-haired bold boys worthy to lead their clan someday. Aye, and get into mischief plenty of times before that.

His kiss gentled. Marianne in his bed, loving him. And he loving her.

She relaxed in his arms, surrendering, even welcoming his kiss, as she had done that first time. He forgot where he was, and that they weren't alone.

He was kissing Marianne, who'd clung so tightly to him when he caught her after she'd let go of the rope. Who'd leaned against him as if for comfort and protection.

His father cleared his throat.

Adair immediately drew back, watching his bride's lovely face. Her cheeks were flushed, her lips slightly swollen, her eyes closed, as sleepy and satisfied as if they'd just made love.

She opened her bright blue eyes slowly. She had remarkable eyes, as direct and forthright as Cellach's had been.

"And him always claiming he hated Normans," Cormag grumbled. "Only took a pretty one to make him sing a different tune and cause us all this trouble."

"Shut it, Cormag, or I'll break your nose again," Adair said without looking at this cousin, for his gaze was still on his bride. "I'll go fetch Father Padraig."

Then he lowered his voice so that only she could hear. "I'm looking forward to my wedding night."

CHAPTER EIGHT

A SHORT TIME BEFORE HER WEDDING was to take place, Marianne sat on a low stool in one of the several small stone buildings within the wooden fortress walls of Lochbarr. The red-haired young woman, Dearshul, nervously combed her hair, clearly no more certain than she what else they should do as they waited for the summons to the church.

This room was as sparsely furnished as her chamber in Beauxville. There was a bed that was little more than a cot, the stool, two large chests and a table bearing a basin that Dearshul had filled with warm water for Marianne to wash. There was no hearth for a fire, or even a brazier for coals to heat the room.

These people must not feel the cold at all, Marianne thought glumly as she shivered, in spite of the thick, ugly gown she wore and the heavy leather shoes and rough woolen stockings on her bandaged feet.

An old woman with wild gray hair had come to her, examined her feet, frowned, exclaimed something to Dearshul, slathered a disgusting concoction on them, then bandaged them again. Whatever the salve was, though, it seemed to be working, for the soles of her feet were not nearly so sore.

The door to the building opened. Marianne half turned, expecting and dreading to see the glowering groom. Instead, her future father-in-law came into the room. The chieftain carried a parchment scroll, a small clay vessel covered by a waxed linen cloth and a quill.

"I hope I'm not disturbing you, my lady," he said with his usual genial courtesy.

She shook her head.

He then said something to Dearshul in their language. The young woman nodded and hurried away, leaving them alone.

Marianne waited silently, not sure what to do or say, if anything.

"My lady," the vigorous old man began, "I hope you know that I'm sorry my son's actions have caused you hardship."

She nodded.

"I appreciate the sacrifice you're making," he continued as he set the scroll, vessel and quill on the table beside her. "I'm sure you hold your honor dear and lying to your brother about the reason for this marriage won't come easy to you."

"I meant what I said about not wanting to cause any bloodshed," Marianne said, grateful for the chieftain's acknowledgment of what this letter would cost her, even if her honor was already lost in the eyes of the world. "My brother can be very…aggressive."

"I'm sure he can, by the look of him," Seamus

agreed. He nodded at the things he'd brought. "Would you mind writing that letter now? The sooner we can take it to your brother, the better."

She couldn't disagree. And of course he would want her to do it before the ceremony, so she would be sure to go through with it.

But she had no intention of changing her mind. She wanted children the way some women coveted jewelry or fine clothes. She'd enjoyed helping the younger girls at the convent with their tasks and lessons, and offering them comfort when they were sad or lonely. She yearned to do the same for children of her own.

She'd also heard the sly taunts and teasing of those girls so unfortunate as to be born illegitimate. Their lives were not easy, their futures uncertain. She wouldn't subject her children to that. She would rather marry…almost anyone.

She resolutely lifted the waxed cloth from the vessel of ink, reached for the quill, unrolled the parchment, and prepared to write.

"You clearly find it hard to believe my son acted without a selfish motive," the chieftain remarked as she was trying to think of an appropriate salutation.

She slid the man a glance, but didn't reply.

As she started the letter, the chieftain drew up one of the chests and sat beside her. "My eldest son is no smooth-talking courtier, my lady. He always means what he says, and you can know his mood by one look at his face. He couldn't be sly if he tried.

So when he says he wanted to help you because he thought you were in trouble, you can believe him."

"Yet you can't deny that his actions served another purpose," she said as she wrote. "Your son didn't approve of my marriage to Hamish Mac Glogan, and now I couldn't marry my brother's choice even if I wanted to."

"Aye, your marriage could have been disastrous for us, but that wasn't the most important reason to Adair. He cannot abide the thought of a woman suffering."

She still found it hard to accept that any man except a priest would help her without a selfish motive. "But why would he put you all at such risk for a Norman? He clearly hates us."

"Because although you're a Norman, you're a woman first, and a woman in trouble. That's what matters to my son."

"Then he is a very rare man," she conceded, although still unwilling and unable to believe that any man would act with so little regard for more serious consequences. In spite of what his father said, it was more likely Adair was guided by selfishness and, in this instance, lust. She was considered beautiful and he'd kissed her passionately. Whatever other reasons he gave, he'd surely hoped she'd express her gratitude in his bed. He just hadn't expected her to insist upon marriage before she did.

"I can see I'm going to have to give you more of an explanation."

She slid the chieftain another glance. This time,

his gray-eyed gaze held hers. "I'm going to tell you about Cellach."

What was Cellach? A person, a custom, some sort of ritual?

"When Adair was growing up, he had a friend, a girl whose name was Cellach."

A person, then.

"They were very close, like brother and sister. One day, when they were both ten years old, Cellach wanted to go berrying. Adair didn't. He'd just gotten his first *claimh mor* and he wanted to practice. So she went by herself."

Anguish came to the chieftain's eyes as he continued. "When she hadn't returned to Lochbarr by dusk, we thought she'd had an accident. Fallen, perhaps, and injured herself."

The old man shook his head. "It was all I could do to keep Adair from going to look for her in the dark by himself. But there was no moon, and the hills can be treacherous. We went out as soon as it was light. I wanted Adair to stay with me, but he ran ahead. And found Cellach."

For a long moment, no sound broke the silence between them. With a sinking feeling in her breast, Marianne guessed what came next, if not the true, terrible extent.

"She'd been raped and strangled."

The quill slipped unheeded from Marianne's fingers. Adair had been but a boy, and to find that girl, a girl he cherished like a sister… "It must have been terrible for him."

Seamus sighed heavily. "There's not a day goes by I don't wish we'd started looking for her sooner, or that I'd been the one to find her and not Adair.

"We had no idea who'd done it. We soon realized it couldn't have been anyone from Lochbarr, thank God. We could account for everyone, even the shepherds, who'd been too far up in the hills. We thought an outlaw, maybe, but nobody'd been robbed or attacked for miles around, not in years. Then we heard that a band of Norman soldiers had traveled past the place where Cellach was found. Adair was sure they were the ones who'd attacked her."

The chieftain's steady gaze never left her face. "So was I. I took some men and went after them. When we found them, I had them hanged from the nearest tree."

Marianne swallowed hard. No wonder Adair hated Normans, and it would be no wonder if everyone in Lochbarr, including the chieftain, hated them, too.

"When the king heard about it, he was furious—at me. He sent a messenger to tell me that those men, who he'd hired, couldn't have done it. He claimed they were miles away when Cellach was killed, fighting for him."

"Then you hanged innocent men," Marianne said, appalled at the Scot's mistake, thankful that her countrymen had not committed that heinous crime, and wondering why Adair still hated Normans if the mercenaries had been innocent.

The chieftain rose. "If I thought the king had no

reason to defend them, I would have believed him. But these were men he'd hired and men he needed if he was to hold on to his throne. If they'd been guilty, all the clans would have demanded every Norman mercenary leave Scotland. Alexander couldn't risk that."

"So you believe those men were guilty?"

"Aye, I do, and so does Adair."

"Then you must hate Normans, too," she said quietly. "I'm surprised you're willing to let one marry your son."

"I've no love for your countrymen, but I can see that the Normans are here to stay, whether I like it or not. We've got to find a way to live with them in peace."

Now she knew exactly why he wanted her to marry his son. She shouldn't be surprised, or disappointed. "You're making your son marry me because you want an alliance with the Normans, just as my brother wants an alliance with a Scot."

"Aye, I think we need an alliance with a few Normans, but as for *making* Adair marry you?" The chieftain laughed softly. "My lady, if Adair was completely opposed to the idea, he would have stood in the hall and argued with me until I gave in from sheer exhaustion. But that's not the only reason I'm pleased you made your proposal. I'm glad for Adair's sake.

"My stubborn son thinks with his heart, my lady, not his head, as should be clear by now. He needs a clever wife, one who can see things with a courtier's eyes, like his brother Lachlann. You'll help to make him a better, wiser chieftain. Indeed, my lady, I truly think you're a gift from God."

So she was to be an advisor as well as a wife. "Perhaps he won't welcome advice from his wife, especially if his brother has the same qualities you think I possess."

The chieftain walked toward the shuttered window, then turned to look at her. "Lachlann's too ambitious for Lochbarr. I doubt he'll stay." He smiled proudly. "Though I expect all of Scotland will hear of Lachlann Mac Taran some day."

Marianne went back to her letter.

A small leather purse of coins clinked down by her elbow. "That's for a wedding present."

She looked at it with distaste. To be sure, this marriage was a bargain, albeit one of her design, but she didn't appreciate the obvious reminder.

"I mean no offense," Seamus said. "You'll be needing new clothes and other things."

To make life here more bearable, she finished in her thoughts, such as a brazier, if she could find one in that little village. "Thank you."

"I'll have Dearshul put it in Adair's *teach*."

"Teach?"

Seamus waved his hand, indicating the building. "This is a *teach*."

"Oh." She stifled a sigh. She was going to have to learn many new things if she was to live here.

Her letter finished, she signed her name, then re-read what she'd written. It was blunt and to the point, adequate but not eloquent. Yet it would serve its purpose, and she would forever be bound to Adair Mac Taran.

She held the scroll out to Seamus.

He didn't take it right away. Instead, his gaze softened. "Are you sure of this, my lady? Are you truly willing to marry my son?"

"I have no choice if I'm to have legitimate children."

"There's always a choice, my lady," the old man said gently. "You can wait, if nothing else."

As she sat in the cold stone building that seemed more like a byre than a bedchamber, she considered the chieftain's words.

Yes, she could wait—but for what? Her brother to come to Lochbarr with an army?

She rose and faced the chieftain squarely. "I've made my choice, Seamus Mac Taran, and I'll abide by it."

His warm smile made her words seem less like a self-imposed punishment. And then she wondered if his son ever smiled like that.

The chieftain accepted the scroll and read it quickly. He began to roll it up. "Thank you, my lady. You have my gratitude forever, and you'll surely have my son's, too, when he stops being stubborn and realizes what you've done for his sake, and the clan's." He smiled again. "As for children, I don't think Adair will disappoint you there."

She blushed to the soles of her sore feet and couldn't meet his gaze.

Seamus held out his hand. "Now, Lady Marianne—daughter—if you'll give me your hand, I think Father Padraig should be sober enough for the blessing."

SEVERAL HOURS LATER, the brief ceremony was over and Marianne was married to Adair Mac Taran.

Nothing about Marianne's wedding had been as she'd imagined it in days gone by. Not the groom, who'd stood stiff and still beside her in the village church, dressed in a fine white shirt and his moss-green and rusty-red plaid garment. Not herself, wearing that horrid brown gown, with only her mother's crucifix for jewelry. And certainly not the doddering, elderly, drunken priest who had blessed their union, binding her to the Scot for life. The only person who'd looked pleased had been Adair's father.

Now she was alone in Adair's *teach,* which was as spartan as his father's with one notable exception: the bed. It was twice the size of the chieftain's, and made up with linen sheets and a woolen blanket in a striped pattern of green and blue, with a thick black fur across the foot.

There were no coverings on the wall or floor to provide some protection from the cold, and the only light came from a small oil lamp that reeked of sheep's tallow. The rest of the furniture consisted of a table, two stools and a painted chest that probably held Adair's clothes.

Trying to ignore the bed, although it seemed to

take up half the room, she went to the window, intending to close the shutters to drown out the muffled sounds of celebrating—the loud, boisterous singing and the Scots' strange piped instruments that made a noise like cats screeching.

After she shut the shutters as tightly as she could, her stomach growled.

Her wedding feast hadn't been as she'd imagined it, either. She could barely touch the strange, unappetizing food, and she'd been subjected to the curious looks and hostile stares of the household and clansmen, reminding her—as if she needed it!—that she was an unwelcome foreigner. It would probably be years, if ever, before she'd ever feel completely at home in this horrible, rugged, damp and uncivilized place.

The door banged open, making her jump.

She turned to find her husband standing on the threshold, his powerful warrior's body silhouetted against the night sky.

The man who owned her had come to collect his reward for saving her from Hamish Mac Glogan.

Maybe wearing only her shift had been a mistake, but she hadn't wanted to seem some timid girl who had second thoughts about her decision.

"Somebody's been in here tidying," he remarked as he came in and closed the door. His voice was casual, almost blasé, as if nothing of any significance had happened between them. "I'm not a neat man. But generally nobody comes in here but me."

She didn't believe that for a moment. Surely a man of his attributes didn't spend many nights alone.

Unless the women here are fools.

She silently commanded her inner voice to hold its wayward tongue. And her heart to stop racing. And her knees to cease shaking. She must behave with pride and dignity, as befit a well-bred Norman lady.

Her husband moved toward the bed and grinned, looking like the devil's own minion. "Clean sheets."

She couldn't help blushing, and hated herself for it. "I assume that's so your family can inspect them in the morning, to be sure I was a virgin."

The amusement disappeared from his eyes. "They wouldn't care if you weren't. Neither would I."

That had to be a lie, too. "Every man wants to marry a virgin."

Every honorable one, anyway, and his father's claims made Adair Mac Taran sound like the most chivalrous man in England.

"The Normans may think a woman's only value is her maidenhead, but Scots don't. My father hand-fasted three times before my mother. Those women all married well afterward."

She'd forgotten about that barbaric custom. The Scots' notion of honor and chivalry was obviously quite different from the Normans'. "Fidelity is not important to you then."

"Of course it is. Now that we're married, they'll be no other women for me." He strolled closer, his gaze questioning. "Or are you asking if you must be faithful?"

"Of course I will be," she replied, determined to stand her ground and not let him intimidate her. "I've sworn before God."

His eyes seemed to bore right into her. "So, I remind you, did I. From this night on, it will be only you I take to my bed, Marianne." His voice lowered, to a seductive purr that set her heart pounding. "At the moment, there's no other woman I *want* to take to my bed."

Oh, sweet merciful Mary! He could probably seduce a woman without even touching her.

But she didn't want him to think she was a naive young woman who didn't know the truth about men. "I may have been a long time in a convent, but I'm not a fool. I know that men may swear to be faithful, yet break those vows—even the ones before God."

"You may have heard a lot about Norman men, but you don't know me."

He was right. She didn't, yet she'd given herself to him in marriage.

"I suppose I should defend my sex," he said. He gave her a sardonic look. "There are probably even some good Normans."

"Several—just as there may be some exemplary Scots."

"There are plenty of good, decent Scots in Lochbarr."

"If you say so."

His brows lowered. "I do. Or do you intend your words to be an insult to my father, my brother, my clansmen and me?"

Sure she'd angered him, well aware that as her husband, he was free to treat her as he liked, she backed away from him until she hit the table.

Her husband's eyes flared with sudden comprehension. "I'm not going to strike you. I've never hit a woman in my life."

She hoped that was true.

He came to her and lightly took hold of her shoulders, the pressure of his hands warm and firm. "I've never hurt a woman and I certainly don't plan to hurt my wife, in bed or out of it."

As he continued to hold her, her gaze flicked to the bed. She remembered what the girls who'd come to the convent in disgrace had said about making love for the first time, the pain and blood. "Not intentionally, perhaps, but you will. I know…things. About the first time we make love."

God help her, she sounded worse than naive. She sounded stupid and frightened.

His hands slid from her shoulders down her arms, the gesture like a caress. "More things you heard from those girls in the convent?"

"Yes."

Now she sounded defiant and strident. And his hands were still touching her.

Instead of regarding her as if she were stupid, frightened, or strident, his full lips curved up in a smile that was as warm and welcome as his father's had been. And more. "Well, my wife, you may be a virgin, but I'm not."

The pleasant feelings within her died. She didn't need to hear about his experience. "I didn't expect that you were," she snapped, pulling away. "I'm sure you've seduced many women."

"Seduced?" he repeated, his smile gone. "You make it sound as if I sneak about with other men's wives, or deflower virgins for sport."

She crossed her arms. Perhaps he did.

He put his hands on his hips and glared at her. "I've known a few women in my time, and I'm not ashamed to admit it. But they were all free, and so was I, and no harm done."

"Just what I would expect a man to say."

"I only told you so you'd know that I won't be thinking only of myself, like some lustful lad."

"How very kind."

"I suppose that's all the gratitude I'm ever going to get from you," he growled as he marched toward the door. "I should have expected no more, after what you said this morning."

"And I was right to think that by gratitude you meant—"

She fell silent as she envisioned him returning to the hall and telling everyone there that he refused to consummate the marriage.

If he didn't, they wouldn't be really married. He could send her away. Cast her out. She'd be abandoned by her husband, just as her brother had disowned her. She'd never have children or a family. She'd be all alone. "Adair!"

His hand on the latch, he looked back over his shoulder.

"Adair," she said, trying not to sound desperate, "please don't go. I…I'm sorry."

He eyed her warily.

"I don't want you to leave." She went toward him. "Please don't go."

He turned back into the room. "You want me to stay?"

"Yes."

His expression hardened. "Why?"

"Because we're married." She halted in front of him, then reached up and caressed his cheek. "Because I want you."

And that, she knew in her heart, was no lie. "Don't you want me?" she asked, sidling closer. She raised herself on her toes and brushed her lips across his. "Don't you?"

He looked at her for a long moment, then, with a low growl of desire, he pulled her into his arms and kissed her with fierce, hungry passion.

This was the bargain she'd made—marriage and safety for passion and security.

But as his kiss deepened, as heat and need exploded within her, she knew the passion had never been only his.

He shifted, moving his hands slowly down her back, pressing her close, arousing incredible sensations with a kiss, with his tongue, with his touch.

She wanted to be closer, too, to feel more of him, her husband. Leaning into him, she ran her hands over his broad, well-muscled back. A warrior's back. Her husband's virile, powerful body.

She gasped as Adair picked her up and carried her to the bed.

He was going to make love with her. He wasn't going to leave—and she was glad. Excited. Hot with desire.

His hands went to the broach at his shoulder. He undid the clasp and tossed it onto the table. The piece of plaid fabric that hung over his left shoulder fell to the floor. Then he started to undo his belt.

Her breathing accelerated. She was his wife. She belonged to him. She shouldn't look away, and yet before his *feileadh* came undone, she did, scrambling beneath the sheets.

She heard the *feileadh* fall to the floor, then another garment. That had to be his shirt. He must be naked now. She felt the sheet rise and risked a glance as he climbed into the bed beside her.

His body was magnificent, from his handsome head, to his broad chest, his taut belly and…she didn't look lower. She didn't dare.

Not sure what to do or what was expected of her, she closed her eyes and lay still, waiting for him to make the next move.

"Marianne?"

"Yes?"

"Will you open your eyes?"

She obeyed, to find him propped up on one

elbow, looking down at her. "You must lead the way tonight, Marianne," he murmured as his hand slid slowly over the chain of her crucifix and across her collarbone toward the ties at the neck of her shift. "I'll do nothing that you do not want and I'll do my best not to hurt you."

"But you're so big."

His eyes widened. "I like the compliment, but how many naked men have you seen to compare me to?"

"None!" she cried, offended, until he smiled.

"I didn't mean…that," she said, suddenly bashful as she nodded toward his groin. "I meant all over."

"I didn't suppose you'd had many opportunities for comparison in a convent. Are you worried I'll crush you?"

It sounded so silly.

He toyed with the ends of the ties of her shift. He was going to undo the knot. She wished he'd hurry up.

"I promise you, I won't crush you," he said as he bent down and brushed his lips over hers. "My arms are very strong."

"I can tell."

He pulled one tie and undid the knot. "Then have faith in me," he whispered before he kissed her, moving his mouth with slow, intoxicating languor.

She entwined her arms about his neck, steadying herself against the sensual onslaught. His hand slipped beneath her shift, sliding gently over her skin like a whisper of silk, barely touching. Then down to her breasts.

This was his right, too, and she didn't protest. How could she, when his caresses felt so...so... wonderful. Arching back, she instinctively pushed against his hand.

"So you like that," he murmured, his lips against her skin. "So do I."

Emboldened by the excitement he aroused, she lightly brushed her fingertips across the flesh of his belly, then his chest, encountering the dark hairs that spread between his nipples. She tentatively moved her hand down his chest, unsure of what to do, wondering if...

The catch in his breath told her he liked to be touched there. She encircled him, exploring her husband by touch.

To judge by his breathing and the increasing passion of his kiss, he liked that very much.

As she stroked him, he ran his palm over her breast. His thumb lightly brushed the hardened nub.

And she thought they had but one purpose.

She'd often wondered why men had them. Perhaps...

Her fingertips swept across his, earning a low moan from deep within his throat.

So, for pleasure. She would never have guessed that.

What if she kissed him there?

She immediately gave in to the impulse, pressing her lips against his hot, salty skin, letting her tongue flick across the tip of his nipple as his thumb had hers.

He groaned, the sound one of such seeming agony, she instantly stilled and looked up in horror at his face.

"No, don't stop," he murmured, his eyes closed. "Please, Marianne, I beg you. Don't stop."

He sounded aroused and yearning, not angry or in pain.

And completely at her mercy, as if she were the commander here. A spirit of mischief, of freedom and liberty, encouraged her. She grabbed his shoulders and shifted forward, raising herself more as she swirled her tongue about the rosy brown circle.

He was breathing as hard as if he'd run a mile.

She switched to the other side, still gripping him tightly, his skin hot and slick.

He insinuated his leg over hers and moved so that his body was between her limbs. She fell back and he followed, taking her mouth again with fierce hunger.

Adair's hand drifted to her leg and began to lift the skirt of her shift. His mouth left hers, traveling lower, resting for a moment on the throbbing pulse of her neck as she caught her breath.

Then he continued, using his chin to nuzzle her shift lower, until her breasts were bare.

She didn't care if he saw her naked. That was his right. More, the shift was a nuisance, an encumbrance. She wanted to be wanton and wild, free of restraint.

As savage as he.

Panting, she sat up, tugged off her shift and tossed it aside.

He sat back on his haunches, his body illuminated by the flickering, dim light of the lamp, as he slowly perused her body. "You're so beautiful."

"So are you," she whispered as she brought him to her for another kiss. He eagerly complied, his hand continuing to caress and stroke her, creating yet more excitement, and need.

She gasped when he cupped her between her legs, surprised by his action—but only for a moment before she closed her eyes and surrendered to a new pleasure.

His finger slid inside her. Her eyes flew open and she stared, shocked, into his handsome face.

"To prepare you," he said softly. "If you want me to stop, I will."

She shook her head. "Not if it helps."

"You don't like it?"

She was liking it so much, she had to bite her lip to keep from crying out so loudly that the men in the hall could hear her.

"You're moist and warm, Marianne. And tight."

Apparently that was good.

Then he leaned down and his mouth suckled her breasts, licking her nipple. Gently flicking.

More tension grew within her, until her body felt stretched as tight and taut as a rope hauling up a stone. She grabbed the bottom sheet, bunching it in her hands.

He moved to pleasure her other breast, and as he did, he removed his finger.

Then he was against her, pushing gently, but inexorably, inside her. She sucked in her breath at the quick, sharp pain.

He instantly stilled. "That's it," he whispered, his breath hot on her ear as he held her close. "That's what you heard about and feared. It should be just this once."

He moved, thrusting slowly once more, and kissed her cheek, her chin. "The pain shouldn't last," he said as he rocked slowly back, then forward. "Tell me if it does, and I'll stop."

She opened her eyes to look at him. "You can stop?"

"If I must. It won't be easy, I grant you, but I can."

"Does it hurt you, too?"

"No. It feels…" He pushed again. "Words can't describe it."

"It doesn't hurt so much anymore."

"Thank God."

"Kiss me."

He did, tenderly at first. Gently, as he'd taken her maidenhead.

But not for long. Not when the passion returned, full force and more, to overtake them both. Then he kissed her with hungry fervor, and she responded in kind, driven by a need, a desire, older than custom and rules and tribes and language.

His passion overwhelmed her and all conscious thought fled. He swept her off to a place of sensation and feelings, where all that mattered was pleasure.

The pain was gone. Forgotten. She found purchase with her heels and began to meet his thrusts.

An urgent longing to join with him, thrust for thrust, filled her. She took hold of his shoulders and arched, encouraging him to pleasure her breasts again.

This was her man, and she was his woman. Completely his woman. And whether he was a Scot or not, she wouldn't give him reason to share his magnificent body and caresses or kisses with another.

Propelled by that desire, anxious with need, she surrendered completely to the passion surging through her body, and his.

"Oh, yes," she gasped, her breathing ragged, her throat rough with dryness. "Oh, please, yes!"

Tension. Need. Desire. Building and building to a crescendo.

Sighs. Moans. His. Hers. Whimpers, almost begging. For what? She couldn't say. She didn't know the words. Only this feeling. This incredible feeling.

His body suddenly tensed and he groaned, a sound rising deep within his throat.

And just as suddenly, she felt him, harder and stronger, pushing inside her. Primitive. Powerful. Virile. Hers.

She gave a cry like someone discovering something they thought lost forever as wave after wave of release surged through her, and left her sated.

Adair collapsed against her, panting. She held him to her, cradling him in her arms, their bodies sweat-slicked.

So that was making love, she thought, still basking in the aftermath. Those girls hadn't done it justice. Not at all.

CHAPTER NINE

LYING ON HIS SIDE, Adair watched Marianne as she slept, the tumble of her blond hair hiding her face like a veil.

Last night had been a revelation. The kisses he'd shared with Marianne before the wedding had hinted at a hidden well of passion. Now he could believe that well might be bottomless, and he'd married a woman capable of deep feelings and heated desire in wondrous combination.

Yet when he'd stood beside her during the wedding ceremony, she'd seemed so stately and so proud, he'd foreseen a reluctant bride who would take him into her bed only as an unwelcome necessity, in order to have children.

Closing his eyes, he savored the memory of the moment she tore off her shift, as if she couldn't wait to make love. The sense that she desired him that much was even more heady and overwhelming than the sight of her naked beauty.

Marianne shifted, unconsciously brushing the hair from her face before turning to her other side, unknowingly presenting her naked back to him. He yearned to run his fingertips down her spine, brushing them over her silky flesh, then following their progress with his lips.

He inched forward with half a mind to wake her, until the shutters trembled from the wind, the edges knocking together.

That wasn't the way to rouse his bride.

He quickly got out of bed and crossed the room. He was naked, but the cold didn't bother him overmuch. As he started to secure the shutters, he peered out at the sky visible between the narrow opening.

It looked to be another fine day, heralding, he hoped, better weather that was here to stay until harvest. He couldn't remember a wetter spring.

He opened the shutters a little, breathing in the fresh, cool air. Voices nearby exchanged greetings, and somewhere a dog barked. He could hear the muted words of women gossiping at the well outside the hall kitchen.

He looked at the sky again and realized, with a start, that it must be late in the morning.

He fastened the shutters tight. Newly wedded or not, he shouldn't have lingered so long. He should be up and about, checking to see if the patrols sent out at dawn had returned, and if they'd noticed anything suspicious. In spite of Sir Nicholas's denials, he wasn't ready to believe the Normans had nothing to do with the missing cattle.

It was sobering to think that one Norman in particular was his brother-in-law. Nevertheless, a legal relationship wouldn't absolve Sir Nicholas or his men if they were caught stealing Mac Taran cattle.

He should also ask his father when they'd inform Sir Nicholas of the marriage, and how many men would go with him to deliver the bride price.

Adair turned back toward the bed and Marianne, still sleeping. She must be exhausted after their journey and…last night. He would let her sleep.

His clothes lay on a heap on the floor and her shift was on top of them. He quickly and quietly dressed in his wrinkled shirt and *feileadh,* fastening it tight about him and putting his dirk in his belt.

He glanced at his *claimh mor,* leaning against the chest. Sir Nicholas might yet come seeking his sister, and if he found her married, in spite of the bride price Adair would pay—five hundred marks, his father had decided, nearly all the coin Adair possessed—there could be trouble. Nevertheless, he decided to leave the long, heavy sword behind. If the alarm was raised that the Normans were coming, he could always run and fetch it.

With quiet, cautious steps, he left the *teach,* closing the door softly behind him. Walking through the yard toward the hall, he called a greeting to the servants and clansmen who were going about their usual business. A few returned his salutations. Most said nothing, giving him the slightest of nods for a response.

As if he'd done something truly unforgivable.

All the good feelings he'd awakened with slipped away.

His father and Barra would no doubt tell him it would take time for the people of Lochbarr to accept his marriage, and his Norman bride. With a mental jolt, he realized that much would depend on Marianne and her ability to adjust to life among his clan.

Supposing she'd want to. Supposing she would try.

Alone with him in their bed was one thing; a Norman woman living among the clan was another. And Marianne was a proud woman.

But she was also an intelligent woman. Surely she'd see the need to fit into life in Lochbarr.

And if she didn't? Or it she didn't think such a thing worthy of effort? If that proved to be so, he wasn't sure what he'd do.

He pushed open the bossed oaken door of the hall and entered the dim building. Cormag sat at one of the trestle tables, his head over a bowl of thick, gray *brochan,* a heel of brown bread beside it.

As Adair looked around for Dearshul, the hearth fire smoldered and smoked, making the air murky.

Cormag raised his bloodshot, bleary eyes. "So, did she bleed?"

"Don't be disgusting, Cormag, if you can help it," Adair replied with a sneer as he headed for the door.

Cormag chortled and dipped his bread in the wooden bowl. "I wouldn't put it past a Norman woman to claim she was a virgin and weep and wail, only to discover she's already been used by half her brother's garrison. Maybe that's why she fled with you—didn't want her brother to find out she's no better than a *striopach.*"

One hand on the hilt of his dirk, Adair slowly swiveled on his heel to regard his cousin. "Shut your damned mouth, Cormag."

"I don't have to do what you say," his cousin replied, baring his teeth in a grin that was more like a grimace.

Adair started toward him. "She's my wife, so you'll keep a respectful tongue in your head."

Cormag threw down the bread. It rolled off the table and fell to the floor, where a large black dog hurried to gobble it up.

Cormag got to his feet, shoving the bench backward so that it scraped loudly across the stone floor. "There was a time you would have agreed with me that the Normans were all scheming bitches and bastards. But that was in the old days, before you were besotted with a bonnie face and a pair of fine breasts."

"I'm not bewitched. And I told you, speak respectfully of my wife. Aye, and treat her as she deserves, or you'll regret it."

"I'd like nothing better than to give her what she deserves," Cormag said, his eyes gleaming in a way that disgusted Adair as he made a gesture that was more disgusting still. "Except that I won't forget she's a Norman while I'm at it."

Adair shoved the table sideways, so that it wasn't between them anymore. "I told you to shut your disgusting mouth, Cormag," he growled, drawing his dirk.

"Oh, aye?" Cormag mocked as he pulled his

knife from his belt. "And what'll you tell your father if you kill me? Not that it'll matter. He'll forgive you. He always does, no matter what you do. If anyone else did what you did, he'd be banished, or staring at a hangman's rope, but not his blessed boy."

Cormag started to circle Adair. "Everyone in Lochbarr knows how you're favored. We've all seen it a hundred times, and never more than yesterday. You came back here with that Norman's sister, putting us all at risk, and what does Seamus do? He gives you leave to marry her. And then this morning, he goes himself to set it right with the Norman while his precious son stays at home in bed, wallowing like a pig in mud with his bonnie Norman bride."

"You're lying."

"About what? The fact that he treats you like a prince's brat?"

"He's never gone to Sir Nicholas without me."

Cormag's loud, mocking laughter echoed in the stone building, the sound and what it meant making Adair's blood run cold. "Has he not?"

Adair turned on his heel, heading for the door.

"That's a surprise, is it?" Cormag called after him. "Then do you not know about the letter he took, the one *she* wrote?"

Adair wheeled around, to see Cormag nearly giddy with the knowledge that he knew something of which Adair was so obviously ignorant.

"You mean to say she didn't tell you? My, my,

Adair, you must be losing your touch with the women."

Adair gave his cousin a frigid smile. "My wife and I had better things to do last night than talk about letters."

Cormag's eyes flashed envious fire for an instant. "But for Seamus not to tell you he was going, let alone leave you behind—maybe you're not the favored son anymore."

"I notice he didn't take you, either, Cormag. You must have been too drunk," Adair retorted as he strode out of the hall.

He wouldn't believe Cormag. The man was a lout, a liar and a lustful, lazy oaf. His father was probably still in his *teach.*

As he headed toward his father's quarters, Adair spotted Dearshul hurrying toward the kitchen. He called to her and she came running, her expression quizzical.

"Is my father still abed?"

She shook her head. "No. He and Lachlann and ten others left for Dunkeathe at dawn."

Cormag hadn't been lying? His father had gone to face Sir Nicholas without him? Adair could hardly believe it—but Dearshul would have no reason to lie.

Cormag probably wasn't lying about the letter, then, either, for his father would want to take that when he went to see Marianne's brother.

Adair glanced upward. The sun was halfway to noon. They'd be nearly to Dunkeathe by now.

"Fetch some food for Marianne, will you?" he asked as he started toward his own *teach* to get his *claimh mor.*

He couldn't catch up to his father and the others, but he could meet them on the way back. If they came back. If that Norman didn't throw them in his dungeon.

He shoved open the door to his *teach*. His bride, his wife, sat up swiftly, holding the sheets to her creamy breasts, her hair an unkempt mass of gold, her eyes wide with shock. "What's wrong?"

"My father's gone to Dunkeathe."

"Without you?"

She sounded as incredulous as he had been.

His anger diminished. Slightly. "Aye."

Her brow furrowed as she considered. "It's probably better that he tells Nicholas what happened without you there. Nicholas might try to kill you on the spot."

Adair stiffened. "He could try."

"Yes, and that surely occurred to your father. A fight between the two of you would only end in more trouble. I think it's best your father went without you after all."

"Either way, he's already gone." He didn't want her to know that he'd been kept completely in the dark. "He took your letter."

"I should think so."

He wondered what she'd said and when she'd written it. Probably before the wedding. "You told your brother we were lovers." He didn't make it a question, but a statement of fact.

She brushed a lock of hair from the side of her soft cheek. "Yes."

He heard something in her voice that gave him pause. "What else?"

She got out of bed, wrapping a sheet around her slender body. Her fair hair tumbled about her shoulders.

The sight was nearly enough to make him forget what he'd come there for, as well as his father and everybody else in Lochbarr.

"I told him that we had married and I asked for his forgiveness."

His mind snapped alert. "You did what?"

"I asked for Nicholas's forgiveness. I thought it best."

"You thought it best to humiliate yourself?" Adair demanded, incredulous and a little disgusted.

She raised her chin and faced him squarely, as imperious as an empress though she only wore a sheet. "I'm surprised you'd suggest marriage to you was humiliating."

"That's not what I meant."

She adjusted the sheet. "I did what I thought necessary to preserve the peace."

He tried not to be distracted by the thought that one tug would send that sheet falling to the floor. "At the expense of your pride."

"Yes, at the expense of my pride," she answered. "Just as some men will do what they consider necessary because their consciences will permit nothing else, and no matter what other consequences there might be."

He hadn't expected that.

Nor was he prepared for her next remark.

"Your father told me about Cellach."

He let his breath out slowly as he wondered what exactly his father had said about Cellach and her fate.

As always when he thought of Cellach, the terrible images quickly blotted out the happy memories of the girl he'd loved with all his boyish heart.

"I'm glad he did, Adair, and you should be, too," his wife said softly. "Now I understand why you hate my people so much."

He grabbed his *claimh mor* and started toward the door. Unless she'd seen Cellach's tortured body, she understood only a small portion of his hatred.

He glanced back to look at her, his bride, his wife, standing in that sheet, so lovely, so regal, so proud in spite of everything. "I'm going to ride out to meet my father when he returns. I'll send Dearshul to tend you."

"Thank you."

Some gratitude at last, he thought as he left the *teach,* walking with some haste lest he give in to temptation, and go back to Marianne and pull off that sheet and—

"Adair!"

He halted as Roban came sauntering toward him, looking much the worse for a night of celebrating. His shirt was unlaced, his belt and *feileadh* precariously low on his hips, and his eyes were bloodshot beneath his light-brown brows. Wisps of straw stuck out of his reddish-gold hair, as if he'd spent the night in a haystack. Knowing Roban, he probably had, although whether he'd done so alone was subject to speculation.

But if Roban was here, and Cormag, and himself, who the devil *had* his father taken with him to Dunkeathe, other than Lachlann, who was a clever lad but no warrior?

Roban gave Adair a grin and a look that asked a host of questions. "I'm surprised to see you up and about, my friend."

Adair ignored the look to ask a question of his own. "Are you fit to ride?"

Taken aback, Roban frowned as if mightily insulted. "Of course."

Adair started toward the stable again. "Then come with me."

"Where are we going?" Roban asked as he trotted after him.

"My wife's written a letter to her brother, and my father, Lachlann and ten others have taken it to Dunkeathe this morning, to try to make peace."

"To Dunkeathe without ye and me?" Roban cried, aghast as well as breathless. "And with only ten other clansmen?"

"Aye," Adair grimly replied. "I'm going to meet them when they return. At least, I hope so," he finished under his breath.

Roban hoisted up his belt and with it, his *feileadh*. "Right. I'm with ye, Adair, just as soon as I can get my *claimh mor*."

"THERE THEY ARE," Adair noted with relief from his vantage point on the rise. He raised his arm and pointed toward the small band of men riding along the road to Lochbarr, the sound of their horses' hooves like a distant echo of thunder.

"They don't look like they've been in a fight," Roban said, also relieved.

Adair silently agreed, and they were going at a gentle canter, not as if they were in any great hurry or fleeing.

Nevertheless, it was too soon to be sure. It could be that they were going at such a pace because some of them had been wounded.

He punched Neas's sides and rode down the hill along a narrow path through the bracken. Stones and pebbles rolled and scattered, some falling into a narrow stream of clear water on their right. Their progress was hardly silent, and they were clearly visible. His father raised his hand and called a greeting, and brought his party to a halt while they waited for Adair and Roban to arrive.

Adair reached them first. Thankfully, he saw no sign of blood or bruises on any of them.

But only his father met his gaze. None of the other grim, grave men did, not even Lachlann.

Worse, there was something in his father's eyes Adair had never seen before—a wariness that smote him to the heart, as if his father was suspicious of him now. "What happened in Dunkeathe?"

"Sir Nicholas will make no trouble for us," Seamus replied.

The words should have brought comfort, but they didn't, because of that look in his father's eyes. "That's good news, is it not?"

Seamus smiled. With his lips. "Aye, 'tis good."

"He took the bride price?"

"Aye."

Then if anyone should be annoyed… "Why are you not better pleased?"

His father nodded at a little stand of pines a short distance from the road and a bit up the hill. "Come with me and I'll tell you."

Adair wanted no more secrets, no quiet conferences in a corner or out of the way. "Surely Lachlann and the others already know what happened."

"I'd rather we talk alone," his father said as Roban came within twenty yards of them on his slower horse.

"You don't think we have to keep anything from Roban?" Adair asked. "I trust him with my life, and so should you."

"It's not because I don't trust him, or any of the clan," his father replied, dismounting.

"Then what?"

For a moment, he thought his father was going to raise his voice—something almost unheard of, unless he was hurt. He didn't, but his frustration and impatience were clear just the same. "Will you not for once just do as I ask without trying to debate me?"

Chastened, Adair immediately dismounted and followed his father to the stand of trees. The scent of the pines was strong, and the morning dew lingered on the grass in the shade.

When his father faced him, Adair was shocked to realize he didn't seem angry at all. "I have to ask youe this, Adair. Did you consummate the marriage?"

Adair blushed like a lad, but he couldn't help it. "Aye."

His father let his breath out slowly. "Good."

"If you had any doubts about it, you should have come to my *teach* before you went to her brother."

"I didn't want to disturb you, and I was fairly certain what your answer would be anyway. I thought you'd need your rest."

Adair didn't know what to say to that.

His father's expression altered to one grave and grim. "And I didn't think you'd be able to keep your temper when you saw Sir Nicholas."

As much as he wanted to, Adair couldn't refute that.

"The man enrages me, too, my son, but we can't risk open warfare with a friend of the king."

Adair nodded, silently conceding the point, albeit reluctantly. "So what happened when you got to Dunkeathe?"

"Things are not as bad as they could have been, yet it wasn't a pleasant meeting."

"We couldn't expect anything else. I don't suppose he even let you through the gates."

Seamus shook his head. "No, he didn't. I doubt any Mac Taran's going to get inside that castle again while he rules it, and that includes your wife. He met us outside the gates. But even so, I didn't expect him to say what he did."

Adair tried to be patient as Seamus's gaze scanned the sky as if searching for the right words before coming to rest on his son.

"The man was filled with anger, Adair," he said at last. "Not hot with it, as you would be. Cold, like the blade of a headman's ax left out in the snow."

Adair could imagine it, and some of the things such a man might say at such a time. "Did he dare to threaten you? You're the thane by right of charter, and a chieftain, and friend of the king—"

"No, he made no threats," his father interrupted, shaking his snow-white head. "Not in the beginning nor after I told him you'd married his sister."

"He didn't say he'd go to Alexander?"

"He never spoke of the king at all."

"Then he'll not have me charged with a crime?"

His father shook his head, and yet he still seemed grave and troubled.

"What of the betrothal with Hamish Mac Glogan? He must have been upset about the end of that."

"He never said a word about it."

"Then what *did* he say?" That could make you act like you were facing execution, Adair finished in his thoughts.

Or perhaps Seamus feared for his son's life. "If he threatened *me*, I'm not afraid."

His hand on the hilt of his *claimh mor*, his father kicked a stone and sent it rolling through the dead needles at his feet. "He didn't threaten you."

"Marianne, then? I can believe the lout'd go after his own sister. But that's an empty threat, as he has to know. We can protect her."

Seamus shook his head again. "That's not what's troubling me, my son." His heavy brows furrowed as he regarded his son steadily. "He wouldn't take the letter she wrote. He said he had no sister."

Adair's jaw dropped with stunned disbelief. "No sister?" he repeated, scarcely able to comprehend what his father was saying. Yet if Marianne wasn't Sir Nicholas's sister… "Is this some kind of Norman trick?"

And if so, who was Marianne?

"It's no trick," his father said, putting his hand on his son's arm. "She's his sister by blood and birth. That's not what he meant. Sir Nicholas said that as far as he was concerned, Marianne was dead, just as if she'd fallen to her death when she went out the window, and she could rot in hell for all he cared."

"The bloody bastard," Adair muttered. He wished the man was there now. He'd give him a lesson in family loyalty Sir Nicholas would never forget.

"His sister's hurt his pride as much as ruined his plans," Seamus said. "And for now, it's the injury to his pride that's the worst, I think. That's why his anger is more at her than you, although I think he'd likely run you through if he could."

Adair had never loathed anyone in his life as much as he loathed Sir Nicholas. "Yet he took the bride price?"

"Aye. He said it'd be some small compensation for the breaking of the betrothal."

Adair remembered what her brother had called her. He'd shouted the word like an accusation of murder. "If he thinks she's a whore, what does that make him for taking that money?" he snapped as he strode past Seamus, intending to go to Dunkeathe and teach that bloody Norman bastard respect.

Seamus clapped a hand on his son's broad shoulder, making him halt. "Leave him for now, my son, and stay away from Dunkeathe. We've got peace, of a sort, anyway. And the Norman does have a grievance, or enough that other Normans will take his side if he chooses to fight, so we should be relieved he's not, and that he's not planning to go to Alexander." The chieftain eyed his son. "Will you obey in this, Adair?"

Although Adair itched to tell Nicholas what he thought of a man who would so easily cast off his sister, his father had ordered him to stay away from Dunkeathe, so he would.

He had to prove that he could still be trusted. "Aye, Father, I will."

CHAPTER TEN

AT THE SAME TIME Adair was talking with his father, Marianne was wearing her ugly brown dress and wondering what she was supposed to do for the rest of the day.

She surveyed the bare stone walls of the chamber. Perhaps with some tapestries, and a few more items of furniture and a brazier, this room could be comfortable, even in the winter.

At least it was mercifully separate from the other buildings in the fortress. She blushed when she thought of the passionate noises she'd made last night, and Adair, too, as they loved. It was a relief to think that nobody had overheard them.

Comfortable chamber or not, and in spite of the delicious pleasure she'd found in her husband's arms, life here wasn't going to be easy. For one thing, she didn't know the language. She'd always hated it when the twins from Paris had jabbered away in their own secret tongue at the convent, shutting out everybody else while obviously gossiping about them. She wasn't going to live the rest of her life feeling shut out from the people of her husband's household, or the village, so she'd have to learn their language.

She'd also have to find out the way things were done in Lochbarr. Her education hadn't prepared her for life among the Scots, but she'd made her choice when she'd demanded Adair marry her, and it was up to her to learn to live here.

A sound made her start. Something was scratching at the door—a dog, perhaps? Or a cat after a mouse? If it was a mouse, she wasn't getting near it, even to catch it. She hated the furry little creatures, and always had since Henry had dropped one down her neck when they were children.

The latch lifted. So, not a dog or cat.

If it was Adair, she would find out what had happened when his father went to Beauxville. She was sure Nicholas would still be furiously angry, and could only hope her letter had served its purpose.

Instead of Adair coming through the door, however, Dearshul appeared, carrying a tray covered with a square of linen in one hand and a steaming bucket in the other. She didn't move beyond the door, but stared at the floor and mumbled something that sounded vaguely like an apology.

In spite of her desire to appear dignified as befit a Norman lady, Marianne couldn't help blushing, too. Everyone in Lochbarr, Dearshul included, would know what had gone on here last night in general, if not in glorious detail.

Nevertheless trying to act as if that thought hadn't

occurred to her, Marianne motioned for the young woman to come inside.

Dearshul said something else again and scurried toward the table, setting the tray upon it and putting the bucket on the floor. As she uncovered the tray, the odor of fresh bread wafted toward Marianne. There was a bowl of something else on the tray, steaming like the bucket, and a bronze goblet.

The bread smelled wonderful. It seemed a very long time since she'd had a proper meal.

The bucket on the floor held hot water for washing, she assumed. That would be very welcome, too. But she couldn't eat yet.

"Mass?" she inquired of the young serving woman, folding her hands as if in prayer and raising her brows in query.

Dearshul clearly didn't understand what she was asking about.

"Church?" she said, trying again. "Priest?"

A look of understanding dawned. Then Dearshul frowned and shook her head.

"The priest doesn't say mass every morning?"

Marianne realized it was useless to question a girl who couldn't understand you. Nevertheless, she mimed taking the holy bread and shook her head. "No mass?"

The young woman said something in a flurry of unfamiliar words, then likewise shook her head. "No mass," Dearshul repeated, saying the French words tentatively.

She should have guessed that they were no more

religious than her brother. Living in such a place might cause one to despair that God could hear prayers, especially for fine weather.

In spite of that disappointment, Marianne was impressed by Dearshul's attempt to speak French. Perhaps as she struggled to learn Adair's tongue, Dearshul could learn hers. It would be nice to be able to speak to a woman in her own language.

Meanwhile, she would do as she'd done in Beauxville—ask God for forgiveness, and eat.

"Food," Marianne said, moving her hand as if bringing something to her mouth.

Dearshul smiled shyly.

"And drink," Marianne said, pointing to the goblet filled with something that smelled like mead as she sat on the stool, feigning lifting it and drinking.

"Drink," Dearshul repeated.

Marianne raised her brows. "Drink?" she asked, pretending to lift the cup to her lips again. She pointed to Dearshul, hoping she would understand that she was asking for the Scots' word.

Dearshul smiled, her eyes bright, as she, too, feigned taking a drink. "*Ol.*"

"*Ol,*" Marianne repeated, nodding and smiling in return.

Too hungry to learn or teach more words, she took the bread and bit into it, while Dearshul scurried over to the bed and started to pull off the sheets, including the bottom one that had small spots of dried blood on it.

So much for her husband's assurance that being

a virgin didn't matter. She shouldn't have been so quick to believe him.

Yet she was disappointed nonetheless.

Her arms full of sheets, Dearshul said something else, nodded at the bed, then hurried from the room.

Apparently it was important that this checking of the sheets be done quickly. Again, she shouldn't be surprised, or even embarrassed. A Norman husband would surely do the same. She should be glad the evidence was there to be seen.

So why did Adair tell her otherwise? To make her think Scots were kinder? To set her at ease?

What did it matter? It was done. She had been a virgin, and she should be proud of that.

Trying not to imagine people commenting about her wedding night and the blood on the sheets, Marianne finished the bread and mead, which was surprisingly good. She studied the unappetizing gray substance in the bowl, then leaned over and sniffed. She'd smelled worse, and she was still hungry.

There wasn't any spoon. Perhaps she was supposed to use the bread to lift it to her mouth. Well, she couldn't do that now, so instead, she tentatively dipped her finger into the gray mass and stuck it in her mouth.

Not the most appealing taste, but edible. She was nearly finished when Dearshul returned, opening the door without so much as a knock. She walked in, saw Marianne with her fingers in the bowl and stared.

Marianne jumped up and instinctively stuck her sticky finger into her mouth, like a very small child.

Hardly something that would inspire respect, she realized, quickly taking it out.

She marched to the door and rapped her knuckles against the wood. "You should knock in future," she commanded.

Dearshul's face reddened and she looked about to cry.

Marianne instantly regretted being so abrupt. "You surprised me, that's all," she said, trying not to sound overly contrite, but sorry enough to tell the young woman she wasn't very upset anymore.

Head lowered, Dearshul scurried forward to pick up the tray, and Marianne was more sorry than ever that she'd reacted with such haste. She didn't want to lose Dearshul's good opinion, too.

She smiled and stepped in front of the door as Dearshul hurried back. "I'm sorry," she said, not caring if she sounded dignified or not.

Dearshul nodded and gave her a shy smile before departing.

Marianne sighed and hoped she hadn't caused another problem.

But what was she to do now? Sit and wait for Adair to return?

She went to the window, opened the shutter and looked outside. For a miracle, the sun was shining and the ground actually appeared fairly dry.

She would inspect her new home, this fortress and the village beyond. There must be a market there, where she could spend the money Seamus had given her.

As she turned away from the window, a boisterous group of young men dressed in their wool plaids and linen shirts, and with daggers in their belts, strolled past a nearby building, laughing and talking.

Would she be safe wandering about Lochbarr by herself?

Adair was the chieftain's son and she was Adair's wife. Surely she would be.

It was either assume she would, or sit here with the stripped bed, alone with her thoughts, while waiting for her husband to return.

WATER JUGS BALANCED on their hips, a group of women by the well in the fortress of Lochbarr fell silent as Adair's wife strolled past. The Norman glanced at them, her expression indecipherable, as she continued toward the gate.

One of the Scotswomen, tall, with thick dark hair and ample breasts, spit in Marianne's direction.

"Look at her, that Norman slut," Fionnaghal sneered. "Strolling about as free and easy as if she's lived here all her life, and we're all delighted that she's wed our chieftain's son." She grimaced. "I'd like to rip the hair off her head."

A middle-aged woman whose light brown hair was streaked with gray, and whose body made it clear she'd borne several children, set her jug on the side of the well.

"You'd better keep a civil tongue in your head when you speak of her, Fionnaghal," Ceit advised as she started to lower the bucket. "She's Adair's wife now, and neither he nor his father or his brother will take kindly to insults to her."

"She's Adair's wife because he was tricked into it by that scheming Norman hussy," Fionnaghal retorted. "Surely you don't think we ought to welcome her?"

The other younger women looked to Ceit.

"Not welcome with open arms," she replied as the bucket splashed deep in the well. "But when all is said and done, she's the wife of the man who'll be the chieftain when his father dies."

Ceit kept her gaze on Fionnaghal as she began to draw the bucket back. "None of us have to have the Sight to know why *you* hate her, Fionnaghal. But Adair never looked at you that way, no matter how you tried, so let it alone."

"So I wanted him. So I'm sorry he didn't want me," Fionnaghal shot back. "But to marry a Norman—and him always claiming he hated them."

"Aye. If 'twas anybody except himself brought back a Norman woman, he'd be frothing at the mouth like a rabid dog," the sandy-haired Isaebal noted, siding with her friend. "And his father, too. Adair's always been able to twist his father 'round his finger. Still, I'm surprised Seamus agreed to the marriage."

Ceit started to fill Isaebel's jug, for she was skilled at that task and didn't spill nearly as much water as the other women. "What else could Seamus do?"

"Maybe taking that woman's their way of paying back the Normans for the cattle they've stolen," the newly-wedded Una shyly suggested as she moved forward.

Una's equally young husband, dutifully at his post by the gate, smiled at her and waved, making her blush and fumble as she lifted her jug to the side of the well. Ceit gave her an indulgent smile as the bucket hit the water again.

"Don't be stupid," Fionnaghal snapped peevishly, making Una jump. "I tell you, she's a lying, scheming whore."

"She was a virgin."

The women turned to see Dearshul approaching, a bucket grasped in her hands and a frown on her face.

Fionnaghal's eyes narrowed. "How would you know about that?"

While Ceit filled Una's water jug, Dearshul halted on the other side of the well across from Fionnaghal.

"The sheets." Dearshul lifted the bucket a few inches. "I've come to get water to wash away the blood."

"It doesn't mean she bled from that," Fionnaghal replied. "I wouldn't put it past her to try some whore's trick."

"She's not a whore. She's a lady."

Fionnaghal's lip curled with disdain. "Oh, well then, no wonder you think she's perfect. I'd wager she could treat you worse than a dog and you'd beg for more." Holding out her woolen skirt, Fionnaghal swanned around the well. "Because you're fool enough to think you can be a lady, too, if only you try hard enough. As if Lachlann'd ever think of marrying you. That's about as likely as—"

"Adair marrying you?" Ceit interjected, her expression mild, but censure in her brown eyes. "You could always try for Hamish Mac Glogan if you want a chieftain."

Fionnaghal sniffed, then slid a sharp and cruel glance at Dearshul. "Maybe I will." She swayed her hips and thrust out her breasts. "At least I've got something worthwhile to offer."

Dearshul straightened her shoulders. "I'm sure you've offered it to plenty, too, which may be why neither of the chieftain's sons want anything to do with you."

Glaring at Dearshul, Fionnaghal started toward her. "You little—!"

"Quiet," Ceit snapped, stepping between them. "Enough chatter, the pair of you. Get your water and be about your work."

Keeping an eye on the scowling Fionnaghal, Dearshul filled her bucket, then marched away. One by one, the others took their water and departed, until only Ceit and Fionnaghal remained beside the well.

"She has no chance with Lachlann," Fionnaghal declared as Ceit poured water into the vessel she held. "Everybody knows it, and it's no kindness to encourage her."

"I would have said no Norman woman stood any chance with Adair, either," Ceit observed.

She regarded the younger woman steadily. "You've lost Adair, Fionnaghal. Find another. As you say, you've much to offer. As for Dearshul, she's been pining for Lachlann since she was eight years old. He won't have her—too ambitious by far, that one—so leave her be and let her have her maiden's dreams. And tread carefully with Adair's wife. She's got the look of fire about her, and I wouldn't want to get burned, if I were you."

AS THE GRIM BAND OF CLANSMEN RODE into the village of Lochbarr, Adair saw something that made him yank Neas to a sudden halt: Dearshul spreading sheets on some bushes near the river to dry. He recognized the mended rent in one of them—the bottom sheet from his bed, where he'd made love with Marianne last night after assuring her that no one would be checking for signs of virginity.

She'd surely think he'd lied. God help him, he didn't need that, too.

After giving his father a brief farewell, he spurred Neas to a gallop and rode toward Dearshul. When he brought his horse to a prancing halt, she nearly dropped the basket she was holding with one hand and balancing on her hip.

"Are those sheets from my bed?" he demanded without preamble, although he was sure he already knew the answer.

Dearshul flushed and gripped the basket tighter. "Aye."

Adair tried to keep a rein on his temper. Maybe

washing the sheets had been Marianne's idea. "Who told you to wash them?"

"N-nobody," the young woman stammered, snuffing his brief flicker of hope that Marianne had made the request. "I just thought, your wife being a lady and all, she'd want them laundered after…after last night."

Maybe she would, but Dearshul should have waited for the request. "Did Marianne see you take them?"

"Aye," Dearshul answered, dashing another brief hope. "I'm sorry if I shouldn't have done this without asking, Adair. I was only trying to help."

When she looked as if she was about to burst into tears, he immediately regretted speaking so harshly. Dearshul was a sweet, kindhearted lass. He shouldn't get angry or fault her for what she'd done, especially given how most people in Lochbarr would treat Marianne. "'Twas kind of you to think of her comfort, Dearshul," he said, meaning it. "You're a very thoughtful lass."

Her lower lip trembled as she smiled.

"I'll be sure to tell my father how pleased I am with your kindness," he said, avoiding any mention of his brother. "Is my wife still in the *teach?*"

"No. I saw her walking toward the village."

He couldn't hide his surprise. "Why was she going there?"

Again, Dearshul looked as though she might start crying. "I don't know. I didn't think it was my place to question her. I thought she must have told you what she planned to do before you rode out."

An obvious assumption, given that Marianne was his wife. "Aye, you don't have to know where she is and what she's about every moment of the day," he replied. "I'm sure she's safe."

Safe? Why had that word come to mind? Of course she would be safe. Nobody in Lochbarr would dare to harm his wife, including Cormag.

Nobody in Lochbarr…but what of Dunkeathe? What if her brother's harsh words had been a ploy to make them think he didn't care about his sister, while his men were on the way to take her back by stealth and force combined? That would be the Norman's way. That was the way they did everything.

He dismounted. "Take Neas to the stable for me, will you?" he asked as he handed her the reins.

He didn't wait to hear her answer as he started toward the main street of the village, a collection of stone houses and stalls clustered around a central open space that served as a market in good weather.

Since the sun was shining, several of the merchants had set out tables in the green, the better to display their wares.

Perhaps he was wrong to suspect her brother, and Marianne had been curious to see what the merchants had to offer.

He was nearly to the green when Fionnaghal stepped out from behind a cottage and blocked his way. "What's the matter, Adair? Lost something?" She smiled slyly. "Like your wife?"

Fionnaghal had been a pain in his side ever since

she'd arrived in Lochbarr with her family five years ago. "I haven't lost my wife. Now out of my way, Fionnaghal."

The young serving woman laughed and twirled a lock of thick brown hair around her finger. "If you do lose her, or tire of her, you know where to find me."

Adair frowned and made no secret of his impatience. "I've known where to find you for years, and never troubled, so why would I now?"

"Because that wife of yours'll ne'er make you happy, with her haughty Norman ways." Fionnaghal sauntered nearer, her hips swaying, breasts out. "I'll make you happy, Adair."

"Have you no sense at all, woman?" he asked, amazed at her persistence, especially now that he was married. "If I'd ever wanted you, you'd have known it. But I didn't, and now I've got a wife, so you've no chance at all with me."

"Aye—a Norman wife!" Fionnaghal retorted as he marched past her toward the market. "A Norman wife you *had* to marry."

Adair ignored her. Fionnaghal was a nuisance. She'd probably be more than a nuisance, if not an outright enemy, to Marianne.

Marianne was no fool. She must have guessed she wouldn't be welcome in Lochbarr before she proposed the marriage, so she must have decided she could manage their resentment and enmity.

She made the proposal because she thought she had no other choice. No matter what came after or

how bold and brave she looked in the hall, she was
alone and desperate, and that's why she married you.

He tried to ignore his conscience as he continued
through the village, paying special attention to
women in brown dresses. Here, too, he wasn't
greeted with the usual good cheer. There was a wariness now, and suspicion.

His father was right. He should have thought of
the possible consequences of his actions. But even
if he had, he would never have guessed the people
of Lochbarr would look at him as they were doing
now.

Marianne wasn't among them. He couldn't find
her in the village.

His dread increasing, he stood beside the kirk
and wondered where else she might have gone,
and all by herself. A familiar, sickening fear came
over him as he looked at the sky. How soon until
dusk?

He put his hand on the stone wall of the church
to steady himself as that horrible memory of Cellach, her body bloody, her dress torn, her eyes staring open at the sky, came to his mind. Breathing
hard, he stared at the ground, trying to force it away.

Cellach had been a girl. Marianne was a
woman—a woman who'd climb down a wall with
bleeding feet and command a man to catch her. Yet
even so—

He started to run back to the fortress, determined
to mount a search without any more delay, his gaze
still searching for signs of his wife as he ran.

A flash of brown wool beneath a willow tree on the bank of the river leading to the loch caught his eye. He halted and looked closer.

Marianne! Thank God.

His heart still racing despite the relief pouring through him, he jogged toward the river bank. A wall of stones formed an enclosure on two sides, where sheep and cattle were gathered for the fall slaughter. At present, the meadow was occupied not by live-stock, but a group of boys playing with an inflated pig's bladder, kicking it and chasing it, and one an-other, as children do. Three dogs also seemed to think they were part of the game, running and barking ex-citedly.

Marianne wasn't alone under the willow. Teassie, the nine-year-old daughter of the village smith, was with her, and Marianne was wiping the little girl's face with the edge of her sleeve.

Murmuring something in French he couldn't quite make out, Marianne gave the girl a quick hug and pointed her back toward the boys. Adair couldn't begin to guess what use the French would do, for Teassie wouldn't understand it.

Apparently, though, whatever Marianne had said or done, it had been enough to encourage Teassie to approach the boys.

Marianne's whole focus was on the child, and when Teassie glanced back, uncertain, Marianne gave her the warmest, brightest, most encouraging smile Adair had ever seen. Her whole face lightened with it. Then she raised her chin a little.

Teassie raised hers in silent imitation before marching up to Donnan, her brother, who was six years older and built like a miniature version of his father, broad-chested and stocky, with a sheaf of dark hair that fell on his forehead.

Hands on his hips, Donnan's lip curled with disdain as he regarded his sister. "Away with you, Teassie. You're too small to play with us."

Teassie straightened her shoulders, reminding Adair very much of his bride. "I want to play," she insisted in a high wavering voice.

"You're too little. You'll get hurt."

Teassie got a stubborn look in her green eyes that also reminded Adair of his wife, who was still watching from the shelter of the tree.

Teassie pointed at a lad easily half a head shorter than she. "You let Curadan play, and he's smaller than me."

"He's a boy."

"I can run faster."

"He's a boy."

"I can kick harder."

"But he's a *boy!*" Donnan persisted, eloquence obviously not his strong suit.

"You have to let me play. *She* says so." Teassie pointed at Marianne. "And *she's* the chieftain's son's wife."

Donnan looked at Marianne. "Wheest, what has she to do with it?" he asked dismissively.

"She's Adair's wife."

As Donnan was turning back to his sister, he

caught sight of Adair. His face reddened and he rubbed his toe in the dirt.

Aware that Marianne had likely seen him now, too—unless she'd been stricken blind—Adair walked toward the lad. "Let her play, Donnan."

Donnan wasn't pleased by that suggestion.

He'd truly fallen far if even the blacksmith's son didn't respect him anymore. Before he'd gone to rescue Marianne, Donnan would have done as he'd asked without question or qualm.

"An honorable man should always be kind and generous to women," he said to the boy.

"Teassie's not a woman. She's my sister."

"Well, what harm could it do to let her play?"

"She'll get hurt."

"Not if you're careful," Adair repeated, and this time, it wasn't a request. "Let her play, Donnan."

The lad grudgingly nodded.

"Go on with you, then, back to the game."

As Donnan ran off, Adair started to turn toward Marianne, when he felt a little hand touch his arm.

He looked down to see Teassie smiling shyly up at him. "Thank you."

He smiled. "You're welcome."

Her bright eyes shining, she gave him a gap-toothed grin before scampering away to join in the game.

Somewhat mollified, Adair continued toward his wife, who was waiting for him, his hands clasped together, a worried look on her face.

He didn't want to have to tell her what had happened with her brother. He wanted to make her smile again.

"I don't know what you said to Teassie," he remarked when he reached her, "or how she understood it, but it seems to have been very effective."

"She was watching the boys play, crying and looking so longingly at them, it wasn't hard to guess what had happened," Marianne explained. "I told her not to give up."

Adair raised a brow. "In French?"

Marianne's bonnie blue eyes sparkled in the sunlight that made its way through the shifting curtain of willow leaves. "Yes. But I showed her what I meant, too."

"Like a mummer?"

"Something like that."

"I wish I'd seen it."

Marianne suddenly frowned, her brow furrowing like an angry war god. Planting her feet, arms akimbo, she thrust out her chin. "She understood that I was telling her not to let them bully her."

"She did indeed," Adair agreed as they started back to the village.

Marianne's golden hair gleamed in the afternoon light, like a shimmering halo, and he'd never known a woman who walked with such a graceful step. Her feet must be healing well, and that was a relief.

"Did you play with boys when you were her age?" he asked, trying to picture her as a nine-year-old, full of spirit and mischief, with bright golden hair.

"Just my brothers," she answered. She gave a little sigh. "It seems boys are all the same when it comes to letting girls join in their games."

"I bet you were good at games."

"I was fast on my feet," she admitted. "That skill served me well in the convent, too, although once, Sister Mary Katherine nearly caught me after I…"

"After you what?" he prompted when she fell silent.

"We have more important things to talk about," she said briskly. "What happened when your father went to Dunkeathe this morning?"

They'd reached the marketplace, and the censorious, curious villagers were watching them with interest. "Your brother accepted the bride price and there'll be no reprisals."

"What about the betrothal with Hamish Mac Glogan?"

"He said nothing of it."

She looked puzzled. "Nothing?"

Marianne was obviously going to require more of an explanation, yet he didn't think this was the time, or the place. "I'll tell you about it when we're in our *teach*."

To his relief, she nodded and didn't press him further.

"What did you do that you had to flee the sister? Steal some holy wafer?"

She flushed, her cheeks blooming pink. "No."

He couldn't resist teasing her a little, hoping to brighten some of that Norman seriousness that now clouded her features. "The wine?"

"Certainly not!"

"Then what?" he asked. "I think if my wife has an outlaw past, I should know about it."

"I most certainly wasn't an outlaw. Or a thief."

"A bit of a prankster, then? You can confess your sins to me, Marianne. I was hardly a perfect child myself."

"I can well believe that," she replied. "I can also believe you were always excused."

"Why would you say that?" he asked, mindful of what Cormag had said that morning.

"Because I suspect you could smile and talk your way out of any punishment."

He didn't like to think she shared Cormag's opinion of him. "We were talking about you, and what made the good sister give chase."

"I was looking over the wall to the road outside the convent."

"That was a serious offense?"

She answered with obvious reluctance. "I was, um, watching some people."

"That doesn't sound such a sin. What sort of people?"

Another blush colored her cheeks as they neared the gates of the fortress. "Just some boys from the farms down the road."

Boys from farms? And she in a convent. "Ah. Too tempting for young girls, were they?"

"The sisters thought so."

He nodded at the sentries at the gate as they passed them, and thought it a good thing they couldn't understand French, or the proud Marianne might not be so forthcoming.

"What did *you* think?" he asked as they approached their *teach*. "Did you find them tempting?"

"Not in the least."

Her answer was swift—too swift. She *had* been tempted, but she didn't want him to know, as if the notion that being interested in boys was something shameful. That was the Normans for you. Hide girls away for years and be shocked when they were curious about boys.

He would have been shocked if she hadn't been. "They were homely?"

"What does it matter what they looked like?"

"I'm just curious, that's all, since they didn't tempt you. Was it a hot day, by any chance?"

"I don't remember."

Oh, yes, she did, and it was, and he'd wager ten marks the lads hadn't been wearing much in the way of clothes. He stifled a smile as he imagined a young Marianne sneaking looks at half-naked farm boys over the convent wall.

She gave him another sidelong glance. "I'm sure you looked at girls all the time."

"Naturally. And they looked right back."

"I've noticed the women here are rather brazen."

Fionnaghal came to mind, and he wondered if Marianne had already had words with her.

"It's not going to be easy for you here," he said as they entered the *teach*. "There'll be resentment and distrust."

Standing beside the bed, Marianne turned to face him. "Especially from one rather buxom young woman, I think." She saw his frown. "You know of whom I'm speaking?"

"I can guess," he said as he sat on the chest. "Her name's Fionnaghal and in case you're curious, I've never taken her to my bed."

Marianne studied the floor. "I didn't ask."

She didn't have to. It didn't take the Sight to guess what she was thinking. People often assumed he must have many lovers. He knew it was because of his looks, but it galled him to have them imply he was no more than a faithless, lust-driven fellow with no other thought in his head.

It galled him even more to realize Marianne thought the same thing, in spite of what he'd said last night. "I'm telling you anyway."

Her gaze flicked to the bed, then back to him.

He'd forgotten about the sheets. "It was Dearshul's idea to strip the bed this morning, not mine or anybody else's," he said, anxious to set her straight about that. "I was telling you the truth when I said I didn't care if you were a virgin or not. Neither would my father, or anyone else in Lochbarr."

"If you say so."

"I do."

She fastened her steadfast gaze on his face. "Then it's also true that Nicholas will make no reprisals?"

He nodded. "Aye. Your brother's not going to do anything."

Her eyes narrowed. "He's not going to accuse you of abduction or any other crime?"

"He's making no charges. He's going to leave us alone."

"Even though he must break the betrothal agreement with Hamish Mac Glogan? He's going to simply do that and not go to your king?"

"My father said he never spoke of Hamish. He accepted the bride price and he's content to leave us in peace."

"I can't believe Nicholas has accepted our marriage with as good a grace as you're implying. Please tell me the truth—all of it," she said, looking like someone expecting to hear the worst, and who feared that the worst would be very bad indeed.

He couldn't bring himself to tell her about her brother's harsh decree. "Isn't it enough to know that we're going to be able to live in peace?"

She faced him squarely, her eyes as bold and challenging as Cellach's had ever been. "I'm not a child, Adair, and I know better than you the sort of ambitious man my brother is. He took the bride price and he's not going to make any charges against you—why not? What did your father have to do to ensure that? What promises did he have to make? What sort of treaty?"

Why couldn't she just accept what he'd told her and leave it at that? "Nicholas asked for nothing more, and he didn't speak of what would happen with Hamish Mac Glogan."

"There's more to it than that," she insisted. "I can see it in your face."

Adair ran his hand through his hair and realized he couldn't keep the worst from her. "He took the bride price, then told my father that as far as he's concerned, you died when you fled with me. He didn't even want to read your letter."

She stiffened ever so slightly. "I see. He would hear no explanations."

"No."

"Yet he took the bride price."

"Yes."

"A trade, then. Me for the money, and he'll probably use some of that to recompense Hamish Mac Glogan, like a merchant buying his way out of a bad bargain."

He thought she'd be upset. That she'd cry. Instead, she sounded hard, cold—so different from the woman who'd loved him last night.

"I can't believe Nicholas is going to let this simply pass without reprisal," she said, clasping her forearms. "This could be a trick. Nicholas could already be sending messages to your king protesting the marriage or trying to get it annulled. He'll probably say you raped me, so I had no choice but to marry you and he had no choice but to agree. He'll likely say the same thing to Hamish Mac Glogan."

So practical. So very Norman.

"I agree he's not a man to be trusted," Adair replied, trying to sound just as composed. "Unfortunately, my father is convinced your brother meant what he said. He's a good judge of men, so you should believe that, too. To your brother, you're dead, and so not worth any effort at all. The money is his compensation."

"And so you all get what you want. Your father has the peace he desires. Just as you wished, you've destroyed the alliance between my brother and Hamish Mac Glogan, and even got a beautiful wife to take to your bed."

Was she *never* going to believe he'd helped her because he thought she needed to be saved from her brother and Hamish Mac Glogan? "I told you—"

"Yes, you did," she tartly interrupted as she yanked her gown over her head and threw it aside, so that she was clad only in her shift.

"What are you doing?" he demanded warily, yet also intrigued, and aroused.

She marched up to him, grabbed his face and kissed him fiercely. "Getting what *I* want."

Kissing him passionately, she tugged at his shirt, pulling it from his belt, and ran her hands up his chest, as if she wanted him to love her standing there.

Whatever he'd been going to say, he forgot it. Whatever proud words had come to mind, they fled. He could no more ignore her fiery desire than he could will himself to fly.

Returning her kiss, he stroked and caressed her body, his hands eagerly roving, skimming over her shift. Her nipples tightened beneath his palms, and she pressed against him, thrusting her hips forward in silent, brazen invitation, until she let go of him to tear at the rest of his clothes. His broach fell to the floor unheeded and his shirt was stripped off in a moment. As she fumbled with his belt buckle, he pushed her shift lower, exposing her breasts to his lips and touch.

Her eyes full of shameless craving, she wiggled out of the shift and kicked it away.

She was naked and perfect and she wanted him. To hell with taking off his *feileadh*.

He picked her up and threw her on the bed, then covered her body with his. His mouth captured hers, rough and hungry, demanding a response she fervently gave. Her body arched and bucked even before he hiked up his *feileadh,* positioned himself and pushed inside her. She gripped his shoulders and shoved her hips forward to meet him.

She was so warm, so tight, so incredibly exciting. He'd never known a woman more thrilling, more impassioned, as eager as he.

He thrust with lustful urgency and wanton abandon. She moaned and commanded, telling him she wanted more, and harder. Deeper.

He thought he'd die, and gladly, to satisfy her.

She tightened around him and cried out, sending him to the climax, where his throaty exclamations joined with hers in a frenzy of desire.

As the throbbing ebbed, he realized she was weeping.

"What's wrong?" he asked as he withdrew and brushed wisps of hair from her flushed face. "Did I hurt you?"

"No," she murmured, moving away.

"Then why are you crying?"

"I'm not," she answered, wiping her face and turning her back to him.

"You are." He raised himself on his elbow. "Was I too fast? Too rough?"

"Can't you just leave me alone? You've had your sport."

Adair stared at her, appalled by her words and what they implied. "Look at me, Marianne."

When she didn't move, he grabbed her shoulder and made her roll over. "What did you mean, 'I've had my sport'? You started this."

Her hair disheveled, she pulled up her wrinkled shift and rose without answering.

He climbed off the bed. "You make it sound like I forced you. I've never forced you, Marianne."

"Oh yes, you did!" she charged as she tugged on her gown. "You forced me to stay in Beauxville when you stopped me that night. You forced me to run away with you when you came back."

"Running away by yourself would have been dangerous," he replied, trying to control his temper, and failing. "If you have to blame somebody for running away with me, it should be your bastard of a brother."

"Yes, insult Nicholas again," she retorted, adjusting her loose gown with quick, aggressive tugs. "Except that he's not a bastard. He's the son of Sir Lucien de Confriere."

"You can't possibly want to defend the man," Adair scoffed, pulling on his shirt.

"How would you feel if your family disowned you because you'd married against their will?"

"They wouldn't," he answered as he reached for the broach to hold the plaid to his shirt.

She went to the table and grabbed the comb. "Not even if you'd courted me in secret, and then gone to live in Beauxville?"

"Dunkeathe."

"Whatever you want to call it," she said as she dragged the comb through her messy hair, her back to him. "Would you be delighted? Would you say, 'Oh, never mind. It's not important?' Whatever you think of Nicholas, he's my brother. My family. And because he's my family, I can't simply pretend I don't care what he thinks. You Scots claim to set such store by your clan and family. You should be able to understand."

Adair walked up to her so that he could see her face. "You seem to forget he was selling you off to Hamish Mac Glogan."

"No, I'm not," she retorted, putting down the comb. "But I could have stopped the marriage on my own."

Was she never going to be grateful that he'd helped her, and at no small cost to himself? "How?"

"Somehow! But you had to play the great hero, the mighty savior, and ruin everything."

"If you'd fled by yourself, you would have been easy prey for any outlaw or mercenary—"

"I'm not Cellach!"

He backed away, aghast, as if she slapped him

hard across the face. To have her bring Cellach into this, and in that tone…

"No, you're not," he muttered as he turned and marched to the door. "She listened to reason."

"Or did whatever you told her!"

He whirled around, glaring. "Don't you *ever* speak of Cellach to me again! And don't you ever forget that you were the one who proposed this marriage. I offered to see that you were taken anywhere you wanted to go, even though you treated me like an outlaw for coming to your aid."

He strode toward her, stopping when they were nose to nose. "And you're not the only one who lost something when I helped you. I've lost my father's trust and the clan's respect because of you."

He gave her a disdainful smile. "But don't worry, Marianne. A bargain is a bargain, after all. We'll wait and see if your stallion brought to stud has fulfilled his purpose. If not, of course we'll try again."

With that, he left her, slamming the door so hard, it splintered.

Marianne stared at the broken wood, then sank down on the bed. God help her, what had she done?

CHAPTER ELEVEN

A FORTNIGHT LATER, Adair sat on a boulder on a low rise overlooking the village, the fortress and the loch. Above him, the sky was dotted with high, white clouds and gulls circling, their cries loud in the silence. Below, he could see the villagers going about their business, and his father and Roban training some of the lads getting used to the weight and heft of *claimh mors*. He could remember the first time he'd held his own.

The day Cellach had died.

"Adair! What are ye doing up here, man? Watching the sky for portents?"

He turned to see Barra, leaning heavily on a stout stick, making his way up the path towards him. He got to his feet. "No. Father and I have been thinking this would be a good site for a watchtower. One made of stone, like the Normans have."

"Oh, aye?" Barra replied. He reached the boulder and gratefully sank down on it. "To be sure, a man could see far from here."

"We could have started it already, if I hadn't had to give all that money to Sir Nicholas."

"Your father could afford it without your contribution," Barra replied. "But he's cautious with his coin, and wisely so. Come next spring, Sir Nicholas won't have need of so many men to work on his castle, and we can hire experienced masons at a better wage. A very wise man, your father."

Adair gave the older man a wry, knowing look. "That was your advice, I'm sure."

Barra grinned. "Well, so I'm wise, too." He gazed out over Lochbarr. "I see your wife's in the market again."

"Is she?" Adair asked, trying not to betray any special interest although he'd already spotted her, walking with her usual grace and serenity, as if she were merely a casual observer of life in Lochbarr.

At first, that air of detachment annoyed him, for he was sure she saw herself as above them all. Yet as the days passed, he began to see a certain wisdom in her aloofness. Since she didn't try to give orders, she didn't add to the feelings of ill will her arrival and their marriage had created. Instead, servants and villagers seemed to be more at ease around her, or at least less inclined to stop and stare. It might be a long time before she would be more than tolerated by them, but at least she wasn't doing anything to make things worse.

"It can't be easy for her here," Barra noted.

"It was her idea that we marry," Adair reminded the *seanachie*.

He did not add that the past fortnight hadn't been easy for him, either. Although he seemed to be back in his father's good graces, the villagers and half the clansmen still regarded him with suspicion. And sleeping in the stables didn't do much to improve a man's mood.

"Your father likes her. So does Lachlann."

"Aye, I know," Adair muttered. He'd seen them talking to her often in her native tongue, in the hall or around the fortress.

"But you don't. There's a pity."

"I don't want to talk about my wife, Barra."

"No? There's another pity, then. Your father often came to me for advice when he was courting your mother."

This was news to Adair.

Barra grinned, looking like a mischievous sprite. "He had a terrible time of it, too. She hit him the first time he tried to kiss her."

Adair stared in wide-eyed disbelief. To hear his father tell it, his mother had fallen in love with him at first sight.

"Not too many people know about that," Barra continued, smiling with wistful remembrance. "He was that embarrassed, we tried to keep it a secret. She told him he was an insolent, arrogant fool, and she wanted nothing to do with him."

Barra eyed Adair as the younger man sat beside him on the rock. "He *was* insolent and arrogant, aye and as stubborn as you, when he was young."

Adair tried to picture his father slapped for a kiss, but he couldn't quite manage it. "So what did you tell him to do?"

"I counseled patience."

Adair frowned. "You always tell everybody to be patient about everything."

"And how often am I wrong?" the *seanachie* indignantly demanded. "If you'd been patient, your father would have put a stop to the marriage between Lady Marianne and Hamish Mac Glogan and you could have courted Lady Marianne properly."

"My father didn't do anything to stop the marriage, and I never wanted to court Lady Marianne."

"You didn't see the messenger he sent to the king, being too busy with other more weighty matters, like riding off in a lather to Dunkeathe."

"He sent a messenger to the king? Why didn't he tell me what he was going to do?"

Barra gave him a look. "As if he needs your permission?"

"No, but—"

"But he keeps his own counsel sometimes, until he makes a decision, especially if it's best nobody knows what he intends to do."

Adair squirmed. He knew he wasn't much good at keeping secrets, for deception didn't come easily to him, but this was disconcerting to hear. "Even if he had sent a messenger in protest to the king, it would have been too late for the king to stop the marriage."

"It would have been too late for Sir Nicholas to get wind of it, either, and send a messenger of his own," Barra replied. "Then your father would have gone to Dunkeathe before the wedding and told Hamish Mac Glogan he'd taken the matter to the king. Hamish Mac Glogan, greedy lout that he is, would think twice before doing anything that might give the king cause to question his actions, so he would have agreed to a delay. And that would have given your father time to persuade the king that this marriage would be trouble for him, too, since it would ally two powerful men. Once you'd brought the lady here, you forced another decision."

Feeling even worse, Adair put his head in his hands. "Oh, God, Barra. Was there ever a greater fool in Scotland?"

"Maybe," the older man speculated, sounding as if he didn't really think so. "But it's done."

Leaning on his stick, Barra hoisted himself to his feet. "Losh, I'm parched. Are ye finished here, or do you want to admire the view some more?"

"No, I'll go back with you," Adair said, getting up to help Barra down the path.

They proceeded in silence until they came to the village. "I'm off to train with the men," Adair said, bidding Barra farewell.

The *seanachie* regarded him steadily. "Adair, what's been done has been done. There's no point dwelling on what can't be changed." He put his hand on Adair's shoulder and gave him a fatherly smile. "It's easy to build walls, Adair, my lad. But once they're up, they're hard to tear down. Don't build walls between you and your wife."

Adair's jaw clenched. He appreciated that Barra was trying to help, but the *seanachie* could never understand. "This is different, Barra."

"A woman is a woman, Adair, wherever she's born," the *seanachie* replied.

"She acts as if I forced her into this marriage against her will, when I was the one who was forced."

"Were you now?" Barra said, regarding him quizzically. "Your father threatened you, did he?"

"No, but—"

"There was no talk of punishment if you did not, was there?"

Adair felt as if he had tumbled off the side of the hill and rolled all the way to Lochbarr, for his father hadn't threatened him—at all. "Then if I'd refused outright—?"

Barra shrugged. "Even I don't know what your father would have done then. Maybe he would have threatened you to make you marry her. Then again, maybe not. Good day, Adair."

With that, the *seanachie* hobbled off toward the village.

Adair headed toward the fortress. He felt like the victim of a vast conspiracy involving everyone he knew and trusted, including his father.

And all because of Marianne, his proud, aloof Norman bride.

"IT'S RAINING AGAIN," Marianne said as she concentrated hard, forming the words in Gaelic while she sat in the *teach* across from Dearshul. Both of them were sewing, Marianne on a garment of dark blue wool, and Dearshul one of bright scarlet.

"Yes, it is. Very hard," Dearshul answered in French, her brow wrinkled as she spoke the unfamiliar language.

"We'll get wet if we go out."

"Very," Dearshul agreed, as solemn as a priest giving last rites.

Dearshul glanced up at Marianne, then frowned. "That wasn't the right word?"

"It was," Marianne hastened to assure her in the combination of both languages that had served them quite well for the past several days. "We both sound so sad, yet we're only talking about the rain."

Dearshul giggled. "Aye," she agreed, nodding. "It's the thinking, I'm thinking."

Marianne forced herself to smile in return, although she felt anything but happy. She'd cursed herself a hundred times for quarreling with Adair when she'd really been hurt and dismayed by what Nicholas had said.

Adair had been all but ignoring her ever since, to the curiosity of most and the delight of some.

"It's the sewing," she said as she put her work down on her lap with a rueful grin. "I hate it. But I've got nothing else to do."

Except wait to see if she was with child. Sadly, she'd felt cramps that morning, which generally heralded her courses. Her first thought had been sorrow, and then she'd wondered what would happen when she told her husband.

"You could probably take on some of Ceit's duties," Dearshul suggested.

"I suppose I can make myself understood well enough now," Marianne agreed.

"Oh, you've learned very quickly, my lady!" Dearshul grew more serious. "But I think you were wise to wait. Ceit likes you, and she wouldn't if you'd gone into her kitchen and tried to tell her what to do."

Marianne was pleased to hear that. "She reminds me of Sister Mary Katherine at the convent," she admitted. "When Sister Sophia arrived and tried to take charge, it was very upsetting for Sister Mary Katherine. We all thought that Sister Sophia should have been nicer about it, and more diplomatic."

Dearshul looked confused.

"Less arrogant," Marianne offered. She picked up her sewing again. "Una seems a sweet girl."

Dearshul nodded. "I like Una. She's always been kind to me, not like…" The maidservant bent her head over her work.

"Fionnaghal?" Marianne suggested. She'd quickly noticed that Dearshul and Fionnaghal were not friends.

Dearshul blushed and didn't answer.

"Fionnaghal doesn't like me, either."

Dearshul glanced up and gave Marianne a comforting smile. "She wouldn't like anybody Adair married."

"I thought as much," Marianne replied, having had plenty of experience with jealousy among the women. Not necessarily over men, although a comely acolyte could make things very tense in the convent. But there was plenty to envy nonetheless—privileges and favors, food and clothes.

"He never liked Fionnaghal that way," Dearshul said firmly.

"So he told me."

Dearshul's eyes widened, and Marianne wished she hadn't mentioned her husband. "Do you need more thread?"

Dearshul shook her head. "Adair values loyalty, my lady, and Fionnaghal's the most faithless woman in Lochbarr. Why, she's been in the hay with two men on the same night, and everybody knows it. So he'd never go with *her*."

Marianne could guess what Dearshul meant by "in the hay." And she could also appreciate Dearshul's scorn.

Dearshul leaned forward, her gaze intense. "Your husband's not been in the hay since he married. Well, not *that* way. He's been sleeping in the loft over the stables."

Marianne jabbed her finger with her needle. "Oh, by the saints," she muttered, licking away the drop of blood and not looking at Dearshul, in case the young woman saw her relief.

"I didn't mean to upset you," Dearshul said anxiously.

"I'm just surprised you know that," Marianne noncommittally replied.

"Oh, everybody knows. There're no secrets in Lochbarr."

There'd been few secrets in the convent, too. "They blame me, I'm sure," she murmured, sticking her needle through the fabric with more zeal than required.

"Well, some do. Fionnaghal, for one. Others think Adair's angry with his father for making him marry a Norman and that's why he stays away. But you needn't worry, my lady," Dearshul went on comfortingly. "Adair will be chieftain, regardless. He's got too many friends and folk who think highly of him for the clan to choose another, no matter what Cormag and his ilk might say."

"Choose?" Marianne asked, surprised. "Adair is Seamus's eldest son. There should be no choice in the matter."

Dearshul shook her head. "That may be the Norman way, but it's not ours. The clansmen have to agree on who'll take the chieftain's place when he dies. There were some who spoke against Adair, but not many."

Marianne wondered what would happen if they were to choose again now, after Adair had married her. "Can they change their minds?"

"Oh, aye, and there's been some mutterings, but not enough to matter."

Maybe these "mutterings" had made Adair even more sorry he'd married her. That would explain why he found it so easy to ignore her, when she had to struggle not to stare at him in the hall and remember the passion they'd shared.

"You'll look like a queen in this," Dearshul said,

holding up the gown she'd been working on. "Did you ever see such a scarlet?"

"Once, in a market near the docks before my brother and I sailed from France," Marianne replied, glad of the distraction. "I thought it very pretty and craved a dress in that color."

"I can hardly wait to see Fionnaghal's face when you wear it the first time," Dearshul said with a smile. "Maybe at the *Hairst.*"

Dearshul had never used that word before. "What's *Hairst?*"

"That's when the…" Dearshul frowned and thought a moment. "The grain. We cut it and…" She acted out pulling something.

"Oh—harvest!" Marianne cried.

She'd seen the ripening grain in the far field on the side of the valley. Sometimes, when the wind was rippling the lake, it made the grain move like water.

"Aye. Lachlann says it'll be late this year, because it was so wet. I swear to you, my lady, this has been the wettest spring and summer I can ever remember."

Perhaps she'd been wrong to think of this country as perpetually damp. "You like Lachlann, don't you?" Marianne ventured.

"Everybody likes Lachlann," the young woman replied in a tone that told Marianne she should ask no more questions about the chieftain's younger son.

Despite her reaction, Marianne knew Dearshul liked Adair's brother, very much. When they were in the hall, she watched him all the time. Still, it was Dearshul's right to keep her feelings private, and Marianne respected that. But oh, how she missed the whispered conversations in the convent about those mysterious male creatures they would eventually marry!

Unfortunately, she could also guess why Dearshul was reluctant to talk about the man she admired. Lachlann didn't seem aware of Dearshul at all.

Perhaps there was something she could do....

An idea came to her and she acted upon it at once. "There's enough fabric left from my gown to make you an overtunic, Dearshul, if not a whole dress. You deserve something for all your hard work teaching me your language. What do you say? Would you like that?"

Dearshul's eyes sparkled like diamonds, and her smile was just as bright. "Oh, my lady! Truly?"

"Truly." Marianne set aside her sewing and went to the chest where she'd put the extra fabric. "If we start on it today, we can have it ready for *Hairst,* I think."

"Oh, my lady!"

Marianne smiled. Perhaps her marriage was a disaster, but at least she'd found a friend.

"So it seems, Father, that the Normans didn't steal the cattle, after all," Lachlann finished as he sat with Seamus in the hall several days later. "Otherwise, we would have seen more signs, or there'd have been more thieving since. I think it must have been out-laws who've moved on."

Seated beside his brother on the bench, Adair shook his head. "Or else they took enough the first time to satisfy them, or they're scared of getting caught after Father's warning."

"Either way, unless more cattle go missing, there's nothing more to be done," the father said decisively. "We can't accuse Sir Nicholas without strong proof, and that we lack."

"You'll keep up the patrols, though?" Adair asked.

"Aye, for now. Until harvest."

Seamus glanced around the hall, which was empty save for his sons and the hounds lounging by the hearth fire. Everyone else, including Adair's wife, had eaten the midday meal and drifted off.

The chieftain fastened his gray-eyed gaze on his eldest son in a way that made Adair want to squirm. "I don't generally care to interfere in people's lives, Adair, but you've given me no choice. How long do you intend to ignore your wife?"

Adair had no desire to talk about his marriage with anyone. Not his father, or his brother, or Barra, or Roban, who'd taken to making late-night observations about women and how to win them. "I'm not ignoring her."

"'Tis true you talk to her in the hall. But you aren't sharing your bed with her."

He should have known he couldn't keep that a secret. "My troubles with my wife are my own business."

"Your troubles with your wife becomes my business when it leads to strife in the clan and talk of rebellion."

Adair's frustrated annoyance fled, replaced by incredulity. "Rebellion?" he repeated. Lachlann looked just as shocked.

"Aye. Some folk are saying you pay her no heed, even though she's a beauty, because I forced you to wed and you're so angry you might even rebel against me because of it."

"I'd never rebel against you, Father," Adair declared without hesitation. "And not just because you're my father. You're my thane and chieftain, and I've sworn to obey you. You didn't threaten me with punishment if I refused to marry, so they can't say I was—"

Seamus held up his hand for silence and gave his son a fleeting smile. "I know you'd never betray me, Adair, and I'm glad to hear you don't hold your marriage against me. But now you know why I must talk to you about this breach with your wife and why it concerns Lachlann, too. I suppose, my hotheaded son, you had an argument."

"Aye," Adair admitted, still reluctant to discuss Marianne.

"You never could hold your temper," Lachlann said.

Adair bristled at the implication that he was solely accountable. "The fault's not all mine," he declared, feeling again the sting of Marianne's words as if she were whispering them in his ear.

"You're the one forced her from her home," Lachlann noted.

Adair got to his feet. "So she kept reminding me. And if that's all you have to say—"

"Sit down, Adair," his father ordered. "I'm sure there were things said on both sides. She's a proud, spirited woman."

Since his father seemed prepared to be reasonable, Adair sat. "You've been talking to Barra, I suppose."

His father looked taken aback. "Not about you. But I've always found his advice sound."

Adair was sorry he'd mentioned the *seanachie.*

"Adair, you're a proud, *braw* man, and I'm glad you're my son, but you can be stubborn and hot-tempered. You should try to see her side of things."

"Aye, you can't expect her to just accept what's happened and be happy," Lachlann agreed. "It might take years for her to reconcile herself to her marriage."

Adair scowled. His little brother couldn't possibly understand what had happened, or how he felt.

"You quarreled with her after you told her what her brother said, didn't you?" his father asked.

"Aye."

Seamus let out his breath in a long sigh. "I thought as much. That had to be hard for her to hear. No wonder she was upset."

"She wasn't angry at her brother. She was angry at *me*—but I wasn't the one who abandoned her and declared her dead. And then…"

He paused, catching himself before he told them everything that had happened that fateful day. "I'm no more to her than a way to get children. She'll put up with me and live in Lochbarr only for that. Why should I talk to her about anything else?"

His father stroked his chin and studied his son. "Some men would be glad to have the chance to bed her, and not care about anything else."

Adair jumped to his feet. "Other men, aye, like Cormag. But I don't want to just share my bed with her. I want…"

He ground his fist in his palm, cursing himself for his weakness. Yet he longed for something beyond acceptance and even affection, something he'd glimpsed in her brilliant blue eyes on their wedding night.

"She said terrible things to you, I suppose, things that seem unforgivable. I understand that, my son. But as Lachlann says, you must make allowances for her. Think of how she must feel to know her own brother can disown her so easily. She's a strong, brave woman, and like many a man it's probably her way to lash out when she's hurt. Not the water of tears for her, but fire."

That could well be true, and yet… "So I'm just to forgive and forget what she said? I'm to humble myself and say I'm sorry, despite all the things she said to me? Maybe she'll think she can rule me if I beg her forgiveness, that she can twist me round her finger with just the threat of getting cross with me."

Seamus regarded him steadily. "Do you really

think any woman will believe she could rule my bold, *braw* son as if he were a bairn? Do you truly believe she could make you do things against your will?"

"But to debase himself before a woman and a Norman," Lachlann said, finally siding with his brother.

His father shot Lachlann a look. "It's no good for a man to be at war with his wife and Adair's troubles are starting to cause strife in the clan. I can't permit that."

He addressed his eldest son, his deep voice firm and commanding. "I won't have this go on another day, so you'll go to her and make it up, Adair. How or what you say I leave to you."

It was a command, not a request, so Adair had no choice but to obey. "Aye, Father, I will."

CHAPTER TWELVE

THE DOOR TO THE *teach* flew open as if a gust of wind had caught it. Startled, Marianne looked up from Dearshul's tunic, which was nearly finished, to find her husband on the threshold.

She swallowed hard and commanded herself to be calm.

He must have heard she'd had her courses, probably from Dearshul or one of the other servants, and now he'd come to try again to get her with child, as he said he would.

In spite of the tumultuous feelings coursing through her, she tried to betray nothing with her expression, except perhaps mild interest. Yet she couldn't even pretend to sew. She set her work on the table beside her and folded her hands in her lap, which would help to still their trembling.

Adair strode into the chamber. He surveyed the dyed woolen cloth hanging from pegs Dearshul had hammered into the wall and the new furnishings: a chair with a thick cushion on its seat, a brazier, a bronze candle stand boasting eight beeswax candles and a second, smaller chest made of plain oak for Marianne's new clothes.

He then ran his measuring gaze over her, making her blush despite her wish to seem impervious to his scrutiny. She was wearing one of the three new gowns she'd made, a simple one of dark-blue wool trimmed with red thread that laced up the front, and with a new shift beneath.

He walked slowly around the room. Perhaps he'd come for another reason.

She relaxed. A little.

"You've been busy, I see," he said at last.

"Yes. Your father was very generous."

Adair glanced at her, his brows raised in silent surprise.

"He gave me some money for a wedding present." A disturbing thought occurred to her. "How else did you think I paid for these things, and the clothes I'm wearing?"

"I assumed the merchants knew they could come to me for payment, and hadn't yet. I should have told you to get what you wanted and leave the payment of the merchants to me."

She refrained from pointing out that would have required him to actually speak to her.

Adair stopped prowling about the *teach*. He faced her, hands behind his back, grimly determined. "My father tells me our…difficulties…are causing unrest in the clan, so he's ordered me to apologize to you."

She couldn't hide her surprise. "He did?"

His expression softened and his shoulders relaxed. "I *want* to apologize for losing my temper with you, Marianne. I should have been more sympathetic." He took a step closer. "This isn't how either one of us envisioned marriage, I'm sure. Yet we're wed now, for good or ill—and I'd rather try to make it for the good. I'm willing to declare a truce, and start over, if you will."

As he spoke, she felt as though a load had fallen from her shoulders. Ever since he'd marched out that door, she'd been wishing she could call back her harsh words. Her anger and dismay and hurt should have been aimed at her brother, not Adair. She shouldn't have defended Nicholas and spoken of the girl who had died. But she hadn't known how to mend the breach between them, and feared his rejection if she tried.

So she would gladly, and gratefully, accept this olive branch, however it came about. "I'd like that, Adair. I'm sorry, too, for the things I said, and what I implied."

Memories of her wedding night trickled into her thoughts. "I…that is, it's not only for children that I…"

His slow smile took her breath away.

"So it isn't only for children you want me?" he asked, sidling closer.

She shook her head.

"I'm very glad to hear that, Marianne," he murmured as he took her in his arms.

Her pulse began to throb faster. Her skin warmed and flushed. He leaned down to kiss her and his hands moved over her body, until she drew back, breathing hard, and began to unpin the silver broach at his shoulder.

As he watched, she slipped the pin out of the plaid. He silently took the broach from her and tossed it onto the pile of fabric on the table, letting the plaid fall from his shoulder to the floor.

Taking her time, feeling the passion unfurling in its own sweet, heated course, she moved on to the laces of his shirt, untying the knot lying against the indent of his collarbone. When it was undone, she pressed her lips against that soft, warm place.

His hands were busy, too, undoing the laces of her loose, unfitted gown and slipping it from her shoulders.

She pulled his shirt out of his belt and slowly, slowly, slowly started to take it off of him. He helped her, and when they were finished, he likewise tossed the shirt onto the table.

Watching him, feeling the growing, exciting hunger, she stepped out of her gown and then, with a smile, she threw it over the chest nearby.

Adair's eyes darkened with blatant desire as he looked at her, and the thin linen shift covering her nakedness. Meeting that hungry gaze boldly, excited by the gleam of desire in his eyes, she reached up and, with a leisurely, languid motion, slipped her finger in the knot of the drawstring of her shift and pulled it undone. She slipped one sleeve from her shoulder, and then the other, more slowly still.

He observed her silently, and as he did, she

sensed the raw hidden passion, the pure power of his desire, restrained and temporarily leashed, yet yearning to be set free.

With her shoulders bare and the drawstring loose, she bent down to remove her shoes, deliberately exposing her soft, round breasts to his ravenous gaze. She was shamelessly enticing him, playing a thrilling game of seduction, but one that excited her, too.

Adair did nothing as she removed one shoe. Then the other. She straightened and gave him an alluring look before walking toward the bed.

His boots hit the floor with two quick thuds. She heard the clink of his belt buckle on the table top, and his dirk along with it. In the next instant, her naked husband pulled her down on the bed.

"No swift loving today, Marianne," he said softly, holding her in his arms and trailing his finger down her neck, pausing to toy with her crucifix before continuing to her collarbone and her breasts. "Today, we're going to take our time as we begin anew."

And they did.

HIS BREATH LIKE WISPS of mist in the early-morning air, Adair hummed to himself as he strolled toward the hall. Little wavelets frothed upon the loch and whisked away the mist that had formed about the upper reaches of the craggy hills. Above, the undersides of the deep blue clouds, darker than the sky, glowed pink and orange from the rising sun. It was a bit chilly, yet soon enough the day would be warm. A bird winged its silent way toward the loch.

Adair was famished, and he intended to get some bread and ale, or mead, maybe some *brochan,* and take it back to the *teach* to share with Marianne, who was still in their bed, sleeping the sleep of the exhausted.

How many times had they made love? Three, and that was only the lovemaking. His count didn't include kissing and touching and caressing until they'd both dozed off sometime before dawn.

Barra and his father had been so wise, and so right.

Adair drew in a deep breath. A brisk breeze had sprung up in the night, bringing with it the scent of rain. If the weather changed for the worse, he would be as cozy as a nit in fleece in the *teach,* made so comfortable with Marianne's changes.

Who'd ever have thought a simple thing like lining the stone walls with cloth would make such a difference? It could be that the Normans could teach the Scots a few things about comfort, anyway, if never about fighting.

He was nearly to the kitchen when Cormag came out of the hall and smirked as he halted, hands on his hips. "You ne'er came to the hall last night and everyone knows your wife won't have you in her bed, so where've you been? Cuddling with a cow?"

Adair ignored him and continued toward the kitchen.

"Or is it true you've gone crawling back to the Norman like a dog with his tail between his legs?" Cormag demanded. "After I thought you'd come to your senses, too. I thought you had more pride than that. What'd she make you do, kiss her feet?"

Adair realized he'd have to say something, or Cormag was going to bother him all the way to the kitchen. "Maybe I kissed her feet, and maybe I didn't, but I wouldn't tell you if I did."

"I'd wager she likes all sorts of things, that one. Face like an angel, body of a whore."

Adair came to a dead halt and slowly swiveled on his heel. "What did you say about my wife?"

Cormag straightened his shoulders and threw out his chest. "You heard me."

"Aye, I did, and I'm thinking you'll be wanting to take it back and beg my pardon for the insult."

"What's afoot?"

Seamus and Roban had come around the corner of the nearest *teach*.

"I was only making a joke," Cormag replied, as if Adair must be dim not to appreciate his humor.

Adair wasn't about to let Cormag get away with that. "He called my wife a whore."

Roban's eyes widened, then he looked at Cormag as if the man had taken leave of his senses. "Never!"

Seamus, meanwhile, regarded his nephew sternly. "She's Adair's wife, Cormag, and for that, if nothing else, she deserves your respect."

A group of clansmen came out of the hall and stood together watching, all of them friends of Cormag. Lachlann came trotting out of the hall and he, too, came to a halt, obviously wondering what was going on.

Emboldened by the presence of his friends, no doubt, Cormag met Adair's glare with one of his own. "So now we've to respect the Normans, is that it?"

"You'll respect my wife, or I swear, Cormag, I'll do more than break your nose," Adair warned.

"You should do as the chieftain says, Cormag," Lachlann advised, coming closer.

Cormag sneered as he addressed Adair's brother. "I would, if she weren't a Norman."

He raised his voice so that it carried to his friends, while ostensibly addressing Seamus. "You're acting like this marriage is a grand thing. Well, it's not, and every man here knows it, even if they won't speak openly against it, or you. Adair's made an enemy of the most powerful Norman in these parts. If any other man had done such a thing, if anyone but your son had brought that woman here, you wouldn't be so forgiving—nor should you be. Those Frenchmen are our enemies, out to take our land any way they can."

Cormag curled his lip as he looked at Adair. "That's what you always used to say, Adair. Remember? Until that Norman whore made you her pet, and grateful for the pleasure of slipping between her legs at night."

Adair reached for his dirk in his belt—and didn't have it. No matter. He'd still get Cormag to take back his words.

Cormag's friends surged forward. Fionnaghal, coming out of the kitchen, stopped and stared.

Roban took a step toward Adair, while Lachlann looked to their father.

His brow thunderous, the chieftain came between Adair and Cormag. "Cormag, put up your dirk," he commanded. "I'll not have bloodshed here. Are you forgetting you're kin and clansmen? Whatever disagreement you have with my son—or me—that was no way to speak of my daughter-in-law."

A flush spread over Cormag's weasel face, and he finally had the decency to look ashamed.

"Apologize, or go out that gate and never come back."

"I'm sorry for insulting Adair's Norman wife," Cormag muttered while his friends exchanged disgruntled looks.

"And have you something to say to me about the way I rule the clan?"

Cormag shook his head.

"I thought not," Seamus snapped. "Now be about your business."

Scowling, Cormag obeyed his chieftain and went to join his friends, who walked away, grumbling among themselves.

"Roban, see if the patrols are ready to leave and tell them where I want them to go this morning," Seamus ordered.

"Aye," Roban said, giving Adair a friendly smile before he trotted off.

Fionnaghal went back into the kitchen, no doubt to tell everyone inside what she'd witnessed and find a way to blame Marianne.

"God save me, Adair," Seamus muttered, rubbing his chin, "can you not ignore the man?"

Adair shook his head. "Not when he calls Marianne a whore."

"Cormag goes too far," Lachlann concurred.

"He's a fool."

Seamus drew a deep breath. "Aye, he goes too far, but he's not a fool, Adair. He's discontented and restless. I'll put my mind to finding something for him to do, something that'll take him out of Lochbarr for a time. Maybe he should go to visit our relatives in Inverness, to strengthen our bonds with them. Maybe he can even find himself a wife."

"Do you really think that'll content him?" Lachlann asked.

"I don't care if it does," Adair said. "I'll settle for getting him away from here."

"Aye," Seamus agreed. "It'll have to do, because he's our clansman and a good fighter." He fixed his eye on his eldest son. "Those are things you should keep in mind when you quarrel with him."

"If he was the finest warrior in Scotland, that wouldn't give him leave to insult my wife."

"I'm not saying it should. I'm saying you should hold your temper with a clansman."

"Aye, Father. I'll try—as long as he says nothing against my wife."

"I can ask no more, I suppose." Seamus gave Adair a meaningful look. "Speaking of holding your temper, I noticed you never came to the hall last night, nor Marianne neither."

Adair had to smile. "I was…apologizing."

Seamus grinned and looked relieved. "Fight and make up, fight and make up again. That's the way it's going to be with you two. I could see it from the first. No hard feelings for my order, then, my son?"

"No hard feelings, Father."

Seamus looked at his younger son. "You're as pinched-faced as an auld woman, Lachlann lad. There's nothing shameful about a man loving his wife."

Lachlann scowled, his dark brows knitted. "I don't need to know what Adair does with his wife."

Adair reached out and ruffled his brother's hair. "And I've not told you. But if you need any advice—"

"Come to me," his father interrupted. "When you learn there's more to life than worrying about the Normans and the king."

"I don't just think about the Normans and the king," Lachlann protested, his face reddening.

"No? Then you're courting some woman I don't know about?"

Adair looked at his brother with surprise. Was this why Dearshul had no luck with him?

"There's no woman I care about that way," Lachlann muttered.

Seamus patted his younger son on the shoulder. "No shame there, my son. You've plenty of time yet to find a wife. And," he continued, winking at his other son, "I hope you find her in a better way than Adair."

Adair didn't take offense, because his father had a point.

"Will you be joining us in a hunt this fine morning, Adair?" Seamus asked.

"I think not," he answered, blushing like a lad. "I thought I ought to spend more time with my wife."

And not just making love with her. He wanted to know more about her. Her childhood. Her parents. What made her happy, or sad. The friends she'd had. To tear down the walls both she and he had made.

"All right, my son," his father said, laughing as he started toward the stables. "Come along, Lachlann. We'll leave your brother to apologize some more."

A FEW DAYS LATER, two men sat close together in an abandoned stone hut on the far side of the loch, long after most of the inhabitants of Lochbarr were abed, including the chieftain's son and his Norman bride. The men wrapped their plaids about themselves for warmth, and the only illumination came from a small, smoldering peat fire at their feet. Half the thatched roof over their heads was gone, giving them little shelter from the soft rain.

This was the usual time and place for their meetings, for secrecy was necessary, and it was difficult to hide from the prying eyes and ears of the people of Lochbarr.

"You're as bad as Adair," Lachlann sneered as he glared at Cormag, who held a wineskin loose in his hands. "Neither of you knows how to hold his temper."

Cormag took a drink of the *uisge beatha* and scowled. "If I can't, it's because your brother's a damn smug bastard, acting as if he's never put a foot wrong in his life. It makes my blood boil just to look at him."

"Even so, you shouldn't insult his wife. You had to know my father wouldn't approve of that."

"It's no insult to call a whore a whore. You've seen them in the hall. They can't keep their hands off each other. He slavers after that bitch like she's in heat. Aye, and she's just as bad."

Lachlann refused the drink Cormag silently offered. "Still, you'd best learn to curb your tongue and put a rein on your lust, Cormag."

"The way you do?" Cormag's eyes gleamed greedily in the flickering light. "You might be able to fool your father and your brother, but you can't fool me. You want her as much as any man here. I wouldn't be surprised to learn you're planning on having her when you're the chieftain."

Lachlann leaned forward, so that his slender face glowed bronze in the firelight. "I don't want Marianne. I'm not like my brother, ready to put the clan at risk for lust. When my father dies, she'll go back to her brother as a peace offering to lull Sir Nicholas into thinking I'm no more of a threat to him than my father."

"I thought her brother said she was dead to him."

"Aye, but she'll go back just the same. Even if her brother doesn't want her, other Normans will be impressed."

"Adair won't let his wife go easily."

"By then he'll be banished, so he'll have no voice to protest." Lachlann's eyes narrowed as he regarded his companion. "I've still got the blessings of your men, do I not? They'll support me as chieftain?"

"Aye," Cormag affirmed. "And there'll be others to side with you, too—those who realize that Adair hasn't got the wisdom to lead the clan, and they were wrong to think his good looks and *braw* way with a sword meant he'd be as good a chieftain as your father. The dolt proved them wrong when he brought that woman here."

"Aye, he made a mistake—and we must not. Which is why you've got to hold back, Cormag. We can't strike until we're sure about the other clans as well as our own men. So don't protest too strongly when my father sends you north. Go without a fuss, and try to find out if anyone'll interfere if our clan decides to pick a new chieftain."

Cormag took a gulp from the wineskin. "North," he muttered angrily as he wiped his lips with the back of his hand.

"It's your own fault he's sending you. You made too much trouble with Adair. But no matter. This can be to our advantage. Just don't stay long, and don't say too much. If our plans are discovered too soon, my father'll banish us, or worse."

Cormag took another drink, then fixed his gaze on Lachlann. "And how long are we to be patient? How long do we let Adair strut about like a game cock while we do what we're told, even as the Normans take our land? You said that if we stole the cattle, it'd spur your father into complaining to the king. Then you said Adair's interference with the Norman and his sister would make your father turn against him, but now we're allied by marriage to that Norman bastard. You thought Adair's quarrel with his wife would work to our advantage, and they're cozy as can be."

"Granted things haven't turn out as we hoped, but plenty of people are angry at Adair because of what he's done. They'll welcome another chieftain."

"But how long are you willing to wait?" Cormag demanded. "How much time do you want to spend watching your brother get away with what he does, while Seamus ignores you? Your father's still a healthy man. He could be chieftain for years yet."

"He's not as healthy as he seems. I doubt he'll live out the winter."

Hope and disbelief warred in Cormag's narrow eyes. "How can you be so sure?"

"Remember when he fell from his horse in the spring? I kept asking what happened, and finally he told me it wasn't the horse's fault. He'd been dizzy. Although he tried to make light of it, he swore me to secrecy. I said he should go to Beitiris for a potion or medicine, but he wouldn't listen to me."

Cormag sniffed. "He never does, never has. But he's not fallen from his horse again."

"That doesn't mean he's well. Look at him when he's tired—his face is drawn and gray and blue about the lips. He's as stubborn as Adair when it comes to sickness."

Cormag shifted, and slowly smiled. "Before the winter's out, you say?"

Lachlann nodded. "Aye. He's old and he's weakening, and it could be the ague will be enough to kill him."

"But if not? We can't wait forever."

Lachlann rose and looked down at his cousin. "We'll not hasten my father's death, Cormag. We'll bide our time and move when we stand the best chance of making certain I'll be chosen as the new chieftain." He gave his comrade a thin smile. "And when I'm chieftain, Cormag, I'll reward you for your support and your loyalty—but not with Marianne."

"Dearshul, then."

Lachlann shrugged. "If you want her, she's yours," he answered before he opened the door and slipped out into the night. "It makes no difference to me."

CHAPTER THIRTEEN

WARM UNDER THE COVERS on the morning of the harvest, Marianne lay on her side and studied her husband's slumbering face in the dawning light. His face relaxed, Adair looked as he must have when he was a boy.

She wished she'd seen him then. He'd probably been an imp, getting into mischief, yet getting out of trouble just as easily with an explanation and a grin.

Smiling dreamily, she rested a hand on her stomach. If their firstborn was a son, he'd probably be just the same. If their firstborn was a daughter, she'd likely have a stubborn, fiery temper, too. How could she help it, with two such parents?

But if their son was like his father, she'd be happy and proud, for Adair was as her father-in-law had said—there was no guile, no deceit, in him. He was as you saw him.

He was a man you could trust.

Her husband's eyelids fluttered and he reached out and pulled her to him. She snuggled against his warm, powerful body. "You're awake?" she asked.

"No, I'm still sleeping," he answered, his eyelids closed, "and I'm having a wonderful dream about having an angel in my arms, so please don't wake me."

She couldn't resist the urge to kiss his cheek. "An angel in your bed? That sounds like a very earthly sort of angel."

"For which I'm very glad." Skimming his palm over her thigh, he slowly opened his eyes. "I think I know this body."

"I should think you do," Marianne replied pertly, even as desire blossomed within her.

Adair moved her so that she lay prone upon him, his arms wrapped about her, holding her close. She realized he was very wide awake. All over.

So was she.

As a familiar, delightful excitement surged through her, she moved so that she was straddling his chest, her shift riding high on her thighs.

"What are you doing, my golden-haired wife?"

"I suspect you're still weary after last night. And the night before that. And the night before that."

"I feel full of vitality at the moment."

"Perhaps, but I don't want you to wear yourself out."

His breathing quickened. "No?"

"Absolutely not. Now are you going to be quiet, or would you rather get out of bed?"

His eyes dancing in a way that made her whole body feel like it was melting, he firmly pressed his lips together and shook his head.

"Good," she murmured as she slowly reached

down and then—even more slowly—lifted off her shift.

His eyes widened as she tossed it aside. She leaned forward so that her breasts brushed his naked chest.

He raised himself to kiss her, but she caught hold of his wrists and held them. "I think you need to rest," she said. "Save your strength…for now."

His only answer was a strangled gasp as she shifted slightly back, his erection against her buttocks. He most definitely wasn't exhausted, yet this morning would be for his pleasure, not hers, she decided.

Keeping hold of his wrists, she tongued his nipple at her leisure, sucking it between her teeth and nipping gently. He made little noises in his throat and began to shift, his legs moving as if he had to do something to keep from rolling her over and taking her swiftly.

Thrilling thought. Arousing motion.

She went to his other nipple and suckled it, too, making him gasp. He bucked, raising his hips and lowering them, exciting her more. "This is torture, Marianne!"

"Is it?" she lazily replied and without any sympathy. He would be begging for more "torture" before she was done.

She moved lower, letting her hair trail over his body. She moved up and over his erection, so that she was sitting on his hips. "The girls at the convent talked about making love. They could be quite…specific."

She slid a little further backward.

"What are you—?" He gasped when she kissed the soft skin of the head of his penis. Then she put her mouth over the head and sucked him inside.

He groaned as if it was both the most exquisite agony and the most incredibly stimulating act. Encouraged and excited by his enjoyment, she did it again.

His hands gripped the sheets and his whole body rose as if offering itself to her. Once more, and his moans filled the air.

Aroused herself, she simply had to have him inside her, so she guided his glistening shaft to her, then slowly lowered herself. A low growl sounded in his throat and his whole body tensed, while she reveled in the sensation of his hardness within her.

Grinding herself against him, she leaned forward again to lick and suck his skin, while he took hold of her shoulders. His mouth found her breasts, and her nipples. With quick, light movements, like the beating wings of a bird, he pleasured her with his tongue. She couldn't keep silent as she raised herself again, but she didn't care if she roused the entire fortress.

She had her magnificent husband inside her, loving her. Arousing her, filling her. And she was going to inflame him as he'd never imagined.

She grabbed his shoulders, pushing him back down. Splaying her hands beside his head, determined to excite him, she begin to lever herself up and then down, varying the rhythm, letting his breathing be her guide. Her hair flowed over his chest and she moved her head from side to side, letting that inflame him, too.

She increased the tempo and watched the cords in his neck tighten. That delicious tension began to build in her own body, until it was like being on the brink of a warm river. One more step would immerse her. One step, and she would be over the edge. One push...and with a cry, she was there, and so was he, his hips bucking wildly, his back arching.

The pulsing continued, then slowed, as she fell against him.

Breathing as hard as she, he stroked her hair. "I wonder if those nuns had any idea what you were learning in that convent."

She laughed softly. "I doubt it, or they would never have given us any time to talk alone."

His eyes twinkling, he brushed a lock of hair from her face. "So, what else did you learn?"

Pulling away, she moved to lie beside him. "Patience, my love, patience. I don't want to share all my surprises so quickly."

He chuckled, the low rumble of amusement wonderfully intimate. "I'll try."

She toyed with the narrow braid at the side of his face, realizing he wouldn't be nearly so attractive with his hair cut like a Norman. "I think you've probably got a few surprises of your own."

"Well, I don't know," he mused aloud. "Those girls seemed to know quite a bit. But perhaps there are one or two things they never learned."

"Maybe now would be a good time for you to show me."

"God help me, the woman's insatiable!" he cried to the ceiling before looking at to her with real regret. "Unfortunately, I can't lie abed with my lovely wife, no matter how much I want to. I don't want to give those who don't approve of our marriage more cause for complaining."

Marianne sighed, for he was right. "At least Cormag is gone."

"Aye, for a bit, but he'll be back," Adair answered as he got out of bed, unabashedly naked. "I'll have to try harder not to let him goad me."

She was sorry she'd mentioned Cormag, and sought a return to their happy mood. "If you're going to parade about like that, it's not my fault if I want to make love with you all day."

He gave her a lascivious wink. "But we'll have tonight, and plenty of nights afterward."

Yes. Yes, they would.

He went to his chest and threw it open. "There should be a clean—"

He hesitated, then pulled out the breeches she'd been working on lately. Usually she hid them underneath her gowns, since she'd intended them for a surprise. She'd thought he should have such a garment for when he went to parlay with Normans. Now, she suddenly realized, that would be as much a mistake as cutting his hair.

"Losh, what are these?" he asked, holding them up.

"They're breeches," she answered, feeling rather

foolish. "I made them for you, but never mind. I doubt they'd fit anyway."

"I appreciate the thought," Adair muttered, turning them from side to side.

"Put them back, Adair. Dearshul probably put your shirt in the other— What are you doing?"

"Trying them on. It's the least I can do after you went to so much trouble."

She scrambled out of bed and tried to snatch them from his hands. "No, really, you don't have to bother. It was a mistake."

He held them away from her. "I want to try them on." He ran a wolfish gaze over her. "Aren't you cold, Marianne?"

"As a matter of fact, I'm freezing. Now give them back to me. Perhaps I can make something else with the fabric, or give them to one of the servants."

His gaze was fastened on her breasts. "I can tell you're cold. I think you'd better get dressed yourself."

She stopped trying to snatch the breeches. She went back to bed and found her shift.

"What, you're giving up?" he asked as he pulled on the woolen garment.

"Yes. If you want to wear them, I won't stop you. Besides, you're right. I should get dressed. I don't want to catch a chill."

After putting on her shift, she reached under the pillow and took out what she'd hidden beneath it the night before. "I'm not good with a needle, but I've been trying to improve, and not just by making clothes for you and me, Adair," she said, hiding the little garment behind her back.

Adair regarded her quizzically. "You've made something for my father?"

She shook her head. "Not exactly, but I think he'll like it."

She held out the little baby's nightgown, embroidered around the neck. "It's for our child."

He blinked. "Child?"

"Yes. Our child."

"Losh, Marianne, truly?" he cried as he rushed to embrace her, holding her so tight, she could scarcely draw breath. "A bairn! Are ye sure?"

He said a lot of other things in Gaelic, too, speaking so quickly, she couldn't make sense of it.

She pushed him back a little, just so she could breathe. "I'm fairly certain."

"Why didn't you tell me?"

"I just did." She smiled, suddenly feeling shy and girlish and delightfully happy, too. "I wanted to surprise you with the garment."

Adair laughed and kissed her on the forehead. "Well, that you did. I was expecting a shirt." He took the gown in his strong, powerful hands and held as if it envisioning the baby wearing it. "Wait till my father hears!"

"Do you have to tell him right away?"

"Why not?"

She shrugged her shoulders. "I want it to be our secret, at least for a little while, before people start gossiping about it and speculating when it'll be born and watching me for signs to know if it's a boy or girl."

He nodded as he delicately folded the little gown and put it on the bed. "All right, I'll try, but I'm no good at keeping secrets and this one's going to be harder than most. I feel like shouting it from the roof of the hall."

"You can do that in a little while, if you truly feel the need. I promise."

He hugged her again. "A child! And so soon! I can hardly believe it!"

"Do you mean to say you doubt your virility?" she teased.

His eyes sparkled with laughter. "No, yet I'm happy to know I can father a child just the same."

She smiled. "So am I."

His grin dissolved as he scratched his thigh. "I appreciate the thought and the work, Marianne, but these damn things itch something fierce," he said, starting to remove the breeches. "They're likely doing a mischief to my body, too. I don't want this child to be our last."

"I don't, either," she replied as she put the little gown away under her clothes. She didn't want Dearshul to find out their secret just yet, either.

"It's a fine morning," Adair noted, peering out of the shuttered window as he put on his *feileadh*. "Not a cloud in the sky, and only a bit of a breeze." He looked back at her with a warm smile that made her heart leap with happiness. "A fine day for fine news."

"When I first came here, I was sure Scotland

never had a sunny day," she said as she began to dress. "Dearshul's since explained that you had a very wet spring and summer."

"Aye, that we did. I thought we'd never be able to get the seed in the ground. And I'll not deny we have a lot of rain most of the time. And fog. And mist. And drizzle. But that only makes the sunny days more special. If tomorrow's fair, we'll go to the site my father's chosen for the watchtower. You can see the whole valley and the loch spread out below you. It's quite a sight."

She heard the pleasure and pride in her husband's voice. He loved this land, even when it was wet. It was too early yet for her to share his love for his country, yet when the sun did shine, she could see a certain rugged beauty to it.

As for the wet days, staying inside the cozy *teach* or the hall, working companionably with Dearshul, or being with Adair, provided much in the way of compensation.

Tugging on his shirt, Adair slid her a questioning glance. "Are you intending to go about in your shift all day? I wouldn't mind, but I don't think my people would approve, especially since it's a special day."

"No, we couldn't have that," Marianne agreed. "Fionnaghal would likely accuse me of trying to tempt the men."

Adair paused in the process of putting on his boots. "Would you like me to speak to her?"

"No," Marianne answered as she lifted her lovely new scarlet gown from her chest. Dearshul had finished it a few days ago, and it truly did seem fit for a queen. Dearshul's overtunic had turned out well, too, for they'd bought some bright green and gold thread to embroider a border around the hem. "Dearshul and I have a plan for Fionnaghal that we've been saving for today."

"A plan?"

"Yes, a plan. And no, you can't know what it is," she finished in response to his silent query. She put the gown over her head and wiggled it on.

"You are a stubborn, insolent woman," he said as he stuck his dirk through his belt. He raised his eyes and saw her in her new gown. "By all the saints in Scotland," he gasped. "I'm going to be the envy of every man in Lochbarr."

"Then you like it?" she asked, turning in a circle, although it hadn't yet been laced.

"Like it? I like it so much, it's all I can do not to come over there and tear it off you."

She gave him a seductive smile. "Come over here anyway, and help me with the laces. Of course later, you can undo them."

"Later, I'll do more than undo your laces."

"Is that a promise, husband?" she asked as he came toward her, a passionate gleam in his eye.

"Aye, it is, wife," he whispered as he took hold of the laces.

She could hardly wait.

HIS BACK WARMED BY THE SUN, Adair stood beside Roban and Lachlann, watching the farmers work their scythes with the speed and skill that came from years of practice. If necessary, they could take down a man with the same sweeping motion, just as Adair could cut grain, if they were shorthanded. Fortunately, this year they weren't, which meant he could watch Marianne.

Seamus, Barra and several of the older clansmen were at the far end of the field, where the farmers would finish. Marianne, with Dearshul beside her, was on the opposite side with the women of the household, several of whom were braiding straw to make the bands to bind the sheaves. His bold, passionate wife and Dearshul were very easy to spot in their red dresses, and Adair's gaze often strayed that way.

He smiled to himself, pleased that his wife had found a friend in Dearshul, whose gaze kept drifting to the oblivious Lachlann as if her eyes were connected to him by a string. Why his brother didn't like Dearshul, he could never figure out. The young woman was pretty, and clever, and got along with everyone—except Fionnaghal—and it was clear she doted on the chieftain's younger son.

Perhaps the last was the reason. Maybe her obvious yearning created the opposite result in Lachlann. Or maybe Lachlann was simply too busy thinking about the Normans and the state of the country to realize a pretty young woman was besotted with him— the way some stubborn fools tried to overlook their wives.

He'd learned the error of that. Never again would he ignore Marianne, or pretend she wasn't impor-

tant to him. She was more important to him than
he'd ever imagined a wife could be.

"Dearshul's looking very lovely this morning," he
remarked, deciding to make Lachlann take a little
notice of Dearshul.

Lachlann glanced at the young woman and
shrugged. "It's the red tunic she's wearing, I expect."

"Not as lovely as your wife, though," Roban
noted. "She looks like a queen."

"Aye, that she does," Adair agreed. He desperately wanted to tell them his wonderful news; however, he'd promised Marianne he wouldn't, so he bit
his tongue and kept their secret to himself. "But
Dearshul's looking very pretty these days. She's
been a great help to Marianne, too."

"Has she now?"

Somewhat to Adair's chagrin, that question—and
a look of interest—came from Roban.

On the other hand, he reasoned, if his brother
wasn't interested in Dearshul, she could do worse
than Roban, who was generous and loyal and the
man Adair wanted nearest him in a fight. "Aye. She's
clever, too."

Even that didn't merit so much as a nod from
Lachlann. He seemed more interested in watching
their father and Barra strolling across the top of the
field.

Before Adair could say anything more about
Dearshul, Fionnaghal sauntered up to them. "So,
Adair, I should have got myself a red dress to get you

to notice me, is that it? Or maybe I should have been born a Norman."

Adair refused to let Fionnaghal sour his mood. "It wasn't that you're not a bonnie woman, Fionnaghal. It's that you've never been faithful to a lover since you came here. I didn't want to be just another in your bed."

"Maybe if you'd come to my bed, I wouldn't have been so quick to take another."

"We'll never know that now, will we? But you've no one to blame but yourself if you're jealous."

"Me? Jealous of a Norman?" Fionnaghal retorted, her face reddening. "You're mad—or bewitched."

"Aye, maybe I am. Bewitched—or in love."

It was the first time he'd ever used that word in reference to his feelings for his wife, even in his own thoughts. Yet now that he said, he recognized the truth of it. He was in love with Marianne.

Roban and Lachlann stared at him, while Fionnaghal sucked in her breath sharply.

Then Roban let out a peal of deep, hearty laughter and nudged Adair so hard, he nearly fell over. "Losh, I should have known it would turn out like this. With her a beauty and you...well, being you."

Adair realized Lachlann was frowning. "Are you not pleased, Lachlann?" he asked. "Surely you didn't want us at each other's throats forever?"

"Aye, aye, I'm pleased for you. I never thought your marriage would turn out so well."

"Fionnaghal!" one of the harvesters shouted.

Adair patted the stunned woman on her shoul-

der. "Did you not hear that, Fionnaghal?" he said
with mock gravity. "One of your bands has broken
again. A pity it is that after all these years, you're
not more skilled. Of course, now you've got to kiss
that *braw* lad."

Fionnaghal made a noise that gave him to understand she was insulted and disgusted before she
flounced off to kiss the young farmer who was eagerly waiting. Adair shook his head. Fionnaghal
surely made her bands weak on purpose.

He turned to watch his wife again, who was smiling at something Ceit was saying. She'd managed
to impress the woman who'd been running their
household for years—no easy task.

"I think you'd better go to yer wife," Roban said,
his deep voice a warning rumble. "Fionnaghal's
heading for her, and she looks ready for battle."

One swift look and Adair realized he was right.
Fionnaghal was marching toward Marianne the way
men went to war, grim-faced and determined. He
started across the cut field, weaving his way around
the standing sheaves.

He was still about ten feet away when Fionnaghal
stopped in front of Marianne, gave her a look of utter
contempt, and muttered a particularly loathsome,
insulting epithet.

"What did ye just say tae me, Fionnaghal?" Marianne demanded, her response in nearly flawless
Gaelic.

Everyone stared in surprised silence, including
Adair. How the devil did she learn…?

Dearshul, of course.

"Whatever it was, I don't think 'twas flattering," Marianne continued, her expression calm, but her eyes flashing with a fire Adair recognized, and that Fionnaghal should dread.

"The first part was 'useless,' was it not?" she said when Fionnaghal didn't answer. "You think I'm useless, Fionnaghal?"

The serving woman recovered and answered with a sneer. "You don't do any work. You don't even give the orders to the household."

"Why should I?" Marianne asked calmly. "Is Ceit not capable? Is she not doing a good job? I think she is, so I see no need to interfere. Do you?"

Adair glanced at Ceit. She was not impressed with Fionnaghal's comment. Some of the other women, however, exchanged sly smiles as if they agreed. Several of the clansmen not cutting grain drifted closer.

Adair wondered if he should say something, or come between them, until his wife glanced his way with a look that suggested he stay out of it.

Fionnaghal tossed her hair and planted her feet. "It's not Ceit I'm talking about."

"What would you have me do, Fionnaghal?" Marianne asked with quiet, unruffled dignity. "Surely you don't think the wife of the chieftain's son should make bands for the sheaves?"

A look of triumph bloomed in Fionnaghal's dark brown eyes and she straightened her shoulders. "You couldn't do it anyway. Like I said, you're useless."

Marianne's smile would have made Adair think twice. "Really?"

"Aye!"

The harvesters realized something was happening and stopped, straightening with the scythes in their hands.

"You think I've never worked in the fields, even when I was a child?" Marianne calmly inquired.

Adair didn't think she had, but she certainly spoke as if that were true. Fionnaghal was clearly wondering if such a thing was possible, too, for her eyes narrowed, and a flicker of doubt crossed her face.

"Perhaps I did and perhaps I did not," Marianne said, "but you've challenged me, so I can't back down now without a loss to my pride, and Norman pride is just as fierce as Scots'. Let's see who can make the most bands, and the strongest, shall we?"

She was proposing a contest? Maybe she *had* worked in the fields. Or maybe this was part of the plan she'd mentioned that morning, the one she'd concocted with Dearshul.

"Are you willing to let your wife do this, Adair?" Fionnaghal demanded. "You won't mind her getting kissed by some other man when her bands break?"

"I'd prefer that she save her kisses for me," he answered truthfully, "but I'd think twice about accepting the challenge, if I were you. I'm afraid your pride is in for a tumble."

Fionnaghal's answer to that was a disdainful sniff.

Seamus, a winded Barra trotting along beside him, strode up to the growing crowd. "What's afoot?"

"Fionnaghal's challenged my wife to a contest," Adair said. He nodded at the field. "Making bands, the most and the strongest."

Seamus's gray eyes widened. "A contest, is it?" His face lighted with a grin. "Whoever wins, I'll reward with a necklace. A *gold* necklace."

"Done!" Fionnaghal eagerly cried. She ran a scornful gaze over Marianne. "Do you want to change first, my lady, out of your fine Norman gown?"

"That won't be necessary," Marianne said, briskly rolling back the long cuffs to her elbows and stepping toward a pile of straw that was ready to be plaited. She picked up an armload and sat on a large stone nearby that marked the corner of the field. She put the straw at her feet, brushed off her skirt, and smiled angelically at her opponent. "I'm ready."

Glowering, Fionnaghal grabbed some straw and sat on another stone.

By now, everyone knew what was about to happen. Those not cutting the grain crowded around the two women. The men and youths preparing to scythe bent low, their bodies tense, their eyes alight, ready to start once they got the word.

Seamus raised his hand and as he lowered it, shouted, "Go!"

Marianne and Fionnaghal's fingers leapt into swift, purposeful action.

As Adair watched, it was immediately obvious that Marianne knew exactly what she was doing.

A scowling Fionnaghal realized it, too. Her brow wrinkled with concentration, she bent to her task, while Marianne looked cool as ice, with a quiet resolve that didn't bode well for Fionnaghal's chances.

Teassie, Donnan and other children hurried to take the completed bands to the men cutting the sheaves, and it soon became apparent that Fionnaghal had been deliberately sabotaging her bands before, because the ones she made now held up very well.

Marianne's were all holding firm, too. Thank God. He really didn't want anybody else kissing Marianne, even if it was a tradition.

A shout went up from the field. "Fionnaghal!"

One of her bands had broken, and a sheaf had fallen apart.

With a curse, Fionnaghal pushed the straw from her lap and ran out into the field to kiss the man whose sheaf had to be remade. This was no lingering kiss of the sort Fionnaghal usually bestowed, though, but a fast buss on the cheek. She ran back just as swiftly, grabbed more straw, and began to plait another band.

Marianne was still cool and calm, barely taking any note of what had happened.

Then another shout came from the field—all the grain was cut. The men harvesting sat down to rest, while everyone else gathered around Marianne and

Fionnaghal and looked at the piles of bands left un-
used, trying to estimate who'd made the most.

Seamus went first to Fionnaghal. Adair held his
breath as his father bent down and counted her
bands. "Eight."

He then went to Marianne's pile. "A dozen. My
son's wife's the winner!"

Adair whooped with delight. His father didn't
hide his pleasure, either. Lachlann smiled, while
Roban laughed, and Dearshul, standing close to him,
beamed. The other men and women regarded Marianne with an awed respect.

As for his wife, her blue eyes fairly glowed with
happiness and triumph.

Fionnaghal jumped to her feet. "You taught her,
you little *striopach!*" she shouted at Dearshul. "Trying to impress a Norman and embarrass one of your
own. Learning their language—think that'll make
you a fine lady, do you? Think that'll make Lachlann look at you with wanting?"

Lachlann frowned and Dearshul's face crumpled
as if she was about to burst into tears. Adair and his
father stepped forward simultaneously, but before
either man could speak, Marianne rose, paying no
heed to the straw tumbling from her skirt.

She glared at Fionnaghal, her intense, angry stare
as fierce as any Adair had ever seen on a man's face.
"You're a foulmouthed, jealous, bitter witch, Fionnaghal. You couldn't beat me, so you'll take out
your rage on Dearshul. She's done nothing wrong.
Apologize for what you called her."

Fionnaghal crossed her arms. "I will not."

Marianne took a step backward and ran a measuring gaze over the woman. "I have to make you?"

People started to whisper and talk among themselves. Adair wasn't sure what his wife meant, either.

Fionnaghal sniffed derisively. "How would you do that?"

"I'll fight you."

Adair stared at Marianne incredulously. She must have used the wrong word. His well-bred wife surely couldn't mean a physical fight.

"Do you think I lived all those years among women without being involved in a few fights?" Marianne asked. "There were girls at the convent who make you look like a lamb."

Fionnaghal blinked. "You're lying. You won't really fight me."

"You don't think so? Then you likely won't believe that before my brothers left home to seek their fortunes, they used to wrestle each other all the time, and when they tired of fighting each other or wanted to try something new, they'd come after me." She crossed her arms. "If you're not worried about a few bruises or a black eye, neither am I."

Adair still couldn't believe she was serious. Why, she was with child. She might get injured, or lose the baby.

Plan or not, he was about to step forward and stop them when Fionnaghal let out a screech and ran at Marianne. Adair cried out a warning—but

Marianne didn't need it. She crouched and when Fionnaghal drew near, she caught the running woman with a blow to the stomach that knocked her flat.

"Are you all right?" Adair cried, hurrying to his wife as Fionnaghal gasped for breath. "She didn't hurt you or the baby?"

Marianne shook her head.

"She's carrying a bairn?" his father cried, his gray eyes alight with joy.

Adair cringed inwardly. He hoped Marianne would forgive him for revealing their secret sooner than she wanted, but it was done now. "Aye."

"I'm going to have a grandson!" Seamus shouted at the top of his lungs.

Adair lost sight of Marianne and Fionnaghal as his friends crowded around him. Roban slapped him on the back and offered good wishes for a healthy son. Lachlann congratulated him, too, if not so boisterously, and so did many others. When he finally broke free, he saw the women gathered around Marianne, while Dearshul, her eyes shining, clasped her hands and looked as if she were too happy to speak at all.

Leaving the women, Marianne went to Fionnaghal, who was sitting on the ground, staring disconsolately at the field.

When Fionnaghal realized Marianne was coming toward her, she scrambled to her feet. "My lady, I didn't know you were with child. If I'd had—"

"It's all right. I'm not hurt. But let this be a lesson to you never to underestimate another woman, or judge her by her looks. And never insult Dearshul again, or you'll have to answer to me."

"Aye, my lady, aye," Fionnaghal hastily agreed, backing away.

"Good, and now that we understand each other, come with me and have some wine."

Although Fionnaghal looked as if she would have preferred an invitation from Satan to join him in hell, she nodded her acceptance.

"I need a wee word with my husband first, so if you'll excuse me," she said to Fionnaghal before heading toward Adair.

He could guess why she wanted to speak to him. "Marianne, I'm sorry I—"

She put her fingertips lightly on his lips. "Never mind. I'm surprised you managed to keep it a secret for as long as you did." Then she raised herself on her toes and kissed him.

It was too bad they weren't alone, so he could make a more thorough apology, he thought as he drew back. "You're forgiving Fionnaghal?"

"I've learned it's best to forgive and forget, but if you wish to apologize more later…"

"I certainly do."

With a smile that roused his desire even more, she went back to join Fionnaghal.

It was all he could do not to grab her and carry her to the *teach* as he watched her go to the hall with Fionnaghal at her side. Behind them came Dearshul, with Roban on her heels like an eager puppy. The other men and women surged after them, likewise heading to the hall for the harvest feast, Lachlann among them.

His father appeared beside Adair, still beaming with joy. "A grandson! Adair, I'm the proudest, happiest man in Scotland today."

"No, you're not," his son said with a smile. "I am."

"We'll argue about it in the hall," Seamus replied, clapping him on the back. "And I hope your son—"

"Or daughter."

His father grinned. "Your bairn leads you the same merry dance of mischief you led me and your sainted mother. Now come, and we'll have a drink on it. Aye, and maybe two or three."

CHAPTER FOURTEEN

ADAIR COULDN'T REMEMBER a better feast. This was a far cry from the grim celebrations of his wedding. For one thing, there was plenty of laughter in the hall. Marianne joined in, too, although it was obvious she had some way to go to appreciate the food. His father, overjoyed with the news of the baby, was offering toasts and salutes as often as he raised his cup.

"You might have told me you were learning Gaelic," Adair said in French, placing his hand on his wife's knee as he leaned closer to be heard above the din.

She blushed, looking like an innocent maid, and the fact that he knew she was not proved surprisingly arousing. "I didn't want to sound foolish," she confided.

"You nearly gave me a fit when you challenged Fionnaghal. What were you trying to do, send me to an early grave?"

She shook her head. "I wanted to show her I wouldn't take her insolence any more, and I honestly didn't think she'd fight me." Marianne looked down, more bashful than he'd ever seen her before. "You don't think I behaved in an unseemly, undignified manner?"

Adair laughed. "With Fionnaghal, that was obviously exactly the right way to behave. I think she'll respect you now."

Marianne smiled a warm, entrancing smile that heated him to the soles of his boots. "I've spent the last twelve years of my life with girls and women. I've met her sort plenty of times before."

"Is it true, what you said about the fighting among them?"

"Yes. Put fifty girls in close quarters for a long period of time, and you'll see."

"I'll take your word for it. And was it true about your brothers, too?"

Marianne nodded, squirming a little as his hand shifted slightly upward, although she didn't ask him to stop. "Oh, yes. If I had to, I could probably take you down."

He gave her a sly, seductive grin. "What say we try it later, when we're alone?"

"Have you forgotten I'm with child—and after you announced it so loudly?"

Adair flushed and removed his hand. "I know I said I wouldn't, but I was afraid for you."

She patted his cheek. "I understand, and I'm not angry. But I really wasn't planning on fighting Fionnaghal. I was sure she'd back down before it came to that. I must confess, she surprised me."

"It was a good thing you knew what to do."

"Yes. All those years of practice stood me in good stead."

Banging his goblet on the table, his father called out for more wine.

"Our news has made my father happy," Adair observed.

"Yes." She chewed her lip and her smile disappeared. "I don't think everyone here shares that joy."

"Of course they do—or they should."

"I can imagine Cormag saying it's part of the Normans' clever scheme to take over Scotland. You might have said the same thing about another Scot with a Norman wife, before we married."

"Aye," he answered, for he couldn't deny it.

"I think our child will turn out to be more Scot than Norman, though. After all, it will be raised here, among Scots."

Adair heard a hint of wistfulness in her voice. "Does that trouble you?"

She smiled, and the shadows fled from her bright blue eyes. "Not as much as it would have if I'd married Hamish Mac Glogan," she said in a way that made him want to kiss her.

So he did.

"Adair! People can see!" she protested.

"I don't care," he said, kissing her again. "And you kissed me in the field today."

"Losh, Adair!" Roban cried from his place at one of the near tables. "Can ye not wait until you're alone?"

"Nay, I can't. And if that's the way you feel, we'll take our leave."

He stood up, intending to go, but there was a bustle at the door and the men who played the pipes, tabor and whistle came into the hall.

"I'll go after I've had a dance with my wife," Adair declared, holding out his hand to lead her forward.

"Oh, no!" she cried as she got to her feet and moved swiftly around the table. "I'm not going to try to dance the way you Scots do, jumping about like you're treading on hot coals."

The slight annoyance he felt at her criticism disappeared as she went to stand beside the hearth in the center of the hall and addressed the musicians. "Play something slow, if you please."

She raised her voice so that everyone could hear. "I'm going to show you how the Normans dance."

Then she closed her eyes and began to sway to the music, her body as sinuous as a snake. She lifted first one hand, then the other, palm out, before she turned, doing a little hop-skip. She made a few delicate steps and turned the other way. She had an enticing little smile on her face and her dusky lashes fanned on her flushed cheeks. Her body undulated like a wave in a way he'd never seen a woman's body move before.

Adair would never have believed anything so simple could be so completely arousing if he hadn't witnessed it himself.

A quick survey showed that everybody else in the hall was staring at her, too. Roban was slack-jawed, and Lachlann looked as if he couldn't tear his gaze from her swaying hips. His father, mercifully, had dozed off, his head against the back of his chair.

"I think that's enough, Marianne," Adair said, hurrying toward her. "We get the sense of a Norman dance."

Marianne's eyes snapped open as the music stopped. "Have I done something wrong?"

"No," Adair said as he joined her. His voice dropped to a whisper. "I'd just rather you showed me how the Normans dance when we're alone."

She tilted her head and gave him a coy, yet knowing, smile. "All right."

He thought he'd die of desire right then and there. Instead, he picked her up and strode to the door, accompanied by cheers, laughter and cries to let Marianne stay.

His father roused and raised his head. "Take good care of the mother of my grandson, Adair, and apologize nicely," Seamus called out, his words slightly slurred.

Outside, the quarter moon, sometimes covered by scudding clouds, was still bright enough to light their way. The air was chill, and Marianne snuggled against her husband. "Was your father ordering you to apologize for telling everyone about the baby? You already have."

Her bold, brave husband blushed. "Oh, he probably thinks I should apologize every night just to prevent quarrels."

"I hope you're not annoyed with me about the dancing," she said as she fingered the edge of his broach. "I was only trying to show you the sort of dances I learned in Normandy."

Never had it seemed so far from the hall to their quarters. "I'm not annoyed."

"I want you to be proud of me."

"I am, although I'm surprised they'd teach anything like that in a convent. What was the place called, St. Seductia of the Swaying Hips?"

"The sisters couldn't watch us every minute of the day, although they did try."

"If we have a daughter, I'm not sending her to any convent. Heaven only knows what she might learn."

"Your father seems convinced our firstborn will be a boy. What if it's not? Will you be very disappointed?"

"A boy will please my father, and I can't deny I'd like sons, but a wee bonnie lass will be welcome, too," he said, envisioning a family of children with Marianne. "We'll just have to keep trying for sons, that's all."

They reached the *teach* at last. Adair shoved the door open with his shoulder and carried her inside, eagerly anticipating making love with her again. And again.

She slipped down from his arms, the sensation nearly enough to make him climax then and there, before she turned her back to him and moved her hair so that the pale nape of her neck was exposed. "Will you untie my laces?"

"With pleasure, my lady," he replied, attempting to control his raging passion. "Will you dance for me again?"

"With pleasure."

He slipped his finger in the laces and tugged gently, undoing the knot. Then he pulled the laces out of the holes, exposing her back.

"Are you finished?" she asked, holding the bodice of her gown to her breasts.

"Not quite," he said, his voice husky with desire. Putting his arms about her waist, he pulled her close and pressed his lips to the nape of her neck.

Holding her slipping gown against her breasts, she giggled. "That tickles."

"What about this?" he asked, sliding his lips lower.

She laughed. "You're still tickling."

"And here?"

She squirmed. "Not exactly." She jumped and whirled around. The gown slipped down a little more. "Did you just…lick me?"

He grinned with a mischievous glee. "Did you like it?"

"Perhaps," she replied, her eyes sparkling with mirth as she backed away from him. Her legs hit the bed and she lost her balance, falling onto it. Laughing, she held out one hand and with the other, pulled up her bodice. "Help me."

"Not yet," he said coming to stand between her knees, looking down at her hair spread across the black fur.

"You want me to lie here in this awkward position?"

"I want to look at your hair against the black fur

for a moment, with that red gown against your skin. Before I undress you."

"I see," she whispered, her eyes darkening, expectant and excited.

He put his hands on either side of her head and leaned down to kiss her again. Slowly. Leisurely.

Her arms wrapped about his neck, the movements as sinuous as when she danced, and she responded with the passion he'd come to expect, and crave.

Someone knocked on the door.

Adair raised his head. "Go away!"

The pounding continued.

With a low mutter of complaint, Adair shoved himself backward and strode to the door, flinging it open.

Dearshul stood in the dim moonlight, her face white, her eyes wide, her lips trembling. "You've got to come quick, Adair. It's your father. He got up from the table and fell down and we can't rouse him."

"Surely there's no need for you to fetch me," Adair said as Marianne sat up. "He had too much wine, that's all."

"Nay, it's not that," Dearshul said anxiously, looking past Adair to Marianne. "It's not from the drink. It's something else."

With a sick feeling of dread, Marianne reached back for the ends of her laces. "This is serious, Adair."

Her husband gave her a look of sudden, deep dismay. Then he pushed past Dearshul, who flattened herself against the frame of the door to let him go by.

Marianne shivered, and it wasn't only from the chill air coming in the open door.

"Help me with my gown, Dearshul, please," she said, trying not to believe her father-in-law, so healthy and vigorous only a short while ago, could be gravely ill now.

Dearshul sprang forward and grabbed the ends of the ties, pulling them tight with quick efficiency.

"How long ago did he fall?" Marianne asked as Dearshul knotted the laces.

"A moment after you left, my lady. He stood up, like I said, to excuse himself for a bit. He was laughing and clapping with the music, heading for the door, when he just…well, his knees seemed to give out. He didn't make a sound. Ceit and Lachlann tried to rouse him, but when they couldn't, they sent me for Adair."

Marianne remembered the older woman who had tended to her feet. "Has anyone gone for Beitiris?"

"Aye. Ceit sent Fionnaghal."

"Good." Marianne started for the door, with Dearshul following.

She couldn't be much help with the nursing, but she could see that Seamus was made comfortable. She could take charge of the servants. She could ensure that Adair and Lachlann weren't bothered, for they'd surely be worried about their father.

The whole fortress seemed hushed and expectant, as if even the buildings were waiting for word of the chieftain.

When she arrived at the hall, the serving women stood clustered in the corner, and even the usually efficient Ceit appeared as helpless and worried as any of the silent, subdued men huddled around the fallen Seamus. Looking bewildered and lost, wringing his hands, Barra was at his feet. Lachlann knelt beside the chieftain, while Adair cradled his father's head in his lap.

Adair raised his head. Their gazes met, and in his, she saw a tormented dread that wrenched her heart.

Yet no matter how upset she was, this was no time to be weak. Strength was needed—a woman's strength, the sort of strength that had nursed generations of men, women and children through illness and injury, childbirth and death.

So she strode down the hall like a conquering general. With a voice that didn't waver or give any hint of dismay, she began issuing orders. "When Beitiris arrives, she is to have anything she needs. Ceit, take some others and go to our *teach* and bring our braziers to Seamus's quarters. The candles, too, and any other candles or lamps you can find in the storerooms. I want the chieftain's chamber well lit and warm. Una, fetch an ewer of cool water, and the freshest bread for when the chieftain wakes. Isaebal, go and see that there is hot water ready, in case Beitiris needs it."

The woman hurried to obey, while the anxious men shuffled their feet and looked at her expectantly, as if they wanted to be told what to do, too.

She opened her mouth to order them to take Seamus to his *teach* when she recalled something her brother had told her on their journey from France, about a comrade-in-arms who had seemed well after a blow to the head, only to die later in the night. "Did Seamus strike his head when he fell?"

"I don't think so," Lachlann answered, his voice strained, his eyes anguished. "He was walking toward the door and his knees buckled and down he went."

"That's a relief," Marianne replied briskly. "His head probably isn't injured. Now we should take him to his own bed. Bring a bench and lay him on it."

The men sprang into action, except for Adair. He stayed with his father, holding him as gently as if Seamus were a slumbering child.

While the men fetched the bench, Marianne studied Seamus's face. He looked as though he was sleeping a deep sleep, except for one thing: the right side of his mouth was more relaxed than the left.

She'd heard of this—apoplexy. Often it led to death, but not always. Sometimes people survived, although they might be crippled afterward.

It was hard to imagine Seamus enfeebled, but surely that was better than death.

"Adair," she said softly, bending down to address him when Lachlann and Roban returned with the bench. "We must move him now."

Adair carefully lowered his father's head to the ground and dispatched Roban and Barra to bring torches. He himself took hold of his father's broad shoulders and helped lift him onto the bench. Then they were on their way, a silent procession with Seamus borne aloft as if this were his funeral.

Marianne glanced at Adair and hoped that notion hadn't struck him, too.

When they reached the chieftain's quarters, Beitiris and Fionnaghal were waiting. Fionnaghal shifted impatiently from foot to foot, while Beitiris, with a basket over her arm, stood still.

This would not be the first time Beitiris had been summoned for such a thing. She'd probably seen all manner of sickness and death.

"Put him down," Beitiris ordered.

The men did as she commanded. In the flickering light of the torches, Beitiris immediately bent over Seamus, examining his face. Touching his cheek. Raising his eyelid.

Seamus didn't stir, except to breathe.

"Inside," Beitiris snapped as she straightened, nodding at the door.

The men quickly moved to obey.

Was there nothing more she could say? Marianne thought with dismay. No suggestion of what had caused this? No hope that he could recover?

"Fionnaghal," she said, trying not to let her distress overwhelm her. "Go to the hall and see that the food is cleared away and the tables taken down. Ceit is too busy with other things."

Fionnaghal nodded. "Aye, my lady," she said immediately, and without so much as a hint of protest before setting off for the hall.

Marianne moved closer to Beitiris. "Seamus… is he…?"

"It's early yet, my lady."

"I thought it best to bring him here, to his own *teach,* where it would be quieter. I hope that wasn't wrong."

"No. Here is better than the hall for a sick man."

"You'll have anything you need to tend to him. And any servants you require."

"Thank you, my lady. I'll do my best," Beitiris replied as she turned to enter the chieftain's *teach.*

Marianne put her hand on Beitiris's arm. "Is there any hope?" she asked quietly, unable to hide her dread.

A look of sympathy appeared on the old woman's wrinkled face. "There's always hope while there's life, my lady. I've seen men live who should have died twice, and men who had little more than a cough go down in a day. Sickness and death are mysteries we can't hope to understand." She gave Marianne a small smile. "Your father-in-law's a *braw,* healthy man, and that's to the good."

Finding some relief in Beitiris's words, Marianne thanked her and sent up a brief, fervent prayer that God would spare Seamus.

After Beitiris entered the *teach,* the men began to file out. Marianne stood in the shadows, watching and waiting for her husband.

Adair still hadn't come out when Lachlann approached her. He took hold of her hands and pressed them between his, gazing sadly into her face. "Lady, I…"

Too full of emotion, he could say no more, and only shook his head.

"Marianne?"

She pulled her hands free and hurried to her husband, who was standing in the open door of his father's *teach*. It closed behind him with a dull thud when she reached him.

"Oh, Adair," she murmured, embracing him, his body warm against her cheek.

He made no effort to hold her.

"Beitiris wouldn't say a word except to order us from the *teach*," he muttered.

Beneath his frustration, she could sense a fear she shared.

"So that she could do her work without a lot of people getting in the way, I expect," Marianne replied, trying to offer him a comforting explanation, and hoping she was right. "Before she went in, she gave me cause to think your father would recover. He is, as she said, a very healthy man."

Adair let out his breath in a great rush, as if he'd been holding it since Dearshul had appeared at their *teach*. "Then I'll try to be hopeful, too."

Marianne managed a little smile. "We should have faith in her skill, and your father's vitality."

"Beitiris *is* skilled."

"Whatever she put on my feet healed them almost overnight," Marianne reminded him as she slipped her arm through his.

"That's true. I'd forgotten."

She shivered and leaned against him. "Let's go back to our *teach*. If there's any news, I'm sure Beitiris will send someone to tell us."

He nodded. "Aye. There's nothing I can do here."

"I understand older people have spells sometimes, a dizziness and swooning," Marianne said as she walked beside him across the yard. "I remember old Sister Mary used to complain of them regularly, and she lived to be over eighty years old. Your father's surely nowhere near eighty. Or perhaps it's the start of an illness, something that requires a potion or some herbs to make him better.

"Maybe it was something he ate, or too much of that drink you Scots make. It tasted very potent. Perhaps all he requires is sleep, or maybe a purgative will make him better. Sometimes food can make people very sick."

She was babbling, her voice falsely cheerful, but she couldn't help it. She wanted to reassure Adair, and herself, that Seamus would be well, and saying such things seemed a way to stave off the worst of her fears.

She thought she was succeeding, until they were alone in their *teach*. Then Adair's head lowered and his shoulders slumped, and she realized that his confident strides as they'd crossed the yard had been as false as her good cheer.

Sitting on the bed, he put his face in his hands and his voice dropped to a strangled whisper. "Oh, God, Marianne, my father's going to die."

"Don't talk nonsense!" she cried as she hurried to embrace her husband. "He's robust and healthy for his age. He'll get better. You'll see."

Again, she tried to sound far less worried than she

was, for she wanted to offer him all the comfort she could. "While he lives, we must have hope, Adair. And pray."

"Pray? Why should I pray?" her husband demanded, jumping to his feet and striding toward the window. "God struck him down—the finest, best man in Scotland."

It was blasphemy, but the blasphemy of a man in pain. She ran to her husband and embraced him. "We should pray because we can't know the will of God. Because there is nothing else we can do, and perhaps God will listen."

"And if He doesn't?"

"Then we'll know it was time for Seamus to go to heaven. Maybe God wants to confer with the finest, best man in Scotland."

As Adair looked down at her, the anguish in his eyes smote her to the core. Then he slowly, awkwardly, knelt at her feet. "Will you help me?"

She couldn't have denied that request for anything. And as she knelt beside him, she realized something more.

She loved Adair Mac Taran with all her heart. She cherished her strong, trustworthy husband and wanted to protect him from whatever blows life might send his way. He was more dear to her than anyone, even her own kin.

Adair clasped his hands and looked at her. "I'm not much good at praying," he said, his voice rough. "I've always left it to holier men. And I have no head for Latin."

"I don't think God cares what words we use. It's the praying that matters," she answered, the realization of her love a balm to her worst fears for Seamus.

She pressed her palms together and closed her eyes. "Dear Father in Heaven," she began, "we humbly beg you to spare the life of Seamus Mac Taran, a good man, a wise leader, a beloved father."

As she continued, the formality of the prayers she'd heard at the convent gave way to her own heartfelt pleas. "Please, God, don't take him yet. We need him here awhile to lead us, like the good man he is. Our land is divided, war may be looming and we need men such as Seamus to keep the peace. Please, God, don't take him away from us. Don't take him from his people and his sons." Her voice broke and she could only manage a whisper. "Don't take him away from me, either."

Adair gathered her in his arms. He held her tenderly and stroked her hair as she wept on his shoulder. "Don't cry, *m'eudail*," he murmured. "Please, don't cry. I believe what you said. He'll be well, *m'eudail*. He'll be well."

She drew back and wiped her eyes. "I should be comforting *you*."

Adair's lips curved up in a small, woeful smile. "We can comfort each other." He rose and held out his hand to help her stand. "I didn't realize my father meant so much to you."

"He does—a great deal," she answered truthfully, realizing how deep her affection for Adair's father had grown. "You called me *m'eudail*. What does that mean?"

"My love."

Adair Mac Taran didn't lie, either with words or expression. As she looked into his eyes, they confirmed the truth of his words. He loved her, and her aching heart rejoiced. However her marriage had come about, whether it was destiny or fate or God's good grace that had brought her here, to this place and this man, she didn't know. But she was grateful. "Adair, I—"

The door to their *teach* burst open.

"Adair!" Lachlann cried, his face full of dismay. "She sent me. Beitiris. She says you must come…that…you must…"

Adair grabbed Marianne's hand, his grip cold and strong as a vice. There could be no mistaking the meaning of that urgent, stammered summons.

Nevertheless, Marianne desperately begged God to spare Seamus as they rushed to the chieftain's *teach*.

But Beitiris's grim expression confirmed Marianne's worst fears, and told her God had already decided.

Adair understood at once, too, and with a groan, he threw himself on his knees beside his father's bed. He laid his head beside him, his arm about the older man's chest.

Lachlann, who'd followed them, went to the opposite side of the bed with slower, more measured steps. With sorrowful eyes, he looked down at his father and his brother.

Beitiris retreated to a corner. Marianne stayed close to the door. This was their family, their grief, and although she shared it, it wasn't the same.

A dog started to howl. Adair stiffened, and so did Lachlann and Beitiris.

Marianne remembered a story one of the young nuns used to tell on dark, stormy nights when the wind howled about the convent walls—of how dogs could foretell a death.

Then another dog joined the first, and another, until it seemed a veritable chorus of howls churned the night air like the final verdict, the absolute confirmation that Seamus wasn't going to live.

Only a few moments later, Seamus gave a great sigh, as if he were about to wake up. Instead, as his breath left his body, he slipped from this life to the next.

Hunched over, still embracing his father, Adair's shoulders started to shake. Marianne rushed to his side, kneeling and holding him close, her face against her husband's broad, quivering back. Lachlann shifted and she looked up at him, expecting to see tears on his cheeks, too.

His expression was sorrowful, but in the light of the several candles, she saw another emotion in his hazel eyes, one that shocked and confused her.

Triumph.

Yet it was gone as soon as the word to describe it came to her, and his expression became anguished.

Her tear-filled eyes must have deceived her, she

thought, desperately hoping she was wrong, even though she knew death changed many things.

Beitiris stepped out of the shadows bearing a small, flat dish of salt that she reverently placed on Seamus's still chest. As she moved back, she reached out to touch him, the gesture almost a caress.

"I'll go tell the people, the clan," Lachlann said, his voice heavy with sadness as he, too, gently stroked his father's arm before stepping away.

She had to be mistaken, in her grief seeing emotions that didn't exist. No one could be pleased that a man like Seamus was dead.

Adair drew in a ragged breath and wiped his eyes with his sleeve before he got to his feet. He looked grimly determined, once more the warrior and not the grieving son. "That is for me to do, Lachlann. Please take Marianne back to our *teach.* I'll speak to you afterward about what needs to be done."

Then he, too, touched his father's arm and, with a silent nod of farewell, left the *teach,* too distraught to close the door behind him despite the cold night air. She went to shut it, until a sharp look from Beitiris stopped her.

What did it all mean, the salt and the caresses and not closing the door?

Whatever beliefs the Scots had, she assumed there was something common to all when it came to death: the preparation for burial.

"I'll help you," she said to Beitiris, even as a great weariness began to overtake her.

Beitiris shook her head and Marianne was suddenly sure that if Beitiris hadn't heard of her condition, she had guessed.

"Not you, my lady," Beitiris said, not unkindly. "We'll manage, Dearshul and me. You touch him, then go and rest."

Marianne had never touched a dead person, and she didn't want to now.

"It's to keep him from haunting you in your dreams," Lachlann explained in French.

"I don't think Seamus would haunt anybody."

Lachlann shrugged. "Perhaps not—who can say? We do it to be sure."

Since it was their custom, Marianne put aside her reluctance and went forward. She gazed down at Seamus's face. Despite everything, he'd been kind to her. He'd been her ally here, when he could very well have been her worst enemy. He was a good man, and a wise one.

"May you rest in the peace you've earned," she whispered as she laid her hand on his arm.

Then she turned away, glad to be spared having to see him like this any longer. She wanted to remember Seamus as he was, alive and vital, laughing with joy at the thought of being a grandfather.

"Lean on me, Marianne," Lachlann said softly, and with great gentleness.

Surely she was wrong to suspect him of anything except grief.

Holding on to her brother-in-law, she left the chamber, and Beitiris to her task.

"The door is open for his spirit to leave," Lachlann explained before she asked. "She'll be opening the windows, too."

She'd thought the Scots were heathens, and it seemed in some ways they were—or perhaps they merely clung to the old, familiar traditions as a way to remember who they were in a changing world. "Why did Beitiris put the salt on him?"

"To keep away the devil."

The fortress was deathly silent, the quiet broken only by the continuing howls of the dogs, as if in lament. Not a person stirred, except the men on guard, and they seemed inexpressibly weary, weighed down by the news.

"I am so sorry this happened, Lachlann," Marianne said when they reached her quarters. "I liked your father very much."

"He was a fine man," Lachlann replied, loss and pain in every word.

Clearly she *had* been horribly wrong to think he derived anything but sorrow from his father's death. "What happens now, Lachlann? I don't know how you…I don't know your customs."

"You're cold. Let's go inside and I'll tell you."

Don't be alone with him.

The thought came swiftly, unbidden, but hard to ignore.

Yet if she was to rid herself completely of her suspicions, she should take this opportunity to speak with him. "Very well."

When they entered, Lachlann looked around him in awe. "This is…amazing."

"A few simple comforts, that's all," Marianne said, facing him. "You were going to tell me about your customs."

Lachlann gestured at one of the stools, inviting her to sit.

As if it were his *teach,* not hers. It could be courtesy, she supposed, yet the action struck her as patronizing, even a bit arrogant. On the other hand, he'd just lost his father, so surely it was unkind to make judgments based on his actions now.

"Men will keep a vigil over my…the body," Lachlann said as he sat opposite her. "For three days."

A vigil for a warrior lord. Of course.

"As eldest son—and being Adair—your husband will likely stay with him for the entire time."

"Without sleep?"

"As little as possible."

"I see. And what should I do?"

"Arrange the feast after the burial. We'll eat and drink and remember my father, and Barra will recite my father's lineage. Then there will be singing and dancing." He gave her a sad little smile. "You dance well, my lady. I hope you'll do so again."

"Not at such a time," she replied. It may be their custom, but it was one she wasn't willing to participate in, at least not yet. "When will Adair be acknowledged as the new chieftain?"

"There's nothing formal, if that's what you mean. Once my father died, Adair became thane and chieftain. He's already sworn his loath of loyalty to the king. He did it before my father named him heir, or he wouldn't have been accepted. My father would have chosen another."

"Like Cormag? Is that why he's so bitter?"

Lachlann shook his head. "Cormag would never have been chosen, and only he believes otherwise. If you have any trouble with him and Adair isn't nearby, please call on me. Cormag can be an insolent dog sometimes."

"He'll heed you?"

"I'm his cousin."

"Thank you, Lachlann." She regarded her brother-in-law steadily. "Do you believe Cormag might cause serious trouble for Adair?"

"They don't like each other, God knows, but Adair is chieftain now, and I expect Cormag to give Adair the respect he deserves." Lachlann reached out and patted her hand. "Try not to worry about Cormag and Adair."

"You'll probably have to stand between them sometimes, the way your father did."

Lachlann shrugged. "Aye."

Marianne entwined her fingers in her lap. "I appreciate that, Lachlann, and I know keeping the peace between two fractious relatives isn't nearly as easy as some people think. Before my brothers left home and I went to the convent, I sometimes had to come between them, or try to, before they hurt each other. It was a difficult, thankless task."

Lachlann gave her a grateful smile. "I hope my brother appreciates what a jewel you are."

"I'm not a jewel. I'm just someone like you, with relatives who quarrel frequently. I wouldn't be surprised to learn that you sometimes had to stand between your father and your brother, too."

She could read nothing in Lachlann's expression as he replied. "Sometimes."

"More often than you'd like, though, I'm sure. It's difficult being in such a position in one's own family and really, not at all fair. I daresay many times you thought you'd done nothing to be thrust into such a situation except been born, and you couldn't help that."

"Exactly," Lachlann replied, his smile growing. "You're a wise woman, Marianne."

"I always resented having to play the peacemaker."

Lachlann rose and took hold of her hands, pulling her to her feet.

What was he doing?

Holding her hands loosely, he looked down at her, his expression mournful. "Beautiful and wise, too. You're wasted here in Lochbarr, Marianne. You should be at the king's court, married to a great and wealthy nobleman."

Very uncomfortable now, she tugged her hands free. "My brother would agree with you about the wealthy part, anyway," she answered, wanting Lachlann gone. "But as that hasn't happened, I'm getting used to living here. With your brother. My husband."

Lachlann's eyes didn't betray so much as a flicker

of guilt. Perhaps his actions had been innocent, after all, and she was finding cause for suspicion where there was none. "Will you leave me now, please, Lachlann? I'm very tired."

"Of course," he said, immediately going to the door. He gave her another woeful look. "I'd tell you to sleep well, but I doubt any of us will sleep soundly tonight."

After he left, Marianne lowered herself onto the stool and rubbed the back of her neck, trying to decide if she truly had cause to suspect that her brother-in-law was pleased that his father was dead. Yet surely she had to be wrong. Surely she would have noticed something before this....

"What was Lachlann doing here?"

Marianne rose as Adair entered. "Explaining your burial customs."

His shoulders relaxed. "Ah."

"What else?"

Adair went to the bucket of water and splashed his face.

"Adair!"

As he wiped his face with the cloth, she snatched it from his hand. "I know you're full of grief, but so am I and even so, I won't countenance that sort of accusation."

"I didn't accuse you of anything."

"No, but you were thinking it!"

"What was I thinking?"

"That it was unseemly for Lachlann and me to be here alone together," she answered indignantly. "I

wanted to know about your customs. It was cold outside. We came inside, and he told me. There was
nothing more—"

Her breath caught as another thought came to
her, one that completely altered her thinking. "Or do
you have reason to suspect Lachlann of being less
than honorable?"

"God, no," Adair retorted, striding toward the
stool and sitting heavily. "I'm sorry. I don't know
what I'm saying."

He put his head in his heads. "Right now, I don't
know anything except that my father is dead. You
have every right to be angry. You've done nothing,
and I'm acting like a jealous idiot. And over Lachlann, too. I must be going mad."

"Not mad," she assured him, kneeling beside him
and wrapping her arms about him. "You're upset and
grieving. I understand."

He lowered his hands and looked into her eyes.
"You're as wise as my father thought. Barra tells me
he said you were the cleverest woman he'd ever met,
and the bravest." He tried to smile, his lips trembling. "I know you are, *m'eudail*."

Her heart was too full of both love and grief to
reply right away.

Suddenly a horrified look came to his face and he
scrambled to his feet. "You shouldn't be kneeling on
the ground! You might fall ill," he cried, helping her
to stand.

"I'm fine."

"I couldn't bear it if anything happened to you,

too," he said, holding her close, as if he was afraid she might disappear. Or wander off, never to return.

"I won't leave you, Adair. You're my husband, and I love you."

"What did you say?"

"I love you," she replied, as sincere as she'd ever been about anything in her life.

"Oh, *m'eudail,*" he whispered, his eyes shining as he held her tight.

They embraced for a long moment, neither moving or speaking, until Adair pulled away. "I have to go, Marianne."

"I know. Lachlann told me there'll be a vigil for three days and that you'd probably stay the whole time."

"It's my duty, Marianne. One last duty to my father, so I must go. They'll have him in the kirk by now."

He went to the chest and got his long gray cloak.

In spite of Lachlann's reassurances, and Dearshul's, too, she couldn't let him leave without asking the question that had been preying on her mind. "Adair, will all the clansmen accept you as chieftain without question?"

There wasn't a hint of doubt in his face or voice when he answered. "Aye."

"You trust them, then? All of them?"

"Aye," he replied as he put on his cloak, adjusting it about his shoulders. He picked up his *claimh mor* that had been leaning against the chest.

"Even Cormag, when he returns?"

Holding his scabbard, the hilt of his sword gleaming in the light, Adair spoke without hesitation. "Even Cormag. He hates me, and I hate him, but he'd never betray me, or his clan. Loyalty's in our blood, Marianne, like the land under our feet. There are few things in this world I'm sure of, but that would be one of them."

He gathered her into his arms for one brief kiss. "Until my last duty to my father is done, *m'eudail*," he whispered.

When he was gone, Marianne thought about Lachlann, and Cormag, and the people of Lochbarr. The looks, the whispered words, the disgruntled way some of the men watched Adair as he walked by.

"Oh, Adair," she murmured as she sank down on the bed. "I hope you're right."

CHAPTER FIFTEEN

ACCOMPANIED BY THE MOURNFUL DIRGE played on their strange wind instrument, led by the same priest who'd performed the blessing of her marriage, Marianne walked in the funeral procession of Seamus Mac Taran as it made its long, slow way toward the loch. The sun shone weakly through the clouds, and mist shrouded both the upper reaches of the surrounding hills and the surface of the lake.

Barra walked behind the wooden bier carried by six men, including Adair and Lachlann. Followed by the warriors of the clan, the *seanachie* loudly recited the long and proud lineage of Seamus Mac Taran.

Shivering and holding her dark-brown cloak tighter about her, Marianne was among the women of the household who came next. Ceit and Fionnaghal wailed and keened, their voices loud and plaintive. Behind them came the people of the village of Lochbarr, grim-faced and silent.

Marianne made no sound as she watched her husband. He walked with his head bent, as if he carried more than the weight of his father on his shoulders.

His eyes were bloodshot and red-rimmed, and his face haggard.

Lachlann looked a bit better than Adair, but he was likewise exhausted and pale from lack of sleep. To her relief, he'd done nothing since his father's death to raise more suspicions, nor had he tried to speak to her alone. She'd obviously been upset and over-wrought when she doubted his loyalty and feared that he wasn't quite what she'd been led to believe.

Unfortunately, she had no such comforting thoughts about Cormag, who'd returned the day before with the man sent to fetch him, their beasts sweat-slicked and foaming from the long, arduous ride.

At last the procession reached the wharf. Dearshul had explained that all the thanes and chieftains of Clan Mac Taran had their final resting place on the small island out in the loch. It would be peaceful, Marianne supposed, with only the calls of the birds to disturb their final rest.

Once Seamus's body was in the boat, along with the priest, piper and six men accompanying it, the women, Barra and the rest of the pipers fell silent. As they watched the boat pull away from the wharf to make its way across the calm waters of the loch, Marianne spotted an eagle circling. It was like seeing Seamus's spirit soaring—a minstrel's notion, perhaps, but a comforting one.

When the boat disappeared around the island, she turned to Dearshul and the other women. "Come. We'll make certain all is ready for when they return."

She led the subdued women back to the hall, where those involved in the cooking went off to the kitchen. Marianne had only to ensure that the tables, benches and goblets were ready, and since they were, she sat down to wait, leaning her head in her hand. She hadn't had much sleep either. She'd lain awake for a long time every night, wondering about Adair's brother and Cormag and these people she couldn't really understand....

She awoke with a start when the door to the hall banged open. Sitting up straight, she rubbed her weary eyes as Adair strode inside, followed by his brother and Cormag, and then the other men.

There was relief in her husband's face as he approached her, as if the worst was over. She hoped it was.

She was about to rise and go to meet him when Lachlann came to a halt. "Adair!"

The word was like a challenge, a slap to the face.

Cold fear gripped her heart as her husband turned on his heel to look at his brother, now standing so defiant beside the hearth, with a sneering Cormag beside him. Everything about their attitude told her she'd been right about Lachlann and Cormag, and Adair seriously, grievously wrong.

Where was Roban? And Adair's other friends? She didn't see any of them in the group facing her husband.

Hands on his hips, Adair cocked his head, apparently simply puzzled. "What?"

Lachlann instinctively stepped back. Cormag didn't move.

"Well?" Adair said, his tone impatient, but not worried. "If you've got something to say that's so important I can't sit down to hear it, out with it."

Could he not see the difference in their attitude? Did he not sense that this was open defiance, perhaps even a challenge to his leadership?

Lachlann reddened. "I don't think the women need to hear clan business."

Marianne wasn't about to be sent away. "I'm not going anywhere," she said firmly. "You can't dismiss me like a child."

Her husband gave her a swift, questioning glance, but he didn't tell her to go. Instead, he addressed his brother.

"What do you have to say to me, Lachlann?" he repeated, his voice stern and, finally, wary.

When Lachlann hesitated, Cormag stepped forward. "We don't want you for chieftain."

"I was chosen by the clan," Adair replied, the only sign of his rising temper the slight flushing of his face. "Are you questioning their decision?"

"Aye, we are."

Adair regarded his brother. "Are you in agreement with Cormag?" he demanded.

Oh, Adair, she wanted to cry. *He's not like you. He's not loyal like you. Trustworthy and honest and honorable like you.*

Recovering his bravado, Lachlann straightened his shoulders. "I agree with them. You're too impetuous, too stubborn and too selfish to think of the clan before your own needs and desires. That woman beside you is proof of that."

"So you wish to call a meeting of the clansmen to debate their choice?"

"No," Cormag declared. "We're telling you to get out of Lochbarr and take that Norman wife of yours with you."

Adair's eyes flared with surprise, then scorn. "You would put yourself above the other clansmen?" He looked at Lachlann. "You know this isn't how this should be done."

"We won't wait for that," Cormag said, reaching back and drawing his *claimh mor*. "Your time as chieftain is over, Adair. Get out of Lochbarr."

Adair stared incredulously at Lachlann, who also unsheathed his long sword. So did the men behind him. "You threaten your thane and chieftain with death? That's no different than treason against the king."

Lachlann pushed his way past Cormag. "You won't be hurt, either you or Marianne. You'll be free to leave and—"

"Traitor!" Adair bellowed, his voice rumbling through the hall like thunder breaking upon the mountains. She'd never heard a man so angry, not even Nicholas. "Do you think I'd leave Lochbarr to *you* after this? You ought to die of shame right now!"

"Traitor?" Lachlann charged. "You call me a traitor? You're the one who went after a Norman woman and brought her here. What have you *ever* done to deserve being chieftain, except being born first, and comely?"

"I'm glad our father's dead," Adair said, his angry gaze sweeping over the men facing him before coming to rest on his traitorous brother once more. "I'm thankful he's not alive to see this shameful, disloyal act."

"And if he were, we all know what he'd say," Lachlann hotly replied. "You could never do any wrong in his eyes. The angriest he ever got was over that woman, yet even then, what did he do? Did he cast you out of the clan? Did he so much as utter harsh words? No. He forgave you, *again*. He even made the marriage out to be an advantage, all because he loved you so much, he wouldn't see the truth—that you've endangered us all with your selfish lust. Well, we won't wait for you to bring a Norman army down on our head."

"What Norman army?" Marianne demanded, no longer able to keep silent. "Has anyone spotted one on its way? My brother is not making a war over my marriage." She gestured at the other men. "Is that how you're getting these men to support you, by lying to them? Because if anybody brings a Norman army down upon Lochbarr, it will be *you* with this traitorous act. By trying to usurp my husband's position as chieftain, you are also acting against the sister of Sir Nicholas de Beauxville. Whoever attacks us will have to deal with *him*."

She hoped.

Seeing the doubt and dismay blooming in Lachlann's eyes, and in spite of what Nicholas had said and done after her marriage, she pressed on. "Do you think Scots are the only families who fight among themselves, yet unite when threatened? Do you think my brother won't come to my aid if I tell him you're trying to rob my husband and me of our rightful places? If you believe that, you don't know Nicholas, or the Normans. My brother will fight you with all the men and arms at his disposal to insure that doesn't happen. *You'll* be the one who starts an open war, not Adair."

"That's a lie," Cormag snarled, all but shoving Lachlann out of his way. "Your brother doesn't give a damn about you, and we all know it."

"Are you willing to gamble your lives on that?" she asked, seeing the other men's confidence flagging as they exchanged wary glances. She turned to Lachlann. "As for what Adair's done, what have you done except prove that you're not worthy to be Adair's brother and your father's son? Adair would have died for you and every man of this clan, simply because you *are* his clan. *That's* what makes him fit to be chieftain. Yes, he's impetuous and rash—but he's not sly and deceitful. He's honest and trustworthy, incapable of lying—not like *you*."

She addressed the clansmen. "Which would you rather have for a leader, a man who acts because of the dictates of his noble heart, or one who'll draw a weapon against his lawful thane, his chieftain, and his brother?"

Before anyone could speak, and regarding his

brother with a stern and grim expression, Adair stepped toward Lachlann, and when he spoke, it wasn't with red-hot rage, but with a cold deliberation that seemed yet more awesome, and terrible. "If you want to lead this clan, Lachlann, you're going to have to kill me. You won't succeed, so I'll give you one chance to turn around and walk out of Lochbarr, never to return while I or my wife or my children live."

Gritting his teeth, his hand gripping his sword, Lachlann shook his head as the men behind him moved forward. "I'll give *you* one last chance to walk out of Lochbarr, Adair," he replied. "Never to return."

The door to the hall burst open and Roban ran into the hall, followed by some of Adair's friends. For a moment, Marianne joyfully thought help was at hand, until she realized how few in number they were.

"What mischief's afoot, Adair?" Roban demanded. "Who decided on three patrols this morning, and most of our friends among them?"

"This traitor," Adair replied, not for an instant taking his eyes off Lachlann.

Roban's brow furrowed as he drew his *claimh mor* from the sheath on his back. "It's like that, is it?"

"Aye, it is," Lachlann replied, likewise not taking his gaze from his brother's face. "And if you're smart—"

Cormag lunged for Adair.

Marianne screamed and threw herself in front of

her husband. Lachlann shouted and Roban charged forward. Cormag roughly shoved Marianne aside. She fell hard on her knees while Adair, snarling like an angry wolf, pulled his *claimh mor* from its sheath and charged his cousin.

Cormag avoided Adair's blow, but as her husband recovered, ready to strike again, Lachlann leapt at him.

Someone grabbed Marianne around the waist and pulled her backward. A rough, callused hand clamped over her mouth.

She struggled and kicked and fought as she was dragged backward toward the door to the yard, away from the fight, and her husband. She twisted and turned, trying desperately to break free, but the arms holding her were too strong.

Her assailant dragged her toward the chieftain's empty *teach*. Where were the sentries at the gate?

Her captor shouldered open the door to Seamus's empty quarters, then threw her inside. As Marianne stumbled to her feet, the door closed.

"Let me go!" she shouted as she turned, ready to fight to get away and back to the hall, and Adair.

She gasped at the sight of Fionnaghal barring the door. "You! Are you in league with them?"

"No," Fionnaghal answered, but not moving, either. "I still think it would have been better if Adair hadn't married you, but what Lachlann is doing is worse."

"Then let me out of here! I have to go back to Adair!"

"Do you want to be killed, too?"

Marianne didn't care about any danger to herself. "I have to go to Adair!"

Fionnaghal moved so that her back was up against the door. "And do what? You'll only get yourself killed—or raped."

Marianne started forward. "That won't happen. Adair and his men—"

"Are outnumbered."

"They'll still win!"

"No, they won't."

"I won't hide in here like a coward!"

Fionnaghal put her hands on her hips. "If Adair's wounded or killed and Cormag finds you, what do you think he'll do?"

"Nothing," she returned, telling herself it would never come to that. "I'm still Lachlann's sister-in-law. He won't dare to harm me."

Frowning, Fionnaghal swore under her breath. "*Gomeral,* Cormag and those others will never listen to Lachlann, no matter what they've said to his face about being the chieftain. They'll do what they want, and he won't be able to stop them."

Marianne felt sick, because she knew Fionnaghal was probably right. Lachlann wouldn't be able to control Cormag. But it wouldn't matter. Adair would defeat them.

"You heard what Roban said. Lachlann sent out most of Adair's friends on patrol. I don't doubt he left Roban and a few others behind in case it came to a fight. This way, he can kill them, too, and claim his men were only defending themselves."

"Defending themselves from what? They're traitors who've attacked their chieftain."

"They'll say Adair flew into a rage and drew his dirk on Lachlann first because he was jealous over his wife."

"What?" Marianne cried. Then she remembered Adair's moment of jealousy the night Seamus died, when Lachlann had been with her in the *teach*. Perhaps some people would believe that.

Fionnaghal looked at Marianne as if she was dim. "It's no secret Adair cares for you and he's got a fiery temper. So when Adair's friends return, Lachlann will claim Adair made jealous accusations and attacked him. He had no choice except to defend himself. Then it got to be a bigger fight."

A cold shiver of suspicion ran down Marianne's back. "How do you know their plans?"

"Because I made it my business to find out, and Cormag is a boastful braggart who can't keep his mouth shut when he beds a woman."

Fionnaghal smirked when she saw the look on Marianne's face. "It's a doughty woman who can beat me at anything, so I decided Adair had done well after all to wed you. It was no secret that Cormag was discontented and bitter with it, but Adair and his father have always been too honorable themselves to believe their own kin would move against them. I didn't share that notion, so I thought I'd find out what Cormag might do. And I did."

If she'd known.... "Why didn't you warn us?"

"Because I didn't know when or where or how he'd make his move. I thought I had time to find out more, and I didn't know that Lachlann was with him, or that they had so many men willing to side with them. Still, I'm sorry I didn't tell you what I heard."

Marianne wished she had, too, but that was in the past. "These other men out on patrol are Adair's friends. Surely they won't believe Lachlann."

"Lachlann wasn't able to convince all those with him now he'd be a better, wiser chieftain because Adair is sweet-tempered and thoughtful."

Oh, God help them, she was right. Yet even so, there had to be a way.... "Adair will beat them," she said, once again starting for the door. "He's too fine a fighter—"

Again Fionnaghal blocked her way, this time spreading her arms wide so there could be no mistake that she meant to keep Marianne there. "Can you not see that you've got to think of yourself now, and the bairn?"

The baby. She'd forgotten about the baby.

"Now that we've got our breath, it's time to run. There's a way through the palisade at the back and a path to the hills we can take. We can hide there and think about what to do after."

Marianne didn't want to leave Lochbarr while Adair was still fighting, but for the sake of their unborn child, she must. "Adair will surely find—"

The door crashed open, knocking Fionnaghal to

her knees. Then Cormag strode into the chamber, his broadsword in his hands. "So, this is where the bird's flown."

As Fionnaghal staggered to her feet, Marianne summoned her courage and her dignity, and pointed imperiously at the open door. "Get out!"

Cormag merely smiled a cold, cruel smile. "You should have more care, Norman," he said. "You can't order me, not when your husband's dead."

Every muscle in Marianne's chest clenched and she couldn't breathe.

But she mustn't—she wouldn't—believe him. "You're lying."

"Lachlann killed him, ran him through with his dirk, like sticking a pig."

"Liar!"

Out of the corner of her eye, Marianne saw Fionnaghal sidling to the door. Leaving her to her fate.

"Lachlann's the chieftain now," Cormag said.

"He'll *never* be chieftain."

Cormag laughed, coming closer. "Of course Seamus's younger son will be chieftain. He's a clever one, if not so fine a fighter. 'Twas his idea to steal the cattle, to make it look like the Normans were raiding ours."

"Why?" she demanded, backing away.

"To spur his father to go to the king. Seamus was too peaceable by far."

"Lachlann wants a war with the Normans?"

"He wants power, and he wants Dunkeathe. When he has the Norman's land, I get Lochbarr."

"You've betrayed your clan for greed and ambition?"

"What else? Honor and glory? That's for fools like Adair."

"Or men who understand what honor and glory mean," Marianne charged. Her back hit the wall and she could go no farther. "And once you've got Lochbarr, will you be content with it, or will you want Dunkeathe, too?"

"You're a clever lass," Cormag replied with a smile that made her feel sick. "I'll let little Lachlann pretend to rule the roost awhile, until Dunkeathe is back in Scots' hands."

"As you say, Lachlann's clever, Cormag," she said, keeping her gaze on her husband's cousin, trying to determine how and where to attack.

His shirt was open, exposing the dip in the collarbone, where there was no muscle. A weak spot, and if she could jab him there with her fingers, it would be enough to shock him.

She'd have to be close to him, though, and keep her hands free and in front of her. She raised and clasped them as if she was going to beg for mercy. "Lachlann will see what you plan and surely get rid of you first."

Splaying his left hand on the wall beside her, Cormag leaned close. "If it comes to a fight between Lachlann and me, who do you think would win?" He put the tip of his blade on her cheek. "If it comes to a fight between ye and me, who do you think will win?"

In one swift move, she unclasped her hands and jabbed hard at his throat.

As he coughed and lost his balance, Marianne shoved him backward, making him stumble. He grabbed the back of her skirt as she ran past him. Hearing the fabric tear, not caring if he ripped the gown right off her, she kept trying to get away.

Then, with a shriek, coming as if from nowhere, Fionnaghal launched herself at Cormag, knocking him to the ground and falling on top of him.

Her dress free, Marianne fell. Although on her knees, she turned, ready to join the fight.

Cormag had kept hold of his knife. Marianne screamed a warning to Fionnaghal just as he thrust it upward, into the woman's chest.

Fionnaghal gasped, then went limp.

"You bastard!" Marianne cried as he struggled to throw off Fionnaghal's body. "You bloody bastard!"

"What's going on in here?" a man asked sternly.

For one brief, wonderful moment, she thought Adair had come.

Then she saw Lachlann, his shirt bloody, his red-stained knife still in his hand, standing in the doorway.

"Traitor!" she cried as she scrambled to her feet. "Where's my husband?"

Lachlann didn't answer her. Instead, he looked at Cormag. "What have you done?"

Cormag heaved Fionnaghal's body off. "She attacked me. They both attacked me."

Lachlann's brow lowered. "And I can guess why.

You'll not touch my brother's widow again, do you understand?"

His brother's widow.

He sounded so sure, so certain, as if it were an incontrovertible fact.

She couldn't breathe. Couldn't think.

His brother's widow. Adair was dead. Her bold, brave, honorable husband was dead.

As she stared at his murderer, sick and weak, a great blackness blotted out the light coming in through the door, like a huge gaping hole in the fabric of the world.

She tumbled into it and was lost.

"LADY? MY LADY?"

Marianne groggily recognized Dearshul's soft voice and slowly realized someone was gently cradling her head and holding a cool cup to her lips.

She didn't open her eyes. She didn't want to wake, because Adair was dead.

"My lady? Oh, God save us, my lady, *please* wake up."

Dearshul sounded so desperate.

And there was the child, growing in her womb. Adair's child. His legacy. The child who deserved a father, cruelly, basely taken.

By a traitor.

She couldn't let a traitor triumph.

Marianne opened her eyes. Although she knew Dearshul was there, she more than half expected to see Lachlann looming above her like an evil spirit.

He wasn't.

"Oh, thank God!" Dearshul cried, tears welling in her eyes. "Are you hurt, my lady? Did Cormag hurt you?"

Hurt? Of course she was hurt. She'd suffered a mortal blow to her heart, her soul. She'd never really known how much she loved Adair until she heard he was dead.

Her gaze swept the room around her. Her chamber. The one she'd shared so briefly with Adair.

This bed, their bed. She lay upon the covers, fully clothed, her gown soiled with dirt and stained with blood.

Whose blood? She wished it was Lachlann's. Or Cormag's, and that she'd killed them both.

She would kill them both yet, or see them dead, for what they'd done.

"Oh, my lady," Dearshul whispered, and she began to shake as the tears started to fall down her cheeks.

Marianne regarded the distraught young woman. Could she trust her?

She didn't dare, she thought as she struggled to sit up. "How did I get here?"

"You swooned, Lachlann said," Dearshul replied, crying. "He carried you here and sent me to look after you."

Then this was her husband's blood on her gown, shed by his own traitorous brother, the man Dearshul still obviously adored, for her voice softened when she spoke of him even now and despite what he'd done.

"Did he tell you why I swooned?"

Dearshul sniffled and wiped her face with the hem of her sleeve. "Because you think Adair is dead."

Think Adair is dead? Marianne's heart leapt and her mind grasped at the hope Dearshul's words offered. "He's still alive?"

Dearshul flushed and bit her lip. "Lachlann says he can't be. His wound was too serious."

In spite of Dearshul's answer, energy hummed through Marianne's veins, as if she'd been half dead herself and was now fully alive once more, because wounded was not dead. "Tell me what happened in the hall after I was taken from it."

Dearshul looked scared, perhaps fearing she'd already said too much. "You should rest, my lady. Lachlann says—"

"I want to know what happened." Marianne reached out and grabbed Dearshul's hand. "I need to know what happened to Adair."

Dearshul licked her lips, uncertain and wary, but she answered. "As Lachlann and Adair fought, Cormag struck at him from behind, and when Adair turned to defend himself, Lachlann stabbed him in the side. Then Roban came and knocked Lachlann down. Young Dougal went for Cormag. Roban carried Adair from the hall, and the others have fled with him to the hills."

Adair, Roban and the others had gotten away. They had more loyal men who'd been sent out of

Lochbarr, which meant Lachlann's usurping of the chieftain's position was not yet a certain thing.

"What of the patrols?" she asked Dearshul. "Have they returned?"

"I don't know," Dearshul mournfully replied. "I've been here, tending to you."

"How long have you been with me?"

"Half the day. 'Tis past the noon."

It was possible the patrols hadn't returned yet, and if so, Adair's loyal friends wouldn't know what had happened. "What do you think they'll do when they find out Lachlann betrayed his brother, the rightful chieftain?"

"I don't know." Dearshul sniffled and wiped her nose with her sleeve. "I think Lachlann will convince them he acted for the best."

Just as Fionnaghal had predicted. "What do you think will become of me?"

Dearshul's eyes widened and her tears ceased. "Oh, you'll be safe, I'm sure! Lachlann wouldn't hurt a woman. He's not like Cormag."

He is, more than you know, Marianne thought. "Then you know Cormag killed Fionnaghal."

Dearshul paled. "Fionnaghal is dead?" she whispered.

"Cormag slew her when she tried to protect me." Marianne pitied Dearshul for giving her love to a man who didn't deserve it, but she wouldn't lessen the enormity of what had happened. "That's what happens in rebellion, Dearshul—death of the innocent as well as warriors. That's what Lachlann brought here, death and dishonor."

The door to the chamber opened and Lachlann, now in a clean shirt and unstained *feileadh,* entered the *teach.* Dearshul jumped to her feet and once more wiped her eyes.

Lachlann ignored her. "I hope you're feeling better?" he asked Marianne politely, as if he hadn't tried to kill her husband that morning.

"I'm much better now, thank you, since I'm sure Adair isn't dead," she answered with that same politeness as she got off the bed and faced him, fighting the wave of dizziness that threatened to make her swoon again. "Poor Lachlann, all your plans don't look so clever now, I daresay."

The young man scowled as he glared at Dearshul. "What have you been saying to her?"

"I told her what you told me, Lachlann—that Adair must be dead."

"I'll believe it when you show me his body and not before," Marianne declared.

"Leave us, Dearshul," Lachlann ordered.

"I—I'm sorry," she stammered. "I didn't mean to—"

"Leave us!"

Dearshul scurried from the *teach,* closing the door softly behind her.

Meanwhile, Marianne went to sit on one of the stools, gracefully moving her skirt to one side, as she'd seen the Reverend Mother do a thousand times. It was a simple, womanly gesture, yet done with dignity, it conveyed a sense of power and control, as if he could rail and scream, but she would move at her own exalted, womanly leisure.

"There was no need to be so harsh with Dearshul," she said evenly, regarding him steadily, her eyes telling him exactly what she thought of him in spite of her tone. "Obviously, some of her judgment is suspect, or she wouldn't still be besotted with you. Otherwise, she's a harmless young woman who means well. You should treat her better."

Lachlann frowned, and did not sit. "The way you Normans treat everybody?"

"The way a gentleman should treat a woman."

"As my brother treated you?"

She smiled serenely. "I have absolutely nothing to complain about when it comes to that."

"I would stop acting like a queen if I were you, Marianne," Lachlann said. "You have no power here, now that my brother is dead."

"Since your brother is *not* dead, we'll see how much power I wield when he returns to take his rightful place as thane of Lochbarr and chieftain of your clan. I daresay I'll wield a lot more power than you ever will, provided you even survive, of course."

Lachlann regarded her scornfully. "What is it about you Normans? You think you own the entire world! Or at least you act as if you do."

"While you're acting like a petulant child, except that your envy has lead to death and bloodshed. You ought to be ashamed of yourself."

Lachlann suddenly lunged, grabbing her by her

shoulders and hauling her to her feet. "Listen to me, woman! I'm the chieftain of Lochbarr now, and my word is as good as law. You're at my mercy and you better start acting like it or—"

"Or what?" she charged, glaring into his red face. "You'll kill me, too? How will you explain *that* to my husband? Your clan? My brother? Your king?"

"I'll tell them…I'll tell them—"

He pulled her forward and kissed her hard on the mouth.

She twisted out of his grasp and slapped his face with all her might. "How dare you! How dare you touch me, you murderer! You traitor!"

His expression fierce, he put his hand to the reddening mark on his cheek. "Is that what you said to my brother the first time he kissed you? Or did you let him kiss you more? Do you enjoy teasing men, Marianne? Does it make you feel pretty and powerful?"

"I don't tease men," she retorted. "If you thought I teased you, or that I was attracted to you in *any* way, it was all in your own conceited mind."

"I'm conceited? I'm not the one walking around Lochbarr with my nose in the air, acting like I'm too good to put my dainty toes on the soil of Scotland."

Marianne struggled to regain her self-control. She must rein in her temper, no matter what he said or did, because this man was a viper, and she *was* at his mercy. "Do you intend to kill me?"

"God, no!" he retorted. "I don't want you dead."

"Do you then intend to force yourself upon me?"

She watched Lachlann's face as he struggled to regain his self-possession. "That kiss was...a mistake."

"A mistake? I would call it unwelcome and repulsive. But whatever you would call it, I warn you—I will *never* give myself to you willingly, and if you rape me, I'll bring down the entire weight of Norman and Scots law on your head and I won't rest until you're executed."

"I'm going to take you back to your brother," he snarled, still not back in control. "You're to be a peace offering, to prove that I have no quarrel with him or his family. You should be thankful, and act like it."

Marianne's mind worked quickly. She didn't want to go back to Nicholas, not while Adair lived, but she had to get out of this fortress and find her husband. So she had to make Lachlann believe she accepted this plan. Once out of Lochbarr, she'd find a way to escape his custody.

She let her shoulders relax a little, but she kept her tone as haughty as before. "You'd do that? You'd take me safely back to my brother? How can I believe you?"

"I'll give you my word, as chieftain of Clan Mac Taran."

She sniffed derisively. "The word of a traitor doesn't mean much."

He stiffened. "It's the only guarantee you'll get."

"And what of my child?"

Lachlann shrugged.

"You don't care?"

"No, and no one in the clan will, either. The child's mother is Norman, you see."

"I should have realized you wouldn't care about family bonds when it came to your brother's child, either. Very well, then. Take me back to my brother."

"You'll tell him I made sure you weren't harmed?"

She nodded, and a flicker of relief crossed Lachlann's face. "And to show my gratitude, I will *not* tell him that you kissed me."

Lachlann took a step toward her. She instinctively stepped back.

His eyes softened with what looked like sincere regret. "I didn't want Adair to die, Marianne. I thought he'd accept the opportunity to leave for your sake, if not his own, yet he wouldn't take the chance I offered to let you both go unharmed."

Marianne tilted her head to study the man in front of her, as she might a strange and bizarre creature. "Because he's an honorable man who wouldn't let a traitor win without a fight."

"I'm not the traitor," Lachlann retorted, his expression hardening. "I'm not the one who went to Beauxville knowing it was bound to lead to trouble, and maybe war. But would Adair listen? No! He'll do what he wants, when he wants. What kind of chieftain is that?"

"The kind who won't let a woman suffer. The kind who sees injustice and tries to end it. The kind who can make men follow him with no more than a word because they know he won't betray them, that he'll die first, and gladly, fighting for his clan. He's the kind of chieftain you could never be, Lachlann."

"You don't understand anything."

"More than you know, Lachlann. I have two brothers who competed in everything. But it was always open warfare, not sly, deceitful tricks."

Lachlann backed away. "I'll take you to Beauxville tomorrow."

"Dunkeathe," she murmured as her enemy went outside and closed the door behind him. "The name of the place is Dunkeathe."

"Two days later, the sky was gray with clouds and the air chill and damp with drizzle. Seated on a horse, her cloak wrapped around her, Marianne waited for Lachlann to take her back to her brother, as he'd said he would.

She'd begun to fear he no longer intended to do so. Imprisoned in her *teach*, anxious and tense, she'd barely slept the past two nights, listening and planning and hoping for the chance to get away. She'd gotten no answer to her questions from Dearshul, who only wept when she brought food, and didn't linger. Then at dawn this morning, Lachlann had knocked on her door and told her the time had come for her to go back to Dunkeathe.

Marianne glanced at the ten men who were to be her guard, likewise mounted and waiting, save one who held Lachlann's horse. She didn't recognize any of them. They passed a wineskin, and she tried to ignore their hoarse laughter and crude jests. She couldn't understand all of what they said, but she understood enough to know she didn't want to.

Finally Lachlann came out of the hall, his steps none too steady. He looked as exhausted as she felt, but she had no pity for him. She boldly met his gaze when he glanced at her. She'd done nothing wrong; let him look away with shame. And he did, but not before she saw that his eyes were bloodshot.

As he joined them, the other men exchanged smirks, regarding Lachlann not with respect, but sly amusement, and she knew he was no more the leader here than she.

Lachlann's face reddened, yet he said nothing as he mounted his horse, either to her or the men. Instead, he called out for the gate to be opened and raised his hand to lead the small cortege out of the fortress. Riding through the village, the men kept drinking and laughing and joking, while Lachlann stared stoically ahead.

Once outside Lochbarr, Marianne constantly scanned the road ahead, seeking an opportunity for escape. Thankfully Lachlann hadn't taken hold of the reins of her horse, as she'd worried he might, and as they moved away from the fortress and village, his head began to dip and his shoulders slump, as if he were falling asleep. A backward glance revealed that the men behind were too busy drinking and joking among themselves to pay much heed to her.

Yet she could find no good place to try to get away. She wished she'd ridden out with Adair, to see more of the land, or that she'd paid more attention the first time he brought her to Lochbarr.

Then, at last, she saw her chance, where the road was bordered by a meadow and a wood. The trees were thick, but not too close together to prevent a horse from getting through them.

Lachlann's chin was practically on his chest. Another swift glance showed that the men behind weren't paying any more attention to her.

So she gave one quick punch to the horse's sides and turned it into the wood as it broke into a gallop. There was a cry, then shouting and she could hear other horses charging through the wood behind her. Holding on for dear life, she turned the horse, again and again once more, until she spotted a fallen log. She pulled her mount to a stop beside it with such force, it sat back on its haunches. Steadying it, she quickly climbed down onto the log, so she would leave no footprints in the dirt. Then she smacked the horse hard on its rump, sending it galloping off through the trees. She jumped onto the ground and lay flat in a little hollow made by the roots of another tree behind the log. She stayed there, prone and panting, while the men following her rode by, chasing her horse.

Still she waited—and was glad she had when she heard the sound of the hooves of one last horse, walking. She pressed herself against the roots, down in the dirt as far as she could go. Holding her breath, she peered through the narrow gap between the log and the ground.

It was Lachlann's horse. For a long, terrible moment, she feared he'd seen some sign, or guessed where she was, especially when his horse halted. Time seemed to stretch, a short while becoming an eternity, until the horse began to move again.

Once it was out of sight, she let out her breath slowly. She also started to shiver, there on the cold ground, but she didn't dare move, not until more time had passed and no rider returned. Only then did she slowly and cautiously rise, her joints aching. She brushed off the mud as best she could, and tried to get her bearings.

She wouldn't leave Lochbarr, not without Adair. She was sure there would be those loyal nearby who would help her. She would find them and get to Adair. Together they would reclaim his rightful place and —

"Marianne?"

CHAPTER SIXTEEN

ADAIR'S EYELIDS FLUTTERED open. His head hurt, his side, his chest. What had happened?

Then he remembered.

Where was Marianne? He'd heard her cry out....

He sat up abruptly, only to gasp in pain and collapse back onto the rock-hard bed.

It *was* a rock, and around him, in the flickering light of a torch, he recognized the walls of the cave under the falls.

His side hurt as if a hot shaft of iron had been shoved between his ribs, but that was nothing compared to his inner anguish as he recalled what had happened in the hall.

Barra appeared beside him, his lined face full of worry. "Adair, ye're awake?"

Without waiting for an answer, Barra broke into a relieved smile. "You gave us quite a scare. I was that fearful for your life. And no way to get Beitiris, neither. I tell you, I feared you'd ne'er last the night."

The night? How long had he been there? "Where's Marianne?" he asked through dry, cracked lips.

Barra turned away, then brought a wineskin to Adair's lips. "Have a wee drink o' this. You'll feel better."

Adair choked back some of the strong, cool *uisge beatha,* then put his hand on Barra's to make him lower the drink.

"Where's Marianne?" he repeated, his voice weak, determined to have an answer.

"Still in Lochbarr."

With Lachlann and the other traitors.

Adair tried to sit up again. "I've got to go back."

Barra put his hands on Adair's shoulders and pushed him down. "We can't go to Lochbarr, at least not yet," he said with unexpected firmness. "Not when you're hurt and your brother and those others hold the fortress."

Those others, the traitors. Including his brother. And Marianne was their captive.

Adair closed his eyes and tried to muster his self-control, to stop the raging torrent of anger and dismay and need for immediate action. As much as he wanted to rush back to Lochbarr, he couldn't let his emotions be his guide—he'd learned the folly of that. He needed to be more like Marianne, more like his father, and *think*. Find out what exactly had happened. How many men Lachlann had at his command. How many *he* had.

He needed a plan. He had to consider all the possibilities, all the potential outcomes. Most of all, if he was to save Marianne, he had to make sure he won when next he confronted his brother and the rest of those who'd fought against him.

"We can't risk staying here much longer," Barra said, looking around at the damp walls. "They'll remember the cave and come looking."

"How did I get here?"

"Roban and the others loyal to you who weren't out on patrol brought you."

"How many men loyal to me are there?"

"Nineteen got away from Lochbarr. There would have been twenty, but young Dougal fell in the fighting."

Young Dougal—Roban's second cousin. He was only sixteen.

Lachlann had even more to answer for.

"We have only nineteen men?"

That would include Barra, he supposed. Although Adair was glad to see the *seanachie,* Barra was no warrior.

Barra looked indignant, almost as if he'd read Adair's mind and been insulted, but the explanation for his expression became clear when he answered. "There are more loyal to you than that, Adair. Remember the patrols? We had some luck there. Roban spotted one of them coming back to Lochbarr, and he warned them what was afoot. Old Creemore sent some of his men to find the others before they went back to Lochbarr, so Lachlann and his traitors can't tell them any lies. That's another fifty men."

It was good news, and Adair was relieved to hear

it. With so many, they could attack Lochbarr, he could regain control and free Marianne.

"Where are they?" he asked, knowing they could not be there, for the cave could hold twenty men and horses at the most.

"Scattered here and there, hiding. The traitors will have a job trying to find us all."

"You didn't have to leave Lochbarr," Adair noted.

Barra made a sour face. "Stay there after what your brother did? Your father would surely rise from the grave and strike me down if I did."

"He didn't rise from the grave to strike down Lachlann," Adair grimly replied. "Or to save Marianne."

"You fear Lachlann will hurt your wife?"

"He'd better not, or I swear to God, Barra, I'll kill him."

"I don't think he will."

Although Adair was glad to hear that, Barra sighed and shook his head in a way that robbed him of some of his relief.

"You're a forthright, plain-speaking man, Adair Mac Taran," Barra said, "without an ounce of deceit in you, so maybe that's why you didn't see it. Your brother wasn't just jealous because you were to be the thane and chieftain when your father died. He envies you your wife, too."

Adair closed his eyes, sick to think the signs of jealousy had been there, and his pride in his family and his clan had made him blind to them.

He'd noticed the way Lachlann watched Marianne.

The quiet conversations. The way his brother had looked at her in his *teach* the night their father died. Marianne had been rightly indignant, because she was innocent of improper feelings—but Lachlann…?

He'd had too much trust in his brother and his clansmen, believing they would be as loyal and trustworthy as he.

He should have been wiser with Cormag, as Marianne had been with Fionnaghal.

His beloved Marianne, now in danger because he refused to believe any Scot could be as sly and deceitful as a Norman.

Ignoring the pain, Adair forced himself upright. He pressed his hand against his side and fought the dizziness and nausea that threatened to overwhelm him. "I'll talk to the men."

Barra gently pushed him back down. "You should rest awhile longer. You're wounded, Adair."

He pointed to the cloth wrapped around Adair's torso. It was stained red, crusted with dry blood and damp with wet. "Look, you've started bleeding again, and I had a devil of a time stopping it before. Now lie down, or so help me God, I'll knock you out myself. It's already been two days, so if there was evil to be done, it's been done."

Adair stared at Barra, horrified. Marianne had been alone in Lochbarr with the traitors for *two days?* His poor wife…his poor brave wife who'd climbed down a wall rather than be forced to wed. His brave, clever wife who'd fled her brother and made a marriage that should have been a disaster into a joy.

This was the woman Lachlann might try to rape and conquer. "He'll be lucky if she doesn't kill him if he dares to touch her."

Barra managed a smile. "Even though he lusts after her, I think we can hope she'll not be harmed. This is Lachlann we're speaking of, after all, and she's more valuable to him safe and untouched. He'll think of that, I'm sure. He was always a coolheaded boy."

Adair let out his breath slowly. Barra had a point. The clever, calculating Lachlann would think of Marianne's value before his own desire. Nevertheless… "We still have to get Lochbarr back, and soon."

"Oh, aye, absolutely," Barra agreed. He reached down and produced a loaf of bread wrapped in some rough cloth. "And we will. But it is not going to be easy. It seems your brother's been planning his rebellion for a long time. Since he took Lochbarr, we've heard other men have come—a motley bunch, by the sound of it. Mercenaries, mostly, as well as some Scots."

"How many?" Adair asked, again trying to be calm and force away images of Marianne hurt or in other danger.

"We make it about two hundred."

Two hundred—and he had seventy at most.

"Is Roban here? And Old Creemore?"

"Aye, I'll fetch them." Barra rose and looked down at him, his eyes full of sympathy. "You're still the chieftain of Clan Mac Taran, Adair. It's what your father wished, and most of the good men in our clan. Never forget that."

"Adair!"

The cry reverberated off the stone walls and the small pool of water, followed by the sound of somebody running, and apparently stumbling.

Adair struggled to his feet, sucking in his breath at the sudden pain, and looking for his *claimh mor*. Or his dirk. He wasn't going to go down without a fight.

But it wasn't Cormag or another traitor who appeared, mud-splattered and soaking.

It was Marianne.

"Adair!" she shouted with relief and happiness as she crossed the space between them and threw herself into his arms.

He cried out with both joy and pain as he held her tight, ignoring Barra, who danced about, exclaiming, "Not so tight! He'll bleed again!"

At the moment, Adair didn't care if he bled to death, as long as he could do so in Marianne's arms.

His lips found hers and they kissed with fierce and fervent passion as if they'd been lovers for years and never thought to see each other again.

Finally a desperate Barra pried them apart. "Marianne, please, for my sake, if not for his. I had a terrible time with the bandaging."

Marianne's eyes widened with horror and remorse. "Oh, sweet mother of God! I'm so sorry. Adair, lie down at once. Barra, have you more bandages? I'm no healer, but I can repair what I've done. Oh, Adair! He's right. You're bleeding."

Holding his breath, and her hand, Adair sat gingerly on the ledge that was acting as his makeshift bed. "I'll not lie and say it doesn't hurt, but this pain is nothing now that you're here. How did you get away? How did you find us?"

"We'll talk of that later, after we've seen to your wound. Barra, can you bring me some fresh water? And linen?"

"Water we've got and plenty of it, but no fresh linen."

Without a moment's pause, Marianne lifted up her skirt, revealing her shift. "We'll use this then. I need a knife."

Barra looked scandalized.

"Don't try and stop her, Barra," Adair said, his mouth tight with pain, but his eyes dancing. "She'll get angry and she's fierce when she's angry."

"Aye," Barra said, although whether that was an agreement to do what she ordered, or agreeing that she was fierce when angered wasn't completely clear. He obediently handed her a knife he took from his belt.

"Where'd you get that?" Adair asked, for Barra never carried weapons.

Barra grinned as he handed the dirk to Marianne. "Just because I don't flash a dirk about like you youngsters doesn't mean I don't have one."

"I don't know where you keep it hidden, but I suspect it's a lucky thing you don't do yourself an injury."

"If both of you are finished jesting, I need to get

to work," Marianne said as she took the long knife. She immediately began tearing the skirt of her shift into strips. "The water, please, Barra."

The *seanachie* dutifully hurried away to the pool.

Marianne frowned at Adair. "And you should lie down."

He wasn't fooled by the downturn of her lips. She wasn't angry—and he was too happy and giddy with relief that she was here to be completely serious. With her by his side, he didn't doubt that he'd overthrow the traitors and return to Lochbarr in triumph. "I want to watch you ruin your shift."

"Why do you men always have to try to act as if you're not in pain when it's obvious you are? You're not fooling anyone, you know."

"So much for my manliness, eh?" he said as he finally lay back down, trying not to groan. "I had a lovely view of your ankles. Very nice ankles they are, too."

She leaned over him and brushed his hair off his cheek with a gentle caress. "You don't have to prove your manliness to *me*."

He laughed, then sucked in his breath. "Losh, woman, don't say such things. It hurts too much to laugh."

"Does it hurt to smile?" she asked as she sat beside him on his uncomfortable bed.

"No. Let's see if it hurts to kiss," he whispered. He reached up and cradled her head in his hand, then pulled her to him for a long, slow, passionate embrace.

Barra cleared his throat and they moved apart. "I've, um, brought the water," he said, as sheepish as a lad.

"Thank you," Marianne said, blushing, too. "If you'll put it down beside me on that rock." She nodded at the loaf of bread. "Would you happen to have anything more to eat? I'm starving."

Adair realized how pale and tired she looked. "What was Lachlann trying to do, starve you?"

"Not deliberately." She sighed as she started to remove the bloodstained cloth from Adair's torso. "I was too worried about you to think of food much."

She gasped when she saw the torn and bloodied flesh along Adair's ribs. "No wonder Lachlann thought he'd killed you."

"He did?"

"He told me so himself."

Barra was still hovering nearby and he quickly moved closer. "It looks worse than it is," he assured her. "The sword went along the rib, you see, not between, thank God. And thank God Roban got him out of there as fast as he did, and Lachlann didn't strike again."

Adair and Marianne both looked at him, surprised.

Barra nodded in confirmation. "Aye, Roban said that after Adair fell, Lachlann just stood there, staring."

Adair closed his eyes as emotion swamped him. Lachlann could have finished him, but he hadn't. Whatever else he'd done, his brother hadn't killed him when he had the chance.

"In the times I've seen him since," Marianne said, "he looks as if he's haunted by what he's done."

"And if he's not, we'll give him cause for regret soon enough," Barra declared.

"Aye," Adair quietly assented.

Whatever mercy Lachlann had shown to him, the drawing of his weapon against the clan's chosen chieftain and the subsequent crimes of his followers had already sealed his doom.

Heartsick, Adair bunched his *feileadh* in his fists when Marianne started to wash his wound. The pain nearly made him pass out again. He clenched his teeth, pressed his eyes shut and listened to Marianne and Barra.

"Lachlann told me he didn't think he'd have to kill Adair," Marianne said.

"Then he's a fool as well as a traitor."

"He's ambitious and jealous of his brother, but not a fool. It would be a mistake to act as if he is," Marianne replied. "If he was a fool, he wouldn't have been able to convince anybody that he should be chieftain and not Adair."

Adair flinched as she started to bandage him again.

"I'm sorry. Am I hurting you very much, Adair?" his wife asked gently.

"It's all right," he answered, his eyes still closed. He just wanted this to be over. "And you're right. We shouldn't underestimate Lachlann. Barra, I'll talk to the men here in a little while. Not just now, though. Will you tell them? Oh, and please bring some food for Marianne."

"Aye, Adair," the older man answered.

Adair opened his eyes to find Marianne beside him. He scanned the cavern, and realized they were as private as it was possible to be. His hand reached for hers, and for a long moment, he simply held it, content to look at her lovely face and be glad that she was with him, and safe.

Her gaze faltered. "Oh, Adair, if you hadn't come for me at Dunkeathe—"

"If I hadn't gone to help you, this would have happened anyway." His grip tightened. "And I wouldn't have a wife I love with all my heart."

She wiped her eyes with the grass-stained cuff of her gown. "As I love you."

In spite of everything, when he heard her words, he had a moment's true and joyful contentment.

But he had questions, too. "How did you get away from Lochbarr? Surely Lachlann didn't just let you go."

"He was taking me back to Dunkeathe, to show Nicholas that he had no quarrel with him," Marianne replied, her expression showing how ineffective she thought that tactic would be. "Nicholas would never trust a man who'd betray his own brother."

"Another mistake Lachlann made," Adair said. "There wasn't just the two of you, surely?"

"There were ten men with us."

"Cormag?"

"No. I never saw him after that first day—thank God. When we reached a turn in the road between the meadow and the wood, I found my chance to escape. I kicked the poor horse so hard, she took off like a shot from a bow, right for the wood." Marianne drew in a deep breath. "I confess I feared I'd fall, but I managed to hang on."

Adair felt faint again. "The child?"

She caressed her stomach and gave him a smile that filled him with new relief. "No harm done." Her expression changed, to one intense and full of meaning. "No harm done to *me*, Adair, not by Lachlann or Cormag or any man."

A wave of relief passed through him. "Thank God."

Although he would love her no matter what had happened, he was relieved to think she'd been spared that humiliating agony, part of the fate that had befallen poor Cellach.

"So you rode to the woods...?" he prompted, moving past those terrible memories to concentrate on his precious wife.

"I got to the woods and as soon as I could make the horse stop, I dismounted and smacked her on the rump to send her running again. Then I hid in a hollow under the roots of a large tree until I heard Lachlann and his men go past, chasing the horse. I stayed there as long as I dared, then got up and started back toward Lochbarr."

"What?" Adair gasped in horrified disbelief and utter confusion. "You went *back* to Lochbarr? Why?"

She gave him a rueful smile. "You mustn't think I was planning to walk through the gate and announce my presence. I was hopeful most of the people of Lochbarr would be loyal to you, and they would help me find you."

"Oh, my God, Marianne!" he murmured. "You could have been caught, and I doubt Lachlann would have risked letting you escape a second time. Why did you risk it?"

"Because Lochbarr is my home and you're the rightful chieftain of Lochbarr." She gave him a glorious smile. "And because you're my husband. I was quite determined to find you and help you fight to get it back."

Had there ever been a braver, more resolute woman? How could he *not* love her?

Adair brought her hand to his lips and pressed a kiss upon it.

"Fortunately, Roban found me as he was on his way to some of your faithful clansmen who are hidden hereabouts. He told me you were alive, and brought me here."

She made it sound so simple and easy, but in her tone he read a deeper tale, of struggle and fear and sheer force of will. "You're a bonnie brave woman, *m'eudail,* and I'm so proud you're my wife, I may burst with it."

"What, and need more bandaging?" she said, frowning, although her eyes shone with love.

"We'll get Lochbarr back somehow," he vowed.

"Of course we will." She covered him with his plaid. "Now you rest, and we'll talk later."

"But—"

She rose and gave him an imperious look. "Rest. You're no good to us if you're weak."

Then she grinned, looking like a beautiful, mischievous imp. "Besides, we'll give Lachlann a few more days trying to control Cormag and the others. Let him see if it's as easy to be a chieftain as he thinks."

"AYE, ADAIR, they stole everything we had that they could carry. Like ravening wolves they were," the middle-aged farmer said, his bright eyes full of hate above his bushy black beard. "Thank God I'd heard of their mischief and sent my wife and daughters into the hills, or…"

Anghas's gaze faltered as he regarded Adair. "We've heard tales about some of the poor lasses in Lochbarr."

Her heart full of sorrow, Marianne glanced at her husband seated beside her in another farmer's byre high up in the hills where they'd taken refuge after leaving the cave. Close by, a mouse scuttled through a pile of straw, while outside, cows lowed, waiting to be milked.

When she'd told Adair they should let Lachlann try to control Cormag and the others for a few days, she hadn't considered the full extent of the evil Cormag and the others might do if left unchecked for even a little while. Now she especially feared for sweet, gentle Dearshul and hoped that somehow, her affection for Lachlann had kept her safe.

Adair shifted and Marianne reached out to take his hand, offering him her silent comfort. As painful as it was for her to hear what was happening in Lochbarr under Lachlann's leadership—or lack of it—she knew it was even more agonizing for Adair.

"What of Lachlann?" Adair asked.

The burly farmer's lip curled with scorn. "He stays in the hall dead drunk, they say. He's been that way ever since you got away."

"Then he doesn't lead these raiding parties?"

"No," Anghas replied. "But he doesn't stop them, either."

"I don't mean that I won't hold him responsible for what's happening," Adair replied. "He'll suffer for it, along with the rest."

"When?" Anghas demanded, his deference giving way to understandable anger and frustration.

"Soon."

"As soon as Adair's fit to fight," Marianne clarified.

"And when might that be?"

Roban, who'd been listening from his place in the shadows of the small stone building, stepped forward. "It's not for you to question what Adair intends to do, Anghas, or when."

His face creased from worry and the pain of his healing wound, Adair addressed his friend. "Aye, it is for Anghas to question, and be assured that I'm going to act soon. It's his livestock got taken, and his wife and daughters put in harm's way because of me."

Marianne heard the heavy mantle of guilt he'd put upon his shoulders. "Adair, nobody will blame you for what they're doing."

His hand on his side, her husband got to his feet. "They should," he said bitterly. "I should have seen which way the wind was blowing. I should have taken steps against Cormag, at least, and not believed no clansman would betray me. I should have paid more attention to Lachlann, too. But I didn't, so now this man has every right to know what I intend to do."

Adair put his other hand on Anghas's shoulder and spoke with determination and sincerity. "I won't let Cormag and his men turn our land into an outlaws' hunting ground. And I'm well enough to do something now."

Hearing the firm resolution in his voice, Marianne decided the time had come to tell her husband of her plan. Afraid he would want to ride before he was well enough, she'd hesitated, but Adair was too anxious and determined to delay any longer.

After hearing Anghas, so was she.

"You can ride, Barra thinks," she said, "but we're outnumbered. We've got to get more men before we attack."

"I'm not going to stay hidden away like a coward any longer," Adair replied, rubbing his fist into his palm.

Looking as if he'd rather be elsewhere, Anghas sidled toward the door. "I only wanted to know how long my wife and daughters need stay in the hills."

"Come with me, Anghas, and have some stew," Roban said with slightly forced good humor. "It's best to leave these two to fight their battles alone anyway."

Anghas looked from Adair to Marianne, then nodded and joined Roban, who was already walking out the door.

"There's an excellent troop of soldiers nearby led by a man who should be very keen to help, and we should seek his aid," Marianne said the moment they were alone.

Adair's eyes narrowed warily. "What man?"

"My brother." Marianne hurried on before Adair could reply. "He should realize that it's far better for him to have his sister and her husband for neighbors and allies than men who'd betray their chieftain. It won't be easy to humble ourselves to Nicholas, but what is our pride compared to what's happening in Lochbarr? I'm even willing to beg, if I must, to see you restored to your rightful place, and those men defeated."

Some of the tension left Adair's face, only to return a moment later. "Marianne, *m'eudail*, I've already been humbled. I'll ask for help from anyone who might provide it. But I fear your brother'll probably bar the gate against us and tell us to go shift for ourselves."

"I'll make sure Nicholas listens to what we have to say," Marianne replied firmly. "And that he'll help us."

More of the tension fled Adair's features as he reached for her. "I'm sure if anybody can get that man to listen and come to our aid, it will be my bonnie wife."

CHAPTER SEVENTEEN

STANDING IN HIS SOLAR, Nicholas studied the soldier before him as if the man were proposing Nicholas jump into the nearest large body of water. "What do you mean, she refuses to leave?"

The garrison commander shuffled his feet and shrugged his beefy shoulders, making his chain mail rattle.

"She says they'll block the gates until you come and speak to them," he replied, his accent revealing his Saxon heritage.

"She's mad," Nicholas muttered, turning and walking toward the window through which weak sunlight shone. "Utterly and completely mad. I wondered before, but now I'm sure."

And he must have been temporarily deranged to think for one moment when he heard who was at his castle gate that Marianne had come crawling back to beg his pardon and forgiveness.

Nicholas looked out unseeing over the completed inner walls, to the hills that he considered the natural outer ring of his defenses against the lawless Scots. It was going to pour rain before the day was done.

He wouldn't worry about Marianne getting soaked to the skin. She hadn't worried about the compensation he'd have to pay Hamish Mac Glogan when she'd run off with Adair Mac Taran, a sum her husband's bride price had barely covered.

The garrison commander's mail jingled again. "Whatever her state o' mind, me lord, they're not budgin'."

"Didn't you tell them I was prepared to use force?" Nicholas demanded without turning, his hands clasped behind his back.

"Yes, me lord."

"Well?"

"Well, me lord, that is, she, um, she…laughed."

"Laughed?" Nicholas turned on his heel to glare at the soldier, who stiffened to attention.

"Yes, sir," the soldier replied. "Laughed and said she knew you weren't the most kindhearted fellow, but she didn't take you for a fool, and what she had to say was important. She said, 'Tell my brother that for his own sake, if not mine, he'd better let us in.'"

"She dared to *threaten* me?" Nicholas demanded, incredulous at her insolence.

The grizzled veteran frowned, as if thinking very hard. "No, me lord, it didn't sound like no threat—more like a warning. Like she thinks you're in danger."

Nicholas snorted. "What danger could I be in from them?"

The soldier didn't reply.

Nicholas turned back to the window. He should let her sit there until she rotted.

Except that they were blocking the castle gate.

He should send out his men against them.

Except that would lead to bloodshed, and he didn't want to have to hire more men.

Finally, exasperated, he strode to the door.

"Get back to your duties," he snapped as he passed the garrison commander.

After trotting down the steps, he marched across the courtyard. Ignoring the guards, who watched him as they might a pot about to explode, he threw open the wicket door in the inner gate.

"Raise the portcullis," he ordered as he proceeded.

Through the slowly rising wooden grille he could make out Marianne, mounted, with that Scot she'd married beside her. Behind them were about twenty other Scots, armed with those enormous broadswords they carried on their backs and wearing their ridiculous skirts.

His gaze returned to his sister, who still sat on a horse like an empress. When he'd arrived at the convent, he'd noticed the proud carriage of her head and the graceful dignity of her posture. That, and her beauty, had made her a valuable asset—until she'd allowed herself to be seduced by a savage Scot. That barbarian bastard still had that same smug, superior smile he'd sported when he'd first met Marianne, too.

He should have run him through and thought of an excuse afterward.

"Good day, brother," Marianne said brightly

when the wheels stopped creaking and the ascending portcullis came to a halt.

Nicholas marched closer. "I thought your father-in-law understood I no longer have a sister."

"Sister or not, aren't you going to behave like a well-to-do Norman nobleman and invite us into your hall for refreshments and rest?"

"No."

Marianne shrugged her shoulders. "Very well. We'll have our parlay here."

She dismounted, and so did the Scot, moving in a way that told Nicholas at once the man wasn't well.

He nodded at Adair. "What's happened to him?"

"That's what I've come to talk to you about."

"If he's sick, I don't give a damn."

"You should. Violence can be like a plague, spreading from one town to the next, or one valley to another."

Nicholas's eyes narrowed. "I've heard nothing to suggest I'm in danger. If the Scots want to fight among themselves, that's none of my concern."

"You think not?"

Quite certain the Scots could all happily kill each other before it would be important to him, Nicholas merely crossed his arms over his chest and raised a brow.

"Have you heard that Seamus Mac Taran has died?"

"Yes."

"A truly fine Norman nobleman would have sent his condolences."

Considering how much he'd paid those nuns over the years, they should have trained that arrogance out of her, Nicholas thought as he scowled at Adair Mac Taran. "You have my condolences."

"Thank you, brother-in-law."

Marianne obviously wasn't the only arrogant one at the gate.

"Since then, dear brother," she continued as if she had every right in the world to arrive at his castle and talk to him as though they were on the best of terms, "we've learned that there's been discontent and rebellion brewing among my husband's clan. Some of the clansmen, including his younger brother, were of the opinion that Adair wouldn't make a good chieftain, and his marriage to me was proof of his unsuitability."

"I'm inclined to agree with them."

Marianne looked at her brother as if she couldn't believe what she'd heard. "You would agree that an upstart faction should rebel against their rightful leader? I had no idea you had such sentiments, Nicholas. Tell me, does King Alexander know you feel this way?"

Nicholas's brows lowered. "What does Alexander have to do with this?"

"If you truly consider rebellion a viable means of obtaining power, the king who rewarded you with this large estate should know."

He was fast losing what little patience he had. "What do you want, Marianne?"

"It's not only what *I* want, Nicholas, but what you ought to want, too."

"For God's sake, why are you here?"

"We're here because Adair's brother has taken Lochbarr and made himself chieftain, against the expressed wish and choice of his late father and the majority of the clansmen."

"What do you expect me to do about it?"

"I expect you to…" She hesitated and some of the color drained from her cheeks.

"I expect you to—" she began again, her words faltering.

She started to slip to the ground.

"Marianne!" her husband cried, rushing forward to catch her as she fell, yet looking faint himself with the effort.

Adair Mac Taran's voice and his expression told Nicholas this was no ploy to gain sympathy. His sister was sick, or hurt.

Marianne's pale face looked like their mother's just before she died.

That realization was like the stab of a knife, and Nicholas immediately leapt forward to help. He gathered his sister into his arms. "Here, I'll take her," he said to the Scot, picking her up. "Inside."

He became aware of the worried rumblings of the other Scots. They could look and sound as concerned as nursemaids; he wasn't letting a heavily armed band of Scots inside Beauxville. "Just Marianne and her husband can come into the castle. The rest of you stay here."

They weren't happy about the order, but they were the least of Nicholas's worries as he carried his sister through the gatehouse. He wasn't concerned whether Adair could keep up with him, either. All that mattered was getting Marianne safely inside.

"Open the wicket! Now!" Nicholas shouted when he reached the inner gate.

The smaller door swung open and he went through sideways, careful not to let Marianne's head hit the frame. He strode across the courtyard.

"Get that door!" he ordered a dumbfounded female servant—the slightly less ugly one with the mole on her breast whose name he could never remember. She sprang into action and did as he commanded.

"Oh, God help us!" she cried as he carried Marianne past her. "Is she dead?"

"No. Fetch water. And wine. And the man who tends the laborers when they're injured."

He took the stairs to the apartments two at a time and kicked open the door to his bedchamber. Gently he laid Marianne on his featherbed. As he looked at her deathly pale features, the image of their mother's face kept surging upward from the depths of his memory, an image he'd kept buried there because it was too painful to recall.

He heard footsteps behind him and turned to find a winded Adair Mac Taran leaning against the doorjamb and breathing hard.

"What's wrong with Marianne?" Nicholas demanded. "Is she ill? She said something about the plague."

The Scot shook his head. "Not ill. She's with child."

Nicholas's dread lessened, but his animosity toward the Scot increased. "Yours?"

"Of course mine," the Scot retorted. "I'm her husband."

Nicholas regarded the man with undisguised disdain. "Yes, I know. You seduced her, so what choice did she have?"

"More than you gave her," the Scot muttered as he went to the bed.

Nicholas refused to feel guilty for what had happened. "So your own brother has rebelled against you," he sneered as Adair bent over Marianne, studying her face and stroking her hand.

"Aye, he has," Mac Taran said absently, as if he was more concerned about Marianne than regaining what had been taken from him. "We've come to ask you to help us get back Lochbarr, and my place as clan chieftain."

"Surely you're jesting," Nicholas scoffed, even as he wondered what was taking the man who tended to the laborers' injuries and illness so long to get there. "Why would I help the man who ruined my sister?"

Adair straightened and his intense gaze seemed to peer into Nicholas's heart. "And destroyed your ambitious plans?"

"You destroyed her future."

"That's debatable and I didn't come here to debate you. I came because Marianne suggested it. It seems my wife believes her brother will help us."

"How?"

"We need more men, and although I've sent to other clans for their assistance, it could be days yet before enough Scots can get here. Meanwhile, the traitors who hold Lochbarr are acting like outlaws. Marianne thought you'd see the merit of helping us because the alternative would be to have those outlaws for neighbors."

The Scot looked down at Marianne, then back to Nicholas. "I don't think that's the only reason she wanted to come here. Is she wrong to hope that a Norman can have family loyalty, too?"

"Family loyalty?" Nicholas jeered. "Where was her family loyalty when she ran off with you?"

"She didn't run away with me because we were lovers. She came with me because she thought she had no other choice—that you'd given her none, and neither had I."

"She didn't choose to go with you?" Nicholas demanded skeptically.

"She didn't think you'd believe her explanation for my unwelcome presence in her chamber."

"And what explanation would that be?"

"That I'd come there to rescue her, although she hadn't asked me to. In fact, Sir Nicholas of Dunkeathe, she refused my help and was trying to make me leave when we were discovered."

Nicholas wouldn't believe him. "Are you trying to tell me you weren't lovers?"

"No, we weren't," the Scot said, shaking his head. "And if you'd been calmer, she would have told you so."

Nicholas still refused to believe him. "She was in her shift."

"She was in her shift because she doesn't sleep in her gowns."

Nicholas would not accept that he was at all to blame for Marianne running off with the Scot. "Yet she married you."

"Aye—and not as willingly as she would have led you to believe, although it was her idea. She wants children and thought what had happened would make men—well, Normans, anyway—loath to wed her. So I was her last hope for motherhood. That's how it began, anyway. Now I love her."

Nicholas frowned. "Love? Love is for minstrels and foolish girls to sing about. You lust after her, that's all."

"At first, I won't deny it was only desire I felt, but I swear to you that now she's as dear to me as my own life."

Nicholas's lip curled with derision. "That sounds exactly like a minstrel's nonsense."

"If you believe that love is nonsense, I pity you."

"And what of Marianne? You don't really expect me to believe she could ever love a man like you?"

"What else but love would compel a woman as proud as your sister to stay with her defeated husband and ask for help from the brother who disowned her?" The Scot tilted his head and studied the Norman. "What else but love for that brother would make her hope he didn't really mean it when he said she was dead to him?"

Nicholas crossed his arms. "Maybe she's afraid and knows I can protect her when you obviously can't."

"Afraid? God save us, man, you ought to know she's as brave as any man you've ever met." Adair shook his head. "But if it pleases you to think that's why she's come, I won't argue. And if you don't understand what love is, I'm sorry for you."

Marianne stirred.

Both men went quickly to the bed, one on either side.

"Look what you've done to her," Nicholas murmured. "She was a beautiful woman—"

"She's the most beautiful woman in the world, and she'd be the most beautiful woman in the world to me if her face was scarred. She'll be the most beautiful woman in the world to me when she's old and gray, if I'm blessed to live so long."

A minstrel could hardly have put it better, Nicholas thought. "You have the soul of a poet, do you?" he asked with dismissive disdain.

"So does every man when he's in love," Adair replied.

Foolishness. Such talk was rank foolishness, or for those weak in the head.

The maidservant appeared at the door, bearing a tray with a carafe and a goblet.

Glad of the interruption, Nicholas watched as Adair hurried to take the wine. Sitting on the bed, the Scot gently raised Marianne's head and helped her to drink.

Whether there was such a thing as love or not, the Scot was certainly gentle with her.

She spluttered a bit, then opened her bright blue eyes and smiled up at her husband in a way that made Nicholas suddenly feel that if there was such a thing as love, the couple before him shared it, and it was something he should crave, not reject.

"What happened?" Marianne asked.

"You fainted," Adair said, rising and handing the goblet back to the maidservant, who was staring, openmouthed.

"You can go," Nicholas said to the young woman before turning his attention back to his sister. "Your husband said you aren't ill."

"No, I'm with child," she replied, shifting so that she was sitting with her feet on the floor. "I felt a bit dizzy and…" She looked around. "Where am I?"

"My bedchamber."

"How are you feeling now?" the Scot asked, watching her carefully.

"I'm fine. I'm just a little weary." She patted Adair's hand, then regarded Nicholas. "Did Adair tell you why we've come?"

Pushing aside useless thoughts about love, Nicholas focused on the problem before him, which was whether to offer his men for their aid, or refuse.

It wasn't a difficult decision to make, because as Marianne had said, it was better to have a peaceable relative for a neighbor—especially one who would now be beholden to him—than a gang of men who'd rebel against their lawful chieftain. "How many men do you need?"

Her grateful smile seemed to warm the entire room. "You'll help us?"

"As you so wisely point out," he replied evenly, "I'd be a fool not to. I'm not a fool. Now, how many of my soldiers do you require?"

"A hundred, if you can spare that many," the Scot answered.

"I can." Nicholas started toward the door. "And I'll come with you."

"This isn't your fight, Nicholas," Marianne said, rising, her arm around her husband.

"Yes, it is," he replied. "Your husband must be restored to his rightful place. We can't allow rebels to run loose." He made a grim little smile. "Besides, members of a family should help one another in times of trouble."

Marianne left her husband and embraced her brother. "Oh, thank you, Nicholas! I hoped you didn't mean it when you said I was dead to you."

Over Marianne's shoulder, the Norman and the Scot looked at each other.

As they did, Nicholas realized her husband knew he'd meant it when he'd disowned her, but that Adair would never tell her.

And for that, Nicholas was grateful.

"LACHLANN, YE WORTHLESS *gomeral!*" Cormag bellowed as he ran into the hall. His gaze flew around the room, passing over the broken furnishings, the empty hearth and the filthy, stinking rushes on the floor before finally coming to rest on the figure sprawled in the chieftain's chair, head hanging back as if he was dead. Lachlann's shirt was stained with wine, and his skin had a sickly pallor.

His *claimh mor* in his hand, Cormag ran up to Lachlann, grabbed him by the shoulder and shook him hard. "Wake up, ye drunken dolt!"

Lachlann's bloodshot eyes cracked open and his hand went to the hilt of his dirk as he tried to focus on his cousin. "Go 'way."

"We're under attack, ye daft shite!" Cormag shouted, shoving Lachlann hard against the chair. "Adair's come back with an army! You didn't kill him. I should have guessed you'd be useless in a fight."

Lachlann blinked and struggled to sit upright. "Adair isn't dead?"

"No! Are you deaf? He's got an army with him— a *Norman* army and that bloody Sir Nicholas, too!"

Lachlann stared at Cormag in stunned disbelief. "The Norman?" he whispered.

Then he started to laugh, his laughter getting louder and harder until tears rolled down his cheeks.

"Are you mad? There's nothing funny about this," Cormag cried as he hauled Lachlann to his feet and raised his hand to strike. "They've come to kill us."

Lachlann caught Cormag's hand in midswing. "Nay, I'm not mad. I'm a dead man, the same as you." Lachlann released his cousin. "Or maybe I was mad to betray my brother and shame my father's memory. And now my punishment is upon me." He smiled coldly at Cormag. "Yours, too."

Cormag glared at him. "So you're not going to fight?"

Lachlann shook his head. "Why bother? We're doomed anyway."

With an exclamation of disgust, Cormag turned away. "Stay here, then, ye shite, and wait for death."

The door opened before Cormag reached it. A woman appeared.

"Ah, it's little Dearshul come to warn you," Cormag jeered, twisting to look over his shoulder at Lachlann. "Although you're such a fool you never took what she offered. Well, she was sweet. Fought me every step but that only made it more enjoyable." He leered at Dearshul. "Am I not right, Dearshul?"

A great roar of rage like that of a wounded beast burst from Lachlann. Raising his dirk, he charged Cormag. Cormag turned, but Lachlann plunged his knife into his cousin's chest before he could lift his heavy sword. Grimacing, Lachlann held Cormag close, as if they were in an embrace, and shoved the dirk deeper still.

Hanging on to Lachlann, Cormag stared up at him in silent, horrified disbelief.

"Dinna fear, cousin," Lachlann said as the man's eyes clouded. "We'll see each other again soon—in hell."

Then Cormag's hold loosened and he slipped to the floor, leaving a trail of blood down Lachlann's soiled shirt and *feileadh*.

Sobbing, Dearshul ran to Lachlann and, regardless of the blood, held him tightly. "Oh, Lachlann, he could have killed you!"

He gently pushed her away and looked down at her tear-streaked face. "I'm so sorry, Dearshul. I've been so blind. So selfish. So stupid. I should have known I could never control Cormag and the others. I should have…" He managed a small smile and cupped her chin. "There is so much I should have done."

He caressed her damp cheek. "Goodbye, Dearshul," he said as he started for the door.

Barely able to see him through her tears, she ran after him. "Where are you going?"

"To meet my brother. He's come back to claim what is his by right."

"But he'll kill you!"

"I expect so."

She ran back to Cormag and frantically started to tug the knife from his body. "Wait! You have no sword, nor knife."

"I won't have need of them," he answered without looking back at the woman who loved him as he went to meet his brother.

And the fate he deserved.

CHAPTER EIGHTEEN

NEAS SHIFTED NERVOUSLY as he and Adair waited with the armed men on the hill overlooking Lochbarr. Around him mounted Norman soldiers, as well as several on foot, were taking their positions along with his clansmen, many of whom were muttering darkly in a way that boded ill for the traitors. The village had obviously been despoiled and pillaged, too, like most of the farms they'd passed along the way. Cormag and his band were worse than the Normans, worse even than the Vikings, and these were their own people they'd robbed.

Adair could guess what assumptions Nicholas and his men were making about the Scots.

He glanced at his powerful brother-in-law, seated on his huge warhorse. Nicholas's chain mail and helmet gleamed in the sun. His raised visor revealed his stoic, battle-hardened face that betrayed nothing of what he felt.

Adair had been surprised that Nicholas had so swiftly and easily deferred to him when it came to planning the attack, until Marianne pointed out that should things go awry, Nicholas would be able to blame his sister's husband.

In spite of that, Adair was grateful for his brother-in-law's aid, and pleased to think that the breach between Marianne and her brother might be mended.

As his horse shifted again, Adair scratched his naked knee. He'd refused Nicholas's offer of Norman armor. He was used to fighting in his *feileadh* and a padded leather jerkin, and mail was heavy.

"Marianne should be able to see everything from that vantage point, since she insisted on being here," Nicholas noted, nodding at the crest of a hill to the west covered with pine, not hiding his disapproval that Marianne had been so stubborn on that point. "She should be safe there. And I've got Herman guarding her. He's not a clever fellow, but he'll obey my orders without question."

Adair's eyes narrowed. "What do you mean, guarding?"

Nicholas's stony visage cracked with a little smile. "I mean preventing her from charging into battle herself. Trust me, Scot, she'll be returned to you after we win."

"Oddly enough, I do trust you," Adair replied.

Nicholas's smile became a wry smirk. "Good, since we're neighbors and related by marriage." He looked at the hill again. "Still, I'd rather she'd stayed in Beauxville until it was over."

"The name of the place is Dunkeathe."

Nicholas regarded his brother-in-law thoughtfully. "That has a certain ring to it. I've been think-

ing Beauxville sounds more…flowery…than I
would like."

Adair barked a laugh. "Then change it, man, back
to what it was. The people hereabouts will think
you've learned some wisdom. As for Marianne, I
wish she'd stayed behind, too, but she refused and
I decided it wasn't worth an argument."

"My sister can be very stubborn."

"Aye," Adair agreed. "She's brave and clever, too.
I'm a lucky man to love her."

Nicholas didn't reply before he rose in his stir-
rups and twisted in his saddle, surveying the as-
sembled men. "We're ready. Let's go get your
fortress back."

Adair drew his *claimh mor* as Nicholas raised
his hand, prepared to signal his mounted troops to
advance.

Then the gates of Lochbarr slowly swung open
and a lone man appeared—Lachlann, his arms
spread wide as if in surrender.

"Wait!" Adair ordered, lowering his sword.
"That's my brother."

"The traitor?" Nicholas asked.

"Aye, and he's alone," Adair replied, mystified,
as he nudged Neas forward.

"Perhaps the other rebels are lying in wait in the
village, or in the fortress," Nicholas said, following
him. "This could be a trap."

"Or else they're surrendering," Adair said, his
gaze still on his brother.

"I find that hard to believe," the Norman said.

"I find it hard to believe myself," Adair murmured.

He continued forward, his grip on his sword still tight, uneasily wondering if this was another betrayal. Nevertheless, he hoped he was right and he could regain Lochbarr without a battle, and more death.

"The others have run," Lachlann shouted, his voice carrying on the wind. "Fled. Scattered. Lochbarr is yours again, Adair. There's no need to attack."

"I still think this could be a trap and he's the lure," Nicholas said.

Adair studied his brother, then the fortress beyond. He saw no sign of men or arms. Only Lachlann, alone, his shoulders slumped with despair. "It's not a trick."

He kicked his heels against Neas's sides. They cantered down the hill and through the village toward the fortress, with Nicholas and his mounted men following behind. After them came the clansmen, their swords at the ready.

The faces of some of the people who remained in the village appeared at their windows, silently watching as Adair and Sir Nicholas reached the fortress, and Lachlann.

Still holding his arms open, Lachlann fell to his knees on the muddy road. "Lochbarr is yours, Adair, and so I am, to do with as you will."

"Why are you still here?" Nicholas demanded.

"Where would I go that Adair wouldn't find me?" Lachlann answered. "Where could I hide from his just wrath and my lawful punishment? Where could I flee from the shame of what I've done?"

His heart aching anew, Adair dismounted. He walked up to his younger brother, who was disheveled and dirty, his shirt stained with blood, his eyes haunted with remorse. "Are you hurt?"

Lachlann shook his head.

"Stand up."

Lachlann obeyed.

Adair knew he should summon his men to take Lachlann prisoner, and then pass swift judgment on him. Yet in spite of that, and in spite of all that Lachlann had done, Adair could only think that this was his little brother, the same Lachlann who used to tag along after him when they were children. Who used to regard him with such awe.

"Why did you do it, Lachlann?" he asked, his voice breaking. "Why did you betray me?"

"Didn't your wife tell you?" Lachlann replied quietly. "Ambition. Jealousy. Greed. And I honestly thought I'd be a better chieftain than you, Adair. But your wife was right about that, too. There's more to being a chieftain than cleverness, and I couldn't control the others."

Nicholas dismounted and approached. "He's giving up?"

"Aye, he's giving up," Adair answered in French, not taking his gaze from his brother.

"And the others?" Nicholas demanded.

"Gone. Scattered," Adair replied. "We'll have to track them down."

"What do you intend to do with the traitor? Take him to the king for trial?"

Before Adair could speak, Lachlann looked at the Norman and answered. "There's no need to take me to the king. As thane, Adair has the right to pass judgment on me. And the punishment for what I've done is death."

Death. To kill Lachlann, his brother.

Who'd tried to kill him, then spared his life. And Marianne's, too.

"Very well," Nicholas said, drawing his sword. "Let's do it and be done."

"No!" Adair commanded, holding out his hand to stop him. "It's my place to decide when and where my brother's punished for what he's done, not yours."

Adair spotted Roban among the men who'd followed him down the hill and called him over. "Cormag and the others have escaped. Take our men and find them. I want them brought back here, especially Cormag."

"Cormag is dead," Lachlann announced. He spoke dully, as if what energy he'd possessed moments before had drained from him. "I killed him. I wish I'd done it days ago."

Adair gave Roban a look, and Roban went back to the other Scots. He quietly began issuing orders.

Adair turned to his brother-in-law. "It seems, Nicholas, that I have no more need of you or your men. I thank you for your help, but now you can go back to Dunkeathe."

"Are you certain you'll need no assistance capturing the rest of the rebels?"

For a moment, Adair wondered if he'd walked into a different trap. Perhaps Nicholas would try to leave an occupying force in Lochbarr and claim it was for their own protection. "Aye, I'm sure," he said, his words carrying a hint of challenge.

Fortunately, Nicholas nodded his agreement. "If you are content," he said. "I'll have Herman bring Marianne to you."

The Norman mounted his horse and returned to the rest of his men waiting on the hill.

A SHORT TIME LATER, Marianne hurried into the chieftain's hall in Lochbarr. She saw at once that Lachlann wasn't dead, although she knew that had to be the traitor's eventual punishment.

Instead, her brother-in-law stood facing her grim and forbidding husband, who was seated in the chieftain's chair. Several of the other men of the clan were on benches surrounding the prisoner. Barra, who'd returned to Lochbarr with her, sidled off to one side and sat among the Scots.

Adair spotted her. Looking very much the thane and chieftain, he nodded toward the empty chair to his right, indicating she was to join him.

As she walked toward her husband, she was aware of Lachlann's bowed head and disheveled state; of Ceit and the other serving women peering out of the kitchen; of Dearshul sobbing quietly near the main door; of the solemn, long-haired clansmen; and the heavy weight of responsibility and judgment that sat upon her husband's broad shoulders.

Full of regret for what might have been, she passed her young brother-in-law. So much promise. So much trouble.

She didn't speak when she reached her chair. With a heavy heart, she sat and waited for what would happen next.

"Lachlann," Adair began, his deep voice filling the hall, "you know the punishment for what you've done is death."

The young man raised his head. His face looked angular, stark, older, wiser—and sickly pale. "Aye," he replied, his voice wavering a little.

"And I *should* kill you," Adair declared. "Your greed and ambition have led to death and rape and destruction. Some would even say a quick end is too good for all that you've brought to our people."

Adair slowly got to his feet. "Yet from all I've heard, you didn't rob or rape or pillage, like the others. My wife has told me that you saved her from Cormag."

Marianne looked from her husband to Lachlann, and saw doubt in the young man's eyes. Doubt, more than hope, although her heartbeat began to quicken with an emotion she was almost afraid to feel. Yet Adair already had so much guilt, so much remorse…if he didn't have to be responsible for his brother's execution, too…

"So I have decided your punishment will not be death."

As relief ran through Marianne, a low murmur of discontent filled the hall. Barra and the men around him exchanged confused looks. Dearshul, her hope like a beacon shining on her face, stopped crying.

"Not death," Adair repeated firmly. "But you're banished, Lachlann, from my lands and all of Scotland. Every clan chieftain and laird, every thane and merchant, every peasant and shepherd, every man, woman and child—aye, even King Alexander himself—will know of my judgment upon you. No one will give you aid or succor, food or shelter, while you are in this land. And if you ever return to Scotland, any Scot may kill you."

Not death, perhaps, but surely for a Scot, with his pride and family feeling, this was purgatory, a living limbo of shame and loneliness and remorse.

Around her, the murmur of discontent continued, but quieter, as the full import of Adair's judgment sank in among them.

Adair approached his brother. "You've lost everything, Lachlann. Home and country, friend and family. But I can't kill you because you did what I couldn't do for Cellach. You saved Marianne."

A tear rolled down Lachlann's cheek. "Be merciful, Adair, and kill me."

Adair shook his head and the look in his eyes nearly broke Marianne's heart. "I can't do it, Lachlann. I can't kill my own brother—any more than you could kill me. Now go, never to see your homeland again."

The heavy silence broke when Dearshul hurried toward them. "I'm going with Lachlann."

"No," Lachlann said brusquely over the murmurs and questioning asides from the clansmen. He turned away from Adair and started walking toward the door, past the censorious gaze of the other Scots.

Dearshul ran after him and grabbed his arm. "I want to go with you! Banished or not, I love you, Lachlann!"

Lachlann halted, then appealed to his brother, and Marianne. "She doesn't understand. Please, make her stay."

Marianne looked at Dearshul and saw the love shining in her eyes, despite everything. "You realize he has nothing, Dearshul? No home, no money, no food, no clothes?"

Dearshul nodded.

"That he is disgraced and banished?"

Dearshul nodded.

"Yet you would still go with him?"

"Yes, my lady."

"Adair, Marianne, please!" Lachlann pleaded, his voice husky with emotion. "She doesn't know what she's doing—and I don't deserve to have her with me." He looked beseechingly at Dearshul. "How can you want to be with me now?"

Her cheeks flushed, Dearshul answered with a determination Marianne recognized. "Because I love you. I've always loved you, and I always will love you." Her gaze faltered a moment. "If you don't want me because of Cormag—"

Lachlann took hold of her slender shoulders and replied with heartfelt fervor, "That doesn't matter to me. It's *you* that matters, Dearshul. Do you not understand? I have *nothing*. I *am* nothing."

Her smile blossomed, and her expression was as resolute as a general's before battle. "You're the man I love."

"Let her go with you," Marianne said softly, slipping her hand in her husband's. "Trust me in this, Lachlann. Where there is a love as strong as this, there is no hardship that can't be overcome."

Lachlann looked at her for a long moment, then his brother, and then he reached for Dearshul's hand and clasped it firmly. "Come, Dearshul," he said softly to her. "Come with me."

Together they walked out of the hall, and out of Lochbarr.

HOURS LATER, after Adair had taken charge of the rebuilding of Lochbarr and Marianne had set about ordering the repairs to the hall and kitchens, seeing to the restocking of the storerooms and trying to undo some of the damage and neglect, she turned her efforts to their *teach*.

It had been looted. All the cloth had been torn from the walls and the bedding stolen. Mercifully, the bed itself—too large and too heavy to take apart easily—remained. The stools had been shattered, and she had to search for the missing braziers and table. One of the few merchants who hadn't fled the village had some linens he'd kept hidden from the rebels that he was willing to give her on promise of future payment.

By the time Marianne was finished, it wasn't as comfortable as it had been, but livable. Soon, she hoped, she could again make it a sanctuary of rest and comfort, a place Adair deserved after all he'd been through.

Exhausted, Marianne took off her gown and got into bed to wait for him. Her thoughts ranged over all that had happened, from the first time she'd seen the handsome, grim Scot from her brother's window, to the last time she'd seen him today, briskly issuing orders, fully the chieftain.

Gone, perhaps for good, was the air of friendly camaraderie he'd shared with his clansmen. He might never again trust any man the way he had before.

Yet it could have been worse. So very much worse.

The door to the *teach* opened. Adair came inside, his shoulders rounded with exhaustion. She got out of the bed and hurried to pour some warm water from the small pot she'd set in the brazier into the basin for him to wash.

He looked around and managed a small smile. "You've been busy, I see."

"Not so busy as you, I think."

He sighed wearily and sat on the bed. "Aye. There's much to be done, not the least of which is finding the rest of the traitors."

"The worst is over now, Adair."

"Almost," he said as he heaved himself to his feet again and joined her. "I've still got to deal with the rebels when we catch them."

Reaching up, she unfastened the broach at his shoulder. "How long do you think that will take?"

He shrugged as he took the broach from her and set it beside the basin. "It's hard to say. We may never get them all."

"Surely they'll know not to come back to Lochbarr."

"I hope so, Marianne. God help me, I hope so."

Marianne saw the anguish deep in his eyes and knew there was more to his distress than the necessity of rounding up the rebels. "At least Lachlann's not completely alone, Adair. He has Dearshul."

"Aye," Adair replied quietly, kissing her hand. "I'm glad of that."

"So am I, and for her sake, too. Her heart would have died if she'd stayed." She gazed lovingly at her husband. "As mine would have if you'd been killed."

"Oh, Marianne, the mistakes I've made," he murmured as he drew her to him and held her.

She stroked his hair, holding him tight. "We all have. But you're a good man, Adair. And merciful. You'll be a good chieftain, as fine as your father."

"I'll try, Marianne. By God, I'll try—and with you to help me, I stand a chance."

They stood together awhile, not speaking or moving, just embracing, feeling the strength that came from being together.

Finally, Adair drew back. "You must be tired. We should go to bed."

Throwing the plaid off his shoulder, he tucked it into his belt, then stripped off his shirt and tossed it aside. He still had bandages around his ribs and she instinctively looked to make sure there was no fresh bleeding.

There wasn't, so as he splashed his face with water, she picked up his shirt and folded it, setting it on the chest. "Would you like some wine? Ceit and I found some in the far reaches of one of the store-houses, behind some flour."

"No, thank you," he said as he dried his face with a square of linen. "But I appreciate the thought."

"Speaking of thoughts," Marianne said as she climbed back onto the bed. "I've had one that I hope you'll approve of."

Tossing down the linen, he turned to face her. He gave her a smile reminiscent of those seductive smiles that had made her heart beat so wildly. "Does it have anything to do with a bed?"

He was trying to be as he was before. Yet there was a shadow in his eyes that had nothing to do with the flickering light from the oil lamp, and everything to do with all that had happened.

She silently vowed she would do everything she could to make that grave shadow go away. "In a manner of speaking. It's about our child."

Adair started to take off his belt. "Yes?"

"I was thinking that if it's a boy, we should name him Seamus, for your father."

As Adair paused and looked at her, the shadow lifted a little. "I'd like that, Marianne. Very much."

"I was very fond of your father."

"Aye, and he was very fond of you," he replied as he removed his belt and unwrapped his *feileadh*.

Warmed by his words, she got under the covers. "I was also thinking that if we have a girl, we should name her Cellach. I know how much she meant to you."

Adair lifted the covers and climbed into the bed beside her. She nestled against him, careful of his wound.

"Aye, *m'eudail,* I loved her—but not as I love you." He stroked her cheek. "There's only been one woman I've given both my heart and body to, and I'm holding her now."

Marianne kissed him tenderly. She was so blessed, so fortunate. She couldn't have found a better, more loving husband if she searched a hundred years, in Normandy or anywhere else.

Adair smiled and she saw the glimmer of mischief in his eyes. "Or maybe, because I'm sure she'll be a spirited beauty like her mother, it should be something like *My-father-is-the-meanest-most-dangerous-Scot-in-Scotland.* Or *Touch-me-and-you'll-be-sorry.*"

"Very long and very unusual. Unfortunately, I doubt she'll ever get a husband with such a name," Marianne replied, happy to hear that teasing tone in his voice again.

"We could always put her in a tower, forbid anybody to wed her, and see what *braw,* handsome Scot will come to rescue her from such ogres."

Marianne tucked a stray lock of hair behind his

ear. "Maybe there won't be any handsome, *braw* Scots. Maybe I got the last of them."

"You still don't know the Scots very well, my wife," Adair replied, lightly stroking her arm. "Some Scot would come for her, if only for the challenge."

"Nevertheless, I don't think we should tempt fate."

He chuckled, and she rejoiced to hear his laughter. "You're indeed a wise woman, Marianne. Spirited, passionate and wise."

"Passionate, am I?" she murmured, sliding her hand down his chest, lower and lower still.

He closed his eyes. "Aye, very."

She thought of the way he looked when he'd arrived. "If you're tired, or your wound troubles you…?"

"I'll just have to make the best of it," he said, opening his eyes as his hand meandered down her hip. "What was it you said in the hall? Where there is love, there is no hardship."

"Because I love you, too, I'm willing to make the best of things," she agreed as she put her leg over his thigh and shifted closer. "I must confess, my efforts have been well rewarded thus far."

He lay back so that she was more on top of him. "Thus far? I'll have to do my best to see that you always think so."

"Then I have nothing more to ask."

"Nothing?"

"Do I have to ask?"

"It might make things interesting to hear exactly what you'd like."

She leaned close and whispered in his ear.

His eyes widened with mock astonishment. "Losh, my lady, such…explicit…descriptions."

She looked at him with wide-eyed, and bogus, naivete. "Would you rather go to sleep?"

His answering smile was seduction incarnate. "Perish the thought, *m'eudail*. Perish the thought."

He reached up and, cradling her head in his strong hand, pulled her to him for a long, slow kiss.

As her smoldering desire flamed, she moved to straddle him, her shift bunching about her hips. She splayed her hands beside his head on the pillow. "I think you should keep still," she whispered. "I don't want to have to summon Beitiris tonight."

His eyes gleamed with passion. "I may be the chieftain of my clan, but I'm beginning to think you're going to be the chieftain in here."

She trailed light kisses down his neck to his chest. "Does that trouble you?"

"I'd have to say…no," he answered, his voice a little strained.

"Would you like to tell me how to pleasure you?"

He arched back slightly as her lips continued their downward course. "I think you're doing a fine job on your own."

She raised her head, and her hips. "You seem quite anxious."

"You seem willing to torture me."

"I just want you to be ready."

"I've been ready since I got into bed."

"Reeeally?" she said, drawing the word out as she reached for him.

Then she guided him inside and lowered her body with a slow sigh. When he groaned not with pain, but pleasure, she wiggled, settling herself more.

"I think you like this," she said.

"Aye, I do—and so do you, you sly wench, because you know you've got me at your mercy."

She raised herself a little. "Would you like me to stop?"

He shook his head. "No."

She moved slowly lower. "Good, because I don't want to, either."

"We might take all night at this pace," Adair murmured, his hands sliding up her shift toward her breasts.

"And we've got much to do tomorrow."

"So what do you suggest?"

She smiled and began to go faster, pushing down with more intensity. More need. More anxious hunger.

Panting, straining, Adair grabbed hold of her shoulders and raised himself to meet her. She slowed for a moment, to catch her breath, then began again when she couldn't resist the building yearning to feel him hard and powerful inside her, especially at the moment of climax.

She threw back her head and, with wild abandon, gave herself over to desire, until together, they reached the pinnacle of ecstasy. A moan burst from her throat as they came together. Throbbing, her whole body responding, she kept moving, wanting to have the joy of him for as long as she could.

The pulsing inside subsided. His breathing, equally ragged, grew more calm.

Sated, blissfully tired, she moved to lie beside him, then raised herself on her elbow to look down at her husband. "Savage Scot or not," she murmured as she brushed her fingertips across his hard nipples, "it's no wonder I've fallen hopelessly in love with you."

His eyes shining, Adair caught her hand and pressed his mouth to her palm, then her wrist, creating new ripples of delight. "And it's no wonder I love you, Marianne Mac Taran. To think I once believed all Normans were coldhearted. I couldn't have been more wrong."

"We were both wrong, Adair, about many things. But out of all our mistakes and our troubles, some good has come."

"Aye, *m'eudail,*" he whispered. "Wrong in many things, but right to marry, after all."

"Aye," she murmured as she leaned forward to kiss him tenderly. *"M'eudail."*

Read on for a tantalising taste of Sir Nicholas's story!

LORD OF DUNKEATHE
by Margaret Moore

Available in February 2006.

She had no desire to parade in front of all these people and be presented to a Norman lord like a fish on a platter. Unfortunately, Uncle Fergus was already hurrying forward, so unless she wanted him to call out for her to hurry up, she had no choice but to follow. As she did, she reminded herself that if she had no wealth, fine clothes or beauty, she still had much to be proud of. Her uncle and cousin loved her, she was as noble as anyone here and she had one considerable advantage they lacked.

She was a Scot.

"Fergus Mac Gordon, Thane of Glencleith," the steward announced. "And his niece, the Lady Riona."

"As if anybody would want to marry *her*," Lord Chesleigh said behind her.

His scornful words lit her pride and roused her anger. Who was this Lord Chesleigh to speak so arrogantly? These men and their mute relatives were all here like beggars at this man's whim.

She would show them what Scots were made of, and that they were the equal of any here, including their host. She didn't care what any of them thought of her, even Sir Nicholas, with his grim face and arrogant method of finding a wife.

So she gave Sir Nicholas a bright smile and said, in Gaelic, and in a voice loud enough to carry to the far reaches of the hall, "Good evening, my lord. Don't you look different in your fine clothes. I might never have recognized you, except for the hair."

Surprise flared in Sir Nicholas's dark eyes and there were more incredulous whispers behind her. They were all surely wondering what she was saying.

Let them wonder.

MILLS & BOON®

Live the emotion

Look out for next month's
Super Historical Romance

TESTING MISS TOOGOOD
by Stella Cameron

Charged with making a brilliant match, Miss Fleur
Toogood reluctantly agrees to be squired around town
by Lord Dominic Elliot. A secretive man, he shows little
interest in her except to give the most annoying advice.

Not inclined to marry without love, Fleur has devised
a list of essential qualities, knowing no man can meet
her high standards. As she is introduced to one eligible
gentleman after another, it becomes painfully clear –
the only man who scores highly enough to interest her
is the mysterious Dominic himself.

**"Cameron blends sensuality, mystery, danger and
some funny moments in this satisfying tale of love."**
—*Romantic Times*

On sale Friday 6th January 2006

*Available at most branches of WHSmith, Tesco, ASDA,
Borders, Eason, Sainsbury's and most bookshops*

www.millsandboon.co.uk